We're lost in the land of dreams
Nothing here is anything like what it seems
Wonders and terrors, a feast
                        of sighs and screams
The sky flickers and the flowers burn
The path takes another unexpected turn
The golden smile of the demon gleams
Deep in the land of dreams....

Cover art by Wales Christian Ledgerwood
Author photo by Barbara Stanton

ISBN 978-1-7360041-1-1

10 9 8 7 6 5 4 3 2 1

The House
of
Broken Dolls

stories, 1982-2008

Also by Jim Aikin

The Leafstone Series:
The Leafstone Shield
The Rainbow Tree
The Heartsong Fountain
The Firepearl Chalice

Other Fiction:
The Wall at the Edge of the World
While Caesar Sang of Hercules

Contents

Foreword

TALKING ABOUT WHAT one has written is not often a good idea, but you may be curious about a few things. I'll keep it brief.

The earlier stories in this collection were written between 1982 and 1988. A more recent batch was written in 2008.

"Leaving the Station," "Statues," and "A Place to Stay for a Little While" first appeared in *Asimov's Science Fiction*. "An Elvish Sword of Great Antiquity," "My Life in the Jungle," "Run! Run!," and "Dancing Among Ghosts" first appeared in *Fantasy & Science Fiction*. "Cleaving" was in *Amazing Stories*. "Dance for the King" was in *Omni*. "Dancing Among Ghosts" was later anthologized in *The Year's Best Fantasy, Second Annual Edition* (published in 1989), and "My Life in the Jungle" was given a second life in a modest 1985 paperback called *Beyond Armageddon*. The other six stories appear here for the first time.

I've tidied up the writing a bit here and there — more than a bit in the case of "Statues," because it was wordy — but none of the stories has been changed in any significant way. I had a go at updating the '80s cultural and technology references in "Dancing Among Ghosts," but they're too tightly woven into the story, so I had to let them stand. The rather shopworn sci-fi tropes in "Cleaving" (published in 1984) had to be left alone for much the same reason.

Now about that elvish sword....

Before the dawn of computer graphics, there were text-based computer games. I had a lot of fun in the late '70s and early '80s playing Adventure and Zork, and thought it would be great fun to write a game of my own.

In the late '90s, I discovered an active online community of hobbyist programmers who were doing exactly that. New works of interactive fiction (the term by which we dignify text-based games) were being written by a number of talented practitioners. So I wrote and released a game called "Not Just an Ordinary Ballerina." I've since written several more. You can download and play my games if you like; they're free, as are hundreds of others, some of them quite clever.

The online interactive fiction community is still active, and from time to time I get into discussions in the forum with other authors. Sometimes we give one another tips on programming techniques. Other times, the talk turns to writing. At some point a few years ago, the question arose, what makes a piece of writing evocative? Someone (I've forgotten who) quoted a line that appears early in Zork: "Hanging above the trophy case is an elvish sword of great antiquity." This sentence, the person who referred to it maintained, is evocative.

Having in mind, I suppose, Gertrude Stein's pithy observation, "A sentence is not emotional a paragraph is," I replied, "It's not evocative by itself. Not unless you've already played Zork, in which case it will evoke the whole experience of playing the game. A sentence like that can become evocative only when it has a context. You could even use it as the first sentence in a short story, and it would acquire a context from the sentences that followed. Hey, we could have a contest to see who could use that sentence most evocatively in a story!"

Nobody took me up on the contest idea. Their loss, my gain.

If memory serves, "A Place to Stay for a Little While" was inspired by another encounter with an assertion of dubious validity. In a book on how to write fantasy stories, I learned that a story should always have just one fantasy premise. I said to myself, "Oh, really?" I promptly wrote a story that had seven or eight of them.

"Statues" was originally published in the November 1984 issue of *Asimov's*. Apparently there was some adverse reaction to "Statues" among the readers of *Asimov's*. When I opened the June 1985 issue, I was surprised and flattered to find that Dr. Asimov had taken it upon himself to defend my story in his monthly column. His essay begins by talking about symbolism, and touches on *Alice's Adventures in Wonderland* and *Lord of the Rings* (exalted company indeed!). He then turns to what must have led him to feel he should make a statement:

> ...sometimes this magazine publishes stories that must not be read only on the surface, and, as is almost inevitable, this riles a number of readers.
>
> I am thinking, for instance, of the novella "Statues" by Jim Aikin, which ... some readers objected to strenuously. There were statements to the effect that it wasn't science fiction or even fantasy, that it had no point, that it was anti-Christian, and so on.

To begin with, the story, taken simply as a story, is undoubtedly unpleasant in spots. I winced several times when I read it, and I tell you, right now, that I wouldn't, and couldn't, write such a story. But I'm not the be-all and the end-all. The story, however difficult to stomach some of its passages may be, was skillfully and powerfully written....

And it was indeed a fantasy. Aikin made it clear toward the end that the statues were not pushed about, and that their apparent movement was not a delusion. They were on the side of the heroine and were ... trying to rescue her from her unhappy life.

But that is only the surface. A little deeper and we see that it is a case of the old gods trying to save the young woman from the new. It is a rebellion against the rigid Pharisaic morality of some aspects of the Judeo-Christian tradition and a harking back to the greater freedom of some aspects of paganism. The story is in the spirit of that powerful line of A. C. Swinburne in his "Hymn to Proserpine," — "Thou has conquered, O pale Galilean; the world has grown gray from thy breath...."

But if you go deeper still, you will find the story is one more expression of the longing for the old. In this story it is expressed by contrasting the frowning new god with the kindly old ones. In *The Lord of the Rings* it is expressed by contrasting the evil technology of the Dark Lord, Sauron, with the pastoral life of the simple hobbits. (Of course, it is much safer to make of the enemy a Devil-figure than a God-figure, so Tolkien got into no trouble at all.)

You can see the value of symbolism, when you compare either of these with Jack Finney's famous "The Third Level," where he demonstrates his longing for the old by a straightforward contrast between 1950 and 1980. It leaves nothing to discover and, in my opinion, therefore, is a weak story.

But "Statues" — like it or not — is a strong story that makes an important point with great skill.

Looking back, I think Dr. Asimov knew what the story was about better than I did when I wrote it. And I don't think I ever thanked him for defending it. So thanks, Dr. A!

—JA, February 2021

Leaving the Station

"The past isn't dead. It isn't even past."
— William Faulkner

By THE TIME SHE TURNED forty, Joan had mostly managed to forget that when she was young she had seen ghosts. She had thrust the ectoplasmic intrusions that roiled her childhood into a big old trunk in the back of her brain, had locked the trunk and thrown away the key.

But then Uncle Frederick died and left her the antique store.

She had never been close to Uncle Frederick, though they lived less than twenty miles apart. He was her mother's brother, and was too wedded in spirit to the inexplicable enthusiasms that had infected and ultimately shredded her parents' lives. Her parents had grown up in the Sixties. Mom read Tarot cards, played the flute while sitting cross-legged on the floor, and changed her name twice because her guru told her to. Daddy made oregami sculpture, fetishistically and inexpertly, and sold it with indifferent success at an endless string of grimy street fairs. Crushed and mutilated birds and frogs made of folded yellow and purple paper littered the floor of Joan's childhood.

She far preferred Uncle Ray, her father's brother. Uncle Ray had inherited the same obsessive gene, but turned it to better use: He taught high-school math. At fifteen, weary of moving from one cramped, noisy apartment to another, weary of her parents' penniless, stoned friends and their droning reminiscences of long-ago Grateful Dead concerts, Joan stormily divorced her parents and stomped off to live with Uncle Ray and his brood, where she cheerfully slept on a futon on the living room floor until she went away to college. She learned trig and then calculus sitting at Uncle Ray's kitchen table, ignoring Aunt Mary's diffident, though unceasing, attempts to interest her in cooking. At college she majored in math. She became a computer programmer.

Somewhere along in there, the ghosts tapered off. Maybe they sensed that she really didn't want them hanging around, or maybe something had changed in her that made her less receptive.

When she was little, she hadn't known they were ghosts. They didn't shriek or walk through walls, though they did appear and disappear with alarming insouciance. Only gradually did it dawn on her that she was seeing people nobody else could see. The woman with the burned hand, for instance, or the old man mowing his lawn day after day, and the lawn standing up just as long behind the mower as in front of it. Sometimes they spoke to her, but not in the normal way — "Hello, little girl." It was as if she had turned on the TV in the middle of a show and was being treated to random scraps of dialog. "I killed my brother," a young black man said to her. That scared her, but he didn't look so much scary as just sad and lost. She knew he was a ghost because she always saw him at the same street corner, and he always said the same thing. Sometimes the ghosts would ask her questions, and if she replied they would look puzzled, as if that wasn't what they were expecting (hoping?) to hear. Mostly, though, they just ignored her and went about their business, whatever that was.

When Mom found out about the ghosts, they became a Big Deal. At the age of eight, Joan was expected to lead séances. But she couldn't summon ghosts; they came and went according to their own whims, and not very often at that. The seances were a flop. Her mother seemed to take this as a personal affront, as if either Joan or the ghosts (or both, conspiring) were hoarding some Ultimate Truth rather than share it with her.

The séances stopped, but her mother never stopped pestering her to know what the ghosts had said. Every spectral utterance, no matter how banal, was poked and prodded in an effort to force it to reveal its veiled cosmic import. After a while Joan started making stuff up and claiming a ghost had said it. When her mother caught on (and that didn't happen for several years), it turned into a kind of game. "Did they really say that? Really? Or is it something you made up? Joanie, tell me the truth, now."

Maybe the ghosts had gone away because she started lying about them. That was a thought. Only now they were back, and the antique store was to blame. It attracted them.

The store was called Station House Antiques. It was housed in an old building that had once, when the town was much smaller, been an actual functioning train station. The train line had been moved down by the bay before World War II, and the rails torn out.

New streets had been laid down when the freeway came, leaving the former station perched in isolated and rapidly fading nineteenth-century small-town civic architecture grandeur on an awkwardly shaped lot with inadequate parking.

The main room was large, high-ceilinged, and crammed with tables, shelves, and display cases. Every available surface, not omitting the walls, was overflowing with merchandise. Faded brown photos in plain frames, a butter churn, cavalry swords, a dressmaker's dummy, a model merry-go-round made of painted tin. Hundreds of pieces of china and glass, some chipped and some pristine, no two alike. Tattered magazines, pewter pepper mills, stuffed birds perched in ornate cages, four or five assorted umbrella stands. The light from the street acquired a patina of dust as it passed through the broad front window, and quickly lost itself among the crooked aisles. Smaller side rooms were packed with dark, heavy furniture and used books.

As a young adult, pursuing her lackluster career in Silicon Valley, Joan was only hazily aware that Uncle Frederick had ventured into the antiques business. Before that he had owned a bicycle shop, which went broke. She had visited the antique store exactly once, and found the teetering stacks of tarnished junk depressing and a little creepy. Having gone to some lengths to unencumber herself of the baggage of the past, she couldn't fathom why anyone would want to surround themselves with old stuff. She hadn't seen any ghosts on that visit, but looking back on it, her urge to get out of the place quickly might have been a clue that they were hovering nearby, dreaming about her.

At thirty, goaded by long-submerged urges, she had swum up out of the depths of database code maintenance long enough to get married, to an individual she now referred to exclusively as "that asshole." Six years later she learned, because he didn't try very hard to hide it, that that asshole was sleeping with his admin. He had also caught herpes from the admin, and bestowed it on Joan as a little amorous gift.

After he trudged off, padded so thickly in injured dignity that her screams of rage had no chance to penetrate, she went through the apartment with furious energy, seizing and removing any item that was even faintly stained by its former nearness to that asshole. She hauled down to the dumpster the pictures he had bought for the walls, the plates he had eaten off of, even the tins of shoe polish he had left under the bathroom sink. She was left with an almost bare apartment. The wind blew through uncurtained windows, and there was no past to weigh her down. Except for the herpes, of course.

And then the company she worked for got acquisitioned and downsized, and she got laid off. The severance package dwindled, and all the programming jobs were moving offshore. But within days after she gave notice on the apartment and started looking around in a gloomy, half-hearted way for a roommate situation, Uncle Frederick providentially died.

Like her parents, and like Uncle Ray and Aunt Mary, Uncle Frederick had lived his life from month to month, never managing to scrape together more than a few dollars in savings. But he had owned the antique store outright, and he left it to her.

Her first thought was to sell it. But until she found another job, a steady source of income, however meager, would be better than a big lump of money that she would eventually burn through. Anyway, she had mastered the intricacies of Fortran, Pascal, C++, Java, and Python. How hard could it be to learn antiques?

There was a room in the back of the store — Uncle Frederick had used it as an office, as had the station master in years gone by — that had a functioning bathroom. She cleared out the back room, set up housekeeping, and went into business as a full-time purveyor of fine antiquities and collectible memorabilia. She pored through antiques trade journals, scoured the websites where aficionados aired their passions and prejudices, staked out auctions and estate sales. Business was never good, but some months she actually had enough extra in the cash drawer to treat herself to a play in San Francisco or a weekend at Tahoe.

The ghosts didn't arrive at the store all in a rush. Maybe it took them a while to notice where she was hanging out, or maybe they were there all along but it was a while before she started to see them.

The first whisper that something might be awry came from the ungovernable inventory. Uncle Frederick had never kept a written inventory that she could find. Either he had stored the cost and likely value of ten thousand things in his head, or he was just a poor excuse for a businessman. Joan suspected the latter. Until she knew what she had in stock, acquiring more stuff would only embroil her in costly mistakes. So she did what any computer professional would do: She set up a database on her laptop.

But a task that had at first seemed merely monumental soon slipped through her fingers entirely.

Not simply because of the size of the store — there were five downstairs rooms, plus the upstairs gallery — or the difficulty in categorizing nearly unique items. Maybe, she told herself, it was because it was so easy to get sleepy on a warm afternoon and miss something. She would list all of the items on the long narrow table by the west wall, filling in the fields for Type, Condition, Description, Price, and Table/Case/Shelf, working in what she was sure was a meticulous and methodical manner, but a few days later her eye would be caught by some striking piece on the table, and she would think, "Now, I don't remember that. Is that in the inventory?" And when she looked in the database, sure enough, there was no fluted porcelain pitcher with pink flowers and twining vines listed on that table. Nor anywhere else in the store, if the database was to be believed. Yet there it was.

How many ukuleles were hanging on the north wall of the east room? She didn't exactly know. The database said six, but when she went to look, there might be seven. Or only six, but their descriptions might not, if you got a flashlight and peered between the strings to inspect the labels on the inside, quite match what was entered in the computer. The cuckoo clocks seemed to flit from wall to wall whenever her back was turned.

She could see at least four possible explanations. First, there might be something wrong with the database software. Being a computer professional, she investigated that possibility methodically, and ruled it out. Second, someone might be altering the database when she wasn't around. But she was alone in the store most of the time, the laptop wasn't even connected to the Internet most of the time, and the database was password-protected, so no hacker could possibly be fiddling with the data — not that anyone would want to. Third, there might be something seriously awry with her inventory methods. But Joan was not a scatterbrain. Fourth, things might be somehow magically appearing and disappearing in the store when she wasn't looking. And that was obviously impossible too.

If it had just been things disappearing, that would be due to shoplifters or burglars. But why would a burglar break in at night (without tripping the alarm) and put an extra Victorian brooch in the jewelry case?

Even before Joan saw the girl, she had started to think maybe the store was infested with ghosts. It was as if the past was not quite dead and buried here, as if history slept fitfully in its bed and tumbled the blankets into knots.

She came upon the girl in the upstairs gallery, just at sunset. The gallery was a narrow floor space above the main room from which you could look down over a railing and see a labyrinth of tables, shelves, and glass-topped counters that looked, depending on the light, not unlike an aerial photo of the ruins of Pompeii. A rainstorm had been pounding all afternoon, and it occurred to Joan (tardily) that she ought to make sure the upstairs windows were securely closed. She hadn't turned on the overheads, so the gallery was dim, and rain thrummed on the roof.

The girl was no more than ten years old. Her dress was long and faded, and she was wearing, of all things, a bonnet. She looked at Joan beseechingly. "Can you help, ma'am? My mama, she's took awful sick."

Questions crowded in — how did you get in here? Why are you dressed like that? But those weren't the most urgent concern. "Sick? Where is she?"

"In the back of the wagon, ma'am. She was burnin' up with fever, but now she's cold, and she won't wake up, no matter how I shake her and call to her."

"The wagon? You mean a station wagon? Where is it parked? I'll call 9-1-1." Joan flipped out her cell phone, fumbled, and dropped it. It skittered under a table, and she had to grope for it. When she straightened up and turned around, the girl was gone. The hair on the back of Joan's neck crinkled, and she moaned aloud. How stupid not to have seen it at once! The girl was a ghost. Hoping she was wrong, Joan ran up and down the gallery, calling, "Hello? Hello? Where are you? Is anybody there?" But no, she wasn't wrong.

If she hadn't been living in the station, she would have closed up shop for a few days — or possibly forever — so as to duck the whole problem. She didn't *want* ghosts in her life. But she did live there.

The shelves next to where the girl had appeared were a repository for tin mugs and tableware, much of it dating back to the Gold Rush. Over the next few days, when not overcome by depression and inertia, Joan read up on the Gold Rush. Many of the wagon trains, she learned, had been overtaken by cholera. Imagine a girl whose mother is lying in the back of the wagon, dead of cholera. It wasn't hard to see how that awful feeling of helplessness might imprint itself on a mug or a plate and show up, out of the blue, on a rainy afternoon a hundred fifty years later. At least it was a workable theory. Joan didn't actually know whether ghosts were stray bits of emotion that had gotten imprinted on physical objects, or whether they were ... something else entirely.

She tried reading up on ghosts, but found it too difficult to pan nuggets out of the tons of black sand. Most of the self-proclaimed authorities plainly knew less than she did. Which was almost nothing.

Not a week later she came out of the lumber room, which was what she called the room full of old furniture, to find a man standing at the counter. She hadn't heard the bell at the shop door jingle. The man was wearing a long soiled coat that had once been gray and a three-cornered hat from beneath which a greasy ponytail curled down his back. Her nose informed her that he hadn't bathed in weeks. He was fingering a flintlock pistol in an engrossed way, as if he had a quite practical interest in its workmanship. The glass-fronted cabinet — she glanced across the room — in which she kept the early firearms was always kept locked, but now its door yawned wide.

"I've a need for this pistol," he said without preamble. "I should like to buy it, thankee." His voice was a gravelly croak.

"Yes, of course," she said. "It's — here, let me see the price tag." She reached for the pistol. She was close enough now to see that it wasn't one she remembered. The lock and barrel were almost free of rust. Also, there wasn't any price tag.

He pulled it back so she couldn't touch it, and glared at her distrustfully. Beneath dark, tangled brows he had the glittering eyes of a hawk. He slapped a coin on the counter. "This be enough?"

The coin was the size of a silver dollar, but yellow. The sun-bright circle almost gleamed with its own light. "I'd have to look it up," she said, stammering. "I think I have a catalog. Wait here while I find it." She had to go around behind a bookcase to haul out the carton of coin catalogs. Probably counterfeit, she said to herself. He's on his way to a costume party. Where he'll win first prize.

When she emerged with the catalog, the frontiersman was gone, and the pistol with him. Again, the front bell hadn't rung. But the coin remained. It turned out to be a gold doubloon — not rare, but in shockingly good condition. And not provably counterfeit, though eyebrows were raised because of its lack of provenance. The property tax bill was due in less than a month, and she paid it by selling that one coin.

The frontiersman's rank odor lingered in the shop for days. Sometimes she thought she could still smell it. More likely it was just the dodgy plumbing, but all the same she felt obscurely irritated. The girl had disappeared before she could do anything to help her, or even try, but she couldn't quite get rid of the frontiersman even after he was gone.

After the frontiersman, the ghosts began showing up more often. The weeping woman, the blind soldier, the golden-haired toddler eating an ice cream cone, the angry old man who thumped up and down the aisle with his walker. They never showed up when customers were in the store, only when she was alone. She tried ignoring them, tried shouting at them, tried chatting with them. When they chose to notice her at all, their utterances were enigmatic.

One of the very nice things about Ted was that he wasn't a ghost. She met him at a party some friends had invited her to. She had been only too glad to get out of the store for an evening. Ted was up from L.A., where he was in accounting with a movie studio. In spite of his superficial physical resemblance to that asshole, she liked him at once. He kept fit by rock climbing, didn't smoke or do drugs, and wasn't a Scientologist or a Republican. On their second date she mentioned in an offhand way (it was kind of a test) that she had been named after Joan Baez, and he had never even heard of Joan Baez. That was when she decided to sleep with him.

Ted wanted her to move to L.A. and live with him and probably get married eventually. The herpes didn't faze him. The only slight impediment to their impending bliss was that she would have to sell the antique store in order to move. By that time the ghosts were showing up almost daily, and she was overjoyed at the prospect of being rid of them. True, they might follow her to L.A., but somehow she doubted it. In L.A. she might expect to see an occasional unicorn, or a centaur, or tiny winged people who left sparkly trails in the air as they flew, but surely she would be able to shut the door forever on her crew of self-absorbed and gloomy shades.

But the store didn't sell, and didn't sell, and didn't sell. The problem wasn't that it was haunted; she wasn't about to disclose that to anyone, not even Ted. No, the shortage of parking was the sticking point — that, and the marginal value of the inventory, and the exorbitant cost of renovating the building to rip out the termite damage and bring the restrooms up to code. After two years on the market, there had been not a whisper of genuine interest. Her agent had gotten lazy about returning her calls, and Ted's weekend flights up from L.A. were getting spaced further apart.

And then one morning as she sat beside the cash register, watching the dust motes drift lazily across a stray beam of sunlight that had bounced off of something in the street and zigzagged in the front window by mistake, the bell above the door jingled and Mr. and Mrs. Behrens came in. They came down the central aisle slowly, turning this way and that. People who came into Station House Antiques usually reacted that way. The newcomers were both in their forties, well dressed, no more than middle height. The woman had mouse-brown hair and a washed-out complexion. The man was pudgy, cheeks florid, hair receding, and wore wire-rimmed glasses. They took their time working their way back through the store to the counter, their eyes wandering, being snagged on this or that, being tugged free, snagging again. "We saw your listing on the Internet," the man said. His English was only faintly accented, but even before they introduced themselves Joan had pegged them as probably German. "Can you tell us, is the property still available?"

By that time, she had forgotten placing the ad in the online marketplace. Figured she was doomed to spend the rest of her life swaddled in layers of cobwebs behind the counter of Station House Antiques.

"Yes, it's still available," she said. "I've had a couple of offers" — a lie — "but my agent felt we could do better." The agent who no longer even bothered to return her phone calls.

"May we take a look around?"

She twisted the key in the cash register. "Better yet, I'll show you around."

"I am Ludwig Behrens," the man said. "This is my wife Anna." He extended his hand and all but clicked his heels together. The light from the window glinted flat off of his spectacles, turning his eyes to round white slices of radish. "Have you owned it long?"

"No, not really. My uncle left it to me a few years ago, in his will. At the time I knew almost nothing about antiques. Are you in the trade yourselves?" She ushered them through the low door into the lumber room. Massive furniture crowded in on them.

"In a small way. We have been looking for a retail opportunity since arriving in this country last summer."

"Something with enough floor space that we can be creative," Mrs. Behrens said, gazing around the lumber room with something like discomfort.

"Of course it doesn't look as large on the inside as it is," Joan said, "on account of the amount of stock. If you look at the numbers for the square footage, it's actually quite impressive. This used to be a real functioning train station. The tracks were torn out years ago, when the railway line was relocated down by the bay. The building is an official landmark, so you have to maintain the exterior, but there are no restrictions if you want to remodel the interior. Let me show you the upstairs gallery." And steer you away from the rusted plumbing.

While she was ushering the Behrenses into the used book room, her cell phone chirped. She flipped it out, saw that it was Ted. "Hi, sweetie. I'm busy right now. Can I call you back?"

"Busy?"

"I'm showing the station to some folks who are interested in possibly buying it."

"Wow! That is great news, hon. Call me later."

She could tell Ted was on the freeway because of the traffic noise. With a sudden fierceness she ached to be there beside him, riding in his Beemer in the land of golden sun, where palm trees swayed like frowzy-topped sentinels above a thousand blue swimming pools, instead of stuck in a mouldering train station in the hills west of San Jose.

Twenty minutes later, Mr. and Mrs. Behrens were back at the counter beside the cash register. The plumbing hadn't sent them rocketing out the door. "And of course you'll want to inspect the books," she said. "I'll have to arrange that with my accountant." Her accountant was the laptop, but they didn't need to know that.

"Oh, I don't think that will be necessary," Mrs. Behrens said. "We will plan to change the nature of the business ever so slightly. A downstairs tea room here, and Navajo pottery, and some things imported from Europe. It's really quite charming. But there are other possibilities on our list. Perhaps you will see us again."

Joan ushered them to the front door. "*Auf wiedersehen,*" she said wistfully, waving.

Two days later, they were back. Ludwig Behrens slipped a hand into his coat pocket and drew out a piece of paper. "We have, in the interim, inspected a number of properties, and yours is still under consideration. If it's still available?"

"I've shown it a couple of times this week" — another lie — "but there are no other offers on the table, no."

"Good, good." Ludwig Behrens straightened his spectacles and peered at the piece of paper. "We have made a list of questions, the dimensions of various rooms and so forth. We have brought a tape measure. Would it trouble you if we were to undertake a detailed inspection?"

After measuring and sketching for an hour, they had a low-voiced conference, their heads bent together, Joan carefully giving them privacy. Then came questions about zoning and parking and the prevalence of earthquakes, which always seemed to arouse morbid fascination in foreigners, and then another conference. At last Ludwig Behrens strode toward her and stuck out his hand for her to shake. "My wife and I have decided. It is very suitable. But we do not want the stock, I think, except for perhaps a few items to be specified later. I assume you will find another dealer who will take the remainder off your hands."

"Yes, of course."

"Good. We shall instruct our agent to draw up an offer. Would it be convenient if he were to present it to you this afternoon?"

When they were gone, she tried to call Ted, but his voicemail picked it up. She left half of an exuberant message and then hung up in mid-sentence when she realized she was babbling.

The door jingled again. An old woman, purse clutched in both hands, advanced into the shop hesitantly. "I was just about to close for lunch," Joan said. But if the woman bought something, it was one less thing she'd have to pack up and try to sell to another dealer. "Can I help you? Are you looking for anything in particular?"

"I don't quite know," the old woman said. "No, my eye was just caught as I was passing by. I must have been down this street a hundred times, and I don't remember ever seeing your store before. That happens when you get old, you know. You think you're paying attention, when you're not. Things jump out at you, and you think, 'Where ever did that come from?'" She gazed around in awe. "Antiques! My goodness, what a trove!" Her face was spotted and deeply lined, her hair silver and sparse, her stockings thick and sensible. She set one foot in front of the other laboriously, as if her knees were unreliable. "I'm practically an antique myself," she said with a pinch of pride. "Can you guess how old I am? I'm ninety-three. Ninety-three. When I was born, Woodrow Wilson was president. Can you believe that?"

"I have some Wilson memorabilia," Joan said.

"Oh, I don't care anything about that. He was a dreadful racist, apart from anything else." The old woman craned her neck to peer at some fussily clothed dolls on a high shelf, but then swayed a little and seemed to have trouble catching her breath. "My goodness." She looked around, spotted a high-backed chair, and sank into it. "Oh, dear. I felt quite faint for a moment there. Could I trouble you for a glass of water?"

"Are you all right? Should I call 9-1-1?"

"Oh, please don't. They always make such a fuss. Just the water will be fine." Between sips, she said, "I was having a — a discussion with my daughter this morning, and I believe it tired me out more than I realized. Which is odd, you know, because we didn't argue. I'm finished with all that. Finally. For years I've tried to help her." She took a tiny sip. "All my life, it seems. And she always ends up as badly off as before, if not worse. At long last I've accepted that. All of it, including my own part in it. I felt quite kindly disposed toward her when we spoke today. I told her I forgave her, and I do." Sip. "What I didn't tell her — I don't know that it would have served any purpose — was that I also forgave myself. Looking back on it, I don't believe I could have done a single thing any differently. There's something very freeing about understanding that. Today I don't believe I'd change a single thing about my entire life. It's all been perfect, perfect, even the parts that at the time seemed quite horrid. I expect you don't understand. You will, one day."

She set the glass on a table at her elbow and looked around. "Is that a gramophone? My goodness, look at that! I haven't seen one since — oh, since the Forties. And you have records! I must look at them." She stood up, a little unsteadily — Joan was afraid for a moment she was going to have to catch her — and tottered over to the gramophone, an old hand-cranked model with a large bell. Three or four records were sitting beside it, and she picked up the top one. "Louis Armstrong — 'King Porter Stomp.' We used to dance to this, when I was a girl. It was so jazzy! It made you feel quite alive, dancing to it, sixteen and you knew you'd be young forever. Could I play it? Does the machine work? I'd love to hear it again."

Joan didn't actually know whether the gramophone worked. Nobody had ever asked. She fitted the disc onto the turntable and inspected the mechanism uncertainly. "Here, let me do it," the woman said. She gave the crank a few deft twists and set the needle in the groove.

The tinny, scratchy sound of old-time jazz rang out in the station. "Oh, yes," the woman said. "Oh, yes." She took a hesitant dance step, then another. She set her purse on the chair, swung her arms, snapped her fingers.

The beat set Joan's toe tapping too. She marveled at the lively sound pouring out of the ancient gramophone. The clarinet and trumpet wailed, the bass and drums throbbed as if the band were right here in the room. The very floor was rumbling. The old woman danced down the aisle, skipping, nodding her head. Ninety-three and moving so nimbly?

The rumble got louder. Quite distinctly Joan heard a railroad train pulling into the station — the whistle, the deep chuff of the engine, the hiss of the brakes. The broad double doors at the rear of the room, which had once opened onto the platform, when there was a platform, had been boarded up for years, the windows painted over, but when the old woman reached the doors and touched the latch they swung slowly, ponderously open.

A dazzle of milky light poured in, flooding the room. The woman danced out into the light, the music rippling around her, and her figure was slim, her hair dark, her step light and eager, and she never turned to look back. A conductor cried, "All aboard!" His bell clanged.

Joan moved toward the doors, almost blinded by the radiance, trying to see. Something big was out there, and yes, it was a train, and the trumpet leaped and darted around the banjo while the trombone slid and the clarinet trilled, and the woman, young now, stepped up into the train as a spray of flower petals fluttered and swirled white and pink around her, and the conductor's bell clanged again and there were ghosts beside Joan now, walking with her as she drifted out onto the platform, the old man with the walker, who cast it aside and strode with a firm step, and the Gold Rush girl and the frontiersman, one by one they boarded the train in a gentle blizzard of flower petals, and Joan was in line behind the weeping woman, whose tears now flowed around a radiant smile, and she reached out to put her hand on the side of the car so she could climb into the train feeling yes of course yes the joy of this flooding her now forever.

But an arm in a dark sleeve reached across in front of her and barred the way. She looked up. The conductor's face was long and pale with bushy white eyebrows, a little like Uncle Frederick's but not really so very much. The conductor said, "Not yet. Your time is not yet. Your task is to watch over the station."

She opened her mouth to wail a protest, it was impossible not to board the train, how could she not? But somehow she stumbled, as if her foot had come down on a step that wasn't there, and for a moment more she thought the train was starting to move, sliding sideways in front of her, she submerged in the engine's bone-deep rumble, and then suddenly she wasn't on the platform at all, she was engulfed in ordinary sunlight, lurch-staggering down the embankment onto the freeway on-ramp where it cut close behind the store. She was hollow. She had been turned inside out. Head spinning, she nearly sat down on the pavement, but a rusty old pickup truck bearing down on her at forty miles an hour honked, and she leaped sideways to dodge it and fell in the grimy bed of iceplant where it sloped up to the back of the station. She sprawled among the wadded candy wrappers, the crushed and mutilated soft drink cups, and started to cry.

All right, she said, get hold of yourself. What just happened? Feeling unbearably heavy, as if she were wearing the train across her shoulders like a great metal stole, she picked herself up, winced in pain when she put her weight on a twisted ankle, and stared up in blurred confusion at the rear of the station. Thirty feet away, the rear double doors were shut as tight as ever.

Cars whizzed past her, their chrome lancing daggers in the sunlight. It seemed to take all day to walk around the building, limping, staring fixedly at the curb in front of her feet as if she might lose her way. A line from an old song, a spiritual, coiled into her mind like sweet smoke: "Don't need no ticket, you just get on board." Was that it?

Inside, the station was blessedly dark and cool. She noticed she was trembling, and shut her eyes and willed the trembling to cease. That didn't work, so she went and got a drink of water. The gramophone needle was going *whicka-whicka-whicka* at the center of the disc, so she took it out of the groove. The double doors were still shut, but strewn around them on the floor was a careless scatter of white and pink flower petals, which certainly hadn't been there before. She went to the doors and touched them, running her hands up and down the rough surface like a blind person. And started to cry again. Out there, just beyond the doors, was an ocean of joy so deep she had never imagined such joy could exist. She had tasted it, it had filled her, and now it was gone and the doors were sealed shut again. She slid down to the floor and sobbed.

The tears dried up. Sitting on the floor, she saw the store at a new angle. It felt empty, though it was still as packed with antiques as before. There were no ghosts now, that was it. The ghosts had gotten on the train.

She might have sat there all afternoon, but the phone rang. She got up, sniffled a little, and answered. It was the Behrenses' real estate agent. "I have an offer here for your retail property," he said, sounding just the right note of suppressed excitement. "I'd like to present it to you and your agent this afternoon. What time would be convenient?"

Her agent. The one she hadn't spoken to in months. "Well, I'll have to—" No, wait. She took a breath, and swallowed. "I'm sorry," she said. "The property is — it's no longer on the market. There's been a — I've changed my mind. I'm not going to sell it."

"If you've received a better offer, I can talk to my clients and see if they might be—"

"No, you don't understand. I'm really not going to sell. I'm going to keep it."

He took a little convincing. He told her how disappointed Ludwig and Anna would be. He vented a gentle rasp of annoyance, testing whether she could be intimidated into feeling guilty. In the end, he signed off with a breezy assurance that he'd call again in a day or two in case she had reconsidered.

She hung up, sat on her stool by the cash register, and thought about that. He'd call again. She could still change her mind and sell. But if she stayed here, before long more ghosts would be bound to show up, and sooner or later the doors would open again and she could go out on the platform for just a minute and maybe wave to them as the train slid away, and touch the tip of her tongue to a drop of glory. If she sold the store and moved to L.A., would she ever find this kind of station again? And where would the ghosts go, when it was shut down?

The old woman had left her purse sitting on the chair near the gramophone. And that was very bad. She might already have been a ghost when she came in, but she hadn't acted like one. If she had been alive, she was a missing person now, and the police would make inquiries. When they found the purse they would ask Joan what had happened, and Joan would have to lie. Her lies had never fooled anyone for very long, apart from her mother.

Toss it in a dumpster. Drive down to Gilroy and toss it in a dumpster. And don't leave fingerprints. But on a whim, she snapped it open. There wasn't much inside — some Kleenex, keys, a billfold with a few dollars, an opened packet of hearing aid batteries, and a postcard.

It was an old-fashioned picture postcard. On one side was what looked like an Alpine ski lodge, but cupped in summer, perched on the side of a mountain amid a gorgeous spill of trees and flowers. On the other side was a three-cent stamp and a brief message written in blue fountain pen in a flowing hand: "Having a wonderful time. Wish you were here!"

When had postcards cost three cents to mail? The stamp was obviously old. It took Joan ten minutes to find the stamp catalog in the book room. When she saw what the stamp was worth, her mouth got dry. She'd be able to pay last year's taxes and then replace her sputtering, asthmatic Geo with a new Honda Civic.

She's still there. If you'd like, you can drop by Station House Antiques and say hello, though you probably won't see any ghosts. They never seem to come out when customers are around. The antiques business is lousy, but once in a while Joan picks up a valuable item that keeps her going for a few months.

She had a repair shop look at the gramophone and make sure it's in good shape. It's always kept dusted and polished, and there's a box of old-time jazz records sitting next to it, in case anybody who drops in wants to play one. Once in a while, somebody does.

And sometimes, when Joan is alone in the store, she puts on "King Porter Stomp." While it plays, she goes over and presses her ear against the double doors and listens for the train.

A Little Something Extra

I HAD BEEN WORKING AT this local coffee place — I'm not going to say which one, it's not Starbuck's but it's one of the chains — for about three months when this guy came in. Big creepy guy, long greasy brown hair that hadn't been combed in a while but it was slicked back with some kind of oil, a patchy beard, and his gut spilling out of his jeans along with his shirt-tail, you get the picture. And he had a glass eye, it stared straight ahead no matter which way the other eye was looking.

Telling you about the guy, though, won't make any sense unless I back up and tell you about Maggie. Maggie — oh, man, where do I start? At the beginning, I guess. Rob hired her either right after he hired me, or maybe before, I don't remember. About the coffee place, I guess you can imagine. It's crappy work, but kind of fun at the same time, mixing beverages for whoever comes in, fishing the muffins out of the display case with the tongs, mopping the crud off of the floor, having a few laughs, whatever.

I'm still there, for a while anyhow. Maggie's gone now.

Everybody who works there is under 25 except the manager, Rob, he's gotta be 40 but he won't admit it. Anyway, Maggie was ancient. Like, over 50. And crabby. Well, maybe not crabby exactly, but she wasn't a real bundle of cheer, if you see what I mean. I don't know why Rob hired her, maybe she reminded him of his mom. It would be useless to ask him now if that was it, because he for sure wouldn't remember. But I'm getting this all out of order. The main reason he kept her, I guess, other than she didn't mess up the drink orders, she would put up with any kind of crap and never complain. That makes anybody an ace in Rob's book.

So I was busy breaking up with my boyfriend for, like, the third time, mainly because I was taking martial arts classes and it scared him dating a strong woman only he would never admit it, so I didn't spend a lot of time at first chatting up this weird crabby old lady, until one day we weren't too busy and I was standing around and I happened to see her whip out a little vial, like a test tube sort of thing, and pop the cork off of it and empty it into this decaf mocha she was making. Not for herself, either. I mean, Rob would fire you if he caught you taking any kind of recreational substance on the job, believe me, it's happened. No, this was for a customer. She tucked the little vial back into the pocket in her apron, gave the mocha an extra stir, and slid it across the counter to the guy like it was nothing out of the ordinary, and he took it and walked away with it.

It was just too weird. I didn't say anything, because what are you gonna say? "Hey, I noticed you poisoning one of the customers. What's up with that?" No, either the guy was going to drop dead before he got to the door or he wasn't, and either way there was nothing I could do about it.

Well, he didn't, he just walked out sipping his mocha. But after that I kind of kept an eye on Maggie when we were on the same shift, which was pretty often.

The next day I saw her do it again. This time it wasn't a test tube, it was a pinch of some yellow powder, which she fished out of this, like, enamel snuff box in her pocket and sprinkled into an iced tea. The guy who guzzled down the iced tea was somebody I knew slightly, Jason something-or-other, and the very next day I heard that Jason's girlfriend, who was bad news on high heels, had been arrested for shoplifting.

No possible connection, right? Not even a coincidence, just two things that happened.

Over the next few weeks, I must have seen Maggie dose a drink eight or ten times. She never took a lot of trouble to hide it, other than turning her back, but it usually seemed to happen when we weren't busy so nobody was around to notice, or else when we were insanely busy so nobody would notice. I don't know how many times she did it that I didn't spot. I kept waiting for the headlines to break out about a wave of mysterious poisonings in the downtown area, but nothing.

So I started chatting her up a little, like do you have any kids, any pets, I saw this great movie, whatever. And she started to open up to me. "I got a son in Boise," she said one time. "But he never writes."

"Do you write to him? Call him?"

"Nah, he don't want to hear from me. He's got a life." Or maybe she said "wife," not "life." Maggie kind of mumbled sometimes. I don't think her teeth were too good. Later I found out more about her life, and it was definitely the teeth. She wasn't stupid, she'd been to college and everything. She could talk about stuff I'd barely even heard of, like chaos theory. Since all this happened, I've been reading up on chaos theory. But I'm getting ahead of the story again.

There was this woman, a regular, I won't say too much about her because she still comes in. Very pretty but kind of distracted, with these worry lines around her mouth. Turns out she had a kid that had autism or Down's or schizophrenia or some crap. A very bad mental case. He was in an institution. I heard her telling some of her friends the latest gory details one afternoon over about three frappuchinos and this really dangerous chocolate chip cookie that I try to stay away from. And the second frappuchino had a little something extra in it, courtesy of Maggie. This time she had it in a vanilla extract bottle, and sploosh, right into the drink, but I know for a fact it wasn't vanilla extract. Later Maggie told me what it was, but there's no point in going into that, it isn't important, and anyway it was disgusting.

So the woman drinks the frappuchino, and two days later she's back at the same table with the same friends, tears of joy streaming down her cheeks, telling them how her kid had this spontaneous remission, and he was getting all better and talking to her in whole sentences and everything, and how they were going to discharge him from the institution and let him come live at home. "Just like any other little boy," she said. "Can you believe it?"

Maggie was standing behind the counter while this whole conversation was going down, kind of chewing on the end of her hair and listening to the Nirvana CD that Rob had popped in the CD player after lunch. I tilted my head at the woman with the kid who was suddenly all better. "What do you think of that?"

Maggie shrugged. "What am I supposed to think?"

"I don't know. Wasn't she one of your little chemistry experiments?"

Maggie shot me a look of muted terror, like a dog that knows you're about to kick him. "I don't know what you're talking about."

"You know what I'm talking about. You think I haven't noticed?"

She sighed and shook her head, staring at the floor. "Is it time for me to move on? Already? You're gonna get me fired, right?"

"I don't know." I folded my arms. "You're kind of cute and cuddly. I get a kick out of having you around."

"You can make fun of me if you like," she said. "I don't mind."

"So tell me why."

"Why what?"

"Don't play dumb. Why you put stuff in people's drinks."

She was holding a towel, and her hands twisted at it as if she was trying to wring it dry. "I don't think I ought to say anything. Anyway, you wouldn't believe me if I told you."

"Try me."

"No, I don't think so." She turned away.

Should I have said something to Rob? Maybe, but I didn't. I let it lay.

So a few days later this guy came in. Not the the guy with the glass eye, he came along later. This was another guy, but he was even creepier. His skin was gray and shiny, like it was sprayed on, and he was wearing this black suit that had so much starch in it, it practically creaked at the joints when he walked. He walked stiff too, so maybe the suit was just an ordinary suit and it was him doing the creaking. He came straight up to the counter — it was the middle of the afternoon, we weren't busy — and he looked straight at me through these square-framed gray-tinted glasses, and I don't think he ever blinked, not the whole time. He said, "I have been informed that a Margaret White is employed in this place." Very mechanical-sounding, like an electronic translation machine that somebody had programmed to speak English, and not done a very good job.

I didn't get the "Margaret" part for a second, because nobody called Maggie Margaret, she was always just Maggie. But then I got it, and I said, "Sure, she's right here." And I turned around, because Maggie had been standing right behind me about five seconds before, but she was gone. She wasn't anywhere. (Later on I found out that was sort of literally true, in a way.) "Hey, Maggie," I called out. No response.

I turned back to the guy and shrugged. "I guess she must have stepped out."

"But she does work in this place, am I correct?" Still in that harsh machine voice.

"Well, yeah. Are you a friend of hers? Should I tell her you came by? What's your name?"

"You may tell her that the Plan has become aware of her activities," he said. "Tell her we will return." And he turned and walked out.

It was only after he left that I noticed how cold the room had gotten while he was standing there. And thinking back on it now, I don't know if the door opened when he was leaving. He walked toward the door, and then he was gone, so your brain just assumes he must have opened the door, because that's what happens when people leave, they open the door.

And then I turned around again, and Maggie was standing right behind me. I guess I jumped. "Where did you come from?"

"What do you mean? I been standing here. Where would I go?"

"You didn't go to the little girls' room and come back just now?"

"No, nothing like that."

"Well, that guy was just asking about you, and I turned around, and you weren't here."

You can probably guess what she said next. She said, "What guy?"

"I don't know. He didn't say his name. A guy in a black suit, with gray glasses."

Maggie kind of moaned. "So soon, so soon. And he was asking for me? He knows my name?" I told her what he had said. "You shouldn't have said anything," she said. "You should have told him you didn't know me. But it's my fault. I should have told you to be careful." She didn't actually start hitting her head with her fists, but she looked like she wanted to.

"Okay," I said. "Are you going to tell me what this is all about?"

"You don't want to know. Believe me."

"Is that guy after you? Is he, like, a private detective or a bill collector or something? Or a cop? Maybe I can help. I mean, I'm not offering to loan you any money or anything, because I don't have any, but...."

She thought about it for a minute. I could see the wheels turning in her head. I mean, not literally. I guess I have to be careful how I say things like that, because some of the things that happened later — well, I'll get to that.

"You know how I put a little something extra in a drink, sometimes. You saw me do it," she said. "Not everybody sees that. Or if they do see it, it's like they don't quite see it. It doesn't register. But it registered with you. So maybe it's all right. I started doing it even before the Light Bulb Man found me. I thought I must be going crazy."

"That guy was the Light Bulb Man?"

"No, not him. Let me tell it. How it started, I would just have to do something. It could be anything. Ride the bus out in the country and go out into a certain field and pick a certain flower. Not any of the hundred other flowers just like it, they won't do, it has to be that one flower. Or walk down an alley and scrape some paint from the side of a building. Or hairs, it can be hairs, or a piece of gum from the sidewalk, or a little piece torn off the corner of a comic book and shredded, only it has to be that one particular comic book, that exact page. Once I had to buy a clay flowerpot from a gardening store, go up to the top of a building and drop it off, and then go down to the sidewalk and scoop up a little bit of the clay dust. I never know what it will be. And then I put whatever it is in somebody's beverage, and it changes something."

"They, like, what? Keel over dead? That would change something."

"It's not like that. I'm not hurting people, I'm *helping* them. It's like this little tiny nudge. What I do changes something, and then something else changes, and then something else, and then something can happen that wasn't going to happen because it wasn't part of the Plan, something that wouldn't have happened if I hadn't done what I did. You see?"

"I have this friend," I told her, "who has obsessive-compulsive disorder. Have you heard of it? I think they have some new drugs now that can treat it."

"Oh, yeah, I heard of it. It's not that. I thought so at first, until the Light Bulb Man explained it to me. It's about the Plan."

By this time I was thinking I had a serious fruitcake on my hands, and not the kind you can buy a slice of out of the display case. But I was all, "Okay, the Plan. Tell me about the Plan."

We got interrupted then by a couple of customers. When they were gone, she said, "The Plan is, like, how it's all supposed to be. Everything. Everything in the world. Maybe in the whole Universe, I don't know."

"Like, God's plan for the world."

"I don't think God has anything to do with it," she said. "If there is a God, I think He's way up there somewhere, way up past all this stuff. I don't know if He even knows about it. But there is definitely a Plan, and there are guys whose job is making sure everything goes according to Plan. The man you say came in here a little while ago, he isn't a man at all, that's a disguise."

"He's what, a robot?" I was getting a little sarcastic.

"Make fun of it if you like," she said. "I'm being serious. I don't know what he is, maybe a robot, maybe something else, but I know he's from the Plan. Only, they can't see me, because I'm not part of the Plan. I'm off the grid. That's how I know where he came from. When he came in, all of a sudden I was nowhere. For just a minute there, I didn't exist. I had never been born, or maybe I died a long time ago. I wouldn't even know about him, or anything at all about the Plan, because I can't see them either. The Light Bulb Man explained it all to me.

"I'm not the only one," she went on. "There's, like, this network of us, I don't know how many, maybe only a few. And maybe I'm the only one who puts things in drinks, I don't know that either. The Light Bulb Man, what he does, he goes into places, mostly public places I guess, and he thumps light bulbs. With his middle finger, he taps them in a certain way, and after that, after he's gone I guess, the bulb will flicker once in a while, and when it flickers something changes, and then something else changes, and then something happens that's not part of the Plan. He introduced me to the Water Lady. She carries around a plastic jug and dribbles water on the sidewalk."

"And then something happens."

"Right. Once in a while I see somebody doing something and I think, 'There's one of us,' but I don't say anything to them. Maybe I should. Maybe they're lonely and they think they're the only one. I don't know. That's how the Light Bulb Man found me. He saw me scraping some paint chips from the side of a building, and he stopped and said hello."

Just at that moment Rob came back from his lunch break, which was probably just as well, because I was about ready to call 9-1-1 and tell them to send somebody from the mental health department or an ambulance or something. I mean, this stuff was seriously around the bend. With Rob there, though, we couldn't talk about it. All afternoon I kept thinking I ought to say something to him, but I didn't.

After the shift ended, I ambushed her. I was waiting outside when she came shuffling out, buttoning up the green sweater she always wore, the one with the baggy sleeves and the place you could still kind of see where she'd tried to wash out a stain, and I fell into step beside her. "So where do you live, anyway?" I said brightly.

"Over on Third Street."

"Okay."

"It's just one room. It's not set up for company."

So we sat down on a bench at a bus stop with the traffic zooming by, and she told me the rest of it. Or as much as she knew, which was not a whole lot.

"It's not just knowing where to find the ingredients," she said. "That's only part of it. I know who to give them to. And I don't know how I know, I just know. I've got lots of stuff that I've had for a long time and I've never needed, and then one day I think, 'The orange seeds from Palm Springs, and that little chip of pink nail polish,' and I get them down and crush them up together, and sure enough, that afternoon somebody walks into the place where I'm working and I just know, 'He's the orange seeds and nail polish.' I know when the person walks in, and I'm always right. Even if there are four of us back there doing orders, I finish up what I'm doing right at the perfect moment to pick up that person's cup and do the order. It's not like I rush or slow down, it just happens."

"Like it's part of the Plan."

"No, no, not like that. Don't make fun of it. Or go ahead, make fun if you like. But it's not what you think. That woman with the autistic kid, and suddenly he's all better — sometimes it's a big thing like that, sometimes maybe just a little thing, but I think it's always something. Usually I never find out. A few times I've followed people, because I wanted to know, was I hurting them? A guy had his car stolen one time, right in front of me, not ten minutes after I gave him a little something extra. But how can you tell that wasn't a good thing? Maybe he needed the insurance money to pay for an operation, or maybe if he had been behind the wheel he would have been in a big pile-up."

My head was spinning. "You're saying you give them something, some kind of useless potion made of stuff you picked up in an alley, and then right after that something happens to them that has nothing whatever to do with drinking the potion? That's crazy!"

Maggie nodded unhappily. "I know it sounds crazy. Sometimes I think it is just crazy. But I took a course in college. I know about chaos. How sometimes a little thing in one place can trigger a big thing in another place, because the universe is so complicated and there's so much energy whizzing all around. They call it the butterfly effect. A butterfly flaps its wings in China, and days later there's a storm in California. It's like that. And you might not see a connection between the little thing and the big thing, but it's there.

"What I think, I think I'm stirring the pot. I'm making it so things don't go exactly according to the Plan. People like me and the Light Bulb Man and the Water Lady, we've all got our spoons, and our job is to stir things a little, here and there. But the men from the Plan, they don't like that. I guess you can see why.

"It feels good to talk about it," she said. "I don't usually tell anybody, because who would I tell? They'd lock me up for sure, and then who could I help? Everything would be down to the Plan."

By that time I was pretty sure it would be better for her, and for everybody else, if she was locked up. Nothing she was saying made sense. I had pretty much forgotten about the guy in the black suit by that time. What I was mainly thinking was that sooner or later she was going to dose somebody with ground glass and tear up their insides, and if I didn't stop her it would be my fault. But she was so *sincere* about it. That's what got to me. If somebody is a lunatic, they're supposed to be convinced they're the Messiah or something, with their eyes spinning around like pinwheels. You don't expect them to be so sincere and down-to-Earth. Or I don't, anyway.

"Is it like hearing voices?" I said. "Do you hear a voice telling you who to give the stuff to?"

"Oh, no, it's nothing like that. I just know. Come on, I'll show you my stuff."

So she took me back to her dingy little room, which was about what you'd expect, but maybe a little neater. There were curtains in the window, and she had more or less made the bed. One whole wall was this teetering bunch of shelves. "I bought the shelves at Goodwill," she said. "A nice man dragged them up the stairs for me, and he wouldn't even take a dollar for doing it." The stuff on the shelves — I couldn't even begin to describe it. Little wood boxes and airline liquor bottles and business envelopes and plastic sandwich bags, and stuff that wasn't in containers at all, seashells and dried flowers and incense sticks and rubber bands and about a million other things, none of it labeled or anything.

"This is my spice rack," she said.

"We've got to get you some help, Maggie," I said.

"Oh, I manage. I know where everything is, and I only need — oh, you mean like a psychiatrist. What good would that do?"

"It might help you feel better."

"I don't think you understand," she said, looking hurt and worried. "I thought maybe you understood, but I guess you don't. I think you'd better leave now."

So I left. But I was torn. We didn't have any health insurance where we worked that would pay for her to see a shrink, I can tell you that. Should I tell Rob and get her fired? She'd only go someplace else and start up again. Should I ask Rob to put me on a different shift from her, so I wouldn't see what she was up to and it wouldn't be my fault when somebody imbibed essence of death cap mushroom, or maybe some nice fresh plutonium? Or should I ask to be put on the same shift so I could keep an eye on her?

I was still thinking about it the next day when the big guy with the glass eye came in. Shirt-tail and guts all spilling out, like I said, no stiff black suit for this guy. There was a line, but he just barged right up to the front. The woman at the head of the line said, "Excuse me!" but he didn't even turn to look at her. To me he said, "You got a Margaret White working here." Like, not a question.

I said, "You'll have to wait in line."

"Where is she?"

This time Maggie didn't pull her vanishing act. She made a little noise, over by the grinder, like, "Uhh-ahh."

The guy swiveled to her and said, "That would be you. End of the line." And he flipped up the gate in the counter and started straight back toward her.

I told you I was taking martial arts, right? I didn't even think what to do, I kicked him in the knee, purely by reflex. And he went down like a bag of wet cement. I flung some scalding espresso all over the place too, but I hardly noticed that until afterward. I shouted, "Run, Maggie! Run!" But where was she gonna run? She was trapped between the end of the counter and the guy on the floor, and she was a little old for pole-vaulting over the counter, even if she had a pole. All she had was this little wooden stick, the kind you shove the beans down into the grinder with.

The guy got to his hands and knees, and I was set to deliver another kick, but then it started to get really weird. He got his hand wrapped around Maggie's ankle, and it was like the whole room froze. Cold, yeah, but not just cold. All of a sudden there was no sound, not any sound at all, except for maybe this icy creaking crackling noise, very quiet, a noise like maybe a glacier would make if you listened to it real close, and when I looked around nobody was moving, only me and Maggie and the guy with the glass eye. Everybody else, it was like they were caught in a black-and-white photograph.

Maggie whimpered and batted at the guy a couple of times with the wooden stick, but that didn't do any good. I kicked him again, as hard as I could. He grunted and let go of Maggie, and the room started moving again, and then he dissolved. Look, I don't care if you don't believe me, that's what happened. Not into smoke, either. He dissolved into this pattern of blue-gray rectangles, like little sheets of glass the size of postage stamps, with more of the ice-crackling noise, and then he wasn't there any more.

The customers were like, "What happened? Where did he go?" I told them he crawled away, and we'd take care of it.

Maggie said, "He'll be back. I got to go. I got to get out of here."

"Where are you gonna go?"

"I don't know. Somewhere. Anywhere." She started to take off her apron. "This happened before, but never so close. I keep moving around. Eight years I been moving around, and it's never been this close."

"Maybe somebody can help. What about the Light Bulb Man? Can he help?"

"That was two years ago," she said. "In Arizona.

People like us, we don't have cell phones."

"We got customers," I said. "You gonna leave me alone back here? Come on, Maggie. Let's leave it for later, okay? Maybe we can figure out something." So she went back to grinding the beans, but she kept glancing at the door, waiting for the guy to come back, or somebody like him,

She should have taken off her apron and run, right then. Maybe she didn't because the guy had touched her and his fingers sucked something out of her. Maybe she knew even if she ran, she wasn't going to get far. Or maybe I should have kept my mouth shut.

About an hour later I had popped this veggie burrito out of the microwave and put it on a plate, and I was taking it upstairs to the guy who ordered it. We don't exactly do table service, but he was a regular, and sometimes he put a five in the tip jar. So that was how I happened to be up on the balcony when they came back. It's this little narrow balcony with only four tables, but it has a solid waist-high railing, which turned out to be important. I put the plate down on the guy's table, and he says thanks, and I turn to look out over the main room just as both of them come back. The door definitely didn't open that time, they were just there suddenly, the big guy with the glass eye and the gray guy in the black suit, and they vectored over straight at Maggie. Rob was behind the counter too, and he said, "Hey, what—" They just powered right past him, and the big guy grabbed Maggie again, by the shoulders this time, and just like the first time, the whole room froze solid, like a photograph.

The guy in the black suit was carrying some kind of remote control thing in his hands, too big to be a remote control but I don't know what else to call it, like a fat iPad except it had knobs, and he fiddled with it for a second while Maggie looked straight up at me, and her lips were moving but I don't know what she was saying because there wasn't any sound. And then a sort of grid of these thin glass pipes started forming all around her and the big guy, a grid with square corners like it was a nest of hollow cubes or something, and the glow from the grid got brighter and brighter with Maggie and the big guy inside it, and then it got too bright to look at, and then it was gone, and Maggie and the big guy were gone too.

Okay, I know you think I'm crazy. I'm just telling you what happened.

The whole room was still frozen, except for some reason I wasn't, I could see it all. The guy in the black suit fiddled with his remote some more, and then he pointed it at Rob. He started around the room, pointing it at everybody, one person at a time. So I ducked down behind the railing. I was pretty sure if he saw me I'd be in big trouble. I crouched down there for a minute, trying not to breathe because I figured he might hear me, and then the people on the balcony started moving and talking again, just like nothing had happened.

I went downstairs and said to Rob, "Have you seen Maggie around anywhere?"

He gave me this really blank look and said, "Maggie? Maggie who?" Right away, I could see what the guy did with the remote control. It was like Rob's brain was a magnetic strip on a credit card and somebody had set it down on the demagnetizer. His memory had been wiped. I pushed a little, and it was clear he really didn't know who I was talking about. The thing about Rob, you can read him. He's not a smooth liar. He had no memory of Maggie at all.

I went outside for a minute to try to get my breath, because I was hyperventilating, and I looked up at the sky and it was almost yellow, this flat bright nasty color, and the noise on the street was so close to me I could feel it crawling on my skin under my clothes, and I thought, this is how it's going to be now. Forever. What if they got the Light Bulb Man too? If they did, maybe the whole world is stuck. Nobody is ever going to come along and make any little adjustments anymore. It's all happening according to the Plan. Nothing wonderful will ever happen to anybody by accident, not ever again, we're all just rats on our little treadmills, and all the treadmills in the world are going around and around and around forever, clickety-click.

Maybe there are lots of other Maggies out there, still off the grid, still stirring things up, but maybe they rounded them all up. How would I know? I'm just saying, how it felt. It was a really awful feeling.

So I went back into the place and started making an espresso for this guy wearing shorts and a baseball cap, because what else are you going to do? I mean, was I going to go around the room telling people, "This guy with an iPad just erased your memory"? I don't think so.

About an hour later this trio of firemen came in, like they did every Tuesday, and I looked at the redheaded one with the narrow shoulders and that was when it hit me. He needed some pine needles in his latte. Not too many, just a little sprinkle of ground-up pine needles. I couldn't tell you why, I just knew. And sure enough, I got handed his order, and I rummaged under the counter and there was a saucer with a few dried-up pine needles in it, which I had never seen before, that's for sure. I guess Maggie must have brought them in that morning. So I crushed them with a spoon. I don't think he noticed the latte tasted of pine needles, he just drank it down.

After work I went over to Maggie's place and started taking down the stuff on the shelves. I don't know where I'm going to store it all, but I have a feeling some of it may come in handy.

Maybe this fall I'll take a trip down to Arizona and see if I can hook up with the Light Bulb Man. Maybe he's still out there somewhere, you never know. Yeah, I'm worried about the guys from the Plan, but Maggie said she went on for eight years, so maybe it was just a fluke how they tracked her down. Anyway, I'm still taking the martial arts classes — more now than before. When they come after me, I'm gonna be ready.

Statues

ALL THE WAY HOME FROM the airport Aunt Edith chattered gaily about people Laura didn't know and places Laura had never been. It was too much trouble to pay attention, so she just sat and stared out the window at the freeway traffic. She wondered dully whether Aunt Edith was being cheerful to help her feel welcome, or whether she made Aunt Edith nervous. She wanted to apologize for making Aunt Edith nervous, but apologizing would only make it worse, so she said nothing. The car was hot and stuffy because the heater was running full blast, and Aunt Edith's perfume smelled like the sickly sweet antiseptic they used in the hospital. Laura couldn't breathe, but there was no crank to open the window, only a confusing array of buttons on the armrest. When Aunt Edith slackened momentarily to negotiate a left turn, Laura said, "Is there a — I'm not sure how you open the window."

"Oh, you don't want the window open, dear. It's freezing out. You wouldn't want to take a chance on catching a chill, not until you're better."

Did Aunt Edith think she had had pneumonia?

How much had Aunt Edith been told? At the thought that her aunt must already know the whole awful story, Laura cringed in shame. She shrank down in the seat and let Aunt Edith chatter on, interjecting only the occasional obligatory murmur. Even that took a great effort. She was tired, so tired. She hoped Aunt Edith already knew everything. That way Laura wouldn't have to try to explain. Explaining was impossible. The streets outside the window slid by in a meaningless blur.

She roused herself when Aunt Edith turned off onto a curving street posted with rural mailboxes and guided the car up a steep driveway. Laura knew that Aunt Edith and Uncle Henry had money. Ever since she was a little girl, she had looked forward to opening the box under the Christmas tree that came from them, because what was in it was always nicer than the things her parents could afford. But she had only imagined what their house must be like. The first thing she noticed was how unkempt the grounds were — certainly nothing like her vision of what a mansion's grounds ought to look like. The scraggly trees marching down the hillside must be the remains of an orchard, and the gully off to the left was choked in brush. Maybe they weren't rich after all — maybe the lavish gifts were a pretense to fool the relatives. Maybe they wouldn't be able to afford to have her stay, and she'd have to turn around and go home on the next plane.

But the house reassured her. At the top of the slope, it was a huge rambling place, white stucco and red tile roof in the Spanish style, with wrought-iron grilles over the windows. They might do things differently in California, but a mansion was still a mansion.

Laura remembered pulling up to another big white building a year ago, the dorm, her parents in the front seat pointing in admiration at the neatly manicured lawns of the college. Her pulse had raced at the thought of starting an exciting new grown-up life. The dorm looked so clean and pleasant, but later she had started dreading it, it was a place where all her dreams turned sick and bloated, and suddenly Aunt Edith's house was full of slimy things too, nameless dead things that wanted to crawl across her naked body and into her mouth and choke her, so she sat in the car trembling and didn't even try to figure out how to open the door while Aunt Edith went inside to fetch the maid to carry the suitcases, and when they came back out Laura had thrown up the airport restaurant lunch all over her new winter coat.

The next morning when she woke the room was quiet and cold and filled with silver light. After the deep vibration of the plane ride and then the roaring confusion of the freeway, the stillness was as thick as cake frosting. She lay warm and cozy under the white blanket and looked around at the mirror on the dressing table, the lace curtains, the pale pastel wallpaper. Aunt Edith and Uncle Henry didn't have any children, so this wasn't a daughter's room where she was trespassing, it was a guest room made to look like a daughter's room. Laura had always wanted to wake up in a room like this. This was the kind of room they gave you when you died and went to Heaven. For a while she had thought the hospital room was like a room in Heaven, but that was while she was still under sedation. The hospital room smelled of chemicals and pain and fear, and even after she was no longer quite so weak physically, she still felt drained and helpless there because nobody listened when she tried to tell them what she wanted. What she wanted was for them to go away and leave her alone, especially Mama. But Mama was always there, sitting at the side of the bed watching her with that dubious, wounded look, trapping Laura's hand between both of hers and scrunching her eyes shut while her lips moved in prayer. The praying was a kind of torture, because it kept Laura from forgetting why she was in the hospital. She screamed sometimes, and threw things, but that only made Mama pray harder.

This room was as cold and white as the hospital room, and there was the same sense that nobody had ever really lived here. But it smelled much nicer — down the hall someone was making toast — and Aunt Edith hadn't tried to do any praying yet.

Laura didn't want to pray, or be prayed for, ever again. And that was a bitterly shameful thing to feel. Mama loved her, and here she was being ungrateful. More important, she was shutting herself off from the love of Jesus Christ. Or had she shut herself off from the Lord a year ago, and been living in Hell ever since?

To escape that oppressive thought, she jumped out of bed and padded barefoot across the cold slick hardwood floor to look out the window. A thin winter fog lay across the hills, shrouding the bare black trees in vagueness. The sun was only a smudged ball sailing in the mist; it gave no warmth, and as she watched it slid behind a gray curtain. Laura had never seen a California winter before. Snow was a trial, but if anything the absence of snow added to the gloom. It was as if this were some ancient season of heatlessness from before the dawn of time, out of which the crystalline winter of Illinois had been born, a bad-tempered child destined one day to be swallowed back into its eternal parent.

At the edge of the grove of trees behind the house, where the fog hung thickest, she thought for a moment that she saw four or five indistinct shapes, whiter blurs in the whiteness. She felt a hot flush of self-consciousness, quite sure suddenly, and for no reason at all, that the shapes were watching her. But when she blinked, they were gone. She shivered. She had only imagined it. There was nothing there, nobody.

⚯ II ⚯

"It's kind of you to let me come visit," she told Aunt Edith at breakfast. Uncle Henry had already left for the office. Uncle Henry was in investment properties. Laura had no idea what investment properties were. She and Aunt Edith were sharing toast and orange juice on the butcher-block table in the big shiny kitchen.

"I'm just pleased that you wanted to come. It's been so long since we saw our little Laura. And you *are* looking well, dear. I was afraid the journey would tire you."

Laura chewed toast. She didn't look well, she knew, and the journey had nothing to do with it. But Aunt Edith seemed willing to sweep the details under the rug. Some things, Laura was pretty sure, could never be swept under the rug. They made lumps, lumps you stumbled over every time you turned around. But if Aunt Edith wanted to help her chart a course around the lumps, that was all right.

"I've been thinking," Aunt Edith went on. "I'm gone so much of the time, with my card club and various obligations, and I hate to think of you here all alone. I'm sure you'd like to meet some girls your own age. Wouldn't that be nice? There are several nice girls right here in Monte Sereno who are daughters of friends of mine."

The toast turned to paper in Laura's mouth. "Please, Aunt Edith, you don't have to do anything special. I don't want to meet anybody."

"Nonsense. You can't possibly have any fun cooped up here all day. I've arranged for you to attend a party next weekend. Now don't fuss, dear, just listen. Sally Lawrence is having a big bash on Friday, and it just so happens that Sally's daughter Amy is about your age. Amy is inviting some of her friends to the party, so I asked Sally straight out if you couldn't come, and of course she said they'd be delighted. So that's all settled."

The tiredness washed over Laura, turning the kitchen a wavering undersea green. "All right, Aunt Edith." Friday was too far away to worry about.

"Do you have something nice to wear? Or should we go shopping? I know some of the most darling little boutiques, and I'd love to help you pick out a new outfit."

"I can wear my wool skirt."

"I must say," Aunt Edith said, "you don't sound very enthusiastic for a girl who's going to a party."

Laura wondered why anybody *would* be enthusiastic about going to a party. There were two kinds of parties, she knew. One kind was where everybody was polite and well-behaved, and there was always a chaperon to suggest playing games that had been fun when you were twelve but weren't much fun anymore, unless you tried really hard to pretend. That was the kind she and her little sisters had gone to when she was in high school. The other kind, the kind she discovered at college, was where everybody was drinking liquor and laughing about things that weren't nice, and the boys were always putting their hands on the girls and trying to get them to go off in a dark corner.

Her father had warned her about the college kind

of parties. The night before they drove up to the dorm he sat her down in the living room and sent her sisters away and lectured her for two hours on morality. "I'm not sure but what it's a mistake," he declared, "to send you fifty miles away to a big city like Champaign-Urbana, where you'll be exposed to who knows what kind of indecent influences. But that scholarship is a blessed opportunity for which we should be properly grateful, so we'll just have to pray to the Lord to protect you from temptation. I want you to promise me you'll go to church every single Sunday, and not ever go to a party where they're serving liquor, and not ever let a boy come into your room. You don't know what might happen. The flesh is weak. The flesh is weak." He was gripping her shoulder so hard she was sure his fingers would leave bruises. The granite lines of his face were inches away, and she couldn't meet his eyes, she could never meet his eyes, so she stared at the front of his shirt and tried not to fidget because if she fidgeted he would demand to know what impure thought she was hiding, and he would hound her until she confessed to something, anything, to escape the awful intensity of his wrath. "I'm going to write to the Dean of Girls," he said, "and ask her to look in on you and report back to let me know exactly how you're doing, and what sort of company you're keeping. And I'd better not hear any stories about you associating with the wrong sort of person."

Even so, it was only the third week of school when another girl at the dorm dragged her off to a party. Laura tried to resist, but she didn't try very hard. She was curious to see what kind of vice and depravity her father had been talking about. He had been forceful, but not very specific. She was quite sure she could resist temptation. After all, she had given her life to Christ. Christ would watch over her, wouldn't He?

And really, the party was nearly as tame as one of her little sisters' birthday parties. It wasn't even one of those notorious fraternity parties; it was in the basement of another dorm. But when she saw them emptying a bottle of something into the punch, she put down her cup without taking another sip and went to find the Coke machine.

That was how she met Stan. The Coke machine took her money and jammed, and she was standing there wondering what to do when a voice behind her said, "That thing busted again? Here, let me." He was a big pale blond boy with snowy wisps of eyebrows, a pouting mouth, and baby fat rounding his cheeks. He was nicely dressed in dark slacks, and his shoes were shined, but his shirt was rumpled where it bulged out over his belt. She stood back gratefully, and he hauled off and hit the machine as hard as he could with the flat of his hand. Laura's ears stung; the whole room seemed to jump and ring. He slammed the machine again. Somewhere inside there was a dark *clunk,* and a can of Coke slid through the little door into the tray.

"Thank you." Popping the top, she sipped.

"There's punch too, if you want any."

"I saw them putting something in it."

He nodded knowledgeably. "Vodka. You ever been drunk?"

She shook her head. "No, I'm a Christian."

"You are?" The boy's eyes lit up. "So am I. My name's Stan. Stan Marshall. Sometimes they call me Marshall Stan." He hitched his thumbs in his belt and swaggered.

She giggled. His face clouded. "All right, make fun of me if you want."

"Oh, no," she said hastily. "I wasn't making fun of you. I didn't mean anything by it, honestly. My name's Laura." His touchiness intimidated her a little, but he was a Christian, and that made it all right. They stood together in the dank cement room with the Coke machine, neither of them sure what to say next.

"Were you raised a Christian?" he said. "I'm Born Again."

"My father is a minister. Methodist."

"Oh." He seemed faintly disappointed. "My mom was a Congregationalist, but she hardly ever went to church. It's only been six months since I accepted Jesus Christ as my personal Savior, but He's made my whole life over. I just can't stop praising His name."

"Would you like to come to church next Sunday?" Laura spoke without thinking, and then blushed furiously at her own boldness.

"Would it be all right? Could I?"

So that was how it started. You never knew what a party might lead to, which was an excellent reason for staying away from parties. Still, Aunt Edith was trying to be helpful. Laura didn't want to seem ungrateful.

Aunt Edith paused with a knifeload of jam poised above a slice of toast. "Are you feeling all right, dear? Did you hear a word I said?"

"About what?"

"About Amy Lawrence and the girls who will be there Friday."

"I'm sorry, Aunt Edith. I'm not feeling too good." And that was the truth. "I think I'd like to go lie down."

She went to her room and lay down, but now that she had started thinking about Stan it was hard to stop. After a minute she got up again. Aunt Edith was still in the kitchen, chattering to the telephone, or else to the maid. Laura put on a sweater and a windbreaker and went out the glass-paneled door that let directly from her bedroom onto the patio.

A silver haze lay along the land, leaching away color, leaving only browns and grays. Beyond the first low hill the second was a ghostly silhouette. The lawn was sodden with freezing dew. Laura's cheeks burned in the chill, and she zipped up the windbreaker. Except for the distant whoosh of traffic on the main road, she might have stepped back in time two thousand years. The houses in this prosperous suburb were tucked away behind tall hedges. Except for a roof-line or two, the scene seemed unpeopled, remote, though she was pretty sure if she walked more than fifty yards in any direction she'd come out by somebody's carport. She crossed the lawn light-footed and found a path among the taller wild growth, a low jungle luxuriantly green in California's paradoxical December spring.

Under the trees there was less vegetation. Low crumbling brickwork suggested that this might once have been a formal garden, but the flower beds had long since gone to ruin in dry scrub and drifts of leaves. She walked slowly, hands jammed deep in her pockets. A squirrel eyed her cautiously from around the trunk of a tree. Here and there among the fallen leaves were white-brown bursts of mushrooms. Somewhere near here, she realized, was where she had seen out her window, or imagined that she saw, the pale shapes in the fog. There was nothing here now. She strolled deeper into the grove, turning aside when she saw the fender of a Mercedes gleaming behind a bush and heading down a gentle slope toward the sound of an invisible creek. There was no more brick underfoot now, only gravel and straggling vines.

Walking with her head down, watching her toes scuff up leaves, she nearly collided with the first statue before she saw it. She gasped and backed up, heart thudding. But the pale figure failed to leap at her, and after a frozen moment she saw what it was and laughed. Standing before her, staring solemnly at her, was the chalk-white figure of a man. He was a little more than six feet tall, broad-shouldered and muscular, dressed in a short tunic that left one shoulder and part of his chest bare. One arm was raised nearly horizontal and held out from his body, palm open in a gesture of welcome, or of demonstration, as one who says, "See; you may." From his tightly curled hair and strong clean-shaven chin to his sandalled feet, he was the dirty white of old plaster or stone.

She stepped to one side, and the statue stayed gazing blankly at the spot where she had been. She had half-expected its eyes to follow her, but of course they didn't.

What was it doing here? Or, to put the question another way, where had her wandering led her? She looked around, and her mouth fell open. The statue was not alone. The grove was peopled with silent white figures, motionless, standing here and there in no particular order. She had walked into the middle of the group without noticing. Back along the path, off to one side and facing inward toward her, stood a middle-aged woman wearing a long flowing robe, her arms open with the palms out in a posture that might have been the beginning of an embrace. On the other side of the path, near the thick bole of an oak tree, an old man with a full beard and mane of hair was leaning on a staff. The hair and beard would be white, of course, but so were the face and robe and staff.

Beyond the man she had seen first was another woman, this one younger, down on one knee, leaning forward as though to examine her reflection in a pool — though there was no pool, only leaves and dirt. Her robe, like the curly-haired man's, fell away from one shoulder, revealing a bare breast. Near her stood a boy of six or seven frozen in the act of drawing a small recurved bow. Unlike the adults, the boy was naked. Opposite these two in the clearing was a heavyset man who sat on a stone bench. Evidently he was an artisan, for his tools were arrayed beside him. And at the far side of the grove, half-hidden behind a bush, was a satyr playing on a set of reed pipes. The nubs of horns — Satanic horns! — peeped from his brow, and when Laura timidly tiptoed closer she saw that his legs were hairy goat's legs. They ended in hooves! That almost sent her bolting from the grove, but she caught her breath and stood her ground, pulse pounding. Since the satyr wasn't on a pedestal — none of them were — it seemed impossible that he could be balanced on two slim hooves without falling over. His center of gravity wasn't even over the hooves, or so it seemed; his bunched muscles showed that he was dancing, and it was obvious he would have to move one leg forward at any moment to catch his weight.

The figures were all like that, Laura saw, not clamped in static poses but held lightly by unseen fingers in a moment of arrested motion, as if time had separated itself from them and flowed on, leaving them to wait with effortless patience for it to return and breathe life into them again. Standing in the center of the grove, turning slowly to take it all in, she felt she was no longer in the world she knew but in another place entirely, a place that had always existed and had no name.

The fog dripped softly from the branches. Her

breath steamed on the air. Somewhere a dog barked once, and was still.

As she examined the statues more closely, she saw that they had not been well cared for. There were no chipped noses or missing fingers, but the surfaces, especially the finely incised lines of detail, were dark with forest grime. The artisan had rings of evaporated rain water in the hollow of his lap, and the angles of the child's bow were clotted with years of spider web festooned with bits of leaf and twig. The satyr was especially filthy; he looked as if he had been buried and dug up.

The sense that the statues might suddenly spring to life was eroded somewhat by the pervasive neglect, and this saddened Laura. It was better not to look at them too closely. It was better to sit with her back against a tree and let her eyelids droop so the grove slurred and starred with light, and pretend that the little gathering was a magic place where nothing could ever be soiled.

✄ III ✄

That night at dinner she asked Uncle Henry, "Who owns the statues?"

"I do, I guess." He spooned onion soup into his big square face. "They were here when we bought the property. Previous owner must have picked them up in one of those antique stores in Saratoga. I keep meaning to have them appraised. Can't be worth much, not the condition they must be in. How'd you happen to stumble onto them?"

"I was out taking a walk."

"Now, dear," Aunt Edith scolded. "I do hope you bundled up and stayed close to the house. I promised your mother we'd take good care of you."

The next morning when Aunt Edith had gone off to have her hair done, Laura went looking for the maid. Victoria was in the living room, dusting. She was a tall, thin Negro girl only a year or two older than Laura, with the flawless features and carriage of a fashion model. But there was no vivacity in her. She spoke and moved with the flatness of a closed door. She was standing in front of the open display case that held Aunt Edith's collection of china dolls, picking up the dolls one by one, polishing each one with a flick of a rag and wiping the area where it had stood before she replaced it. The dolls — shepherds and shepherdesses and ballerinas and huntsmen and clowns — were far too cute, with the smug, coy painted faces of children whose lives are devoted to convincing adults how adorably nice they are.

"Excuse me," Laura said. Victoria stopped, holding a doll — a milkmaid with a brace of pails balanced on a yoke. Both maids looked at Laura. "Could you tell me where I could find a bucket and some detergent and a scrub brush?"

"In the garage," Victoria said. Flick, flick went the rag across the doll's shoulders. "On the shelf beside the washing machine."

"Thanks.

"You got somethin' you need cleaned?"

"No," Laura said — and then felt foolish, remembering how she had vomited the day she arrived. Victoria must think she was in the habit of making messes like an ill-trained puppy, and now was trying to clean up the latest one without letting anybody know. "It's not — it's nothing. I'll take care of it myself."

Victoria accepted this information gravely. "You

change your mind, just let me know."

The sudsy water steamed in the cold morning. Today the fog had retreated a few hundred feet into the air, where it hung, a gray blanket threatening rain. The bucket handle dug into Laura's fingers, and she had to change hands twice before she reached the grove.

Now where to start? With seven statues and only one of her, the task was formidable, but for some reason that she could not have articulated, it was vitally important. After wandering from one to another, peering into their faces and touching them lightly, lingeringly, with her fingertips, she set the bucket down beside the boy with the bow, dug the brush out of her pocket, and went to work.

When she wiped away the first suds, his shoulder was hard and smooth and white. The surface lacked the grain of marble, and not being an expert in stone, she had no idea what it might be. It was hard enough that the brush bristles left no mark, that was the important thing, so she worked onward patch by patch, dipping the brush again and again into the bucket. The suds weakened and her shoulder began to throb, but she paid no attention. The rhythm of the scrubbing filled her, and the pleasure of watching the shining area grow. Briefly the sun poked through the clouds and shone down golden on the boy's torso. Laura stood back to admire her work, wiped a lock of hair away from her eyes with the back of her hand, and bent to pick up the bucket. It was time for more hot water.

"Did you have a nice day, dear?" Again the dinner table, the long white cloth and the asymmetrical Scandinavian candelabra, again Uncle Henry shoveling food into his face and chewing, as methodically as if he were refueling a robot.

"It was all right."

"What did you do?"

"Oh, nothing much." She wasn't about to share the statues with anyone, but especially not with Aunt Edith, who would be either uninterested or far too interested.

The next day it rained, so Laura stayed indoors, but the day after she went back to work, getting thoroughly muddy kneeling on the ground. Alone with the statues, she had started talking to them — or to herself, which was the same thing. "There, that's better," she declared when she finished an eye and a nose. "Isn't that better?" Or, scraping away at the loose dirt covering a foot, "Look at that mess. It's a shame you can't take better care of yourselves. What would you have done if I hadn't come along?" The statues listened placidly, never interrupting her, never correcting her or criticizing her or telling her what to think. The silence was a balm that seeped up out of the Earth. "My mother used to spank me," she murmured, "when I didn't clean behind my ears."

Cleaning below the boy's waist was awkward, because he was naked. She didn't want to do it, but she could see it would look funny if she didn't. "Why couldn't they have put some clothes on you?" she asked him. She tried scrubbing with her eyes closed, but then she had to work by feel, which was even more embarrassing. She didn't think the boy's genitals looked quite right. She didn't know it was because he wasn't circumcised. She had never seen a penis, other than Stan's, and Stan's didn't look anything like this one. The memories rose up as she scrubbed. She shuddered, and swallowed back the bitter taste in her throat. But in this place, somehow, remembering lost a little of its sting.

During those first weeks after they started going to church together, it seemed she ran into Stan everywhere

— in the halls outside the classrooms, in the cafeteria, in the rec room at the dorm. He was always friendly, in that nervous way she never quite got used to, laughing a little too loud and then suddenly turning apprehensive, as if he had seen a snake. In the evenings they went to the coffee shop together to study. Walking back to the dorm afterward, he was unfailingly polite. He never tried to hold her hand or kiss her, though sometimes he clenched and unclenched his fingers while he breathed hard through his nose, which made her think he must want to. But where was the harm in making whuffing noises? "I really did start to think he was nice," she said to the statue.

Until the weekend in January when her roommate had gone away for the weekend. By now Stan had taken to dropping by whenever he felt like it, which was practically every day, or else explaining the next day why he hadn't come by, as if he thought she had been worrying. That Saturday night he came by with an armload of books, but instead of suggesting that they go to the coffee shop to study he paced and fidgeted and alternately babbled and turned morose in the little room for three solid hours until she wanted to scream at him, and then suddenly he leaped at her and grabbed her and hugged her so tight she couldn't breathe and bruised her lips against her teeth kissing her.

She was too bewildered to struggle, so she only stood limp, waiting to be released. But the kiss went on and on, and he began easing her backward toward the bed. She did struggle then, but her arms were feeble weightless things. They thrashed against his sides and did no good. He got her down on the bed on her back, still gripping her tightly. Except for a couple of discreet pecks on the front porch, with the porch light on and the curtains twitching, Laura had never been kissed, but she could tell Stan wasn't a good kisser. His whole face was tensed with the effort of keeping his lips pressed together and pressed tight against hers. She rolled her face away, but his head followed, his mouth pushing against whatever part of her face it could reach. He was snorting through his nose like a steam engine. Freeing one arm from the embrace, he reached down and began tugging at her skirt, pulling the folds of cloth up around her waist to expose her underwear. Then he began tugging at his own belt.

"Stan, no, please Stan, don't, please, you mustn't, no, stop, I don't want you to, Stan, don't do that, please don't, you're hurting me, let me up, Stan, don't, don't, no, no." Strangely, it didn't occur to her to scream. The situation was so far beyond anything she had ever envisioned that her mind plunged into a blanket of numbness. The room and the two figures on the bed were something that was happening to somebody else, very far away. She could only plead in a scared little voice and squirm as he pulled her panties down. There was more fumbling then; she couldn't see what he was doing, because she had her eyes squeezed shut.

The dry, tearing pain took her by surprise, and she did yell then, and Stan clamped a hand over her mouth. She opened her eyes to see his face hovering over her, brow furrowed with intensity. He wasn't looking at her; he was looking at a corner of the pillow. The burning pain deepened. He was pushing something into her, over and over. His body was so heavy on her she thought she'd be crushed.

It was over quickly. He made a noise in his throat, part gasp and part moan, and an unfamiliar wetness was spreading inside her. His breathing slowed.

After a minute he let his hand up from her mouth. They lay together, not moving, not looking at one another. The room seemed emptier than it had been a minute before. Somewhere down the hall a stereo was blaring. Belatedly it came to her that the door wasn't locked. Unless he had locked it; she couldn't remember. If he hadn't, someone might walk in at any moment.

Stan rolled off the bed, pulled his trousers up, and fastened them. She curled up on her side, knees drawn up, staring at the wall. He leaned over and pulled her skirt down to hide her shame. Say something, Stan, she pled silently. Say anything. Tell me you love me so I can scream. She could hear him moving around the room, the scrape of a chair, the thump of a book against the desk. Then the door opened and closed and he was gone. She was alone.

It hurt a lot, but she never touched herself down there if she could help it, and it didn't occur to her to examine herself to see how badly she was injured. The pain was the price you paid for sin, that was all. She guessed she must have led Stan on, encouraged him somehow without knowing it. She wondered whether he would be ashamed and not want to see her again (which didn't seem such a bad thing), whether he would boast to his friends (if he had any friends), whether her life was ruined. She didn't feel ruined; she didn't feel much of anything.

The next morning as she was putting on her good shoes there was a shy, tentative knock at the door. Not even wondering who it might be, she answered it. Stan was standing there in his slightly rumpled suit, looking somewhat more ill-at-ease than usual, watching her doubtfully from under his feathery brows. "Are you ready for church?" he asked.

He had forced the night before back into non-existence by an effort of will. She was so grateful for the deceit she almost wanted to hug him. Almost, but not quite. She said, "I'll be ready in a minute."

So their relationship entered a new phase. They never spoke of it. Outwardly they went on as before, studying together, carrying their trays to the same table in the cafeteria, going to church every Sunday. He never tried to take her hand or put his arm around her. But nearly every weekend, in her room or his, he did what he needed to do, and she lay still and let him. After the first time it didn't hurt quite so badly. There was always a little bleeding, but she had no reason to think that wasn't normal.

She couldn't have explained why she let him keep doing it. It was easier than resisting, that was all. If he had apologized, if he had tried to be affectionate, her anger and fear and shame might have broken through. But in the vacuum of diffidence and outward respect, there was no catalyst around which her resistance could crystallize. There was only Stan, moon-faced omnipresent Stan, Stan with his nervous swings from hectic activity to moody withdrawal, Stan whom she gradually, as the weeks turned to months, began to loathe even when he was being nice. He was an intrusion like a cancer, impossible to eject, and as they smiled and nodded to the people at church she wondered whether any of them might suspect, whether it would show, but nobody gave any sign. The timid girl and her large rumpled boyfriend were good Christians.

"And we were," she said to the statue of the boy, dipping the brush in the bucket to apply suds to his backside. "I was, anyway. I used to pray, 'Dear sweet Jesus, please make Stanley stop. Make him leave me alone.' But praying didn't do any good, so then I thought it must be that the Lord wasn't listening because I was a sinner. He had cast me out of His heart. I wasn't worthy of Him. But I kept on praying anyhow. I didn't know what else to do."

The statues accepted her confidences with boundless placidity.

❧ IV ❧

By Friday afternoon she had finished cleaning the boy and the kneeling woman. She was working on the old man with the staff when gathering darkness forced her to stop. Trudging up the lawn with the bucket, she saw Aunt Edith standing on the patio waiting. "There you are! I've been looking all over for you. You'll have to hurry or we'll be late for Amy's party."

Laura had forgotten about the party. Her heart sank. "Aunt Edith, I wonder if — would it be all right if I stayed home? I really don't feel like going to a party."

"Nonsense, dear. I won't hear of it. They're *expecting* you, and I'm sure you'll have a wonderful time. Now come inside and get cleaned up. Look at you! You're a dreadful mess."

In spite of her aunt's assurances, she didn't have a wonderful time. There were close to a hundred people at the party, or so it seemed, a dozen Laura's age, none of whom she knew, and the rest older. Laura was barely introduced to Amy Lawrence and her mother before they were whisked away to meet somebody else, so she sat on the couch by herself and drank tepid pink punch and watched the Christmas lights strung across the mantel blink and twinkle among the tinsel. Wherever she went, she was sure, she would be this alone. The things that were important in your life were things you couldn't talk to anybody about, it was too painful, and compared to the important things anything else you might talk about was oppressively trivial, so you might as well say nothing.

"Hello."

Laura looked up. The woman was thirty or a little older. She stood with the poise of a dancer, and there was a kindly sparkle in her eye.

"Mind if I join you?"

"No, I guess not." Laura gestured vaguely at a vacant chair.

"You don't look like you're in a party mood."

"I don't know anybody here. I just came because my aunt said I should. I'm out here in California visiting, and she thought I should meet some people my own age."

"How old are you?"

"Twenty."

"You remind me of myself when I was twenty," the woman said.

"Really?" Laura had been admiring the strong planes of the woman's face, the air of confidence, the elegant earrings. That's what I'd like to be like someday, she had been thinking.

"Really. I was convinced I didn't have a friend in the world. A couple of very nasty things had happened to me, and I thought my life was over. But it was just beginning." She smiled at Laura.

Laura was curious what the nasty things might be; they couldn't possibly be as nasty as her nasty things. But it wouldn't be polite to ask. Instead she said, "What do you do? I mean, do you have a job, or are you married?"

"You make it sound like an either-or choice. Most

married women work. But no, I'm not married."

"Oh, I'm sorry."

"Sorry? Don't be. I like living my own life."

"I didn't mean that," Laura said hurriedly, though in fact she had. "I meant, I shouldn't pry."

"You're not prying. We're talking."

"Do you — do you work in an office?"

"I used to," the woman said, "but not any more. I'm a sculptor. Here, I'll show you." She dug into her purse, which was large enough to hold a full complement of mallets and chisels, and fished up an object wrapped in soft cloth. Unwrapping it, she revealed a figurine about eight inches tall, carved of dark wood and polished until it glowed. "I'm doing a series of these. I just finished this one yesterday." She held it out. "Go ahead, you can hold it. It's all right."

Laura reached out and then drew her hand back. Her cheeks burned. The figurine was carved in the likeness of a very pregnant, and very naked, woman. The features were stylized, exaggerated, but there was no doubt what they represented. "It — she doesn't have any clothes on."

"So? Neither do I. Neither do you."

"What?" Laura's gaze dropped in alarm from the woman's stylish satin blouse to her own sensible wool skirt.

"Underneath our clothes, silly. We're naked all the time. They used to make these in the Stone Age — ten or fifteen thousand years ago. They made them from clay or stone, not just wood. Probably they made them by tying dried grass together too, but those are gone now."

"Why would anybody — I mean, what did they make them for?"

"Nobody knows. They might have been dolls for the children to play with. More likely they were religious objects. This is the Great Mother — the Mother Goddess, the Earth Goddess. I'm reviving a lost art form." The woman set the figurine on the coffee table.

That was surely some kind of sacrilege, but Laura didn't know enough about sacrilege to say so. After hesitating, she picked up the figurine, holding it gingerly by the ankles and the top of the head. "It's very pretty," she said. It embarrassed her, even aside from the scandalous talk of goddesses, but it *was* pretty, the smooth grain of the dark wood highlighting the curves of the belly and breasts and buttocks, the inscrutable heavy-lidded face, the large peasant hands, the sturdy flat feet. "You must be very talented, to be able to make something like this."

"Oh, I don't make them. I find them."

A chill teased the back of Laura's neck. "You find them? I thought you said you carved them."

"I do. What I mean is, I find them inside the wood. It's — how can I explain it? Every piece of wood is different, because every tree is different. The tree was alive. You can't just sit down and carve something according to a set of instructions. What you do is, you live with a piece of wood. You sit and look at it, and you keep turning it over and over, and pretty soon you start to get inside of it, you kind of scrunch down in there," swaying her shoulders gently from side to side, "and then you start to see what shape it is on the inside. That shape, whatever it is, is the shape of the figure that's waiting in the wood for you to release it. It might be a wolf or a deer. I don't just make Earth Goddesses.

"When you start to see what's inside the wood, that's when you have to get very slow and move very lightly. If you jump — if you say, 'Ah-ha! That's what it is, it's a seal, and I know how to carve seals, so here goes!' — if you do that, you lose it. What you get when you're finished may look like a seal, but it won't be the seal that was in the wood to start with. That seal you won't ever be able to get back. So you have to be quiet, and wait until that particular seal comes to you and lets you touch it and hold it and feel it and play with it. When you really know that seal, when you're already holding it in your hand, *then* you pick up your tools and carve away the part of the wood that isn't the seal.

"That's what I mean when I say I find them. The important things in life, you don't make them by forcing them. And most of all, nobody hands them to you and tells you to put them together in such-and-such a way. You find them. If you're lucky. Or sometimes, they find you. They come to you in the night, and if you have the courage you follow them, over the hills and down into the valleys," tracing the contours of the carving with a fingertip, "and you never know where they'll lead, you only know you want to go with them and be there with them forever."

Laura shivered, and hugged herself. "It sounds nice," she admitted, "but it's scary. I mean, if you don't know where you're going, or what's going to happen...."

"Life *is* scary sometimes," the woman agreed. "Don't let anybody tell you it isn't."

"But it isn't scary if—" Laura had been about to say, it isn't scary if you accept Jesus Christ as your Lord and Savior. But she had been scared of Stan, and loving Jesus with all her heart hadn't helped.

"If what?"

"Never mind. Nothing."

"You know," the woman said, "when you're growing

up everybody has ideas about how you ought to live your life. They'll tell you they know what's best for you, and they'll keep after you to make sure you believe them. They might even tell you if you do exactly what they say, you'll never have to be scared or lonely. When times are good, it's easy enough to believe that. But when bad things happen, you can't afford to listen to those people. You have to listen to your heart. Your heart knows what's right for you.

"The trouble is," she went on, "sometimes your heart doesn't talk very loud, and everybody else is shouting at you, so you get confused. The thing to do when you get confused is to get real quiet and just listen until you can hear your heart speak its truth."

"But what if your heart is mistaken?" Laura said. "What if your heart wants things that are wicked?"

"Words like 'wicked' are words other people use to try to run your life for you. They're not heart words." The woman held the figurine out to Laura. "Would you like to have this? It's yours, if you want it."

"Oh, I couldn't. It must be worth loads of money. I couldn't possibly afford—"

"Did I say anything about money?"

"I can't, honestly. It's very nice of you to offer, but...." She shrugged helplessly. She was imagining what Aunt Edith would say if she brought home a doll that was naked and pregnant.

"I'll tell you what," the woman said. "I'll keep it for you. It's yours, and it will be there if you change your mind. If you decide you'd like to have it, just let me know. Okay?"

"All right, I guess. Thank you."

The woman swaddled the figurine in its cloth and tucked it back into her bag. She stood up. "One more thing," she said. "Smile a little. It's good for the face muscles."

Laura managed a wan smile.

The things the woman had said spun in her brain. She didn't understand most of it, but it left a feeling like wind blowing through an open window. Vague questions began to form in her mind, like creepers poking up cautiously out of a moist forest floor. But after the party, when she was back home undressing for bed, she realized she hadn't asked the woman's name. Even if she decided she wanted the figurine, she might never be able to claim it.

During the next few days she finished washing the old man and the standing woman and started to work on the artisan. The peacefulness of the grove drew her back again and again. It was a palpable quality, quite different from the peacefulness of Aunt Edith's house, which was merely silent and empty. Laura always brought her bucket and scrub brush, but sometimes instead of working she simply sat, on a fallen log or on the cold damp ground, watching the play of light across the statues' faces.

Beneath the peacefulness, however, or along the edges of it, was something faintly disturbing, an elusive something that slid away from her when she tried to think about it, the way smoke slides between fingers. Gradually she figured out what the source of the disturbance must be. It had to do with the poses and positions of the statues. At first she assumed she was only imagining it, but day by day this idea became harder to maintain. What she found, comparing mental notes with herself about yesterday and the day before, was that the statues were moving.

Not, she hastened to assure herself, actually *moving*

— no matter how long she sat and watched, they remained perfectly motionless. But between one day and the next there were small changes, like grains of sand shifting as a dune crawls inland from the sea. She hadn't consciously noted anything at first, only felt that the grove was somehow mysteriously different every time she came into it, even though it was obviously the same as before. But as she grew quieter and more watchful, she began to notice the changes, not as they occurred but afterward. The standing man's outstretched arm was at a different angle today than yesterday. She walked around him very slowly, measuring the angle with her eyes. The change was so small it was hard to be sure. Still, it *felt* as though the arm had moved.

A chill that had nothing to do with the winter air prickled her shoulders. Statues didn't move. That was impossible.

But it wasn't just the arm. It was the spot on the ground that the kneeling woman was looking at, which sometimes shifted as much as six inches, as well as Laura could judge by the pattern in the roots and pebbles. One morning the woman was staring directly at a single blue wildflower, which had sprung up overnight in defiance of the season. But the next morning she was staring at bare dirt, and Laura looked everywhere for the flower without finding it. The satyr, too. On some days, sitting on the log, she could see him clearly from the waist up where he stood behind the occluding moon of a fat bush. On other days he was entirely hidden but for his face, the sensual curves of lips, cheeks, eyebrows teasing her. (He was easier to look at then, because she didn't have to think about the cloven hooves. She *wasn't* going to wash him below the waist, that was already settled.) And the old man with the staff. When she had first seen him, he had been looking out of the grove at a distant hill. Hadn't he? But as the days passed his body turned slowly, so that he was looking into the grove, nearly toward the spot where Laura liked to sit.

She puzzled all of this out bit by bit, not really believing any of it. Somebody must be sneaking into the grove at night and moving the statues. But wouldn't they leave footprints or something? And why would they do it? To make her think she was going crazy? Neither Aunt Edith nor Uncle Henry would do any such thing, they had no reason to. And certainly it couldn't be the maid.

In the end, the very peacefulness of the grove drew the blood from the hypothesis. Nobody ever came here but Laura. Slowly she let herself begin to imagine that the statues might indeed be moving.

"But they only move at night," she said to herself. "If I want to catch them at it, I've got to stay all night and watch." Aunt Edith would never approve — and that was an excellent reason for not telling her. The best thing would be to slip out the outside door of the bedroom onto the patio, and go back in the same way at dawn.

She fortified herself with a Thermos of hot coffee, which she made stealthily in the kitchen after Victoria had finished the dishes, Uncle Henry had vanished into his study, and Aunt Edith had left for her canasta game. Laura put on a sweater under her coat and added a second pair of socks. California winters might be mild compared to Illinois winters, but that didn't mean you couldn't catch cold.

It would be safer to wait for everybody to go to bed. If Aunt Edith looked in on her at bedtime, there would be trouble. But if she waited too long, whatever happened in the grove might already have happened before she got there. So she wrote two notes. The one in the kitchen read, "Aunt Edith — I'm tired and I've gone to bed early. Please don't wake me when you come in." The one pinned to her pillow read, "Aunt Edith — I couldn't sleep, so I went out for a walk. Please don't worry. I'll be back in a little while." These preparations completed, she slipped out the door onto the patio.

The sky had been scoured by an arctic breeze, and the stars glinted like flecks of glass in the blackness. In the east a nearly full moon hung, blotchy and lopsided. It watched over Laura's shoulder as she walked down the lawn, so that her shadow walked beside her.

Under the trees it was so dark she nearly lost her way. She stumbled over rocks and roots, and once a bush scratched at her face. But in the grove the statues seemed to glimmer faintly with their own light. She chose a spot off at one side, where she could see them all without turning her head, and sat down to wait. There was no wind, and the muffled mutter of distant traffic had thinned. Except for the occasional rustle that might be a small animal foraging along the ground, the night was silent.

Laura's gaze shifted from one pale shape to another, seeking to capture a flicker of animation. But the light was so poor that after a few minutes her eyes rebelled. The whole grove seemed to melt and flow like wax. She rubbed her eyes, and the scene settled down briefly, but before long it was bathed again in milky haze.

Annoyed at her own frailty, she poured a cup of coffee. The rich aroma and the sting of heat on her lips restored her. Eyestrain was a problem she hadn't counted on. She wished she had thought to bring a flashlight, but she couldn't very well go back to the house for one, especially since she didn't know where one was kept. There was nothing to do but close her eyes occasionally to rest them, and hope that the false impressions of movement wouldn't mask the real movement when (if) it came.

The wait became a head-spinning struggle. In spite of the coffee, Laura kept nodding off. Dream images of satyrs dancing, of naked boy archers flying through the sky, of pale, noble men and women strolling among the trees, surged up, but when she jerked awake the grove was just as it had been before. She heard voices too, murmurings out of which strange fragments leaped: An old man saying, "She must rest now." A woman saying, "She could be beautiful." A child: "Come on! Come play! Come fly!"

It felt so good to lie down. She could see nearly as well lying down. All she had to do was keep her eyes open. Before long she was fast asleep.

She woke to gray dawn, feeling not cold and stiff but curiously warm and refreshed. She lay, head on her curled arm, examining in detail the knots and turnings in a fallen twig close by her face. With only a little more effort, it seemed, she would understand what mysterious forces had guided its growth. Confused scraps of the night's dreams came back to her. None of it made sense, any more than dreams usually did, but certainly it *had* all been dreams. She hadn't actually seen the statues move. The experiment was a failure.

But when she moved to sit up, she discovered she was blanketed by a mound of leaves. They poured away from her in a dozen small avalanches, and the dust made her sneeze. She ran a hand through them, puzzled. How had they gotten there? She hadn't buried herself; somebody had come along during the night and covered her. The leaves on the forest floor were damp and mouldering, but those she had been covered with were dry and whole, as if they had been selected by hand.

Fear gripped her, and she scrambled to her feet and looked around wildly. Invisible forces were awake here, forces that came to life when nobody was watching. Somehow the fact that the forces were hiding from her made them more sinister than if she had been able to see them. The mound of leaves frightened her precisely because there was no way she could confront whoever had done it. She grabbed the Thermos and set off at a trot toward the house, looking over her shoulder again and again, unable to shake the feeling that something large was following her. When the statues were out of sight the woods seemed to close in even more, and she ran faster, gasping for breath.

The bedroom door opened on silent hinges. She stepped inside, locked it, and leaned against it while her heart slowed. Of course there must be a rational explanation for how the leaves had come to be there. The wind. A passing stranger. Squirrels and raccoons. Not the statues. No, please, not the statutes. Because if the statues had done it, she saw suddenly, then they weren't statues at all. And if they weren't statues, *what were they?* What forces had she awakened, and what did they mean to do to her? Or — could it all be her imagination? Could she be having a breakdown? Why had she been so foolish? If the statues were moving, that was their business. She didn't want to know about it.

The clock on the dresser said 7:21. Time enough to get the Thermos back to the kitchen, if she hurried. Then she could crawl in bed and "wake up" when

Aunt Edith called her. She wanted very much not to have to explain where she had spent the night. She was too confused.

She unscrewed the top and tipped the Thermos into the sink. But the liquid that ran out wasn't cold coffee. It was thick and golden. She righted the Thermos with a jerk and stared into the mute silvery circle of its mouth. The aroma wasn't coffee, either. It was fragrant with spice. She had a panicky urge to pour the rest down the drain, but curiosity stayed her hand. She poured a little into the top, sniffed again, and very slowly brought it to her mouth to touch the liquid with the tip of her tongue.

The flavor blossomed like a flower unfolding. There were apples, and honey, and cinnamon, and something else — blackberry? Mint? She put out her tongue again, but stopped, rigid, when she realized what she was doing. Whoever had piled up the leaves had filled her Thermos with this stuff, hoping she would drink it. Why? What would it do to her? She up-ended both the top and the Thermos over the sink, turned the tap on full, and rinsed them savagely. Wiping them with a dish towel, she suppressed a pang of regret. Even little kids knew you mustn't eat or drink anything you found in the woods. The flavor of the drop she had drunk still tickled her tongue, so she rinsed her mouth with clean water.

Going back to her room, she felt much more tired than when she awoke.

※ V ※

It was closing on Christmas, and during the next few days Aunt Edith, her conscience presumably stung by her earlier neglect, found a great many things that Laura simply had to help with. Presents and wrapping paper had to be bought, and nothing was ever quite what Aunt Edith was looking for, so Laura was dragged from shop to shop like a wooden duck on a string behind a three-year-old. Then there were cookies and candy to be made and packed in baskets with bows on top for a long list of people, all of whose likes and dislikes Aunt Edith had catalogued in detail.

Laura was grateful for the distraction. Her earlier fascination with the statues had turned to a muted terror. As she avoided going back to see them standing reassuringly motionless, her fright fed on her imaginings. At night she lay awake, knowing they would come to plague her dreams. She knotted the blankets tossing, and woke drenched in sweat.

In one dream she was in a huge schoolroom with hundreds of other students at tiny desks. The old man with the staff was lecturing, but Laura couldn't understand a word he said, and the letters on the blackboard writhed, alien and incomprehensible. Then without transition she was following him along a narrow mountain ledge on a night full of wind and rain, and he was far ahead carrying a lantern. As she watched, he vanished around a corner, leaving her alone in the howling dark. She ran after him stumbling and scraping her knees and crawling on, until finally she slipped off the ledge and fell and fell and fell forever.

That was bad enough, but the dreams of the satyr were worse. She was on a farm she had visited once, watching them feed the pigs, and the satyr crawled up out of the mud at the bottom of the pig pen, covered from head to toe with slime, and clambered over the fence toward her, leering and slavering, his long red tongue licking out obscenely.

In spite of her revulsion, she saw that there was something familiar about the satyr's face. She was sure she had known somebody who looked like him. Except for the horns and the cloven hooves, of course. She frowned at the tray of chocolate chip cookies, the spatula poised in one hand, motionless. If only she could remember, maybe that face would lose some of its terrible power.

Somewhere between the coconut clusters and the candy canes, she remembered. She had been at the coffee shop with Stan. He was hunched over a chemistry textbook, chewing his pencil, and she was trying without much success to memorize irregular French verbs. The air was greasy with the smell of burgers. At the next table a discussion was in progress, one of those terribly earnest debates that only undergraduates seem to have because everybody else is too busy or comfortable or over-specialized to care. The young man holding forth was taller and slimmer than the satyr, and he didn't have horns — at least, they weren't visible — but his black beard was trimmed the same way, and his eyes snapped. What caught her attention was when he declared, "Christianity stinks. It's not just worthless, it's actively bad for you. Don't mess with it."

Laura's heart lurched. How dare he speak that way!

"Oh, come on," another boy objected. "Who are you to say that? You're talking about one of the world's great religions."

"So I'm not entitled to an opinion? Anyway, religion has nothing to do with it. Christianity hasn't been a religion since 300 A.D. It's a Fascist political and social organization whose primary purpose is to keep people scared so they'll obey orders."

Stan slammed his chemistry book shut. "Come on," he said to Laura. "We're getting out of here." He avoided looking at the boys at the next table, but his face was blotched an ugly red. Laura gathered her French papers, fumbling at them because she was busy listening. What she was hearing horrified her, but almost against her will she wanted to hear more.

"What about the teachings of Christ, huh?" the second boy persisted. "How can you say that isn't a religion?"

"Sugar coating," the satyr sneered. "You know as well as I do that Christians only follow the teachings of Jesus when it suits them. I know a guy who's a Christian gun nut. When it comes to his beloved guns, 'Thou Shalt Not Kill' doesn't apply. But I'm not complaining about hypocrisy. That isn't a Christian failing, it's a universal human failing. The reason Christianity isn't a religion is that it doesn't do what a religion has to do. It doesn't enrich people's lives; it tramples on them."

Stan was tapping his foot impatiently. Laura got her arms into her coat, scooped up her homework, and followed as he wove a route among the tables. She wanted to hear more of this scandalous conversation, but not badly enough to defy Stan. That night, lying in bed, she tried to imagine what the boy's objections to Christianity might be — not, she assured herself, because of any merit they might have, but so she could exercise her faith by refuting them. But she found that she was staring at a wall.

The second time she saw the undergraduate satyr was a month or so later. Needing desperately to get away from her room before Stan dropped by, she accepted a casual invitation from one of the girls in the dorm to go to an off-campus party.

Going up the narrow, well-worn stairs to the apartment, hearing the music thundering down, she felt a tingle of excitement. The apartment was a dim grotto under red and blue bulbs, and there was no furniture except pillows on the floor. She knew nobody, so she stood against a wall, getting a headache and wondering whether she should leave. The satyr, clad in a sheepskin vest, materialized in front of her and held out a stubby, lumpy cigarette. It was smoldering unevenly, and smelled sweetly unlike tobacco. "Want a toke?" he asked.

"Is that—" she said, and stopped, knowing what the answer would be. "No, thanks. No." She shook her head stiffly.

He waggled the stubby cigarette under her nose. "Just suck it into your lungs and hold it there. C'mon."

Something — a force entirely outside of her — lifted her arm. She took the cigarette from him gingerly, trying not to touch his fingers with hers. The smoke raked her throat, but she held her breath as long as she could, until the tickle made her cough. The boy had already disappeared back into the milling throng, taking the cigarette with him. Belatedly she remembered the conversation in the coffee shop. Maybe she should search for him, demand that he explain what he had meant, argue with him, prove him wrong. But she didn't see him, and anyway she was pretty sure she'd lose any debate she got into. Not because she was wrong — in this case she couldn't possibly be wrong — but because she wasn't good at debating.

The marijuana had no effect on her that she could see. When being alone got too depressing, she walked back to the dorm. She never saw the bearded boy again.

"Oh, there you are. I've been looking all over for you." Aunt Edith broke into the reverie. Laura was in the living room, wearing her candy-making apron, staring at the china dolls in their glass case. Their droll little painted faces made her queasy, but at least they were a distraction from dreams and memories. "I do hope I haven't been working you too hard," Aunt Edith went on. "You were beginning to perk up, but for the past few days you haven't been the same. If there's anything bothering you, all you have to do is tell me about it. You know I'm happy to listen."

"I'm all right," Laura said dully. "I was just looking at these."

"Aren't they precious?" Aunt Edith said gaily. "I'm always so pleased when I find a new one. They're quite valuable, too. You'd be surprised." Her eyes lit up. "I know — would you like to take a couple of them to keep in your room? To cheer you up?"

"Oh, no, that's all right. I might break one. I wouldn't want—"

"Nonsense. I know you'll be careful with them. Here, let me see. This one, I think, and this one. Yes, that's perfect. Aren't they lovely?" She held the dolls out for Laura to admire.

Laura's hands hung at her sides. "They're very nice," she said.

"Well, come on. Let's see how they look on your dresser." Aunt Edith led the way, and Laura, a knot pinching her throat, followed. After Aunt Edith had found the perfect spot on the dresser for the little figures, chirped happily, and departed, Laura sat on the bed staring at them. A plump boy in short pants and a pink-cheeked girl twirling a parasol. She wanted to like them, because Aunt Edith *was* being kind, but they were loathsome. The plump boy looked faintly like Stan, and the girl — what was she happy about? Laura considered sneaking them back into the case in the living room, but Aunt Edith would notice, and Laura would have to try to explain, and what would she say? In the end she left them where they were.

That evening Uncle Henry arrived home with the tree, a magnificent fir specimen whose tip reached within inches of the living room's ten-foot ceiling. The next afternoon Aunt Edith enlisted Laura and Victoria to help bring the ornaments in from the garage. Victoria, being the maid, was allotted the more hazardous task of standing on a stepladder and handing boxes down, while Laura and Aunt Edith ferried them into the house. Laura set the first box down on the couch in the living room, but Aunt Edith said, "No, dear, let's put them in Henry's study, where they'll be out of the way. We can bring the ornaments in from there."

"It seems like a lot of extra work," Laura said.

"But the clutter is so distracting," her aunt explained. "I can't think properly about where to hang things when I'm surrounded by clutter."

Laura had only glanced into the study before. It was decorated in a determinedly male style, with dark wood paneling, a deer's head mounted over the fireplace, bookcases copiously stocked with leather-bound, gold-embossed volumes, and, standing in one corner, a genuine head-to-toe suit of armor, complete with louvred visor and spikes at the elbows. Though the armor was thoroughly polished, ineradicable spots of tarnish left little doubt about its age. It reminded Laura of her father. He was as stern-looking as that, and he might be as hollow; if there was anything inside you could never touch it. He had never complimented her that she could recall, seldom even smiled. It didn't matter what she did; if it was good it wasn't good enough, and if it was bad she was punished.

To her father, raising children was a problem in human engineering. You applied the necessary leverage to keep them from leaning in the wrong direction. If they persisted, you increased the pressure. Setting the boxes down one by one at the foot of the suit of armor, she found herself whispering, "Yes, Daddy. Yes, Daddy." It was crucial that the boxes be set in a neat array, and not too close to the feet. When she came back from the garage and found that Aunt Edith had put a box in the wrong place, she hurried to set it right. Good girls keep their rooms neat, and never speak unless spoken to. Yes, Daddy.

Her care went for nothing, because when they started unpacking, tissue paper was strewn around the armor's feet like a snowdrift. Laura rushed back and forth carrying strings of lights and delicate glass balls and stars stitched with sequins and angels flocked with sparkly flecks. Holding an ornament, she would search for a vacant spot on the tree, but when she had hung it Aunt Edith, who was standing halfway across the room observing the aesthetic effect, would shake her head and say, "Oh, dear. Oh, no, that's not quite right, is it?", and come and snatch the ornament off and hang it somewhere else. Eventually Laura wearied of this routine and brought an ornament directly to Aunt Edith. Aunt Edith said, "No, dear, you go ahead and hang it. I don't want to have all the fun."

Laura was used to stringing popcorn and cranberries with her mother and sisters for a smaller, scruffier tree. She wondered how her sisters were. She hoped they were all right. She supposed she ought to phone them, but her father might answer — and anyway, what could she say that wouldn't embarrass them all?

The last box held the figures for the manger scene. At first she wasn't sure what they were. They were crudely and amateurishly carved of wood, and gaudily painted in thick reds and greens and blues. Several of them actually seemed misshapen. But yes, here were the Three Wise Men, who had always been Laura's favorites, and here was a cow — or was it a donkey? "Aren't they quaint," Aunt Edith said, leaning over her. "We got them on vacation in Acapulco. Genuine hand-crafted artifacts. The natives down there aren't so sophisticated as we are, but they're quite devout. I feel sure these have a real spiritual aura. Don't you agree?"

"I've never seen anything quite like them," Laura said truthfully. She unwrapped the objects one by one. This one was a shepherd with his staff, so these had to be sheep, though they looked like pigs. Here was Joseph, or at any rate somebody with a beard. This must be Mary. And here was the matchbox manger. Now where was the Baby Jesus? The carton was still half full of crinkled tissue, evidently padding, although the figures certainly didn't look fragile. Laura pawed through it looking for the Baby, at first in annoyance and then with mounting panic. She was sitting on the floor surrounded by empty boxes and piles of loose tissue, with the suit of armor watching sternly over her, and she couldn't find the Baby Jesus anywhere. She started rooting frantically among the paper, throwing it in the air. Where was He? The empty manger stared up at her accusingly. Still tossing paper, she began to whimper. How could the Baby be gone? How could a thing like that happen? Somebody must have done something. They must have hidden it. She looked up at the armor. "You saw," she said. "You were looking. What happened? What happened?" The visor remained closed. "I keep losing babies," she said. Somewhere inside her a sick giggle started. She tried to hold it down, but it bubbled to the surface. "I keep losing the baby," she repeated, gasping.

It was spring when she first began to suspect, spring with its obscene profusion of flowers, butterflies, and couples shamelessly nuzzling by the bike racks. She said nothing to anybody. Who would she tell? Anyway, her period had always been irregular. Any day now it would come, and she could relax. Mid-terms were looming, too, and she had more important things like French and history to worry about. So a month went by, and then another. By now she was sure. When anybody looked at her her face burned, and her leg muscles twitched when she walked across the campus. She was on a tightrope. She was certain everybody could see the soft swelling. Her roommate did notice how ill she was in the mornings, dragging herself out of bed and down the hall to the bathroom, and, eyes, narrowed shrewdly, finally did ask, "Hey, you aren't pregnant or anything, are you?"

Laura pressed her lips together and shook her head tightly, savagely.

"Because if you are, a friend of mine went to this clinic. I could find out where—"

"No! There's nothing the matter. I'm fine."

"Suit yourself." The girl shrugged and turned away.

An impulse stirred in her to tell Stan, one night when they were sitting in the coffee shop and he was droning on about the chain of shoe stores he was going to open someday, a wicked impulse to blurt it out and see how his mouth would fall open, how his upper lip would start to perspire. But she couldn't do it. She was terrified that he would abandon her and leave her to raise the baby by herself, and even more terrified that he would insist on doing the right thing and marrying her. The prospect of being subjected to Stan's attentions every night for the rest of her life was more than she could face. But at the same time, she needed somebody to cling to, and however unpleasant he might be, Stan was indubitably *there*. So she pretended everything was the same as usual, and said nothing. The weeks ticked by. At night, shivering in bed, she prayed as fervently as she knew how that this be only a delayed period, but her prayer went unanswered.

Somehow (afterward it was only a blur) she made it through finals, chewing her fingers bloody, drinking endless Cokes and eating a mountain of potato chips. She was constantly sick to her stomach, and her head wouldn't stop aching. When her parents arrived, she had barely started to pack. Her father scowled at the disorder and went to sit in the car while her mother bustled around helping. On the way home she crawled into the back seat and made herself small in a corner and pretended to take a nap, which turned into a real nap, which left her feeling not rested but muzzy and confused.

She knew she would have to tell them, but the right moment never seemed to arrive. Sitting at the kitchen table drinking a glass of milk while her mother stood at the stove, she drew in a breath and opened her mouth and the phone rang. Or the neighbors were due over any minute. Or Tracy and Ann were underfoot. Or her mother was too busy talking to listen, going on about gardening and the church fair and what a good girl Laura was, how proud they were of her going to college, how they knew she could never disappoint them. And what could you say after that?

"Mama?"

"Yes, dear?" It was after supper. They were alone in the living room. Her mother was knitting.

"Mama, I need to talk to you."

"Yes, dear? What is it?"

"Mama, I'm—" Pregnant. But she couldn't shape the word with her lips. "I'm—" She swallowed with a great effort and sat dumb, her fists clenched.

"You're such a wonderful girl, Laura," her mother said, trying to be helpful. "Your father and I have always been very proud of you."

Laura shut her eyes. "Baby," she said. "Baby."

"Why, no, dear, you're not a baby. You're practically grown up."

"I'm — going — to — have — a — *baby*." Her eyes flooded with bitter tears.

The knitting needles stopped. Laura sat blinking back the tears, afraid to look at her mother, looking at the rug. In the silence the refrigerator kicked on.

"What did you say?"

"A baby. I'm going to have."

"I — I don't understand. You're not secretly married. Are you?"

Laura shook her head.

"Who's the boy? Is he going to marry you? Do we know him?"

"He's a boy at school. I couldn't stop him."

"How often did this happen? More than once?"

She swallowed again. "Maybe ten or twenty times. Maybe more. I wasn't counting."

Her mother took in a sharp breath and let it out. "How could you?" she asked. "How could you?"

"I don't know." Laura sobbed and snuffled. "It just

happened. After the first time it didn't seem to matter so much."

"Nothing 'just happens,'" her mother said. "If you're weak, you may be tempted, but the Lord always gives us the strength to resist temptation. You know that. When you persist in evil, it's no good trying to excuse yourself by saying it 'just happened.'" She set her knitting on the lamp table. "Your father will have to be told. I think you'd better tell him yourself."

"Couldn't you tell him? Please? I don't—"

"Laura. You know the rule."

Of course. When she was little and she broke the cookie jar, Mama made her sweep up the mess and then made her march into her father's study and tell him what she had done. Her father made her go get the belt. The next Sunday he preached a sermon on the waywardness of children and the importance of obedience.

She was startled now to see how old he looked, sitting stiffly in the stuffy little room, the Bible open on the desk before him. A vein meandered like a twisted blue river up his temple. She entered on leaden feet and stopped just inside the door.

"Go on," her mother said, and when she hesitated said again, more forcefully, "Go on."

"Daddy, I'm — I'm in some trouble."

His eyes flashed like a hawk's when it sees a rodent. "What kind of trouble?"

"I'm — I know you don't — I just — oh, please! Please!" She fell to her knees in front of his chair and buried her face in the cool plastic chair arm and groped for his hand, but he had withdrawn it. "It was horrible, and it was a sin, and I'm sorry! Please, please say you forgive me! I didn't mean it, it'll never happen again, never, only please tell me it's all right, I didn't mean to but he made me, and afterwards I couldn't stop it, and now I'm going to have a b-b-baby!"

"Stand up, young lady." His voice was a lash with barbs in it. "Stand up this instant. You may have no respect for yourself, but you shall show some respect for your elders. Stand up straight, and stop blubbering, and explain the meaning of this outburst."

She managed to get to her feet, and snuffled and wiped her nose with the back of her hand. "It was a boy I met at school. I didn't want to, but he made me. I didn't know how to stop him. I prayed, Daddy, please believe me—"

"She says she did it twenty or thirty times," her mother interjected.

"Is this true?"

"I was afraid to tell him no. I was afraid he'd tell everybody I led him on. I didn't want to let him, but he kept coming around—"

"Slut," her father said. "Whore. You make me ashamed to be a father. Engaging in indecent, lascivious acts and then blaming the boy for it. The Devil has had an easy time with you, that's plain to see. Lust and fornication, and now lying to your parents."

"I'm not lying!" Laura wailed. "I tried to stop him, but he was too strong! He made me—"

"Liar. Filthy. Did he make you take drugs, too? Did you take any drugs? Answer me!"

"I — I smoked some marijuana. Just once."

Her father's face was twitching with rage. "I believe I've heard enough. I had hoped, when we sent you away to school, that you had learned to be a responsible, respectable Christian girl. Plainly I was wrong. Go and get the belt."

"Daddy, please! I didn't—"

"The belt. Now. You know the rule. Every second you delay means an additional stroke. One. Two. Three. Four."

"Daddy, please, you can't mean it! How can you possibly—"

"Seven. Eight. Nine."

Her eyes were streaming. She looked to her mother for support, but her mother only stared grimly at the wall and said nothing. Laura wheeled and sprinted from the room — but not toward her parents' bedroom, where the belt hung in the closet. She raced to the bathroom, slammed the door, and locked herself in. Her hands were shaking so badly she barely got the lock fastened before her father was rattling the knob and pounding and shouting, "Laura! Come out of there! Come out this instant! Hiding won't do you any good. You cannot escape what is due you, and I will brook no disobedience! Do you hear me?"

Laura cowered back against the wash basin, trembling. She heard her mother's voice: "Here, I've got the key." She lunged forward and threw her weight against the door, but it swung open anyway, forcing her back. Her father grappled with her, trying to seize her wrists, and she writhed sideways and slipped on the bath mat and fell and he fell on top of her his knee in her stomach knocking the breath out of her and she grabbed the side of the tub to try to stand up and he grabbed her from behind and she fell again and struck the edge of the tub hard across her abdomen and he hauled her to her feet and she lurched into him so he bumped against something and they both fell down again and he pinned her arms and her mother was holding out the belt and her father was forcing her across the floor so she was kneeling in front of the toilet, and he said, "Now, now you'll learn, now I'll teach you," and he was pulling her skirt up and pulling her underwear down and suddenly she barely felt the sting of the belt a cramp started deep inside her and grew and grew until she was screaming gasping and he was still whipping her thinking she was screaming because of the belt he was yelling telling her say she was a filthy whore say it or he'd keep on 'til she said it only the cramp was so bad she couldn't say anything she was being torn in half all she could do was scream the sweat pouring out on her face the disinfecant smell of the toilet the cramp had her in its fist it was crushing her belly squeezing burning and then there was wetness between her legs and she was shuddering in spasms and her mother was yelling, "Stop, you're hurting her, can't you see you're hurting her," and her father grunted and said "She's hurting herself, I'm only doing the Lord's will," and the wetness was running down her leg now and the cramp was squeezing again harder than before and the belt had stopped she was shivering and her father's harsh breath behind her and her mother said, "My God in Heaven, look what you've done," and the wetness was pooling on the floor around her knees the cramp was a fist hitting her and when at last she twisted sideways across the toilet and looked down she already knew what it was, the blood all streaked milky yellow and the transparent pink thing no bigger than her thumb the tiny dark veins like hairs lying there curled in its jelly sac floating in the mess on the floor.

She still hurt — there was a lump of hot metal swelling inside her. But with a kind of weird underwater clarity she saw that somebody had slammed into the medicine cabinet during the struggle, because there were aspirin scattered on the floor and an open packet of her father's single-edge razor blades. Rolling off the toilet, she was hit by a cramp that brought fresh tears to her eyes, but through the tears a loose razor blade swam up and she grabbed it and hid it in her palm and levered herself shakily to her feet and stood bent over tugging at her panties. Her mother was in the hall outside the door, face averted. Her father stood in the doorway, still holding the belt, the rage in his eyes smoldering. "The Lord's judgment—" he began.

Laura swung the razor blade at him. The first slash cut diagonally from his shoulder down across his chest, shearing the fabric open. He looked down at it stupidly, and she swung again, this time at his face, drawing a line from cheekbone to chin that spread wide like a dark flower opening. The third cut went down his arm, and she felt resistance as the blade sank into muscle. He made a noise in his throat and jumped or toppled backward out the door. She slammed the door and locked it again. Then, suddenly dizzy, she slid down the door until she was sitting on the floor.

The little cabinet under the sink was standing open. In it was a blue-and-white plastic jug of Clorox bleach. After staring at the jug for a minute — it was very far away — she crawled toward it, ignoring the sticky mess her knees slid in, and unscrewed the cap and tipped the bottle up and drank.

VI

"Are you all right, dear?" Aunt Edith asked.

Laura looked up from the mound of tissue and empty boxes. "What?"

"I asked if you were all right. You seemed awfully quiet."

"I'm okay. I was just — I lost the baby. The Baby Jesus."

"Oh, is that all? Well, He's got to be here somewhere, doesn't He? Yes, here He is."

Aunt Edith bent and retrieved the tiny carved figure — it had fallen behind the suit of armor — and held it out in her palm. It was no larger than her thumb, and the bulbous forehead, tucked-in chin, and black dots for eyes rang the horrid bell of memory. Laura pushed Aunt Edith's hand away. "Take it away," she said. "Get it out of here! I don't want to see it."

After a moment of shocked silence, Aunt Edith said, "Very well, dear. I can see you're upset. Perhaps you'd better go lie down. You'll feel better when you've taken a nap."

Laura trudged off to her room. But she wasn't sleepy, and she couldn't lounge in bed and relax because of the two repulsive little china dolls on the dresser, whose grotesque cheerful innocence was a mocking accusation. She picked up a hairbrush, meaning to smash them — but she was a guest here. They weren't hers. Instead she jerked her arms into her coat and went out the door onto the patio.

The fog had come in again. The day was gray and silver and wet and cold.

Down at the edge of the lawn, under a tree, stood the old man with the staff, and beside him the older woman with her arms open.

Laura gasped. Her heart hammered wildly. They were still white, still motionless. They were still statues. But they had come up from the grove somehow, and they were looking directly at her. With a little cry, she turned and stumbled back into the bedroom and slammed and locked the door.

When she peeked out the window a moment later, the statues were gone.

She blinked and rubbed her eyes. Had it been a hallucination? Surely it had been a hallucination! Or had they come up to the edge of the lawn specifically for her? To tell her something? Or because they needed her? She whimpered and tugged at her hair. What was happening to her? And why?

After that there was no question of going back to the grove. She stayed in the house, watching television, playing solitaire, trying to read and losing interest. At night when she went to her room she turned off the light and, after bracing herself, looked out at the yard. It would be worse not to look, because then she would imagine things. Always, when she looked, there was a statue or two standing just under the shelter of the trees, watching, waiting for her. Sometimes it was the old man. Sometimes it was the young man, or one of the women, or the child with the bow. "Go away," she would whisper, her words fogging the glass. "Leave me alone." They gave no sign that they had heard. And in the morning they were always gone.

Christmas came. Aunt Edith gave her a fluffy pink sweater. Uncle Henry gave her a Japanese doll in a display case, a doll with lacquered hair and a red kimono embroidered with gold thread. Using money provided by Aunt Edith, Laura bought Uncle Henry a bathrobe and Aunt Edith a cut glass serving dish. On Christmas morning her mother called from Illinois, and after Aunt Edith had chatted for twenty minutes she came and hunted up Laura, who was hiding in one of the other guest bedrooms pretending to be absorbed in a magazine.

She picked up the receiver and held it to her ear, but

for a moment she didn't say anything. The line hissed and crackled in a slow rising and falling rhythm, like something old and huge and feeble lying in its cave up by the North Pole and breathing on the world.

"Hello, Mama."

"Laura? Laura, is that you?" A pause. "Are you all right?"

"I'm fine, Mama."

"Are Edith and Henry treating you well? I hope you're all right. I hope you're feeling better."

"I'm fine, Mama. How's Ann? How's Tracy? Are they all right?"

"They're fine, dear. So is your father. He sends his — he said to tell you — well, he's concerned about you. We all are."

"I don't think I want to talk any more, Mama. Goodbye." No, he hadn't sent his love. He probably hadn't said to tell her anything at all. He just sat there in his big chair — she imagined it, not having been home since that night — brooding, his face ashen around the fresh scar.

"Laura," her mother said quickly, "we miss you, honey. When are you coming home?"

"I don't know." She handed the receiver back to Aunt Edith.

Wandering back to her room, she asked herself, "Well, when *am* I going to go home?" She couldn't impose on Aunt Edith and Uncle Henry forever. But she couldn't go home either, not and face her father.

Also, as long as she stayed here she would have to contend with the menacing presence of the statues. Every night they came a little closer to the house, standing plainly visible on the lawn, holding their silent vigil, vanishing back into the woods before dawn. Nobody else ever saw them — or if they did, they said nothing, and Laura was afraid to ask. She knew they would think she was crazy, and that might mean a trip to a different kind of hospital. All the same, she wasn't imagining things. Aunt Edith and Uncle Henry's bedroom was on the other side of the house, that was all.

The statues went on invading her dreams. She dreamed she was walking in the grove when it was dappled with summer sun, her hand in the old man's as he strode along marking the path with his staff. He led her past the familiar clearing, down a slope she had never noticed before, and now the boy with the bow was holding her other hand and skipping beside them. They came out from under the trees into a valley that sparkled green and gold. People in strange robes standing in the fields waved at them. Laura waved back, feeling that she had known them for a long time. Solemnly the old man presented her with a sturdy wooden goblet, and when she lifted it to drink she saw it was the same golden nectar that had been in the Thermos. But when she sipped, the nectar stung her throat with the vile burning of Clorox. She gagged and dropped the goblet and spilled the nectar on the ground.

She woke filled with a great sorrow, an ache of emptiness and loss, as if the sea itself had drained away during the night and left her staring out across its rocky desolate bottom.

When the wheel turned again, carrying them into January, Aunt Edith said, "You know, dear, if you're planning to stay much longer, you really ought to consider what you're going to *do*. The community college is only ten minutes away. I think perhaps you might want to go down there and register. I'm sure there won't be any problem about your not being a California resident. Henry will take care of that. But you mustn't stay cooped up in the house all day, that's the main thing. It's not healthy. Ever since Christmas you've been getting more and more withdrawn. Isn't that so, Victoria?"

"That's so," Victoria said, not looking up from the ironing.

"I'm only thinking of what's best for you, dear. Your mother entrusted you to my care, and she'll be so disappointed if I tell her you're just moping."

"All right, Aunt Edith. I'll see about getting into school. Is there a bus stop where I can catch a bus to the campus?"

"A bus stop? I don't actually know. Is there a bus stop, Victoria?"

So they talked about transportation. Laura didn't want to face the other students. A gulf separated her from them, a gulf that they wouldn't know existed and that she could never explain. But she was trapped. If she didn't register at the community college, she'd have to go back to Illinois.

That night, lying in bed, she heard an eerie flutelike melody leaping and cavorting outside on the lawn. She knew instantly what it was — the satyr, piping on his pipes. Lively, lascivious, the piping crawled under the covers with her and made her sweat. She got up and made sure the patio door was locked and the window latched. For good measure she propped a chair against the hall door. Even so, she slept feverishly, the piping insinuating itself into her dreams.

In the morning when she woke, the piping had stopped. The room was as still and silver as on the first morning after she arrived. But on the pillow beside her lay a single freshly picked blue wildflower.

She moaned aloud in fear. The bedroom wasn't safe any more. Not content to watch from the lawn, they were coming inside while she slept. She looked around the room very slowly, breathing through her mouth, expecting to see a statue standing in the corner or crouched behind a chair. But she was alone. And when she checked the doors and windows, there was no sign of forced entry.

Standing in the window in her nightgown, she looked down at the woods. The golden flood of morning sun slanted down into the trees. "What do you *want* from me?" she said softly. "Why won't you leave me alone?" There was no answer, only a single broad-winged bird, gray and white like a seagull, that took wing and flew east toward the sun. "Whatever you're trying to do, it won't work. I'm going home now. I'm going back to Illinois. You can't stop me, so please don't try."

"Aunt Edith," she said at breakfast, "I've decided I can't impose on you any longer. You've been very nice, and I appreciate everything you've done. But it's time for me to go home."

"Well, I think perhaps that's best, dear." Aunt Edith placidly spread butter on toast. "Not that your Uncle Henry and I don't enjoy having you here. We do. But now that you've had a chance to get your strength back, you'll be able to face your problems squarely. In the long run it's no good hiding from things. They always catch up with you sooner or later."

Out in the woods there were things that Laura didn't want to catch up with her, not ever. But that wasn't what Aunt Edith meant. Laura said, "You know what I did?"

"I'm not so sure it's any of my business, dear. That's between you and your conscience. I'm sure at heart you're a good Christian girl. Whatever trouble you've had was out of inexperience, not willful perversity. My goodness, how could a man like your father raise a child who was willfully perverse? Now that you've had a chance to rest and think things over, I'm sure you'll agree that your parents do know what's best. After all, they're so much older — well, perhaps not so *very* much older, but they've seen far more of the world than you, and their faith has assured them of living happy, fulfilling lives, the kind of life you'll want for yourself someday. Don't you agree?"

Laura stared at the crumbs scattered in the egg yolk on her plate, trying to read an answer in them that wasn't there. "I guess so," she said.

Two thousand miles away, the phone was ringing. Laura held the receiver to her cheek and said silently, Please nobody answer, please nobody be home, please....

"Hello?"

"Mama? Mama, is that you?"

"Laura! It's so good to hear your voice. How are you, dear?"

"I'm fine, Mama. How are you?"

"Oh, I can't complain. We had more snow last night. I've just been out shoveling the walk, and you know how hard that is, with my back."

"Why can't—" Why can't Daddy do it? But you weren't to criticize your parents. Instead she said, "How are Tracy and Ann?"

"Tracy had the sniffles last week, but they're both fine now."

"Mama, I'm — I want to come home. If I can. If it's all right."

"All right?" Her mother's voice vibrated like a taut string. "Oh, honey, of *course* it's all right. That's wonderful! Your father will be — I mean we'll all be so happy to — oh, there's something I have to tell you. Honey, we've got a surprise for you. Just *wait* 'til you hear. You know that boy you got to know at school? The one you were — you know, that you were friendly with? Stanley? Well, when the Christmas vacation started at college, Stanley came down here to Mattoon to find you. He was worried because you hadn't been at college this fall. So we made him welcome, because at first we didn't know who he *was*, you hadn't told us his name, and it turned out he didn't know anything about the trouble you had, because you hadn't written to let him know. Well, he explained how guilty he'd been feeling, and he said that now that he knew, he felt ten times worse, and the only way to make it right would be for him to marry you. Isn't that wonderful? He was so *noble* about it. And at first your father wouldn't hear of it, because he was pretty angry when he found out who Stanley was, but by and by they got to talking, and it turned out they have a great deal in common. Did you know Stanley is thinking of becoming a *minister?* Isn't that wonderful? So your father saw the light, and he's given his blessing. You can be married just as *soon* as you'd like. It's all settled. I knew you'd be thrilled when you heard, but we didn't want to rush you, we thought it would be best to wait until you called of your own accord, and now you have, and everything is going to be all right again. Isn't it wonderful? Praise the Lord!"

Laura's whole body had gone numb. In the pause at the other end of the line she found she had nothing to say. So she said nothing.

"Laura? Did you hear me? Are you there?"

Yes, I heard you. But the words didn't have enough force to become speech. They hung inside her, suspended from the roof of a great dark cavern, swaying slightly.

"Laura? Laura?"

Very gently she hung up the phone. Somehow her feet guided themselves out of the kitchen and down the hall. Behind her the phone rang, and Aunt Edith answered it. Laura kept walking.

"I don't know. She was here a minute ago. You were? Hold on a minute. Laura. Laura?"

She went into Uncle Henry's study. It was as good a place as any. She sat down on the floor beside the suit of armor. The metal was cool against her cheek. She considered how nice it would be to live inside a suit of armor. The armor would be stiff, so you couldn't move around much, but that wouldn't matter. People would attach ropes to your arms and legs, and they could move you wherever they wanted and you'd just stand there until they moved you again. Some of the positions they put you in might be painful, but you could never be hurt too much, because you'd be inside the armor. You wouldn't have to worry, you wouldn't have to think at all, you wouldn't have to do anything or try to escape from anything. It would be cool and dark and quiet.

She became aware that Aunt Edith was shaking her shoulder. "Laura — Laura, are you all right? Your mother's on the phone. She says you were cut off."

Laura looked warily at Aunt Edith's face. It was still impossible to say anything.

"I'll tell her you'll call back later," Aunt Edith said firmly. Her face went away.

Moving mechanically, Laura got to her feet and went down the hall to her bedroom and got her suitcase out of the closet and set it on the bed and opened it and started putting things in. I'll go away to San Francisco, she said to herself. I'll get a job. But where she would stay, and what kind of job she would get, were questions without answers, so after a while she sat down in the chair, leaving the suitcase open on the bed with clothes strewn around it, and stared at the wall and didn't think about anything at all.

Aunt Edith came in, frowned worriedly, and perched on the edge of the bed. "Your mother told me the good news," she said. "I think it's wonderful that you and this boy are going to be married. He sounds like a fine young man, and I'm sure you'll be very happy. I'm afraid I don't quite understand why you're reacting this way. Naturally when you've been single it takes some getting used to the idea of being married. There are compensations, believe me. Security, for one thing. I understand this Stanley is a fine upstanding Christian boy with big plans for the future. I'd hate to see you pass up an opportunity like that, dear. There's no telling *when* another boy like that will come along. I was lucky to catch your Uncle Henry, believe me. And I had sense enough to know it. Why, I remember when he first...."

Laura let the words flow together into a gurgle. After a while she noticed that her aunt had gone.

She might have sat without moving forever, but eventually she had to go to the bathroom. Sitting on the toilet with her jeans around her ankles, she looked down at her naked body, seeing it as if for the first time. She touched herself, felt the firm flesh of her thighs, the wiry luxuriant hair where they met. She remembered the pain, but when she probed with her fingers it was entirely gone. She traced the soft folds lingeringly, a thing she had never done before. She was a mystery to herself. She rubbed — and gasped at the strange sensation and jerked her hand away. Suddenly the air was cold on her legs. She reached down and pulled her pants up. But before she fastened them she touched herself once more, so she would remember the place.

Uncle Henry came home from work, and the three of them sat down to dinner. Aunt Edith told him all about how Laura was going to marry the nice boy from college, and Laura found that she could say, "Mmm-hmm," and even form short, polite sentences without the slightest trouble. They were talking about somebody else. After dinner she watched television for a while, and then went to her room. The suitcase was still sitting open. Outside the window a three-quarter moon was high, casting brilliant shadows, haloed by a circle of stratospheric ice. She looked out across the lawn, her breath flickering on the glass. Gradually the sounds of the house and the city beyond submerged in stillness. At the edge of the woods, then, she saw pale figures — three, four, five, six. Without seeming to move, they shifted up the lawn toward the house, shimmering shapes that swam in and out behind the moonlight.

The piping started. It trilled. It tickled. It curled into her ears and slid in loops along her limbs. Somewhere in her a small leaping spark answered it.

Turning her back on the window, she crossed the room to switch out the light and put on her coat. In front of the dresser she paused. The two ludicrous little china dolls were standing there, smirking cutely in the reflected moonlight. She picked them up, one in each hand, and dropped them on the rug. Carefully but firmly, she brought her heel down on one and then the other, crushing them to powder. Then, not looking back, she went to the door and unbolted and opened it and stepped outside.

An Elvish Sword
of Great Antiquity

HANGING ON THE WALL above the trophy case
was an elvish sword of great antiquity. During dinner
my eye was drawn to it again and again, so that I fear I
was somewhat inattentive as the conversation flowed
around me. We were nearly a dozen — Portnoy James,
our host, and his charming daughter Patricia; Mimi
Selkirk the celebrated actress; the industrialist Rupert
Savage and his wife; Bishop Choat; and three or four
others whose names, I am sad to say, I no longer recall.
James's dining-room was paneled in dark oak, which
had been rubbed to a high gloss, and a fire had been
laid on account of the chilly November weather. The
firelight danced across the blade of the sword, rendering
it in shifting shades of red and gold.

The sword was small, suited to an elvish hand, and
had a hilt of fine silverwork. From my seat at the dining-
table I could see that its blade was incised with runes,
but I was too far away to read them. I say that it was
"of great antiquity" because I subsequently got a closer
look at the runes, when the sword was passed from

hand to hand around the table.

The servants moved in and out noiselessly, replenishing our wineglasses at need, bringing the soup and the meat and later the dessert. Silverware clanked against the tableware, and I can still hear Miss Selkirk's warm peal of laughter as if it were a sable fur draped across my arm. Miss Patricia James was rather starstruck by Miss Selkirk, and lost no opportunity to draw her out on the subject of her numerous successes and the male film stars with whom her name had been linked in the popular press. I believe the bishop may have snorted audibly at one or two points during this discourse. Rupert Savage, a large man with a heavy jaw, merely chomped; his wife tittered, and drank more wine than perhaps she should have.

As James stirred sugar into his coffee, he turned to me. "You seem quite taken by my sword."

I may have flinched a little. I had scarcely known my eye was so captivated by the weapon. "It's a curious piece," I said. "Elvish, by its look."

"Indubitably. We had a warren of them down by the river — a regular hive. After it burnt to the ground, I spotted this one day while riding through the rubble. Evidently they had left it behind when they fled. Not surprising. Elves are often careless."

"Your own servants seem quite punctilious." I gestured at the silent, black-clad elf who was at that moment tilting a crystal decanter to fill Mrs. Savage's wineglass. The decanter was large, and the elf was small; he had to hoist it in both hands practically over his head to pour; yet never a drop spilled.

"They'd better be. They know the consequences. One lad I had to horsewhip. Made a thorough mess out of polishing my best boots. I had to get new ones."

Bishop Choat cleared his throat. "Had a man once beg me to baptize an elf," he said. "Couldn't do it, of course. They have no souls, elves. Our Savior's irrelevant to them, as there's nothing there to save."

"Oh, but surely elves have contributed so much to our popular culture," Miss Selkirk said. "Their wonderful songs, the famous elfin code of honor — to say nothing of the fine needlework!"

"Elf honor's naught but pagan rubbish," the bishop said. "You won't find it in the Bible, I can promise you that. And the pointy-eared devils ignore it when it suits them to, which is most of the time. They kill their own babies, did you know that, if they even suspect the father's human? Won't raise a half-breed child, for all it would improve the bloodline."

James pushed back his chair and rose. "Would you like to see the sword?" Without waiting for an answer, he strode to the trophy case and took it down. He brought it to the table holding it horizontally in both hands, with the blade flat against the flesh of his fingers. It glinted brighter in the firelight than before, except where his shadow fell across it.

He held it out to the man on his right, who took it and brandished it experimentally, feinting at the nearest candle. "Feels like a toy. Looks sharp enough, though." He passed it on to Patricia James, who took it nervously and passed it hurriedly to Miss Selkirk.

Miss Selkirk was seated beside me, so while she inspected the workmanship I had an opportunity to look at the runes. They were in an archaic style, as I knew from having taken a course in comparative linguistics while at Oxford. Thus I inferred that the sword was not newly wrought, but a relic of some earlier age. I saw the rune for "king's hand," the one for "unerring flight," and the one for "violence turned," which is often mistranslated "vengeance." Some of the others were unfamiliar to me, but while I would not have attempted a faithful translation, the purport was appallingly clear.

Miss Selkirk attempted to hand the sword to me, but I put my hands in my lap and would not take it. She raised a glamorous eyebrow at me. "I'd rather not," I said lamely. "Forgive me, but I have an unreasoning horror of weapons of any sort."

Portnoy James's laugh boomed out across the dining-room. "Squeamish, eh? Wonder how you shave."

I touched the smoothness of my cheek. "I manage," I said.

"A week in the country'll put the steel in your backbone," James went on. "Tomorrow we'll be up early and shoot some grouse. You'll love it."

Miss Selkirk made a delicate moue of distaste, but her eyes twinkled, as if to say, "Men! What else can you expect?" Rupert Savage, on my other side, grunted. He pushed back his chair with a heavy scrape; its rear legs caught on the carpet, and the dining-table shuddered so that the candles swayed. He stepped behind my back and grabbed the sword where Miss Selkirk had laid it on the table. "Not much use against a repeating rifle," he said, swinging it casually in the air. "Is it true elves won't use firearms?"

Not long after, I excused myself to wash my hands. As I was passing down the long hall between the dining-room and the library, one of James's servants stepped out of the shadows. It was not, I think, one of those who had waited table at dinner, but they were none of them known to me. He had the long narrow face and slanted eyes of the Irish elves, and tufts of white hair as fine as down grew from the tall tips of his ears. "You should not linger here this night," he said softly, and passed on.

I considered the matter gravely while studying my face in the bathroom mirror. I may have trembled a little; when I combed my hair, I believe my comb fell into the basin. On returning to the dining-room, I made effusive apologies to our host. Pressing business in the city, a busy week ahead, certainly not a reflection on the charming company (with courteous bows to Miss Selkirk, Miss James, Mrs. Savage, and the other ladies), and so forth. All of the ladies, I may say, had handled the sword as it was passed around the table, some of them gingerly and others with evident relish. As I wrapped myself in coat and scarf and took my leave, James had not yet hung the weapon back up in its accustomed place; it rested on the table at his elbow, like common cutlery.

The hour was already late. I started the engine of my motorcar (no small feat, in such icy weather) and drove off down to the end of the lane. There I stopped, and switched off the headlamps and engine. I wrapped myself in a heavy lap-rug; while I did not much fear for my safety, I saw no reason to risk catching a chill.

Several hours passed. At one point I thought I saw three or four small black-clad figures slipping through the trees, moving down the lane away from the house, but the moonlight was fitful; I could not be certain my eyes weren't playing tricks on me.

Along toward 2:30 in the morning by my watch, the still of the night air was pierced by a long and hideous scream, which came from the direction of the house. I waited, wondering if the scream would be repeated.

I suppose I might at length have climbed out of the car and gone back up to peer in through a window, in order to bear witness to what had transpired, but the need to do so was taken from me. No more than a minute had passed since the scream, when a white-clad figure rushed down the lane. It was Patricia James, her face contorted by terror, the long loose nightgown billowing out behind her as she ran.

She saw my motorcar and veered toward me. "Thank God," she cried. "Father, and the bishop, they're all — that hideous — you must save me!" She gripped the side of the car in a hand whose bones stood out beneath the skin as stiff as a claw.

No sooner had the words escaped her lips than I saw her nemesis plunging toward us. The moon had emerged from behind a cloud, and the blade of the sword flickered with silvery radiance as it flew, swift as an arrow, beneath the skeletal boughs of the trees. Perhaps she heard the thin whistle it made as it sliced the air, or perhaps something in my face hinted at what was to come, for her eyes opened wider just for a moment.

The sword thudded into her body from behind, so forcefully that its tip emerged through her breastbone. It poked the fabric of the nightgown into a new little peak, higher than her breasts. Her mouth opened and blood gushed forth. As she fell to the ground, her head struck the running board with a heavy thump.

The sword wrenched itself from her body. Twice more it plunged into her, just as viciously, guided by no hand that I could see. Then it rose into the air, twirled, and flew back toward the house.

I started the engine once more and drove off toward town.

The newspapers were full of the story for days afterward — how the groundskeeper had come up the lane at daybreak and found Miss James lying butchered in an ice-crusted pool of frozen blood. Tyre-tracks led to the main road, and vanished; as they were of a common tread, not even Sherlock Holmes could have traced them any further. Within the house the groundskeeper found the entire party slaughtered. James's head had been cut clean off, and Miss Selkirk was mutilated most horribly. The bishop — well, some things are best left unsaid. The servants had vanished, as elves will, and inevitably the blame for the tragedy was placed squarely upon them.

The newspaper accounts said nothing, however, of the weapon that was used; nor was I able to find any mention of an elvish sword being found at the scene. I should have been very surprised if there had been.

The bishop was quite wrong on one point, though I forbore to correct him at the time: It is not true that the elves always kill half-breed babies born of elf-maidens who have been raped. Some of us are so loved by our mothers that they cannot bear to part with us, no matter how painfully our rounded ears and gross stature might remind them daily of the infinitude of wrongs done them.

My Life in the Jungle

AT ONE TIME, INCONGRUOUS as it must now seem, I was a professor of mathematics. I'm not sure that that fact is of any importance, but I *am* fairly certain that it's of no importance to anybody but me. Perhaps I think and feel more deeply because of it. Perhaps my remembrance of the past provides me a better perspective on the nature of recent events than those around me are privy to. It's difficult to be certain, if only because I have no idea what those around me think and feel, if anything. I can speculate, but speculation in the absence of evidence is the habit of fools.

There are thousands of us here, perhaps hundreds of thousands, wandering perpetually in this desolation of heat and dust. We all, I'm sure, suffer the same torment. Nevertheless, I do feel that I'm different from the others in some intangible but vital way because of my former circumstances. But while at one time I could recall my life as a professor of mathematics in great detail (indeed, such fond recollections of the rolling lawns of the campus, the classrooms, the cool quiet of the library, the meticulously reasoned papers I wrote for academic journals, occupied at one time many happy hours), of late the memories grow dim and fragmentary, and what I can still recall, I take no pleasure in. On the contrary — the contrast between my remembered life and my current situation is a source of added pain. If I remembered more of the details of the past, the pain would, I'm sure, be worse. Fortunately, those memories have been largely overlaid and blotted out by more recent, more brutal scenes, by more pressing needs and immediate concerns.

Bananas, for instance. As a professor of mathematics, I knew little about bananas, and cared less. They were yellow and grew on trees. I knew, in a general way, what one tasted like. Today I can identify more than a dozen distinct varieties of bananas, including too green to eat, green but edible, overripe but edible, rotten, wormy but edible, lying on the ground forgotten but still edible, half-masticated and spit out, bitter for no apparent reason, and just right. Then there are somebody else's bananas, bananas stomped into the floor of the jungle and pulped by somebody who was angry, bananas smeared over the body (one's own body or someone else's), and bananas hanging too high in the tree to reach. Bananas are a subject of vast and consuming importance to all of us here.

In recent months the band with which I am associated has shrunk by attrition to a fraction of its former size — which, considering the drastic alteration in our environment, is hardly surprising. Originally we numbered between twenty and twenty-five individuals. From the beginning, the number fluctuated a bit from day to day as individuals wandered away and were replaced by others upon whom we happened in our travels. Today the happy state that we enjoyed in the weeks following my arrival is nearly as remote from me as the campus life that preceded it. I look back wistfully on the leafy paradise in which we roamed; nowhere now in this wasteland is such a luxuriant habitat to be found. Had I known then what deterioration would occur, surely I would have tried to find some way to prevent it. Probably nothing I could have done would have done the slightest bit of good. Perhaps, indeed, I would have found myself incapable of acting differently than I have done. In any event, at the time I was far too busy mourning my lost academic life to pay more than cursory attention to the direction in which events were tending. Thus, I did nothing.

Even in those days, it was difficult for me reliably to distinguish one individual within the band from another by sight; now, of course, the problem is compounded a thousandfold. Certain individuals did, however, possess characteristics that enabled me after a time to identify them. I gave them names, in my own mind. The one who was more or less our acknowledged leader I dubbed Blackie, because of the broad irregular stripe of black fur that ran down his back. In addition to Blackie, there was a particular nervous, excitable little fellow I called Phil; a toothless old female I called Granny (whose principal distinguishing feature, other than her grizzled visage, was a a severe chronic case of diarrhea); and — always at the center of my thoughts — a gentle, doe-eyed female I called Arabella. Ah, Arabella!

Perhaps I should call us a tribe, and Blackie our chief. Not that his chieftanship went unchallenged. Far from it. We were constantly quarreling amongst ourselves. Indeed, next to foraging for bananas, quarreling has always been our chief occupation. Whenever we happened upon a band of strangers, we set aside our petty internal squabbles and put up a united front, screeching our challenge at them from the treetops and trampling and crushing whatever vegetation might be handy in order to demonstrate our ferocity and our utter contempt for them. They, of course, were simultaneously doing likewise. These noisy, destructive encounters were by far the grandest, most festive events punctuating our life in the jungle. But when no band of strangers was available, the young males not infrequently exhibited the same sort of aggressive behavior toward Blackie. He was not reluctant to reply in kind, and since he was larger and noisier than any of the rest, he inevitably emerged the victor, after which he would swagger around for hours with a self-satisfied smirk pasted on his repulsive features, deliberately bumping into anybody who was not quick enough to move out of his path and grabbing their bananas away from them.

These, then, were the parameters of the new life into which I was thrust — bananas and quarreling and roaming through the trees, or along the jungle floor when the trees were spaced inconveniently far apart for arboreal travel. At first the abruptness of the transition from the quiet life of a college professor left me shocked and appalled — only natural, I suppose, under the circumstances. For some weeks I remained in a rather befuddled state, and I am sure that I seemed odd and distant to the others. Fortunately the new body in which I found myself already knew the arts of jungle survival, else I would surely have perished. Sitting on a limb peeling a banana (a task I executed as expertly as though I had devoted a life's intensive study to it, though I now possessed only incompletely opposable thumbs), I pondered how such a thing could possibly have happened; but I was unable to arrive at any very satisfactory hypothesis.

It seemed impossible. In point of fact, it still seems impossible.

Nevertheless, the clarity and reliability of my perceptions made it clear at once that I had not been precipitated into a hallucination or a dream. If I had gone to sleep at night a college professor and wakened the next morning in my present situation, I might have found the dream hypothesis more attractive, but the transition was not cloaked in unconsciousness, nor even accompanied by any sense of movement. At one moment I was standing at a blackboard, explaining the techniques of differential calculus to a class of freshmen, most of whom were thoroughly bored and trying to conceal the fact; and then, in the blink of an eye, the classroom, the students, all had vanished, and I was sitting on a limb peeling a banana. When I saw how far above the ground I was, I became dizzy and had to cling to the limb to keep from falling, but the dizziness was, I am convinced, a consequence of my reaction to the height, not of the transition itself.

When, a few moments later, I first came face to face with those who were to be my new companions, again I reacted badly. I was, I regret, somewhat less than cordial. Far from embracing them, I was seized by terror and turned and fled headlong through the jungle, screeching in alarm and confusion.

I might easily have become separated from them and thus lost (hardly a serious matter, since I would soon have been bound to stumble upon another virtually indistinguishable band), but when they saw me running, they instantly concluded that this was some grand new game in which I desired their participation. Without hesitation they followed after me, crashing loudly through the underbrush and screeching in concert.

Hearing this commotion, I in turn naturally assumed that I was being pursued by those who wished me ill, and thus drove myself to greater exertion attempting to escape them. Eventually I would have outpaced them — except for the unfailing fascination of quarreling, their attention span was not long — but before me suddenly the jungle fell away, and I was brought up short at the edge of a wide grassy plain dotted with distant herds of elephant and zebra.

Even then I would have continued, save that directly before me, lolling comfortably in the dust, was a family of lions. Before I quite realized what I was doing, I had altered the direction of my progress from the X to the Y axis and scampered up the nearest tree — where, of course, Blackie and the others speedily joined me. For some hours, until the lions moved off, we had no choice but to remain where we were. Given this forced opportunity to make acquaintance with the band, I quickly lost my fear of them. Certainly they had their shortcomings, but I was not insensible of the fact that to be alone in the jungle is less desirable than to be with others with whom one has interests — survival not least among them — in common.

For some time after the transition, I did wonder whether I might shift back to the classroom as suddenly and unexpectedly as I had left it, whether I might begin shuttling back and forth as a regular thing, or perhaps with as little warning find myself in a third set of circumstances unrelated to either of the others. I no longer think this likely. I seem to be stuck very firmly and permanently where I am. I also wondered whether my new companions might be newly transplanted like myself; but their behavior has never given me any firm evidence to support this hypothesis. My attempts to communicate with them by means of grunts and gestures, by drawing signs in the dirt, were met with blank indifference, or on occasion with crude and mocking imitations of my behavior that could not possibly conceal anything of semantic significance.

I was forced, then, to consider whether *my* overt behavior, however precise or articulate my intentions, was any different from theirs. This is a question I still have not been able to lay to rest. I feel that I am far more intelligent than they, but as I have no method of observing myself from the outside, I am unable to determine whether this inner condition is manifest in any perceptible way. Conceivably, they are as intelligent as I, and we are all equally incapable of communication. As time goes on, admittedly, I am less inclined even to try to establish any meaningful interaction, and I acknowledge with regret that I am no longer much more attentive to matters of personal cleanliness than they. While I still think of myself as a professor of mathematics, so much time has passed that I might find it difficult to explain the calculus, should the occasion arise, or even to take a square root. I am reluctant, truth be told, to try to remember the details of such operations, for fear I might find that my recollections are by now only a muddle. As long as I don't dwell on the details, I can cling to the notion that I am in fact, if not in semblance, a professor of mathematics. If I tried to remember and failed, I would be forced to consider that after all, I may be no more than what I seem.

It is even possible, though I shudder to think of it, that my memories of that previous life are illusory. I may always have been as I am now. While I may consider myself to have been at one time a professor of mathematics, I would be hard pressed to offer any proof.

※　※

Once over the initial shock, I found that my new life offered certain consolations. For instance, I no longer had any professional obligations. There were no faculty meetings to attend, no undergraduates to advise, no thesis proposals to evaluate, no examinations to administer, no appointment calendar, no clocks to watch. My new environment, while perhaps less than idyllic, was in the main quite pleasant. The weather was uniformly warm, and although embarrassed at first, I shortly found that I didn't much mind not being constantly chafed by clothing. I suffered somewhat from boredom, but not excessively. While the course of events was more narrowly circumscribed here, there were endless matters of detail — such as learning to distinguish the many varieties of banana — to claim my attention. And most of all, by way of consolation, there was Arabella.

It was during my first days in the jungle, when I was still cautiously trying to discover the nature of my situation, that Arabella and I became aware of one another. Far from being impudently, raucously lewd like most of the other females, she was shy and retiring by nature, and even fastidious compared to the others (though admittedly the general standards of grooming were deplorably lax, and her own accomplishments in this regard were relative rather than absolute). I no longer recall whether it was she who first approached me or vice versa, but before very long we had become steadfast companions.

Companionship among the tribe was a simple matter, consisting chiefly of long sessions spent picking lice from one another's fur — a necessary task if we were not all to succumb to terminal itching. It was this activity that formed the primary basis of my relationship with Arabella. How well I remember the gentleness of her fingers as they roamed delicately over my back and shoulders! I also from time to time offered her an especially delectable-looking banana; I wish I could report that she reciprocated, but alas, the exchange of such tokens of generosity seemed to be entirely unknown among the tribe. At most, she favored me perhaps with a fleeting glance of appreciation before devoting her attention wholly to the matter at hand — that is, to the banana.

There was a time when I thought Arabella and I could be happy together. I pretended to myself that within her must reside, hidden, a soul akin to my own, though she never gave me any concrete evidence in support of this idea. I seemed to recall a student I had had once who possessed such soft, compassionate eyes, such a sweet disposition, and I fondly imagined that it was with this student that I was passing the hours in our leafy bower. I found, however, that I was unable to remember the student's name. This dampened my enjoyment of the fantasy somewhat.

No matter. In the evenings, when the tribe had settled down for the night in the boughs of a banana grove, when the air was fragrant with the scent of wild orchids and the occasional sleepy roar of a lion could be heard in the distance, Arabella would come to me and pick the lice from my fur, and I the lice from hers. I am sure she would have allowed a greater degree of familiarity had I sought it; couplings among the tribe were indulged in quite casually and openly, with no consideration whatever of propriety or decorum. But I could not quite bear to disturb the tranquility of our time together. Nor, to be honest, could I ever wholly divest myself of the knowledge that I was after all a professor of mathematics, for whom such a scene must remain too grotesquely undignified ever to take part in.

I have no idea how long this period of arboreal contentment lasted. More than a year, surely; perhaps several. At one time I considered whether I might be able to fashion a crude calendar by carving each day a new notch in a convenient tree branch. But even had I possessed a suitable carving tool, it would have availed me naught, for in our wanderings through the jungle we rarely spent two nights in the same place. To have carved a single notch in a new tree every night would have been an exercise in perfect futility.

All during this time, our encounters with other roving bands continued. These were occasions of some devastation to the jungle, for when we saw strangers, so like us and yet so utterly unlike, we flew into paroxysms of rage. To demonstrate our ferocity, we uprooted whole bushes and young trees, or trampled them into the mud. If the strangers had not begun doing so before us, they imitated us without delay. This activity was accompanied by prolonged screeching, gnashing of teeth, thumping of chests, and (though it shames me to admit it) the flinging of excrement. Actual hand-to-hand combat was a rarity, though we sometimes worked ourselves into such a frenzy that no lesser measures would suffice to slake our rage. Generally we preferred to take up a safe strategic position, from which, after a thorough display of animosity, we would begin pelting the enemy with bodily wastes — or, when none came readily to hand, with bananas. After an hour or two of such excitement, both sides would retire grumbling, leaving behind a battlefield strewn with trampled vegetation and quantities of dung.

At first there seemed no harm in this enterprise. The jungle was large, and the scars of battle quickly overgrown. As time went on, however, I noticed that our encounters with bands of strangers were becoming more frequent and the injuries to the jungle slower to heal. Often in our migrations we came upon old battlegrounds, bedraggled and foul-smelling. On some of these occasions, I could recall that it was we who had participated in the depredation, while on others the landmarks were unfamiliar to me. I concluded that we were far from alone in provoking and relishing such hostilities.

Unquestionably, we did our share of the destructive work. There was one band in particular with whom we fought repeatedly, in a series of skirmishes that ranged up and down the jungle. If I had been transported originally into their midst rather than into Blackie's group, I don't suppose it would have made the slightest difference, for on the whole we were quite indistinguishable from one another. Nevertheless, we were bitter enemies. On one memorable occasion we became rivals for a single stand of banana trees, an unusually large and fertile grove whose bananas were among the finest I had ever tasted. In truth, the grove was large enough easily to have fed both our group and the others, but there was no possibility of our reaching an accommodation. Arriving one morning at the grove simultaneously from opposite directions, we both took umbrage; each group was determined that it and it alone should occupy the entire site. As a result, we threw more bananas at one another than we ate, and tore more and more leaves from the banana trees in our furious displays of aggression.

When the trees on all sides were wholly denuded, we had no alternative but to uproot them; failure to do so would have been proof of cowardice. The labor of uprooting full-grown trees was prodigious, and required a greater degree of cooperation than our band had shown before, or has since. But we were determined. When we finished, the trees lay about on the ground like matchsticks. We slammed them down, and grimaced and howled. I cannot say whether our group or the detested strangers uprooted more of the trees; it would have been a victory of sorts, if only symbolic, though I am bound to suppose that nobody but myself was counting, or even capable of counting. Perhaps my failure to keep a tally was, under the circumstances, a form of disloyalty. In any event, the upshot was that we completely destroyed the grove, and both tribes had to look elsewhere for sustenance.

One remarkable aspect of these battles was their effect on the one I called Phil. As if in compensation for the fact that he was unable to best Blackie in our domestic uproars (or, to put it more accurately, that he was unwilling to challenge him), Phil became in our encounters with strangers the most hysterically aggressive of our band. He screeched the loudest, he trampled bushes the most enthusiastically, and he flung excrement with such glee that he generally got more on himself (it not having hardened enough to make proper projectiles) than on the enemy. Not that the rest of us were immune to this unfortunate scattering effect. Phil, however, was nervous and excitable at the best of times, and these bouts did him no good.

For hours after a battle, he would lie on the ground twitching, eyes rolled far back in his head and foam dribbling from his mouth. He was a pitiful sight, and would have been easy prey for a lion had one happened along. Fortunately for him, he was victimized only by the other young males of our own tribe, who lost no opportunity to urinate on him and otherwise display their contempt while he was helpless.

Nor did I, to my everlasting shame, abstain from this ritual of debasement. Although I had only pity for poor Phil, I feared that to hang back when the rest of the tribe so eagerly pressed forward would make me conspicuous, and might lead to my being singled out for the same sort of abuse. Even Granny, the aged and incontinent female, participated on these occasions. Since this was the only time she got the better of anybody, I found it hard to begrudge her the opportunity, though unquestionably it was a disgusting spectacle.

To an outsider it might have appeared that we were demonstrating our disapproval of Phil's extreme pugnacity, but nothing could have been further from the truth. Our vociferousness in encounters with strangers was nearly equal to his. Rather, we were deflecting onto Phil the aggressive impulses we had been unable to vent on any less helpless victim. If the band of strangers had been so considerate as to lie down on the floor of the jungle and allow such treatment, our deepest longings would have been fulfilled.

It was on the evening following our destruction, with the collaboration of our habitual nemeses, of the banana grove, that I lost my Arabella. For some time before, to be sure, she had seemed somewhat distracted. Once or twice she actually pushed away a banana I was offering her. But until it was too late, I attached no significance to this. Perhaps if I had — well, such speculation is of no value now. It happened that during the battle, Blackie's usual consort, his favorite of the five or six upon whom he customarily lavished his lecherous attentions, had wandered away — where or why, I never learned. In her absence, his roving eye fell upon Arabella; and she, to my sorrow, seemed not to find his overtures distasteful. Disdaining even to undertake a preliminary picking of lice by way of courtship, he mounted her straightaway, as I watched in horror. The lust in his eyes was acid in my heart — and as for Arabella, she continued placidly eating a banana all the time he was at his business. A banana I had given her! Faithless Arabella! I fought him, naturally; I had no choice, if I were to salvage even a tattered remnant of honor. Of course he beat me soundly. I fear I have always been too inhibited to screech and trample with the necessary abandon.

But while I remained furious at Blackie, it was hard to hold Arabella blameless. Far from being distraught by the change, far from pining for me or casting longing glances in my direction, she took to the new arrangement as placidly as she had to her time with me, and seemed to want nothing further to do with me. When I approached, humbly beckoning for her to search my back for lice, she pushed me away roughly. At night I was forced to listen to her grunts of pleasure mingled with his. Dismally depressed by this turn of events, I gorged myself on bananas. Briefly I considered leaving the tribe entirely and striking out through the jungle in search of new companions, but I knew I would carry the unhappy memory with me wherever I went, and would have no peace. As long as I stayed nearby, I could cherish the hope that eventually he would tire of her, or she of him. I was unsure whether I would wish, in that case, to resume our former relations, whether I would be capable of so blithely putting the past behind me, but it seemed wrong to deny myself the opportunity should it arise.

From this time on, it seemed, a change came over our life in the jungle. Or perhaps it was only that, no longer distracted by Arabella's sweet presence, I noticed for the first time a change that had already begun. Indeed, as I was now searching for distractions, I may have noticed the change long before it became apparent to the others — if indeed it has ever become apparent to them. To this day, I sometimes think, they have not noticed the cataclysmic deterioration in our surroundings. They continue to behave exactly as they did before, though it is no longer appropriate (if it ever was). Perhaps they have no memory of what once was, and thus no way to gauge the extent of their loss. Perhaps it is only I, among the myriad here, who am aware of the disaster we have brought on ourselves.

Could I have averted it, if I had seen what was to come? What could I possibly have done?

We moved on, then, from the destroyed banana grove in search of unspoiled forage. But more and more, the groves we came upon were already in the possession of bands of strangers, whom we had to drive off in order to enjoy the bananas. The jungle was thick with evidence of past combats, and virgin stretches of wild growth increasingly rare.

The first time we came upon two separate bands of strangers fighting for possession of a grove, we retreated in confusion, never having seen such a thing before. But before long we were inured to such sights. We learned that we could pitch in, making it a three-way fight, taking advantage of the fact that the others were already in a debilitated condition to promote our own cause, and on occasion we emerged the victors. For our victory celebration, naturally, we stuffed ourselves with bananas, whether or not they were ripe and continuing long after we had eaten our fill, continuing until we vomited up undigested banana and then reaching greedily for more — for who knew when we might have the chance for such an orgy again? Just as often, we found ourselves unequal to the contest, and were driven off; if not initially, by those who had taken the grove before us, then certainly at a later date, by those who came after. It proved impossible to retain control of any given grove for very long, especially as the roving bands were becoming more numerous and virgin stands of banana trees more scarce. When we could secure victory only by uprooting the trees, naturally we did so; nor have I any reason to suppose we were alone in this improvident behavior. And always, sooner or later, we were compelled to move on, searching, ever searching for a grove where we could eat and remain unmolested.

It was after one of these raids that I noticed Arabella was gone. Though it had galled me to look on her now that she was another's, I found that I mourned her loss none the less keenly. I hoped that she had found a haven with another band like ours, new companions who would devotedly pick the lice from her fur. The thought that she might lie crushed under a fallen banana tree, her warm doe eyes forever cold and vacant, was for a long time a source of torment for me. I am compelled to wonder, however, whether such a fate might after all be better for her than to have survived. Our circumstances now are so wretched that, though I may wish she were here to ease my loneliness, I cannot in good conscience desire that she should suffer this pain. Perhaps, nevertheless, she has survived, and wanders here as we do. Perhaps someday I will stumble upon her, and not recognize her, and pass on. Perhaps I have done so already. Ah, Arabella, truly you are lost!

Today our encounters with bands of strangers are no longer frequent; they are continual. Of the jungle, nothing remains. As far as I can see in every direction (which is not far, unless I climb for a moment onto somebody else's shoulders), there is nothing on this arid plain but thousands of bands like ourselves roaming through the dust and filth, screeching foul imprecations at one another, bespattering one another with excrement and stumbling occasionally over the dried bleached bones of a lion, as we seek perpetually and in vain a leafy grove where grow bananas.

Of our group, only myself and Blackie and Granny remain. Wanting nothing to do with Granny, but needing release, Blackie has taken to mounting me instead. I find this humiliating, and rather painful, but I am powerless to prevent it. Also he demands that I search his fur for lice, while showing no inclination whatever to reciprocate. I itch constantly, agonizingly. When I scratch, my fur comes out in clumps, leaving raw, red sores.

The heat of the sunlight is so intense as to raise blisters, and in the thick dust I am dreadfully, excruciatingly thirsty. There being no trees left to uproot, some of the more foul-tempered among us have taken to tearing off one another's limbs and belaboring one another about the head with them. The delicious wetness of the blood as it spurts from these horrid wounds goads my thirst unbearably.

Once the blood has mingled with the dust, of course, its usefulness as a means of allaying thirst is a thing of the past. I find myself wondering whether I could become so crazed by thirst as to do what I am now continually contemplating. I have seen a few others do it. Am I actually capable of such savagery? I would like, even in this extremity, to feel that I still possess some tattered measure of dignity, of rationality. After all, I was at one time a professor of mathematics.

Run! Run!

AN ADULT UNICORN IS larger than a pony, though smaller than a horse. Its limbs are as lean and lithe as a deer's, its mane and tail equine, generous, and silky as spider-weave. The males have a goatee of the same hair, which gives them a contemplative look. All unicorns are pure white, but the horns of the males have a thin spiral of blue that runs from the base out to the tip, the females a spiral of gold. At night the horn of a unicorn glows faintly, with a cool unwavering light.

Unicorns have a distinctive odor, somewhere between cinnamon and candle wax. They will eat grass, but they prefer fresh flower petals. An adult can eat seven or eight pounds of flower petals a day, after which its droppings are a swirl of colors, a clotted rainbow.

My daughters know nothing about unicorns. As far as I know, they have never seen one. They may not even know the word. Certainly no one has ever told them about the unicorns their grandfather once kept on his farm outside of Elmira, New York. They never knew their grandfather, for that matter. I wonder — what should I tell them? How much should I tell them?

When I was their age (Cecile is eleven, Faith eight — how quickly they grow!), unicorns were a fact of our lives. We knew we mustn't talk about them, my sister Leonore and I, not to anybody, but they were always there, off in the south paddock nibbling on flower petals, which in the winter my father had flown in from Central America in large bales. I suppose the truck drivers might have wondered about those shipments, but my father had a way of putting people at ease without saying much. He was a quiet, comfortable man, and I miss him very much. My mother had died when I was only a baby and Leonore not much older, so I never knew her, and Father seldom spoke of her. Once in a while he would say, "Your mother's looking down from Heaven, and she's smiling" — or, if we were misbehaving, "Your mother's looking down from Heaven. Do you want her to see you doing that?" But he took good care of us, and our life on the farm seemed to me complete.

The south paddock was well screened from the road by a line of trees, and there was little traffic on the road. If the unicorns — there were usually seven or eight of them — were glimpsed from the road, they would have been thought horses. At night their horns, twinkling among the trees as they ran, might have been mistaken for boys chasing across the field with flashlights.

Father brought the first unicorn home the year before I was born. I suppose Mother must have thought he had gone mad, but he never spoke of that. The unicorn — I knew her, years later, as Sparky — was a foal, and had no horn yet, only a nub on her forehead. He found her at the edge of the woods, a trembling little thing. He thought at first the foal must be an albino deer, its mother shot by a hunter. Deer hunters were not uncommon in the woods around our farm, so he may have been right about the fate of the mother. When the foal failed to thrive on mare's milk, I believe he brought the veterinarian in to look at her. The vet, Dr. Land, must have known at once what she was. In later years my father paid Dr. Land what he called a monthly retainer for his services, though by the time I was five or six we had no animals left other than the unicorns, an aging, arthritic spaniel, and an entirely self-sufficient cat. Dr. Land was a Godly man, and it would be a slander to say he took my father's money to keep quiet about the unicorns, but I can't think of any other explanation.

I was born in the seventh year after the Final Conversion of the Heathen. All the world at last was Christian, which must have set Satan gnashing his teeth! The Mohammedans, the Chinese Communists, even the Jews had converted, one and all, and been baptized. At last, after centuries of struggle, the United States was a Christian nation. Prayer was heard every morning in every school, every unborn child was safe in the womb, and not one soul would have dreamed of giving voice to the atheistic ideas that had once been so disgustingly common.

Or so it's said. I'm entirely in the dark about what those atheistic ideas might have been, because no one repeats them anymore. Why should we?

What I hope my daughters would understand, if I were to tell them about the unicorns, was that their grandfather was a Godly man too. Perhaps not as fervent as some, but Leonore and I were taken faithfully to church every Sunday in Elmira, and on Wednesday nights to Bible study at the Christian center down the road. There was no evil in him, not that I ever saw. But there is evil in all of us, I know it's true. I can't deny that Father strayed from the Word of the Lord.

The last summer when there were unicorns at the

farm, I was fifteen and Leonore was seventeen. She had fallen very much in love with Timothy McFadden, the son of our local pastor. It was expected that Tim would follow in his father's footsteps and join the clergy. Poor Leonore! It was hardly to be expected that Tim would notice her, with so many girls vying for his attention.

She would have had an easier time of it if we lived closer to town, because she was pretty, and had truly accepted Jesus Christ into her heart. She would have made a wonderful wife for a minister! But Father had too much work to do on the farm to drive her to Monday night choir practice or to the Saturday youth picnics, which was where the boys and girls mainly had a chance to socialize. He had acreage in alfalfa, and apple orchards, and he never had quite enough hired hands to do the work. I don't know whether it was because he couldn't afford the hands — the unicorns must have been a constant drain on our finances — or whether he worried that the hands would wander out to the south paddock and see something he didn't want them to see.

I never knew how the unicorns arrived on the farm, or when one would. They may have scented one another. One day there would be seven in the herd, the next day eight, the newcomer not hard to spot — burrs in his mane and tail, perhaps with a limp or scratches left by barbed wire, wild-eyed when Father approached, bolting to the far end of the paddock and not easily soothed.

How did a newcomer get into the paddock? I've often wondered that. Sometimes I think any of them could have leapt the fence at any time, that they stayed only because they wanted to. Sometimes I think they knew how to lift the latch of the gate using their horns, and let the newcomer in themselves. But I suppose it's possible that Father was part of a network of secret unicorn fanciers, and was known to be good with wild ones. Possibly a truck would pull up, well past midnight when Leonore and I were safely dreaming, and the animal would be unloaded and led out to the paddock.

Father never cajoled a newly arrived unicorn, or tried to coax. He just set out the feed, saw to the water, and let the beast get used to his presence in its own time. A month might pass before it would let him curry it. Occasionally they favored me instead of Father, especially as I got older. There was one male that I named Charger, who would always come close when I appeared at the fence. After I fed him, he would — sometimes, not always — permit me to comb his silky mane with my fingers.

"Could I ride Charger?" I asked Father once. "Could we saddle him like a horse?"

Father shook his head. "A unicorn can never be saddled. They won't stand for it. Years ago I heard it said you could possibly mount one and ride it bareback, but you wouldn't want to, Mary."

"Why not?"

"If you mount a unicorn, it will run off bearing you, swift as the wind. It will never tire and never stop, and you'll never be able to dismount again. When at last Jesus calls the faithful up to sit beside Him in Heaven, you'll still be astride the unicorn, and you'll be left behind."

I think he must have made that up, just to keep me from spooking Charger and possibly breaking my leg or my skull when I got thrown off. I don't honestly know where he might have met anyone who could tell him a single thing about unicorns. He told me once about a thing called the Internet, which had flourished when he was younger. You could meet almost anyone on the Internet, he said, or read about no end of wicked, sinful things. But after the Final Conversion of the Heathen, Godless things like the Internet were no longer needed.

I think he would have found a way to manage to take Leonore to choir practice and Saturday picnics, if I had wanted to go too. That's why I have to shoulder some of the blame for what happened. I should have been more interested in socializing, but I had always been a shy, moody, awkward girl. I knew if we went, Leonore would get all the attention while I'd be left standing off in a corner by myself, a miserable lump. I much preferred to stay home and look after the unicorns. Not that they needed much looking after; but if I held out a handful of tulip petals, one would edge closer, curious but skittish, and eventually nibble daintily from my hand.

Sometimes I think Leonore was jealous. They would never eat from her hand, but then she never truly tried. She was always too impatient. She would twitch, or make some wry comment under her breath, and then the unicorn would bound away to the far side of the paddock, where it would gaze at her reproachfully or go back to cropping daisies.

But saying she was jealous isn't fair to her. In truth, our father should not have had the unicorns in the first place. Reverend McFadden delivered several heartfelt sermons every year describing how Satan would tempt the faithful with seeming miracles. Father sat there and listened to the sermons, and nodded and said, "Amen," but it was as if he never heard a word. So maybe Satan had entered into his heart. I don't like to think so, but Satan never rests. He's always looking for an opening. I know this.

Leonore would have done anything — well, almost anything — to get Tim McFadden to notice and approve of her. But Father and I were being no help. It was as if we had entered into a sort of pact and shut poor Leonore out. At the dinner table we would talk mostly about the unicorns. Was Sparky or Noble the faster runner? Would Desdemona foal this year? Leonore would sit there, poking at her food. Through gritted teeth, when she could stand it no longer, she would say, "Could we please talk about something else?"

In the end, it was too much for such a good Christian soul to bear.

The first we knew about what she had done was when Reverend McFadden and four or five of the church elders appeared at our gate one Saturday morning. They wouldn't enter the property, but called out to Father: "We need to speak with you, Mr. Pritchard."

He went striding out to meet them. I had heard them drive up, and came out on the front porch to listen.

"We've received a disturbing report," Reverend McFadden said. He was a portly man, always well dressed, but his eyes were set close together, which made him look as if he was squinting even when he wasn't. "We understand you're harboring horned animals on the property."

"I don't know who would have told you that," my father said.

"Someone who is in a position to know. Can you tell us, then, on your word as a Christian, is it true or is it not?"

"If I tell you it's not, that's as good as calling another man a liar, am I right?"

"That would be one way of looking at it, I suppose."

"Well, I don't think I could do that," Father said. "If a man utters a falsehood, or says anything against me meaning to hurt me, it's between him and his God. It's not for me to judge him."

That set them back, but not by much. "Would it disturb you," Reverend McFadden went on, "if we were to come onto your property and see for ourselves?"

"No!" I cried. "Don't let them!"

Father never turned toward me. "Go into the house, Mary," he said over his shoulder. "Let me deal with this."

I slipped through the front door, and I think the screen banged a little, though I didn't mean it to. My heart was skipping so fast I couldn't breathe.

Leonore was standing at the foot of the stairs, her hand on the newel post. She was smirking.

"You!" I clenched my fist. "You told them!"

"What if I did?" she said archly. "There's no place in God's creation for devil-beasts. You'd know that perfectly well if you hadn't been picking your nose all through Bible study. We'll all be happier when they're gone."

I would like to think she truly believed that. I wouldn't like to think she did it to hurt Father and me; she is far too pure and good ever to have let such a temptation into her heart. Of course she must have thought she would impress Tim McFadden with how upstanding a Christian she was, how vigilant against the wiles of Satan. That was the main reason.

I stomped past her up the stairs to my room, and threw the pillows across the room and wept. Out the window I saw Father leading the men toward the back paddock. They weren't out there more than five minutes before they came back. Reverend McFadden was leading the way almost at a trot, as if he couldn't wait to get off of our place. "Put them down, Mr. Pritchard," he said. "Put them down! You have a rifle. Use it."

Father went out to the front gate to see them off, and then came into the house. I heard him moving around downstairs, and then the awful creak of the rusty old hinges as he opened the gun cabinet.

I knew what I had to do. But when I burst out of my room, Leonore was standing in the hall right in front of me. "Where do you think you're going, missy?" I tried to get past her to the back stairs, but she shifted to block my path. "Want to say goodbye to your precious Charger?" She laughed. "The sooner you forget about him the better."

May God forgive me. I hit my sister with my fist and knocked her down. I think surprise showed in her eyes, but I was already past her, leaping down the back stairs three at a time.

I raced out to the paddock. All the way, I kept looking over my shoulder, but I didn't see Father coming.

I threw open the gate, charged into the paddock, and ran at the unicorns, waving my arms. "Run! Run! You have to run!" They tried to stay away from me in the enclosed space, shy creatures that they were, so when I got to the far side of the paddock and circled back I was able to herd them out the gate, even that year's half-grown foal, Jewel.

Unicorns are much faster than horses, when they want to be. They can run like the wind itself. By the time Father came down from the house carrying his rifle, they had raced away. I could still hear their hoofbeats receding, or thought I could, but they had vanished from view. I was standing at the open gate hugging myself, shivering, though it was a warm day. "They're gone," I said.

"Did you open the gate, then?"

"No, it was open when I got here. I think the men

from the church must have forgotten to latch it." I don't know why I lied. Was it because I didn't want Father to punish me? Or because I wanted the church elders to bear the blame for the unicorns being gone? Either way, it was a sin.

Father may have known I had lied, but he never said a word. He put his arm around my shoulders and led me back into the house.

It turned out I had split Leonore's lip when I hit her. She had bled all over the upstairs hall carpet, and Father had to drive her into town to get stitches. She wouldn't speak to me for a month, and I don't think she ever quite forgave me. Father never said a word about what had happened that afternoon, never again spoke about the unicorns at all. But it was as if someone had switched off the light in his heart. After supper he would sit in the front room and not turn on a lamp or listen to the Gospel hour on the radio, just sit there in the dark all evening.

Once I walked in on him, sitting there in the dark, and saw he had the rifle cradled in his lap. That scared me a lot. But the next morning the rifle was locked up in the gun cabinet again, and later I found the key to the gun cabinet lying on my dresser. I hid it, which I guess was what he wanted me to do.

Leonore married a man named Howard Stith and they moved away to Indiana. She sends me Christmas greetings full of chatty news about her family, but we almost never talk on the phone. The year after she got married, Father died, and I closed up the farm and sold it. That was when I found the key to the gun cabinet, still tucked away in the bottom of my sock drawer. This was all a long time ago. I got married too, to a fine upstanding man, and now I have two daughters of my own. I wish they had known their grandfather, but I never talk about him. What would I say?

At night sometimes, as I lie in bed waiting for sleep to come, I think I hear, somewhere very far away, unicorns galloping, galloping like the wind. I imagine their manes and tails streaming out behind them as they run, the cool glow of their horns flickering among the trees like loose moonlight. I imagine what it would be like to ride one.

The House of Broken Dolls

THE GIRL LOOKED ABOUT eighteen. She had long straight straw-colored hair and large, wide-set hazel eyes. She was standing very still, looking straight at him, one slim-fingered hand parked on the hip of her jeans.

"You should write to my sister," the girl said. "Maybe she can help. She can file some papers or something. Anyway, it's time."

He had never seen her before.

Afterward he remembered her shadow, knife-sharp where the sun threw it across the rough surface of the stone bench where he was sitting. Hallucinations didn't cast shadows, did they?

It was a warm afternoon, the sun pouring down through the dusty leaves of the olive trees. He had come outside to sit on the old stone bench and feel sad and tired and lost. He took no joy in the warmth of the day, nor in the mockingbird gibbering its cheerful nonsense in the nearest treetop. The bench squatted at one edge of the lumpy, patchy lawn, not far from the outer wall that screened the property from the street. Sitting here you could look across the lawn at the little old house, its brown stucco and red tile roof as comfortably weathered as if the house had grown there, and at the boxy little outbuildings camped in what had once been a very large back yard.

His name was John Renagle. The stone bench was a favorite place to sit and think slow, peaceful thoughts, which he often liked to do. One of the outbuildings was his workshop. In it he made musical instruments out of wood, and (more often) repaired instruments that had been damaged. When he wasn't sure whether to use abalone or mother-of-pearl for an inlay, or needed to wait for some inner certainty before he applied the saw or chisel, he would come outside and sit on the bench.

In another month or two, the bench and the outbuildings would be gone. He would still have a workshop — he'd find a place somewhere, probably in some horrid little industrial park jammed up against the freeway, where diesel fumes would eat away at the wood while they ate away at his lungs and his soul. But the Ambrosia Center for the Arts, not just his workshop but the studios of the four other artists who rented space here, was about to be scraped into oblivion. And there wasn't a damn thing he could do about it. All of them together couldn't raise enough capital to buy the place. They were artists, and this was Palo Alto, where residential lots sold for a thousand dollars a square foot.

Suddenly the girl was standing in front of him. He hadn't seen her approach, but the gate was always open during the day. People from the neighborhood, out for a stroll, sometimes detoured onto the grounds, and an occasional customer dropped in to visit one of the studios. Doubtless he had dozed off for a minute without realizing it.

"What did you say?"

"I said you should write to my sister. I think maybe she can help you."

"Who's your sister?"

"I don't know. She's a lawyer. Her name is Beth. She stayed here one summer, a long time ago. You should look in the house for old letters."

Afterward he remembered the serious set of her almost colorless lips and the way the hazel eyes stared at him so fixedly. Had she even blinked? "Well?" she demanded. "Are you going to? If you do it, maybe you won't have to move your workshop."

"One summer a long time ago," he echoed.

"Years and years. She'd be old now. As old as you, I bet."

He let that pass. "There's cabinets and boxes full of stuff in the house," he said. "Stuff the old owners left behind. But how would you know what's there? It's kept locked. Did you break in?"

She rolled her eyes. "Didn't have to. I live there."

"Nobody lives there. It's a doll museum, or it was. It's been closed up for, what, three years now."

"Look for the letters," she said. "Mommy and Daddy wrote to her from Europe. And she's a lawyer. That's all you need to know."

She turned aside and sauntered past him with a confident stride, not quite close enough to touch. She passed between two of the big oleander bushes that screened the outer wall, moving without hesitation, as if the wall, solid brick and seven feet tall, weren't straight in front of her, blocking her path. And then she was gone.

He turned as he stood up. Except where the bushes hid it, he could see the whole expanse of wall, from the northeast corner of the property clear down to the driveway. He didn't see her.

"Okay, enough with the hide-and-seek," he said. She had to be behind one of the bushes. He waited, heard no footsteps.

Marta came out of her studio and crossed the lawn toward him, a big-boned woman, sloppily dressed as usual in a paint-spattered smock, with a heavy mass of black-gray hair that sat on her head like a dead raccoon. "Did you see a girl, just now?" he said. "She was right here."

Marta stood and watched, skeptical but obliging, while he scouted behind the bushes. The narrow dirt lane between foliage and wall was deserted. There wasn't a gate at this spot, and no footholds anybody could use to climb over the wall, only a little niche, a recess with an arched canopy, in which sat a lichen-encrusted stone bust. He had set the bust there, on a whim, some months before, after he found it half-buried down by the creek. It seemed to be at home in the niche. It was of a woman's head and shoulders, and carved of soapstone, not marble. He gazed skeptically at the bust. "Did you see her?" The bust only smiled in its changeless seraphic way.

Talking to statues, now. The day was getting a little strange. But unless the girl had dropped into a hole, a hole that had swallowed her and then closed without a trace, she had walked straight through the wall.

"Was there somebody here?" Marta said when he emerged from behind the bushes.

Had he dreamed her? "Yeah. A girl. She popped up out of nowhere. She said her sister could help. I think she meant, help with the Center closing. It was like she was reading my mind. She said her sister was a lawyer, that she could file some papers. Oh, and she said she lives in the house. Her, I mean, not the sister."

"The house is locked up. The plumbing doesn't even work."

"That's what I told her. And then she walked right past me and vanished."

"She didn't need to read your mind to know the Center is closing," Marta said. "It's not like it's a secret." And that was certainly true. A big white-and-blue For Sale sign stood beside the gate, and agents had shown the property a dozen times, tramping through the artists' studios with scarcely an apology. "I came to ask if I can borrow your scissors," Marta said. "I can't find mine." Her disorganization was legendary. Her studio always looked as if a cyclone had passed through only moments before.

"Sure, if I can borrow the key to the house." Before the owner died, Marta had been the on-site property manager.

It took her ten minutes to locate the key, and the search turned up her scissors, so John escaped without having his own scissors swallowed up by the cyclone. Feeling silly and a little irritated with himself — looking for old letters because a mysterious stranger told him to — he unlocked the front door and prowled through the house. It was a modest bungalow, built in the 1920s, when walls were thick and windows small. The interior was cool and dim, the air close and stuffy. The most recent owner, Axel Taubin, had never lived in the house. After he inherited the property from his brother, in a fit of philanthropy he turned the walled quarter-acre into the Ambrosia Center for the Arts, and the house — for reasons sentimental or fetishistic, it was never clear — into a doll museum. At one time the museum had had a curator, whose main job, in the years after John set up his workshop, seemed to be dusting. Even in its heyday, the museum seldom had visitors. As Axel's health declined, the curator was laid off and the museum closed up. And now Axel was gone, and soon the Center would be shut down as well.

But for now, the dolls were still there. As John passed from room to room they stood in silent ranks on tables and shelves. Of course they weren't staring at him; they took no notice of him at all; but it was hard to escape the feeling that he was in a crowd, a lonely crowd where everyone carefully stood very still and no one ever spoke to anyone else.

A few of the dolls had fallen to the floor — possibly due to a minor earthquake, more likely because prospective buyers being shown the property had carelessly bumped into the display tables. One doll had lost an arm in its fall. A sad-looking rag doll had been kicked into a corner, where it was leaking woolly viscera.

Not fallen but standing on a sideboard shelf in the dining room was a doll that looked a little like the girl who claimed she lived here. The doll was larger than a Barbie and less anorexic, but it had the same long blond hair and the same sense of graceful poise. Hazel eyes, too, he noticed. Eyes that never blinked.

"Okay, you do live here," he said. "I get it." And then chided himself. First talking to a stone bust, and now talking to dolls. He was a man who worked with his hands. He was not given to flights of fancy. He must subconsciously have remembered that doll, and turned it into a drowsy summer hallucination.

But he wasn't in the habit of leaving things half-finished. Having begun to look for letters, he would damn well look for the letters, even though he knew perfectly well there were no letters to be found.

Every closet in the house had its share of cardboard boxes jammed with untidy jumbles of this and that. He could waste days searching. If there were letters, how did the girl know about them? And why exactly was he going to so much trouble to do what the girl suggested? "Maybe she can file some papers or something." That was why. A thread of hope. It would be another hour before the coat of varnish he had applied to the back of the Martin steel-string would be dry enough to buff. Until then, he had nothing better to do.

An hour later, dusty and increasingly grumpy, he pulled down the pocket stairway in the hall and climbed the steep, narrow, creaking stairs to the attic. At first he thought he would need to retreat and find a flashlight, but when he flicked the switch a naked overhead bulb cast its faltering glow among the cobwebs.

An old trunk squatted in one corner, beneath the slope of the roof. In the trunk, tucked away under a moth-eaten blanket, he found a thin packet of old letters. The packet was held together with a stiff rubber band that promptly broke. He gathered up the scattered letters from the floor and took them back to his shop to read.

The postmarks were from the summer of 1978, from the East Coast and Europe. The letters were brief and uninteresting, the handwriting slanted and hard to decipher. Apparently Albert and Judith Drury had been on an extended vacation, and had left their daughter Beth in the care of Donald and Muriel Taubin. Three of the letters were addressed to Beth, three more to Donald and Muriel. There was mention of money enclosed, "in case Beth needs anything special." In the last of the letters to Beth, her mother hinted that she was feeling a bit impatient. Evidently Beth had written to them asking them to break off their vacation and come home early. "Donald and Muriel are very nice people," her mother chided her. "I can't imagine why you wouldn't be happy staying with them. Your father and I will be home at the end of August, as we planned. Please remember to thank Mr. and Mrs. Taubin for their generous hospitality."

John hadn't known the name of Axel Taubin's brother, but the family connection was plain. Donald and Muriel must have owned the house in 1978, and when they were gone it passed to Axel.

The Internet made the next step easy. The girl had said her sister was a lawyer. John had no trouble hunting down an attorney named Elizabeth Drury. He found three of them, in fact, but one was years too young and another had grown up in Anchorage. The third was a Stanford alumna, which made the connection clear. If she had changed her name when she married, it would have been harder, but she hadn't. Her law practice was in Chicago.

And what good was it, knowing that? Should he send a letter to a Chicago attorney saying, "You don't know me, but I found some old letters in a house in Palo Alto. A strange girl I just met thinks you can file some papers or something, but I doubt filing papers is going to help. Would you care to send me six million bucks? It's for a worthy cause."

He spent the rest of the afternoon buffing the varnish on the Martin and taking detailed measurements of the neck of a lute. He did his best not to think about the letters or the mystery girl at all.

The next morning, as he was carefully applying a

second coat of varnish, a shadow fell across his doorway, and the girl came in.

"You're back," he said. "Why am I not surprised? I want to talk to you. I have some questions. But you'll have to wait while I finish this."

She settled down on a tall stool and waited while he stroked the soft brush across the back of the guitar, dipped it in the varnish, stroked again. When he had put the lid back on the can, she said, "There were some letters, weren't there?" She looked smug.

He started cleaning the brush. "You knew there would be. You broke in and searched the attic. Or planted them there for me to find. What's your game?"

"Are you always so obtuse? Wasn't the house locked? How would I get in?"

"You said you live there."

"That's different. I didn't even know for sure there were letters, I just thought there probably would be. I knew Mommy and Daddy sent letters, that summer. I knew they sent money."

"Sent money from where?" He was testing her.

"Europe, of course. You read the letters, didn't you? The postmarks? Hello?"

He still wasn't satisfied. "Before, when I was sitting outside, you walked past me and then you were gone. Where did you go?"

She giggled. "Nowhere. I mean literally, nowhere."

"You went somewhere. I looked behind the bushes, and you were gone."

"Okay, have it your way. I went back into the house. I don't want to argue about that. I want to know if you're going to get in touch with my sister. How are you going to do it? What are you going to say?"

"You're calling the shots," he said. "You tell me."

"Oh, good. You're going to be sensible. Now listen. There's a lot I don't know, but I know a few things. First of all, she remembers me perfectly. My name is Eleanor. You won't forget that, will you?"

"It's engraved on my soul."

"Be that way." She made a face at him. "The thing is, there's some kind of mystery about me. She doesn't know what happened to me. She's sure something awful happened, but she doesn't know what it was. So tell her you know what happened to me, that's the way to do it. Tell her I need her help. She'll come. She'll be on the next plane. After that it's up to you."

"But I don't *know* what happened to you."

"Well, nothing did. I mean really. Nothing. She made it all up. But you mustn't tell her that. A lot happened to *her*, and you mustn't ask her about that either, because it will scare her, and if she gets scared she'll run away. She's been running away her whole life. She's tired of running, really really tired, but she's really good at it too. So you have to convince her it's about me. Which it is, in a way. I'm her long-lost sister, who she hasn't seen since she was eleven years old."

He frowned at her. "Those letters were from forty years ago. They don't even mention you. And you can't be more than eighteen. How can you be her long-lost sister?"

Eleanor looked faintly exasperated. "You ask too many questions. Just tell her. Tell her like I said. Oh, and if you have a picture of the house. She'll remember the house. Send her a letter with a picture."

"You talk like you know her."

"Well, I'm her twin sister. Of course I know her."

He was opening his mouth to ask another question, though he wasn't sure what the question would be, and suddenly she was gone. This time she didn't walk between two bushes, nothing subtle or ambiguous like that. She was perched on the tall stool, right there in the middle of the room, and she just vanished. Without even a little pop. He was looking straight at her, and then, without transition, he was looking at the sunlit doorway behind where she had been, and he was alone.

II

From the windows of her office on the 32nd floor of One Prudential Plaza, Beth Drury had a broad, unobstructed view of Lake Michigan. This morning the lake was layered with a silvery haze that blotted out the distant shipping and left the horizon a mystery, but her desk was situated so that her back was to the window. Except when a client was admiring the view, she seldom even glanced at the lake.

Toward mid-morning, after handling a minor crisis that had sprung up, she used a gold letter opener to slit open the envelopes in the in-basket. While opening the mail, she sipped from a mug of excellent coffee that her paralegal had brought in. Plenty of real cream, no sugar.

The letter was on heavy beige stationery. The letterhead was a sort of logo, an embossed brown pen-and-ink drawing of a small, tile-roofed house. Seeing the house made Beth jittery, for reasons she couldn't have explained. Her eyes slid down the page to the letter itself. Printed in block capitals in heavy pencil, it said, "I KNOW WHAT HAPPENED TO YOUR SISTER. SHE NEEDS YOU." That was all it said.

Quite suddenly, sourceless rage roared up through her like lava. She would have thrown the letter in the wastebasket, would have torn it to shreds, but that act wouldn't have been violent enough to slake the rage. Her teeth and fists were clenched, her heart was pounding.

She must have stood up. What happened after that was not entirely clear, though it was worse than embarrassing. Beth Drury, a senior partner at Hampton, Meade, was *not* subject to fainting spells. It was unthinkable. But when Jackson came into the office — surely only a few seconds had passed — he found her slumped in a heap on the floor, and with a nasty nick bleeding on her forehead from having clipped the corner of the desk on the way down.

After solicitously helping her up and offering to call a doctor, an offer she firmly rejected, Jackson picked up the letter where it had fallen. "You dropped this," he said. She would have snatched it away from him, but her hand shook badly and refused to touch it. He was left holding it out, so he read it.

"I didn't know you had a sister."

"I don't. At least — it was a long time ago. She disappeared when I was eleven. She was kidnapped. They never found her."

"That must have been hard on you."

"I don't want to talk about it. Give me that." She forced herself to take the letter. Beneath the drawing of the house, in the same brown embossed ink, were the words "Ambrosia Center for the Arts." The address was in Palo Alto, California. And that made it all horribly clear. Now she knew why she had fainted. That was the house they had been staying in, the summer when Eleanor disappeared.

She threw the letter down on the desk. "It's some kind of sick joke, that's all." Her forehead was stinging. She touched it with a fingertip, which came away glistening with a drop of fresh blood.

"Then forget about it. There are too many sick jokers in the world. Don't waste a minute on them. I'll get you a BandAid." Jackson departed with alacrity. On his way to spread gossip about her fainting, she had no doubt. The BandAid would be an afterthought, if he remembered to bring it at all.

Jackson's advice was usually impeccable, but as the minutes passed (with no BandAid), she found she couldn't forget about the letter. Couldn't stop staring at it where it lay on the desk, as alien and nauseating as if it were a giant mushroom that had suddenly sprung up. What sort of monstrous prank did somebody think they were playing? And who had done it? Whoever was responsible, they had picked the wrong cookie. Beth Drury was not going to sit idly by and be anybody's victim. Not ever.

She swiveled to her computer and did a little online research. The Ambrosia Center, she found, was nothing much — a small, private art colony not far from downtown Palo Alto. On the premises were the studios of four local artists, none of them famous, and a musical instrument maker. The owner of record was Axel Taubin, but apparently he had died a few months before.

She didn't remember an Axel, but he must be a relative. She remembered Mr. and Mrs. Taubin in a vague, misty way, as faceless shadows drifting through the house. She remembered the house itself more clearly. It was where she and her twin sister Eleanor had been staying, the summer when they were eleven. Mommy and Daddy had gone off to Europe. Beth and Eleanor shared a bedroom at the back of the house, and Mrs. Taubin would make them pancakes whenever they wanted — and then one hot August afternoon Eleanor disappeared, kidnapped from out of the walled yard in broad daylight. As if it were a movie she had watched a thousand times, Beth could still see the police tramping in and out of the house in their big black shoes, smelling of cigars and asking loud questions. She remembered how Mommy and Daddy broke off their trip early, rushed home from Europe, gathered her up, and swept her back to their house in Los Altos, where she would be safe from whatever had happened to Eleanor.

Eleanor had never been found. Whoever kidnapped her had never been apprehended. And now, forty years later, some sick bastard was claiming to know what had happened to her. Worse, pretending she was still alive. Monstrous. Unbelievable.

Beth dialed the number for the Ambrosia Center. It rang and rang and nobody answered. The Axel Taubin number was picked up by a machine; she hung up without leaving a message.

She checked her calendar. There was nothing pressing for the next few days, and the firm owed her six months of vacation that she never seemed to get around to claiming. As she was calling her travel agent, Jackson came back — bearing, miraculously, a BandAid, though by that time the nick in her forehead had started to scab over.

He listened while she finished talking to the travel agent. "Going to fly out to Palo Alto?" he asked.

"Whoever is responsible for this needs to be taught a lesson."

"And you're just the person to teach it to them."

"Thanks, Jacks." She surprised herself by sounding sincere.

"If you need some help," he said, "there's a private detective agency out there that I've used a couple of times. They're reliable."

"Give me the contact info. I'll tell them you recommended them."

And that was all there was to it. She had never married, had no children, and she was a senior partner, so there was nobody she needed to ask for permission to take a few days off. She didn't even have a cat, so there was no need to find a cat-sitter. She just went home and packed.

⚘ III ⚘

The first thing John Renagle did, within an hour after the girl vanished, was phone his doctor and set up an appointment with a neurologist. "I'm seeing things," he said. "People who aren't there." The fact that someone who wasn't there might tell him about some old letters that *were* there, he didn't bother to mention.

Three days later, after two uneventful trips through an MRI machine, he was no wiser than before. The neurologist shook his head and said, "I can't see any abnormality. Whatever is causing these phenomena, I don't think it's organic. Nothing in your description suggests a typical epileptic seizure. You certainly don't strike me as a drug addict, so assuming you're being truthful about your use of drugs and alcohol, we can rule out the DT's. You're not on any medications that could cause hallucinations." The neurologist shrugged unhappily. "All I can suggest is, if it happens while you're driving, pull over and stop immediately."

Even with that reassurance, he felt a little foolish writing an anonymous letter to a lawyer in Chicago. But having begun, he could see no reason not to go a little further. Ride with it, see where it went.

After he mailed the letter — there were no fingerprints on the stationery, he took his time and did it right — he kept an eye out for Arthur Schoeps. Arthur usually wandered in two or three afternoons a week to putter around in his studio and pretend to be working. Arthur was past eighty, and was one of the original tenants of the Center. He wasn't always sure what day it was, but his long-term memory was still sharp, and he liked nothing better than to reminisce.

"Do you remember any stories about people around here appearing and disappearing?" John asked. "Into thin air, that type of thing?"

Arthur took his time about replying. He was hunched over his work table, using a razor blade to scrape a fresh point on the end of a light gray pastel. The half-finished still life on the easel had been sitting there for months, and it never seemed to get any further along. "There was the Case of the Vanishing Lothario," Arthur said at last. "I'd forgotten about it. This was before the Center was opened — back before the Taubin couple bought the house, in fact. I was at Stanford in the Fifties, not so many years after the War, you know, and I took an archaeology course from Lionel Graber. This was his house. He built the house — or had it built, I suppose, though he was the kind of man who could have built a house. He used to go out to Europe on digs and bring back snapshots of himself holding a shovel, that sort of man.

"When he wasn't overseas, he would throw garden parties for his graduate students. The studio buildings were constructed later; at that time the yard was a sort of overgrown ornamental garden decorated with souvenirs he had brought back from Europe and Africa and the Middle East. Mainly Europe, I think, he was a specialist in pre-Christian antiquities. But he wasn't a tomb-robber, you mustn't think that. This was long after the bad old days of archaeology had ended. I'm sure the artifacts he brought home were things he found in antique shops, already removed from the sites and therefore of less scientific value. It was quite a nice collection. After he died I believe most of it went into one of the museums on campus. Anyway, I attended a couple of those parties, that's how I happened to know of it, though I was only an undergraduate at the time. I was dating a girl named Noreen, who had a really marvelous — well, you don't care about that. Where was I?"

"The Case of the Vanishing Lothario."

"Oh, yes. That was my private name for it. I used to read a lot of Perry Mason mysteries, and the name seemed so fitting. Now bear in mind, I only had this second-hand. I never met any of the principals. So I may have it all wrong. But there was a girl who lived in the neighborhood. Not a pretty girl at all, I believe — quite plain and shy. It developed she had been sneaking onto Graber's property in the evenings — this property, where we're now sitting — to meet a young man. Quite strikingly handsome, the way she told it. Well, she got in the family way, that was the phrase we used in those days. So much pleasanter than 'knocked up,' don't you think? And when her father and brothers found out, they were determined to put handcuffs on the Lothario and make him pay for his outrage.

"The way I heard the story, they set a trap for him. The girl came onto the property as usual one evening, and her swain was there to meet her, as romantic and attentive as ever. The father and brothers had the place surrounded, but when they burst in the Lothario was gone. The girl swore he had been there, and I believe they may even have heard his voice or seen him when they peered over the wall, but in the blink of an eye he was gone, and he was never seen again. Graber was overseas at the time, and his gardener was as old as I am now, so no suspicion fell on them.

"A few months later the girl gave birth, and there was a story about it in the paper, which was how I came to learn of it. Apparently the baby had horns, little nubs on its forehead. And a club foot, and a tail. Naturally, the doctor and nurse in the delivery room put it out of its misery. They would have hushed it up entirely, but the girl was awake during the delivery and heard the baby cry, so she accused them of infanticide. That was how the story came out."

John had another thought. "That bust, the one I dug up down by the creek, that would have been one of Graber's archaeological treasures?"

"I would assume so. I thought you knew that. I didn't say anything when you found it, because — well, technically I suppose it's the property of Stanford University. He willed his collection to them. But at this late date, it can hardly be of urgent concern to them, and I rather liked seeing it in the niche in the wall. Such a suitable place for it. An informal shrine, I suppose we might say.

"The collection, now: After Graber died — and again, this is a story I read in the newspaper — his executor sold the house and property to Donald Taubin, and arranged for Stanford to pick up the collection and cart it off. But there was a complication. One of the pieces in the collection was a fragment of a wall, a section about four feet by four, though very irregular. Probably from the ruins of a Roman villa. On the wall was painted an image of the god Pan, or at any rate a faun of some sort, with horns, playing the pipes and dancing. Capering, that's the word. And with cloven hooves, of course. Graber had had this Roman wall section mounted in the outer wall of the property, next to the front gate. It was mortared in. I suppose it amused him to have it displayed so it could be seen from the street, as a sort of advertisement of his august presence.

"When the Stanford crew started to chisel it out, Donald Taubin raised the very devil. Claimed that his purchase contract included anything that was permanently attached to the property. I don't know whether he was genuinely fond of Pan for some reason, or whether he was just cantankerous and ac-quisitive. In any event, there was a lawsuit, which was covered in the local papers, and he won it. The god Pan remained here."

"There's nothing like that by the gate now."

"No, but you can see where it was if you look closely. One section of the wall is smoother than the rest. Some years later, a drunken driver lost control of his vehicle and plowed into the wall, just at that spot. Knocked the Roman wall section loose, and it toppled out and broke into pieces. At that point Stanford claimed the pieces. You can see it at the museum on campus if you like. They mended it, but the cracks still show. By that time, Taubin was in no position to object. He had troubles of his own. So Pan went away, and now we have — who do you suppose your bust is? Brigid? It looks more Celtic than Roman, I'd say. Not that I'm an expert on antiquities."

While fitting the inlay for a Celtic harp he was building, John mulled over what Arthur had said. Pan and Brigid and a vanishing Lothario. Well, if the Lothario could get a girl pregnant without actually existing, it was easy enough to believe that a hallucination named Eleanor could know about some letters in the attic.

The Celtic harp had been a commission from a fairly well known New Age musician, an acoustic guitarist and harpist named Shell Star. (The name on her check was Sheila Stark.) After the deposit payment, which John had spent acquiring the expensive woods Star selected, she ran off to Sri Lanka to study meditation, leaving her record company, her fans, and, incidentally, John Renagle holding the bag. Since he already had the wood, he had decided to go ahead and make the harp. Maybe, he thought, he'd learn to play it himself. It was a low-priority project, something he worked on when he had nothing more pressing.

After gluing the last pieces of inlay in place, wiping off a glistening drop of glue, and cleaning his hands, he went out to the east wall, ducked behind the bushes, and had a fresh look at the bust in the niche.

From the chipped and mottled surface, the bust was obviously very old, but other than the tip of the woman's nose and the top half of one ear, it was still surprisingly intact. John could readily believe that Lionel Graber had found it languishing in an antique store in Provence. How it had gotten half-buried in an embankment at the edge of the creek that ran along the south side of the property, so that the Stanford people missed it and it was still there forty years later for John Renagle to notice peering up at him, muddy but unmistakable, one afternoon after a rainstorm — that was another mystery, but not an important one.

The bust had a Mona Lisa smile, which seemed almost to change as the sunlight shifted. The corners of the woman's lips were quirked up in a way that might be compassionate or mischievous. He had spent hours last month sketching the bust. The design of the inlay on the Celtic harp was patterned after it. He had changed the hair, because the hair of the bust was coiled in a braid atop the woman's head and the design on the harp called for it to be flowing free, like water. He knew he hadn't quite captured the elusive quality of the woman's smile, but he thought he had come close.

"What do you know about it?" he asked the bust. It said nothing, only smiled. "Not very talkative, are you?" The bust only smiled. "Just so you know," he added, "I don't believe in magic."

When he emerged from behind the bushes, a man was cavorting in the middle of the lawn. Fortyish, balding, no more than middle height, dressed in an ordinary shirt and slacks. He would have been unremarkable if he weren't engaged in an impromptu dance, hopping from one foot to the other and waving his arms above his head.

"She's coming, she's coming!" the man cried. "Oh, it's been so long, I've missed her so very much, and now she's coming back at last. Oh, I must get her room ready!" The dance turned into a mad dash as the man sprinted up the steps to the back porch, knees and heels flying. He banged open the screen door and plunged into the house.

When John followed, moving more slowly, he wasn't even faintly surprised to see that the the back door was closed and the screen still securely hooked on the inside.

After mulling it over, he decided he needed to know more about Donald and Muriel Taubin. He went back into the house and dug through the boxes again. He remembered, vaguely, where he had seen the faded snapshots, so it didn't take long to find them. It was hard to be certain, but he thought the man on the lawn had to be Donald Taubin. Who had died twenty years before, in prison.

✣ IV ✣

Forcing herself to set foot on the property was wrenchingly difficult. It shouldn't have been. Yes, something bad had happened here, but that had been a very long time ago. The olive trees and the eucalyptus swayed peacefully behind the wall, and what was the problem, really? Beth had faced tougher situations in her law practice and powered through them without a quiver.

That blank spot beside the gate. Hadn't there been something there? Oh, Goat-Foot. She shuddered. She had forgotten about Goat-Foot. She had to walk past him every day when she and Eleanor came back from the library or the park. Sometimes the wind in the trees made it sound as if he was whispering to her.

On the plane she had debated calling the detective agency Jackson recommended, and decided she could handle it herself. Whoever had sent the letter was clearly a coward. There was no physical danger, no more than there had been from Goat-Foot. Hammering the bastard into the ground would be a pleasure.

The little buildings to the left of the driveway, set on concrete slabs and equipped with rustic-looking plank doors and fake shutters, she didn't remember at all, though the planks were weathered, not new, and little clots of fallen leaves poked up out of the gutters. The house was exactly as she remembered it, and her stomach lurched when she saw it. She turned her back on the house, her heel crunching in the gravel of the drive, and strode through the open doorway of the nearest outbuilding.

A stocky woman with a heavy mat of black hair was standing at a table, staring in concentration at a large canvas that was laid flat. The room was small, disastrously cluttered, and crowded with large abstract paintings that leaned against the walls. The floor had long since vanished beneath a rainbow layer of dried paint droppings, and the warm air was thick with the mingled odors of paint and turpentine. Beth fumbled in her purse, nearly dropping her keys, and drew out the letter. Without preamble she said, "I want to know who wrote this." Her voice scraped harsh in her throat.

Marta saw a well-dressed woman near fifty — expensive understated jewelry, an expensive understated scarf that failed to soften the hard lines of the heavy gray business suit, and expensive understated makeup that failed to soften the hard lines of her face. The straw-blond hair was pulled back in a short, severe ponytail held by a silver clip. The woman was holding out a sheet of cream-colored stationery, and it twitched as her hand trembled.

"Hi," Marta said. "Can I help you?"

"I want to know who is responsible for this outrage. It's your stationery, isn't it? This is the Ambrosia Center for the Arts, I take it."

Marta took the letter and examined it. "I don't recognize the handwriting."

"It's obviously disguised. You didn't write it? Then I expect you to help me discover who did."

Marta decided she'd make allowances. The woman was obviously under some kind of strain. She stuck out her hand. "We haven't been introduced. I'm Marta

Volcik. You're...."

"Elizabeth Drury. I'm an attorney. From Chicago." She ignored the outstretched hand. "This is not a social call. I'm being harassed, and I intend to put a stop to it."

Marta said, "This was sent to you?"

"How would I have acquired it, otherwise?"

"Then this is about — it mentions your sister."

"It's a cruel joke," Beth said. "A sick prank. I want to know who did it, and when I find out, I intend to go straight to the police."

"The police. Mmm."

When Marta hesitated, Beth said, "Are you going to help me, or are you a party to the harassment? Should I call the police right now?" She dug in her purse and pulled out her cell phone.

"Look, I'm sorry. I can see you're upset, but I really have no idea what this is about."

"It's about this letter. This is your stationery, are you denying that?"

"We don't keep it locked up," Marta said, shrugging. "I have some. I expect John and Arthur and Glenda may have some too. Anybody who comes through here could pick up a sheet. We've had realtors." In her own ears, that statement sounded like, "We've had mice." She started to laugh, but Beth's bitter glare cut the laugh short. "Maybe John can help sort this out," Marta said. "I heard him come in a while ago. Why don't you wait here while I go get him? Would you like some herb tea?"

"This is not a social call. What do you do here? Are these your paintings? Do you call this art?"

"Let me go get John. Wait here." Marta backed hurriedly out the door, leaving it ajar.

Left alone in the studio, Beth transferred her scowl to the painting laid out on the table. It was a large and visceral abstraction, part Jackson Pollack and part Sixties psychedelic light show, the thick glops of pigment rescued from looking alarmingly fecal by the liberal application of swirls of glitter. It was grotesque. Left-over California hippies, calling themselves artists. She had seen the For Sale sign on the way in. Whoever bought the property, she fervently hoped they would bulldoze it and put up condos. Toss this bunch of bums out in the street. She might even fly out to watch the bulldozers crunch their way through the house, that would be a pleasure. Get rid of the bad memories once and for all.

A shadow fell across the floor, and she turned, expecting to see Marta. Standing in the doorway was a balding middle-aged man not much taller than her. She could barely see his face, the sunlight was behind him. He reached out a hand toward her. "Beth? Beth, how are you, honey? It's so *good* to *see* you."

It was the voice she recognized, that and the very facelessness of the figure, the way it blocked the light streaming through the doorway. "Mr. Taubin?"

He moved toward her. "I've been waiting for you, honey. I've been so *lonely* without you. It's been such a long time." His eyes glimmered with a damp, hopeful charm.

Her arms and legs were jelly; she couldn't move. She couldn't even breathe. He sidled closer to her. His warm breath stirred the hair at her temple. She stared at his lower lip. He touched her side, her face, her shoulder. "You've grown," he said softly. "But I still remember you as a little girl. That's how I like to think of you, Beth, honey. You're the sweetest little girl in the whole wide world."

It was the paint fumes. He was all over her, touching

her, and the paint fumes were so thick they made her gag. She tried to say something, anything, and the words turned to thick slime that filled her throat.

When John and Marta came through the door a moment later, she was alone — kneeling on the floor, doubled over, vomiting, adding her breakfast to the rainbow carpet of paint spatters.

"Oh, jeez." Marta knelt beside her. John found a towel that wasn't too paint-smeared, soaked it under the faucet, and handed it to Marta.

After a minute Beth sank down to sit on the floor, gasping and sobbing. "Need fresh air," she managed. "Fresh air." So they lifted her between them and helped her stagger out across the lawn to the old stone bench. Her hair had come loose from the clip. "My hairbrush," she said. "Where's my purse?" John went back and got her purse. He filled a mug with water, too, figuring she'd probably want to wash out her mouth. She brushed her hair, got it back into the clip, and used a handkerchief to dry her face.

The newcomer — Marta had called him John — was somewhere between forty and fifty, with a patchy graying beard and broad square hands. He was wearing a plaid lumberjack shirt. He wasn't the man who had been trying to — the man who had been — the man she had thought.... She shook her head and said, "I'm not making a very good first impression, am I? It was the paint fumes. No, it wasn't. There was a man. I thought it was — but it couldn't have been. Where did he go?"

John said, "You saw a man, and then he wasn't there?"

Pain clenched behind her forehead. "Is it part of the — did you hire someone to, oh God, where's my phone? I *am* going to call the police."

"That's been happening around here lately," he said. "I've seen a couple of different people who weren't there. Maybe the same man you saw."

"That's ridiculous," Beth snapped. "Do you think I'm an idiot? You people are playing some kind of sadistic trick. It's a con game. There was a man in there, don't lie to me. He was pretending to be — someone I knew a long time ago."

"Who would that have been?"

"But he wasn't — Mr. Taubin wasn't — he was a *nice* man. He was always kind to me, and to my sister, he wasn't — he wasn't doing anything, he was just being friendly! This is some kind of awful sick game, that's all it is."

Marta said, "You mean Axel Taubin?"

"No, no. Axel would have been his brother, or a cousin. Donald Taubin. Donald and Muriel. They lived here."

"You knew them," John said.

Beth nodded. "My sister and I stayed here with them, one summer while Mommy and Daddy were in Europe."

"That would have been a long time ago."

Beth's eyes drifted away. In a quiet voice she said, "We didn't want to go to Europe that summer, because we'd been the year before and we hated it, so Mommy and Daddy arranged for us to stay with the Taubins. Mr. and Mrs. Taubin were nice people, from the church. It was nice. These buildings weren't here then, it was all just a big back yard. Eleanor and I would play jump rope, or we'd take the bus down to the library. Sometimes in the evenings we'd play three-handed canasta with Mr. and Mrs. Taubin." She paused, confused. "I mean, with one of them or the other. I guess if they had both played, it wouldn't have been three-handed, would it? Anyway, for two months we were living here and everything was fine, until — until Eleanor was kidnapped. After that it was all a nightmare. Our parents flew home, and the police came and investigated, but they never found a trace of her. She was just gone.

"Nothing was ever the same after that," she went on. "Nobody liked to talk about it, because what could you say? After a while my parents got rid of all my sister's things, even the photographs. It was too painful looking at them. I don't even have a photo of my twin sister!" Beth's voice jiggled with suppressed tears.

"Were you identical twins?" John asked.

"Fraternal. But we looked so much alike people used to get us mixed up. And now somebody sends me a letter claiming they know what happened to her! After all this time! It's monstrous! Was it you? Did you send it? Because if you did, or if you know who did, and if you lie to me—"

"Whatever happened to your sister," John said carefully, "it happened here. Maybe there's a clue here, something that didn't mean anything to anybody at the time, but it might mean something to you now. Would you like to see the inside of the house? Maybe it would bring back memories."

"I don't know. No! Maybe. I mean, I've come all this way. I don't know."

Marta went and fetched the key, and they escorted Beth up to the front door. But at the threshold she balked. "I can't," she said. "I think I'd just like to sit outside for a while. And then I'll go. I shouldn't have come here at all." She pressed her palm against her forehead. "This was a huge mistake. I'm not — I'm not usually this disorganized. Whoever sent that letter, they can go to hell." She said it again, louder. "They can go to *hell*. I don't care."

"Speaking of letters," he said as they walked back to the bench, "I've got something you might like to see. Last week I found some old letters up in the attic." He wondered whether he was being foolish. The woman was still very much on edge, and she was certainly sharp enough to see that he could have located her using the information in the letters. But whatever was going on, keeping her in the dark could hardly be productive. Eleanor hadn't specifically said, "Show her the letters," but what else could she have had in mind?

Beth said, "Letters?"

"I think they were written by your parents, while you were staying here. I'll get them."

Beth read the letters slowly, sitting on the stone bench in the sunlight. After frowning for a minute she read them again. "I don't understand," she said at last. "Mom never mentioned Eleanor at all. Not once. And these were written weeks before the kidnapping."

"Why wouldn't she have mentioned Eleanor? Was there some problem between Eleanor and your parents?"

"No, no! Eleanor was a bright, happy, carefree girl. So much fun to be around. Everybody loved her. Everybody!"

"And yet, after she was gone, they put away her things. Did they still talk about her at Christmas, or on birthdays?"

Beth pressed her lips together and shook her head. "We never talked about her. It was too painful. It was like she never existed. Like she'd never been born."

John stood up. "Why don't you just sit here and relax for a few minutes," he said. "Take your time. No hurry. It's a nice place to sit." Marta gave him a peculiar look, but he only jerked his head, and she followed him without a word.

When they had stepped into his workshop, Marta said, "Would you mind telling me what's going on? What is this all about?"

"It's about people who aren't there," he said. "You remember the nursery rhyme? 'Last night I saw upon the stair a little man who wasn't there. He wasn't there again today. Oh, how I wish he'd go away!'"

"You are so exasperating sometimes."

"Maybe I should say it's about archaeology. It's about digging up the past. Did you know Donald Taubin was sent to prison?"

"I think I knew that."

"Do you know why?"

❧ V ❧

It was a warm afternoon, the sun pouring down through the dusty leaves of the old olive trees. Beth sat on the bench, fingers fussing absently at the edges of the letters on her lap. She was looking across the lawn at the bungalow. She remembered Mrs. Taubin coming out the kitchen door and shouting, "Elizabeth! Eleanor! Dinner time!" She remembered clothes hanging from the line. The car parked in the driveway. The plum trees, which must have been cut down when the studios were put in. Oh, the plums had been so tart!

"You got a tummy-ache one day from eating so many. Remember?"

The shock of seeing the girl standing there was like ice in her veins — warm ice. Eleanor, exactly as she had always pictured her. A little older now, eighteen or so, because people did get older. They grew up. "How—?"

"Hush." The girl sat down beside her. "Now, listen. I'm only going to explain this once, and then I have to go."

"Who are you?"

"You know who I am," the girl said. "You read the letters, right?"

Beth nodded.

"Was I in the letters? Did Mom mention me at all?"

"But you're not her!"

"Stop being dense. Was I in the letters?"

"No. And that's—"

"That's because I never existed. No, don't shut your eyes. Don't go away on me. Look at me. I never existed. You made me up." The girl's face was earnest, and her hand gripped Beth's arm hard. "You made me up so it wouldn't hurt so much. At first you knew you were just playing a game. But after a couple of years you forgot it was a game. The game was part of you. It was easier to think about the awful things that supposedly might have happened to me, because then you would never have to remember that they *had* happened to you. When you thought about me you could remember all the nasty things, but it didn't matter, because it was just your imagination. It all happened to somebody else. To your sister Eleanor."

"No, no. Who are you? You're not—"

"Yes, I am."

"Nothing awful ever happened to me. It happened to Eleanor! You're lying. This is all an awful trick."

Eleanor said, "You saw him a little while ago, didn't you? And you freaked out. What was he starting to do to you? He had his hands all over you, and you've almost forgotten already, haven't you? Try to remember

— try! Try to remember what he did. Every night. In the bedroom right over there. After you turned out the light. After you were snug in your bed. How he came into your bedroom and laid down beside you and got on top of you and the things he made you do, and how it hurt and you couldn't get away and he made you swear never to tell anybody, and you thought sure nobody would believe you so you never did."

"No! No, no, no! I won't listen! I won't! Nothing like that ever happened! You're making it all up!"

"I can't make things up, Beth. I'm not even here. You're the one who made up a bunch of stuff, all about me. All about how Mommy and Daddy interrupted their vacation and rushed back from Europe to take you home where you'd be safe? They never did." Eleanor shook her head vigorously. "They never did. They came home at the end of August, just like they planned. You wanted so much to believe they cared, because you were sure they didn't. You even asked them to come home early, and they wouldn't. Why would they have left you here all summer with that awful man if they cared about you? The way you worked it, you could pretend it was *me* they didn't care about. They threw away all my things and the pictures of me and everything and shut me off like a faucet. That proved it."

Beth was weeping now. "No, no, no!" She shut her eyes tight and hugged herself and clenched her fists and rocked. "No, no, no, no, no!"

The next voice she heard was not Eleanor's. "Beth, honey...."

Her eyes flew open. She screamed. Donald Taubin was leaning toward her, blocking out the sun, reaching out to stroke her shoulder. She lurched up off the bench, and she must have hit him in the chest with her shoulder because he fell back, and then she was running toward the gate, toward the street, toward her rental car and freedom, but somehow he got in front of her, standing between her and the gate with his arms outstretched, beaming with affection, moving in toward her again. She turned and ran back toward the house and up the front porch steps into the house where it was dark and cool but for some reason the house was full of dolls, which she didn't remember at all, dozens of them on every side standing staring at her, and she blundered into a table and dolls went crashing to the floor and there he was again, coming at her, saying, "Beth, honey, come here, sweetie, be nice, be nice," and she moaned and backed away from him into the dining room and he came after her, getting closer, so she grabbed a doll, grabbed it by one leg and started hitting him with it, hitting him again and again, swinging it at him, but he didn't seem to notice, he kept groping toward her, touching her, touching her all over with his moist hands, and she turned and ran into the kitchen but there he was again, between her and the back door, smiling, coming toward her. She hit him again with the doll but then it broke, and her hand found a kitchen drawer and yanked it open, it was the drawer where Mrs. Taubin kept the carving knives and there was still a knife in the drawer and she got it in her fist and started stabbing him, stabbing him over and over with the knife and they were both on the floor, rolling back and forth, he had his hand over her mouth and he was gurgling and she was stabbing him and stabbing him and stabbing him.

John and Marta heard the screams and the crashing. By the time they rushed in and found her, it was all over. The living room and dining room had been swept by a

171

tornado, dolls flung everywhere. In the kitchen, Beth lay sprawled face-down on the floor, not moving. Not far from her lay a butcher knife and a broken doll. The doll's head had broken off and rolled under a table.

Marta knelt and felt the woman's neck for a pulse. "She's alive. Fainted."

"She didn't cut herself, at least." He picked up the knife. Other than a few spots of ancient tarnish, its blade gleamed silver.

He set the knife on the counter and was inspecting the broken doll when Marta said, "Uh-oh. Tell me I'm not seeing what I'm seeing."

She had rolled Beth over onto her back. Still unconscious, the fallen figure breathed easily, and her color was good. But who was it? The heavy, dark business suit was the same as before. But in place of the hard-bitten face of a fifty-something corporate lawyer, they were gazing at the face of an eighteen-year-old girl.

He said, "That's Eleanor."

"The sister?"

"There wasn't any sister."

"This is crazy," Marta said. "It's impossible. People don't just...."

"I know," he said. "They don't. Maybe this isn't what we think it is. Let's wait and see."

Beth's eyes fluttered open. "I feel *very* strange," she said faintly.

"I'm not surprised," John said. "Do you remember what happened?"

With Marta's arm around her shoulders, she sat up. "I think — that man. Did I kill him?" She looked around. "Where is he?"

"He was never here."

"I attacked him with a knife. I stabbed him. A lot."

"Well, that's good. I'm glad you did."

"And I found my sister. She came and talked to me. She told me things, crazy things. None of it made any sense! It never happened that way! But she couldn't have been my sister. I — I feel very strange. I don't feel like myself. I drank that water you gave me. Did you put some kind of drug in the water?" She picked at the thick folds of the business suit. "My clothes don't fit. And my hands. What's — oh, my God." She stared at the backs of her hands, and turned them over. Then very slowly she touched her face, her neck, her hair.

"I've got a mirror in my workshop," he said. "I think you might like to look at yourself in a mirror."

Marta tried to help her to her feet, and Beth pushed her away stiffly. "Don't touch me." She walked across the yard in a wobbly drunken gait, as if not sure how to operate her legs.

Back in the workshop, she stared at herself in the fly-specked little mirror for long seconds. Abruptly she threw the mirror to the floor, where it shattered. "This can't be happening," she said finally. "Things like this don't happen. It's some kind of trick. I need a drink."

Marta said, "I can make some herb tea."

"No, I mean a drink."

"I'll make some tea. I don't think we have anything stronger." Marta ducked out.

Left alone with the girl, John wasn't sure what to say, so he said nothing. She was gazing at the floor, trembling a little, her breath shallow. Recollecting herself with an effort, she said, "I'm sorry I broke your mirror. Is this your workshop? What's that?" She pointed at the Celtic harp.

"I made it."

"You made it? It's beautiful. I used to — when I was in college I had a roommate who played one of those. She taught me a couple of songs."

"Would you like to try playing it? I tuned it this morning."

She said hurriedly, "No, I couldn't." Shaking her head stiffly, she backed into a corner and went back to staring at the floor. "That man — did he — did I—" Her breath caught in her throat.

"He's gone now."

Marta bustled in with a tray on which were three steaming mugs. "Thank God for microwaves," she said. "Heat the water in no time. Here, dear." But the girl wouldn't reach out to take the mug. Marta stared at her, exasperated. "You'll feel better."

"What makes you think I *want* to feel better?"

The stand-off was interrupted by a light but insistent tapping at the door. "Excuse me." A woman stood in the doorway, peering in at them. She was broad, rather squat, and not young. An elaborate straw hat festooned with drooping ribbons and a straggle of dried flowers perched crookedly on her head. Slung from one arm was the largest paisley-decorated fabric purse John had ever seen. A live cockatoo gazed at them solemnly from her other shoulder. "Is this the Ambrosia Center for the Arts?"

John admitted it. "Can we help you?"

"Well, I'm not entirely sure," the newcomer said in a breathless gush. "It may be the other way around. I rather think I'm supposed to help *you*, though I'm sure I couldn't say why, or how. I've received some Divine Guidance." The capital letters were plainly audible.

"This would be the morning for it," John said noncommittally.

"I was looking at one of your brochures," the woman said. "And I felt the strongest pull, one of the strongest I've ever felt. 'I must go there,' I said to myself. 'At once. I'm needed.' But you see, it took a few minutes for me to dress and gather my things, and as I was putting on my hat, the mirror clouded over and I saw what I can only describe as an *apparition*." She paused, panting. "One doesn't like to talk of these things. People get the wrong idea. I have a dear, dear niece who tried to have me committed! But there's no doubt in my mind. It was an apparition. It — or I suppose I should say 'she,' as it appeared in the form of a woman — told me I was to find the girl. I suppose that would be you," she said to Beth. "And I was to say to her — let me see, I wrote it down so I wouldn't forget." From the depths of her purse, she produced a crumpled piece of paper. After smoothing it, she held it out at varying distances, as if trying to find the best focus for her eyes, cleared her throat a couple of times, and recited, "'If you would remain as you are now, you must make your home here.'"

The woman shrugged. "I'm afraid that was all the spirit said. After that it simply faded away. I can't tell you what it means, about remaining as you are. I don't in the least know."

Marta said, "Would you like some herb tea? I think we have an extra cup."

Abruptly Beth said, "Here? Stay *here*? You people are insane. This is bullshit." She shoved past them, out the door, and ran lurching crookedly across the lawn toward the gate. They watched from the workshop. Almost to the gate, she turned and dashed back to the stone bench to scoop up her purse. In another moment she was gone. They heard a car's motor start, and the screech of tires.

John shrugged sadly. "Well, it seemed like a good idea at the time."

Marta said, "Are you going to explain now what's going on?" But she interrupted herself to turn to the older woman. "I'm sorry. We haven't been introduced."

The newcomer's name, she told them, was Madeleine Oakley. John had to resist the temptation to call her "Madame Oakley." She wasn't a professional psychic, just a dotty old woman with a ridiculous hat and a live cockatoo. He said, "Could you describe the apparition? You said it was a woman."

"Rather a handsome-looking woman. Her hair was coiled in a braid on top of her head."

"There's something I'd like you to see," he said.

He led her to the niche in the wall. Madeleine Oakley gasped when she saw the bust. "It's her, it's her! There's not the slightest doubt."

Marta said, "John, I really am going to strangle you if you don't tell me what's going on."

"Magic."

"A middle-aged lawyer turning into an eighteen-year-old girl — that's not magic, that's a freaking miracle. And it didn't happen! It couldn't have. Things like that don't happen."

"Maybe they happen oftener than we know, but nobody talks about it, because who would believe them?"

"Well, I'm not going to tell anyone about it," Marta said stubbornly, "you got that right. I saw it with my own eyes, but it Did, Not, Happen."

"Strange things do happen, you know," Madeleine Oakley said. "Not very often. Not nearly often enough, I should say. But they do happen."

John gestured at the stone bust. "And from what

Mrs. Oakley — is it Mrs.? — said about her apparition, I'm thinking Brigid here may be behind it."

Marta stamped her foot. "That's ridiculous. It's absurd. It's a freaking *statue*. Not even a statue, it's what's *left* of a statue."

Madeleine Oakley said, "Sometimes things are absurd, dear. Not that it's any of my business, and I'm sure I have no idea on Earth what you're talking about. But it's no good objecting to Divine Guidance on the basis that it's absurd, I can tell you that much."

✸ VI ✸

By the time Beth reached the stop light and turned left onto El Camino Real, her heart had slowed enough and her vision cleared to the point where she was more or less in control of the car. Three blocks down, she swerved into the parking lot next to a bar, left the car parked crookedly across two vacant spaces, and didn't bother to lock it. She was gritting her teeth. She almost never drank, but God, right now she needed a drink!

The interior of the bar was cool and dim. Only a couple of people were perched on stools, and the tables were mostly vacant. She slipped onto a stool, struggled to get control of her voice, and said, "Bourbon. Double."

The bartender, a well-muscled young man with a five-day beard and an incongruous black bow tie, said, "ID?"

"What?"

"Can I see some ID please, miss?"

"You're *carding* me? Nobody has carded me for — oh, shit." She fished in her purse, pulled out her wallet, and flipped it open.

The bartender inspected her driver's license

impassively. "Illinois. Did you really think you could fool me with your mother's license?"

"My mother's...." She caught sight of herself in the mirror behind the bar. A wide-eyed, white-faced teenager stared back at her, a teenager in a conservatively cut business suit that hung from her, several sizes too large. "No, look. I can explain." But of course there was no possible way to do that. "Just give me a double bourbon. What's it worth to you? A hundred dollars? Here." She pulled out a hundred-dollar bill and slapped it on the bar.

"Just a minute." The bartender moved smoothly away from her, down to the end of the bar, and picked up a phone. He glanced at her while talking.

She had enough sense to scoop up the hundred-dollar bill on her way out the door. Back in the car, she drove a lot more carefully. If a bartender didn't believe it was her license, the cops wouldn't either. And if she got arrested, who was she going to call? Jackson?

Her hands were shaking on the steering wheel, but she kept the car steady. Her foot kept trying to jam down on the accelerator, so she had so spend half her time looking down at the speedometer to stay under the limit, and almost missed a red light. Taking the freeway was out of the question; she stayed on the El Camino clear up the Peninsula until she could cut east to the Airport Hilton.

Room service didn't ask for an ID.

Driving had been good, because she was too confused even to try to think while driving. Back in the hotel room, though, she had nothing to do but think. Eleanor and Donald Taubin chased one another around and around in her head. She didn't understand any of it — and then the next minute she did understand and it clutched her throat and chest tight. But most of all she didn't understand what she saw in the mirror. While putting away half a pint of bourbon, she kept going into the bathroom and staring at her reflection, pulling at the skin of her cheeks with her fingers as if that would change something. She ordered dinner from room service, and when it arrived the smell nauseated her. She made it to the bathroom, threw up, staggered back into the suite, opened the door to shove the tray out into the hall, shut the door, put the chain lock on, phoned the airline to make a reservation for tomorrow morning, poured more bourbon, lay down on the bed, jumped up, stared around wildly looking for something to hit, swung her suitcase savagely against the wall a few times, collapsed back onto the bed sobbing, poured more bourbon, spilled as much as she drank, and somehow tumbled into sleep. In her dreams, wild animals tore at her flesh.

She would have missed the flight if the front desk hadn't phoned to wake her. She managed to pry her eyelids open, put on a pair of slacks and a blouse that sagged less on her than the suit, got everything else stuffed into the now somewhat battered suitcase, turned in the rental car with her head throbbing, climbed on the shuttle with her head throbbing, managed to get through airport security with her head throbbing, sank into her seat in first class with her head throbbing, and went back to sleep.

Somewhere over the Rockies she woke up. This is ridiculous, she told herself. Nothing happened. Nothing goddamn *happened*, goddamn it. They had put some kind of drug in the cup of water they gave her. LSD or something. The hell with them, and the hell with the Ambrosia Center for the Arts. They could rot in hell.

O'Hare was a madhouse, as usual. By the time she got her suitcase she was starving, but her stomach rebelled at the thought of food. Maybe a sandwich when she got home. She took a taxi. The taxi driver called her "ma'am," not "miss."

Her apartment was gray and very empty. Everything seemed to be coated in a thin layer of dust, as if she had been gone for years rather than for two days. She ran her finger along the lid that hid the keyboard of the piano, and her finger left a trail. She made a sandwich, poured a glass of lemonade, and sat down at the computer to check her email. She was only able to eat three bites of the sandwich, but the lemonade washed away some of the misery.

After a while she realized what she was doing. She was avoiding going into the bathroom because she didn't want to look in the mirror. Get tough, she told herself. Don't let it get to you. She said, "Get tough," to herself half a dozen times, the last few times out loud, before she was able to stand up and totter into the bathroom.

The face in the mirror was the one she had grown into over the years, the face of a successful, no-nonsense, middle-aged attorney. Precise lines bracketed the corners of her mouth. Frown lines between her eyebrows. Crow's feet at the corners of her eyes and the start of puffy bags underneath. None of it had ever happened. She didn't know whether to laugh or cry. A thought surfaced, unbidden: "This is what happened to Eleanor." She pushed it away savagely and went back to the computer to answer emails. Her fingers hit the keys so hard she broke a nail, but her wording was no more terse or brutal than usual.

The next morning, Jackson was effusive. "Glad to have you back. We were afraid you might like the Coast so much you'd go on to Hawaii. Were you able to solve your little problem with the anonymous letter?"

"Get the files on the Stanley merger."

"Ooh, we're feeling a bit touchy this morning, are we?"

She glared at him. He raised his eyebrows, unperturbed, then shrugged and went to get the files.

The whole week went like that. She couldn't focus. She would read a paragraph three times and realize she hadn't absorbed a word of it. She forgot a meeting. In the break room, people glanced at her sideways and stopped talking when she came in.

Twice she found that she had pressed the edge of the letter-opener into the flesh of her forearm so hard she drew blood. The pain felt oddly freeing, but she had heard about girls who cut themselves, and she was far too stubborn to go that route. She put the letter opener away in the back of a bottom drawer.

At the end of the day she went home too exhausted to even think about making it to the gym. She couldn't eat, and no amount of ibuprofen would banish the lurking and tenacious headache. She slept badly, tangled in the sheets, and in the morning didn't hear the alarm go off.

It was the house that invaded her thoughts. She refused to think about the people, but the little tile-roofed house crept up on her, the house and the rooms full of dolls. Sometimes in her dreams she was playing with the dolls. Sometimes the dolls turned on her and started biting her.

On her seventh night back in the apartment, she

woke in the wee hours to the sound of the piano. At first she thought it was a dream, but no, it was real. The music was coming from the living room. Someone was picking out the melody of a song, slowly, one note at a time, on the piano.

She slid the drawer of the night table open as quietly as she could and picked up the revolver. Reassured by its cold hard grip, she rose and tiptoed out to the living room.

No lights were on, but a little moonlight sifted through the curtains. A girl with long blond hair was sitting at the piano, poking at the keyboard with one finger. Her back was to the hall door, and she was leaning in toward the keyboard; Beth couldn't see her face. The melody was familiar. It was one her college roommate had taught her, or tried to, on the harp.

She hit the light switch and said, "How did you get in here?" And in that moment, the piano bench was empty. She was alone. But the lid that covered the keyboard was up. She knew perfectly well it had been down when she went to bed, because it had been down a week ago, when she first came home and ran her finger along it through the dust. She certainly hadn't raised it since.

She shouted, "Where are you? Where did you go?" She rushed from room to room, switching on all the lights, waving the revolver, sobbing. But she was alone in the apartment.

She went back to bed, but not back to sleep. The song her midnight visitor had been playing spun through her mind over and over again. Her fingers remembered seeking and finding those notes on her college roommate's simple folk harp.

By that time the piano lessons were a thing of

the past. After the summer when — when Eleanor vanished, piano lessons had become a grind. Every time she sat down to practice, she started getting nervous and flustered and weepy. She couldn't breathe. So she didn't practice. There were arguments with her parents. Mercifully, the lessons stopped. But she still had the piano. Hadn't touched it in years. It sat there, a dead hulk, and she walked past it and around it every day and no stray thought about any of that ever drifted up to trouble her.

After tossing and turning for an hour or so, the melody cycling through her mind insistently, she got up, put on a robe, went out to the living room, sat on the piano bench, and stared at the keys. And suddenly the melody was gone — not a note of it remained. A vast gray void resonated endlessly.

She touched a key, and cringed. The piano was horribly out of tune. That wasn't surprising. She hadn't had it tuned since she moved in here ten years ago. Or even before that, in the other apartment. Now how did that blasted song go? She jabbed more keys at random, and nearly wept in frustration. It was gone.

She banged her forearm down hard on the keys, again and again. The piano roared, clanked, almost groaned.

℣ VII ℣

Enough was enough. Time to put a stop to this. Put it behind her once and for all. The next morning she phoned her bank and talked to a loan officer. Then she found the listing agent online. The photo showed a streaky blond named Cindy McRoberts. She picked up the phone again. "I'm calling from Chicago. I'm looking at investment properties, and I noticed your listing for the property at the corner of Atwell and Maude. Is it still available?"

The agent replied with the kind of bubbly optimism in her voice that was probably a job requirement. "We've had several buyers considering it very seriously, it's a wonderful property, so peaceful and picturesque, but there's no offer on the table just at present. You said you're calling from Chicago?"

"I grew up in Palo Alto. I know the property. I was out there just last week. I — I actually stayed in that house one summer, when I was a girl. Can you tell me, is it zoned so that it could be subdivided for high-density housing?"

"Yes, it is. Is that what you're considering? Because it's a charming cottage, you know, but not entirely modern."

"And I imagine the outbuildings aren't up to code."

"Well, no, they're not. Of course that would all be disclosed. But if you're thinking of subdividing, it shouldn't matter."

"I'm thinking of bulldozing the whole thing and putting up townhouses."

"I think that's a wonderful idea. I'm sure you could make a nice profit. The zoning shouldn't be a problem, but I have to tell you, Palo Alto does have design restrictions on new construction. Have you talked with a local architect? Because I can recommend a friend of mine...."

"How much are the owners asking?"

"Six, five. Six million five."

"Let me make sure I have your fax number. You'll have an offer by the end of the day for six even."

"Do you have an agent locally?"

"I'm a lawyer. I know how to draw up a contract."

"And we'll need a good-faith deposit. Shall we say twenty thousand?"

Beth grabbed a sharp pencil from the jar and pulled the yellow pad toward her. "Give me your bank transfer number."

She downloaded a California real estate contract, made suitable alterations, and fed it into the fax machine herself. This was not a task to delegate to Jackson. She didn't want anybody in the office to know about it, though she wasn't sure why. Her colleagues invested in real estate all the time. Because he had seen the letter, that was why. He could guess why she had flown out there. If he knew she was buying the property, the office gossip mill would grind into high gear.

She'd have as little as possible to do with the tenants, too. Send them eviction notices. That madwoman painter — what a frightful creature! And the guitar repair man. She was sure by now that he had sent the letter. He could act innocent and not say much, but that just proved he was sneaky and manipulative. Bulldoze it all, scrape the ground clean. She was *not* going to get sucked into dwelling in the past.

She had stopped thinking about how she got carded in the bar on El Camino Real. That had happened to someone else. Nothing to do with her.

There were three other apartments on her floor. When she stepped out of the elevator late that afternoon and started down the hall, a doll was lying abandoned outside one of the doors. She picked it up. Not a rag doll or a baby doll, just an ordinary plastic doll with long eyelashes, a puckered mouth, and a ruffled skirt. She didn't know the other tenants, but the management wasn't supposed to rent to people who had children. People always ignored the rules! But someone had dropped the doll. Before she complained to management, she needed to know more. She thumbed the doorbell button.

A man opened the door. He was wearing a tee-shirt, his hair was tousled, and he hadn't shaved. He said, "What?" Behind him, within the apartment, a girl was sobbing quietly. Beth tried to look around him, tried to see the girl, but he moved so that his body blocked the doorway.

She said, "Someone dropped this."

He held out his hand. Reluctantly, she gave it to him.

She said. "Is it your daughter's?"

He didn't answer. He didn't even say thanks. He just shut the door in her face.

His rudeness flared rage in her. She aimed a stiff finger at the doorbell button again, meaning to jab it, but her arm locked. Whatever was going on in there, it was none of her business. Nothing bad was happening, just a father whose daughter had scraped her knee, or who was crying because she had lost her doll. Nothing bad.

The next morning at the office, trying grimly and without much success to concentrate, she jumped when the phone on her desk rang. It was the chirpy real estate lady in Palo Alto. "Are you ready for some good news? The heirs of the estate have accepted your offer! Congratulations!"

Beth spent the rest of the morning on the phone with her broker, liquidating her portfolio. The market was having a good week. He told her she could count on six million with a bit to spare. He tried to talk her out of it, naturally. "Just do it," she told him.

Jackson overheard the last part of the conversation. "You're up to something," he said. He sounded pleased.

"Don't start on me, Jacks." She smoothed a stray lock of hair away from her forehead. "Jacks, what kind of person am I?"

"You're tough as nails. That's why we love you."

"You mean I'm a bitch."

Jackson pressed his lips together, pretending to think. "I decline to answer on advice of counsel."

VIII

All the paperwork was handled electronically. The eviction notices for the so-called artists could be handled from Chicago too — no need to see or speak to them ever again, and she certainly had no intention of doing so. She sealed the eviction notices and left them sitting in her out-basket for Jacks to send by registered mail. She got two phone messages from Marta Volcik, who she now knew was the on-site property manager. Beth didn't return the calls.

At first she thought she'd wait to fly out until the bulldozers came to level the house. She wanted to be there to see that. But before that could happen, she would need to meet with an architect and a contractor. She spoke to three architects via Skype, made an appointment with Robert Bruno of Bruno & Bruno, and booked a flight. On the plane, leaning back in her seat high above the Rockies, she started thinking she'd like to drive the bulldozer herself. The crunch as its blade bit into the side of the house would be a fine thing. She'd have to draft a liability waiver. And buy a hard hat.

Robert Bruno ("call me Bob") was fortyish, trim, and no-nonsense in a pale blue shirt and gray silk tie but no jacket. He answered her questions, showed her drawings, and didn't try to patronize her because she was a woman. When they had inked a preliminary letter of agreement, he said, "I drove by the property when I knew you were coming, but I need to get my feet on the ground. Do you have time this afternoon to take a look, kick some ideas around?" That brought up a flutter of nerves — but why? She had been thinking she'd drive the bulldozer herself. What difference would it make, seeing the place now? Anyway, she needed to make sure the tenants had vacated.

The tenants hadn't vacated. When she marched in through the gate, Bob Bruno in tow, she could see at once that the art studios were still occupied. Metallic banging noises came from one of the little out-buildings, doors stood open on the summer afternoon, and the guitar maker's instruments were hanging in his display window.

"Go ahead and look around," she said to the architect. "I need to take care of something." She angled across the yard and barged into the woman painter's studio.

Marta Volcik stood in front of a large canvas that stood on an easel. She had a paint roller in her hand, but paused brandishing it.

Beth said, "What are you doing still here?"

"Oh. Hello again."

"You're supposed to have vacated the premises. Are you looking for legal action? Because I can assure you—"

"Wait a minute." Marta set the roller down in its tray and wiped her hands, not very effectively, on a towel. "You didn't answer my phone calls. We've been waiting to hear—"

"You got the eviction notices."

"What eviction notices?"

"The notices I sent!" Beth's voice was rising toward a shout. She controlled herself with an effort.

"I'm sorry. We never got any notices. There must be some mistake."

"You people are impossible. There will be consequences." Beth whipped out her cell phone and speed-dialed. "Jacks? Glad I caught you. About those registered letters you mailed last week...."

Jackson's voice: "What registered letters?"

"The ones to my tenants — my former tenants — in California. They were in the out-basket. I know I gave you instructions."

"The out-basket? Let me go look."

She ground her teeth.

Jackson was taking his sweet time. Just inside the door of the studio stood a large cardboard box, its lid yawning open. Phone pressed against her ear, she wandered over to the box and peered in. A jumble of little painted faces, frizzy plastic hair, tiny pink limbs. Dolls.

"I've been boxing them up," Marta said. "I thought if you didn't want them maybe we could give them to Goodwill."

"Not that it's any business of yours. Is there a dumpster here? Throw them in the damn dumpster."

Jackson came back. "Nothing in the out-basket," he reported cheerfully. "Do you want me to look through your desk?"

"Yes. No. Wait. Let me think." Where had she put the letters? She *knew* she had left them in the out-basket and told Jacks to mail them. Why was he lying? She stared down at the dolls. Innocent blue eyes. Eyelashes. Fluffy skirts. Paint fumes. The paint fumes again. Her shoulders were stiff. Her neck stiff, arms stiff, legs. Jackson's voice, very far away now. She couldn't move, couldn't breathe. The box, the dolls, a mad tangle of arms and legs, nothing moving, darkness down at the bottom of the box, nothing moving ever, nothing, that awful tangled darkness, stiff, dizzy, stiff....

Can't move. I'm in a box and I can't move. Wearing a frilly yellow skirt and I can't even blink, staring at nothing, at brown cardboard pressed against one side of my face and a hand reaching toward me not even a real hand the fingers fused together can't look away from it can't move and a rumble of voices *what's happening to me*, where am I, what is this? My name is Elizabeth Drury I'm a lawyer in Chicago and and I'm, I'm in a box full of dolls I was looking down into the box and now I'm in the box and I can't move, no, no, this isn't possible, scream, I have to scream and I can't scream I'm not even breathing I'm just here and staring not blinking, the architect, he'll come in and rescue me he'll see, what will he see? I don't know. Am I out there standing up there looking down still looking down in here at me is anything happening, will he see anything happening, did they drug me again, what if they put the box in the dumpster, no, no, don't put me in the dumpster *please* don't, not the dumpster, I'm hallucinating, it must be the paint fumes, that's it, paint fumes, I fainted, this is a dream, in a minute I'll wake up and flickering light, scraping sounds, and no no, someone is closing the box, it's dark. It's dark it's *dark* and I can't move I'm not breathing I'm in a box.

I'm not going crazy. I *will* not go crazy. I will not. My name is Elizabeth Drury. I'm an attorney. I have purchased a property in Palo Alto and I am here inspecting my property and why is it so dark, why are other arms and legs pressing against my arms and legs against my sides and back I feel them pressing but I can't move, I am not going crazy. I am *not*. Aerosol psychedelics? Have I been poisoned? Hypnotized? Am I dead? How long has it been now? Ten minutes? An hour? A week?

Tenaciously determined not to go insane, she reviewed, in meticulous detail, everything she knew. The names of the people in her law office. The cases she had been working on. Cases she had won. Everything she knew about contract law. The furniture in her apartment. The important events in her career. Her medical history. The suits in her wardrobe. The name of her hairdresser. The route from her apartment to the office. And again. All of it again.

A couple of times she was joggled and bumped into things, into other dolls. Dolls are things. I'm a thing. Somebody must be moving the box. Not to the dumpster, please, not the dumpster! I'm not garbage! Don't throw me in with garbage! I own three purses — the gray leather one, which I bought at Saks, the blood-red leather clutch, which I use only when I go to a party, when was the last party I went to, the office Christmas party? Who all did I see there? Purses, the faux hemp one with the pewter snap fasteners....

How long has it been now?

There was no time in the box, just darkness and motionless stiff limbs pressed against her, the smell of dust and plastic, distant rumbling sounds, more bumps sometimes, voices too muffled to make out words, vibrations, was the box in a truck, thump thump, the truck hitting potholes, she thought her head was pointed down now, her legs higher up toward the lid, but how could you tell?

And then the lid opened and light flooded in. Light! Oh, the darkness is gone, I can see! I still can't blink, I see everything, everything, going home from Mr. and Mrs. Taubin's when Mom and Dad came home from Europe and how it was my fault Eleanor was kidnapped because I was the one who hadn't wanted to go to Europe Eleanor would have been happy to go and why didn't they ever talk about Eleanor? Oh. Oh. That's why.

The light came and went. She couldn't see much, her head wasn't pointed down at the bottom of the box it was sort of sideways, but she could see there was a wall and another shelf up above, the box must be on a shelf at the Goodwill a box full of dolls that nobody wanted and I am *not* going insane, I still know who I am, my name is Eleanor, no I mean Elizabeth, I'm Elizabeth Drury, I'm a lawyer in Chicago and now it's night the lights in the Goodwill store are off and now it must be daytime again, days coming and going I'm losing track of time, don't lose track, please don't, voices now and people moving around and a hand, a hand reaches down into the box and picks up one doll and puts it back and then another and then picks *me* up around the middle and it's that woman! The crazy woman with the bird on her shoulder and the hat with all the ribbons and dried flowers, and she turns me around to inspect me and there's a blond girl standing beside her a girl I almost think I must know, young, maybe eleven, and crazy woman turns to the girl and says, "Do you like this one?", and the girl says, "No, I hate it, it's ugly."

The crazy woman starts to put me back in the box, but then she looks straight at me, not at the girl, and says, "Do you want to be like this? Is this how you want to be?" And I can't answer because I don't have a voice, I'm not even breathing, I want to tell her no! No, I don't want to be like this, trapped forever in a box! But I can't say anything.

Very gently, the woman put the doll back in the box and closed the lid. Dark again. Dark forever. Beth wanted to scream and couldn't. What was left of her mind swirled, sagged, was sucked down fiber by fiber into a whirlpool of razor blades. Everything she had ever been, all of it spinning, sliced apart, the scraps dissolving. Nothing. Everything. Nothing.

Voices. Darkness, but a different kind of darkness now, and voices. A gentle hand pressing against the side of her neck. A woman's voice saying, "She's alive. Fainted."

A man's voice. "She didn't cut herself, at least."

Hands rolled her over. The woman's voice came again. "Tell me I'm not seeing what I think I'm seeing."

Beth took a shuddering breath. She could *breathe*! How long had it been since she had breathed? A year? Forever? Her eyelids felt gummy, but she forced them open and blinked several times. She was on her back on the floor, staring up at — what were their names? John and Marta. Hadn't this all happened before? Her memories were like shards of glass all tumbled together in a glittering heap. "This is — you're — I was in a box."

With Marta's arm around her shoulders, she sat up. She was in a kitchen. The kitchen of the house. Dolls standing on the kitchen counter stared down at her. She shuddered. "A cardboard box. I remember now. This is where I stabbed him. And then a woman came, a woman with a bird."

"Woman with a bird?" John frowned at her.

"You don't remember. It hasn't happened yet. But it's just like it was before." She picked at the thick folds of the business suit. "My clothes don't fit me again."

Her legs were wobbly, so she let them help her walk across the yard. Thinking about the bulldozer. Thinking, they don't know the architect is coming, and then the bulldozer. That hasn't happened yet either.

Back in the workshop, John handed her the fly-specked little mirror and she stared at herself for long seconds. A shaky giggle started, and she stifled it. She set the mirror on the workbench and hugged herself. Still cold. Wanting to be warm.

And there was the harp. She pointed at it. "You made that."

"I did. How did you know?"

"You told me. But you don't remember. There's a name for it, when this happens. I took a psych class in college, because I wanted to know why I was so — never mind about that. It isn't *déjà vu*, it's called *déjà vécu*. Where you're not just remembering, where it's all happening again."

"Never heard of it."

"Well, you have now. Maybe it'll come back to you." She snickered, still too out of breath to laugh but so glad to be breathing!

Marta came in with mugs of tea on a tray. As Beth was sipping, grateful — tea seemed so normal, and right now nothing else was — a shadow slid across the doorway. She said, "Oh, the woman with the bird."

And there she was, tapping lightly on the door frame, straw hat, cockatoo, and all. She said, "Excuse me. Is this the Ambrosia Center for the Arts?"

John admitted it. "Can we help you?"

"I'm not entirely sure," the newcomer said. "It may be the other way around. I rather think I'm supposed to help *you*. I've received some Divine Guidance, you see. A vision. I was told to find the girl, and I was to say to her — let me see, what was it?" After pressing one finger against her chin and staring upward for a moment, she nodded firmly. "Yes, I remember now." She fixed her eyes on Beth and said, "You must choose. This will not happen again."

They went on talking, something about an apparition in a mirror, but Beth wasn't listening. The woman said her name was Madeleine Oakley. John took her outside to show her something. Martha hovered, staring at Beth uncertainly while trying not to, and then she went out too.

Beth sipped tea and gazed out the door of the workshop at the little house. The house with all the dolls. Dolls that she would never, *never* allow to be stuffed into cardboard cartons and hauled off to Goodwill. Except, she was getting ahead of herself. I don't own this place, she realized. I haven't bought it yet, haven't even talked to the bank about getting the loan. That was next week. What am I going to do about that? What had Madeleine Oakley said the other time? If you would remain as you are, you must make your home here. That was it.

Here? Live in that house? *Live* in it? With awful memories oozing out of the walls to smother her? But it was either that, or go back to Chicago, back to the person she had become.

First things first. She got her phone from her purse, texted her broker, and gave instructions about liquidating her portfolio. He would want confirmation, of course, but she could manage it, as long as he didn't see her. Maybe rough up her voice on the phone so she sounded older.

Am I really eighteen again? Another trip to the mirror. Yes, she was eighteen. With the memory of a fifty-year-old woman and some other memories too, of things that couldn't possibly have happened.

John and Marta came back.

"Mrs. Oakley?" Beth said. "She's gone?"

"She wanted to see the dolls," John said. "I told her maybe another time."

Beth suppressed a shiver. That was something else to think about. What if Madeleine Oakley came back and knew things she couldn't possibly know?

"Did you understand her message?" Marta said. "I didn't. And she couldn't explain it. Said it didn't make sense to her either."

Beth nodded. "It was the second message. Or the third, I guess. I don't think I want to try to explain. Maybe this is only a dream I'm having."

John said, "Maybe all of life is only a dream. How would we know?"

"Here's the thing, though. I'm kind of rich. I know this property is for sale. I — I think I'm going to buy it. You can all stay here, keep doing what you're doing."

A gentle smile lit up John's face.

"And I guess maybe I'll move into the house."

"You want to live in the house?" Marta said.

"No, I don't want to. But I think I have to."

"The plumbing doesn't work."

"I'll hire a plumber. I think maybe it will be all right. Maybe not at first, but eventually." She paused to fidget. "The trouble is, once I'm here, I don't have a way to earn a living. I can't pass the California bar. I don't have an ID that makes any sense. Any job at all, I'd need ID."

She stared longingly at the harp, where it sat on the workbench. For a moment she thought the inlay on the harp, the woman with the enigmatic smile and the hair that flowed like a river, was glowing with its own light. The sunlight must be playing tricks as it drifted in through the open doorway. "I might as well play the harp on a street corner," she said. "That's all I'm good for. Would it be all right if I—" She gestured at the harp. "I used to know a couple of songs."

He held out an open hand. "Be my guest."

She took the harp down from the bench, sat cradling it, and touched the strings tentatively. The song the girl had been picking out on her piano, the girl who wasn't there, days ago or days from now, somewhere off in the future, before the cardboard box — how did it go? Now she was remembering.

She stumbled through "Carolan's Dream" and went on, with a bit more confidence, to "The Rising of the Lark." And then "Greensleeves." Her fingertips tingled. John and Marta listened.

She stopped and rubbed her fingers. "I'll get blisters."

Marta said, "That was very nice. You could, you know. Play on street corners, I mean. Or in a coffee shop."

"Oh, I couldn't. I don't remember much about music. I remember things that haven't happened yet, and things that could never have happened even though they did, but things I used to know have slipped away from me." She touched the harp again, a single note that shimmered on the air. "I think I don't want to let things slip away from me anymore."

Who am I now, she wondered. I'm a new person. A doll that came to life. "You sent the letter, didn't you? The one about my sister."

John raised an eyebrow, pretending to be puzzled. "Did you have a sister? What sister?"

"My sister Elea — no, I need to get this straight. She never existed, did she? But the one who never existed, that wasn't Eleanor. That was Beth."

"Beth Drury has a law practice in Chicago, or so I heard."

"And money. But that was never real. None of it. Except for the money, I mean. I hope the money is real, but the rest of it was all just a bad dream. This is real. I think — I think I'm finally about to start being me."

"It's worth a try," John said.

A bright-eyed old man poked his head in the door. "I heard voices," he said. "And music. Are we having a party?"

John said, "Ah, Arthur. This young lady is poised to become our new landlord. This is Arthur Schoeps. And you're—" He let the question hang in the air.

She took a very deep breath, and let it out. "It's very nice to meet you, Mr. Schoeps. My name is Eleanor."

Dance for the King

TONIGHT I WILL DANCE FOR the king tonight I will caper and leap and cavort and turn handsprings for the king. The king sits on his throne made of stone in a room made of stone a huge throne a vast room all dark rough blocks of heavy gray stone, and the king is made of stone, a dark rough giant who never moves only sits on his throne towering high above me as I dance towering above me when I dance when I laugh cry sleep I am in the vast stone room with the king all the time there is nobody here but us there are no doors no way out of the room at all. I will wear my clown suit when I dance. Sometimes I think the king likes it best when I wear my clown suit the red bulb nose and big floppy shoes even though the king never shows what he likes or doesn't like never moves at all only sits there.

I wear the clown suit on special occasions tonight is a special occasion tonight is the anniversary of when we began being here together. I cannot say "of when I was brought here" since I don't remember being brought here or being anywhere else before I was here all I know is being here in the vast stone room with the giant silent unmoving king. Sometimes I wonder what other places might be like if there are other places what it would be like if I were there instead of here. Would they have dark walls of rough heavy stone? Would they have kings? Perhaps there are no other places only here. That would explain why there are no doors.

There are no windows in the room either the light is never very bright it is always the same would light change in a window would light changing be a way to measure time is there a way to know a way to measure time. When I say tonight I am being arbitrary whenever I feel like dancing for the king it is always tonight. Also anniversary is arbitrary. There is always a way of dividing up time to make this the anniversary of the beginning of however long we have been here it seems a very long time although I have nothing to compare it to. But I do not always wear the clown suit only on special occasions.

Sometimes I climb up the king's leg and sit in his lap. Since there is not much to see from up there I always climb down again. When I am down here I can look up at the king and that is something to see he is much larger than I am and he is always up there whether I am down here looking up at him or up there with him and can't see him and can't see me down here either the way he can when I am down here since I am up there not down here when I am up there and he is certainly not down here for me to see when I am up there not ever. The king is very large I am not much bigger than his little finger but I am different colors and I move and his finger is always gray and it never moves. I wonder if the king likes me sitting in his lap. I would like to climb up to his shoulder but I never do I am afraid he might not like it and it is so far up I might get dizzy sometimes I get dizzy when I dance around in circles very fast being dizzy is not fun.

Since I will dance for the king tonight I must put on my clown suit. I sit down on the floor to pull on the baggy polka-dot trousers and the big floppy shoes. I tie the puffy droopy bow tie around my neck and stick the red bulb nose on my nose. I mess my hair up so it is wild and smear chalky white on my face now I am ready.

But before I can begin to dance a strange thing happens a thing that has never happened before. At first I do not know what it is it is only a low rumbling that rolls and echoes between the stone walls. Then I see the king's lips beard and chin are moving. He is speaking! His eyes do not move they are staring at the spot on the floor they always stare at, sad weary eyes, and his arms do not move where they rest on the arms of the throne but he is speaking yes! The words are low and slow filled with weight as though the air itself were stone creaking and groaning like boulders grinding together in the dark inside of him.

He speaks and I strain to understand the words I know they are important they are the only words the king has ever spoken since I have been here he and I are alone here with only each other so whatever is important enough to him to make him speak after so long must be important to me too maybe not as important to me as to him him being a king but still important. The words roll on, the kings's face moves slowly inside the sound like the face of a mountain when the wind blows across it or the light slowly changes on it or the seasons I do not know what a mountain is or wind or seasons but I know the king's face is like these things.

I run closer to the king my floppy shoes flopping if I can hear better maybe I can understand the words but still they mean nothing to me. I fall on my knees in front of him. "What are you saying?" I cry. "Tell me what you are saying!"

The voice rolls on and on my ears buzz my head throbs and aches with it. I cover my ears with my hands shut my eyes tight still the voice rolls on inside me rolls and echoes between the stone walls. At last the pressure on my ears grows less so I think my ears are growing numb from the sound but then I realize the sound itself is growing fainter. I look at the king expecting to see his face moving less but no it is not just the sound but the king himself growing fainter! His features are indistinct he is becoming transparent I can see the rough gray stone on the back of the throne through his body a thing I have never seen before. He continues to speak his lips move as long as I can see them but he and his voice fade slowly very slowly I watch helpless numb unable to move or cry out. The king is vanishing. The king is leaving me here alone.

After a long time the king is completely gone. I still seem to hear echoes of his voice faintly but I think it is only my ears still buzzing from before. I walk slowly toward the throne and look up at it. I can walk across bare floor where the king's feet rested they left no mark. The king is gone.

The room is emptier with the king gone only me and the huge empty throne left here. I wonder where the king has gone to. I wonder if he will be happy there if there is a there maybe he will be happier there than here maybe not as happy. Was he happy here? Will anybody there dance for him will there be anybody there to dance? Will he speak to them as he spoke to me or only sit silent staring at the floor? Will there be a floor? Perhaps if there is a they there they will understand him when he speaks I wish I understood what he said when he spoke it is a sad thing not to understand when a king speaks.

I wonder why he went away. I wonder will he ever come back here to sit and watch me dance. I climb up one of the carved legs of the throne and sit on the seat my legs dangling over the edge staring out at the vast empty room. Once a king sat here and stared out like this now there is only me in my clown suit with the red bulb nose and floppy shoes swinging back and forth I am not a king. After a while I climb down again. First I think I will take off my clown suit but then I think no, I will wear it tonight and dance anyway. Tonight was to be a special occasion for me and the king the king is not here but nothing has changed. Once there was a king. Tonight I will dance for the king.

Flute Lessons

WHEN MARYAM WAS NINE years old, her mother said to her, "If you wish for something with a pure heart, your wish can come true. You must always believe this."

Maryam and her mother and father and three brothers lived in a small house. Her sister had lived there too, until her sister was married. Now that her sister was gone, Maryam had a bedroom all to herself, which was nice, even though the room was very small. Her brothers had to share a bedroom, but it was much bigger.

Sometimes Maryam went outside and played in the alley behind the house. Several houses and apartment buildings backed up on the alley, but nobody ever came into the alley except to put trash in the trash barrel, and when she heard them coming she always slipped back inside. Her mother never told her it was forbidden to play in the alley, only that she must never, ever go out the end of the alley onto the street. Going out onto the street unescorted was strictly forbidden for girls and women.

Maryam liked playing in the alley. When she played in the house her brothers teased her and sometimes broke her things, because she was a girl. In the alley nobody bothered her, and sometimes a skinny cat with patchy brown hair and a scar by its eye would come sit on the lid of a trash barrel and watch her while she played. The cat would never let her pet it, it always jumped down and skittered away when she came too close. But she liked the cat anyway.

One day the lid of the cat's favorite trash barrel was on crooked. Probably it had been crooked lots of times, but she had never noticed. The cat came and looked up at the top of the trash barrel, thought about it, and went away again.

Maryam sat on the back step looking at the trash barrel for a long time. She thought about how people put things in the trash barrel that were broken, or smelled bad. She wondered if anyone ever put anything beautiful in the trash barrel. After a while she started to wish. She wished that someone had put something beautiful in the trash barrel, the most beautiful thing in the world. She wished that when she walked over to the trash barrel, she would find this beautiful thing.

For a long time she sat on the back step wishing. Then she stood up and went over to the trash barrel.

In the trash, resting right at the top so she didn't have to dig for it, was a narrow black box. The box was half a meter long, and not much wider or thicker than her arm. The box was scuffed and dusty, but there was a silver clasp on one side.

When she flipped up the clasp and opened the box, she saw something amazing — something she had never seen or even imagined. There were three silver tubes in the box, all nestled in a cushion of deep green velvet. Along the longest tube ran a row of round things like tiny saucers, with holes in the tube beneath the saucers.

Maryam knew at once that her wish had come true. She didn't wonder how, or why. She didn't even know what the silver tubes were. She only knew that they were the most beautiful thing in the world.

She closed the box, tucked it up under her burqa, and took it into the house to show to her mother. "See what I found? What is it?"

Her mother drew her away from the doorway, so that the men in the front part of the house wouldn't see. "Where did you find it?" Her mother didn't look pleased; she looked nervous.

"It was in the trash. I wished for it, and there it was. What is it?"

"It's a musical instrument. It's called a flute. It's a European instrument, like a surnai but I think the sound is prettier. We mustn't talk of that. Give it to me."

Maryam pulled the box back, away from her mother's grasping fingers. "I don't want to. Why should I give it to you?"

"Because you are a very bad girl, and I'll smack you if you don't."

"But why?"

"Music is not for girls, that's why. Don't ask 'why.' Asking 'why' will get you in big trouble. Your father and your brothers will be angry."

"They're always angry anyway," Maryam said. "They're angry because of the American soldiers. It doesn't matter what I say. If I stay quiet, it won't make them any less angry."

"No, but if you stay quiet they won't be angry at *you*."

"I'd like to play a musical instrument. How do you play it?"

Maryam's mother dried her hands and tilted her head sideways to look out through the door at the living

206

room. It was quiet out there right now. "If I show you, you must promise never to speak of it. And then after I show you, you'll have to put it back where you found it and forget that you ever saw it. Do you promise?"

"Show me." Maryam held out the flute. She hadn't promised anything.

After another glance out the door, her mother took the silver tubes from their case and fitted them end to end. "It's one long tube," her mother said. "You hold it sideways and blow in this hole, I think. I never tried it. And while you blow, you put your fingers on these and wiggle your fingers different ways, and it makes beautiful melodies." She tried blowing into the mouthpiece, but no melody came from the flute. "Anyway, that's how they do it on television." Maryam and her mother were not allowed to watch television, so this statement was rather shocking. But before Maryam could ask any more about it, her mother heard the men coming. She pulled the flute apart, thrust the tubes back into their places in the case, and made urgent motions with her hands. "Take it," she said softly. "Get rid of it. Hurry."

Maryam didn't put the flute back in the trash barrel. She didn't quite dare keep it in the house, but she found a safe place in the alley, a little niche between some boards, and tucked the flute in the niche. All night she worried about whether the flute would be there the next day, but it was, almost as if it were waiting for her. After looking around to make sure no one was watching, she took it out of the case and figured out how to fit the tubes together to make one long tube. But no matter how she tried blowing into the hole or wiggling her fingers, no melody came out.

Every day for a week she tried blowing into it, and she couldn't figure out how to do it. Afterward she always pulled the tubes apart and put them back carefully in the case. She felt very sad that she couldn't make the flute play a beautiful melody, but very pleased that she had a beautiful flute. She wondered if maybe she should be satisfied just to look at it, and never think about making it play a melody.

That week, her mother looked at her a little differently than she ever had before. Her mother looked like she was worried about something, but didn't want to say anything about it. Her mother was always worrying about things, so that wasn't any different than usual. Maryam couldn't quite figure out what was different.

One day her mother said, "Did you get rid of that thing you showed me?"

"Oh, yes."

Her mother looked sad when she heard that.

"I mean, it's gone," Maryam said carefully, "but I guess I could probably find it again if I wanted to. I know where I put it. It might still be there." After a minute she added, "I did try to make it play a melody, after I took it away, but I couldn't see how."

Her mother pressed her lips together. "There are people who teach people how to play music," she said. "I wish — but not girls, not women. It is not allowed, for women."

"I wish somebody could teach me how to make the flute play a melody," Maryam said. "Even just one melody, just one song."

"I wish that too," her mother said, cupping the back of Maryam's head gently with her hand.

Nothing more was said about it that day, nor the next, but a few days later Maryam's mother said, "You must put on your street clothes. We're going to visit someone who has some spices for cooking, which we will buy." With Maryam's brother Mahmoud escorting them, they went out and up and down several streets. Mahmoud scowled the whole way. Maryam guessed it embarrassed him to be seen on the street with his mother and little sister.

When they came to the apartment of the person who had the spices to sell, Mahmoud went inside with them to look around and then went back outside, where he leaned on the railing and scowled. Maryam and her mother sat on the couch of the woman who lived there, and removed their veils. "This is my little girl," her mother said. "Maryam, this is Tamara. You must be nice to her, for she is a very nice person. She can help us."

Tamara looked like a nice person, Maryam thought. There were some books in the room, so Tamara's husband must know how to read. Or maybe Tamara could read the books herself. Maryam thought it would be wonderful to know how to read, but she knew better than to say so.

"Your mother tells me you wanted to know how to play music on the flute," Tamara said.

"Oh, no," Maryam said, suddenly alarmed. "I would never want such a thing!"

"It's all right," her mother said.

From underneath the couch, Tamara brought out a flute. It wasn't as nice as the one Maryam had hidden in the alley: The metal was tarnished, not shiny. But it looked as if someone had played it a lot.

Tamara brought the flute to her lips, pursed her lips in a certain way, and blew across the hole at the end of the tube. Very softly, a note blossomed in the room.

Maryam thought she had never heard anything so lovely in her entire life. She gasped and said, "Oh!"

"Would you like to try?"

"Oh, no, I couldn't! I don't know how! How do you do that?"

"You blow across the hole, not into it."

Maryam felt stupid. It had never occurred to her to blow across the hole. Tamara held out the flute, and very gingerly she took it. She brought it toward her mouth, but twice she had to stop and look at the two women for reassurance. They smiled and urged her to go on.

She blew across the hole. The flute made a sort of ugly squawking noise, and Maryam gave a little shriek of alarm.

"Your brother is just outside," her mother said. "You mustn't make any loud noises that would alarm him."

"Try once more," Tamara said. "Here, let me show you how."

At the end of half an hour, Maryam had made several nice-sounding notes on the flute, and Tamara had shown her how to hold her fingers so they could push the little saucers down over the holes in the tube. Then they bought some cooking spices from Tamara, put their veils across their faces, and went home. It was all Maryam could do to keep from skipping down the street. She walked stiffly to keep her knees from knocking together. Her brother noticed and said, "What's the matter with you, scabby worm?"

"Nothing, honored brother."

After she got home she couldn't wait to go out to the alley and get her own flute out of its case. Her hands were trembling so badly that she almost dropped the pieces before she could put them together. Then she was afraid to play a single note for fear her father or brothers would hear and come and take the flute away from her. At last she played one hurried note, rather louder and more tremulously than she had intended, and scrambled to take the flute apart and hide it as quick as she could, before anyone came.

Days passed before she could steel herself to try the experiment again. But eventually she did. After that, she went out into the alley every day wiggled her fingers while blowing across the hole. The sound wasn't a melody, exactly, but she loved hearing it anyway. No one, it seemed, ever noticed the flute noises coming from the alley. If they did, they must have thought it was a radio in a nearby house. By experimenting, she figured out that if you pressed more of the keys down, the sound was lower, while if you didn't press them down it was higher. After a while she was able to pick out, more or less, the melody of a song she had heard the men singing when they came home after her sister's wedding.

One day her mother said, "Would you like to go back and visit Tamara again? She's been asking after you."

"Oh, yes! Can we?"

After the next visit to Tamara, Maryam brought the flute into the house and hid it under her bed. She even played in her room, very softly, in the afternoon when her father and brothers were away. Her mother found a little pink radio somewhere, and they put it under the near edge of the bed, while the flute case was kept tucked back against the wall under an old blanket. The radio didn't work at all, but her mother dropped careless comments that let the men understand that Maryam had a radio in her room, which was why they might hear music sometimes. She mentioned that it was a little pink radio, and worked badly, so they wouldn't want it for themselves.

The flute lessons went on for three years. Not

on a regular schedule. Sometimes weeks went by. Maryam could do nothing but wait. Once or twice she grew impatient and asked her mother, "When are we going to visit Tamara?" Her mother would only frown and shake her head rapidly, as if to say, "Don't talk about that." But always, a week or two later, her mother would smile at her and say, "Time for a visit to Tamara. Get ready."

Eventually it dawned on Maryam that her mother was paying Tamara for the lessons. Her mother was setting aside a little out of the household food money so that Maryam could learn to play the flute.

"You mustn't do that," Maryam said. She was growing up now, and understood the way things were. "We'll have to stop. I don't want you to get in trouble."

"Nonsense," her mother said. "You let me worry about that. You just worry about playing the flute. You must do it as well as you possibly can, or I will have wasted your father's money."

Maryam knew how lucky she and her mother were to have a home, how lucky she was to have a father and brothers who would protect her and work to bring in money for food. Many other women in Kandahar didn't have these things. She argued with her mother. "I will teach myself to play. We must not do anything to make father angry."

Her mother said, "This is not your decision. You will have flute lessons. Do not argue."

One day when Maryam was thirteen her mother was weeping in the kitchen. At first she wouldn't say why, but Maryam persisted. "Tamara," her mother said. "They threw acid in her face, because she is a woman and dared play music. They said it is against the Koran. She is blind and disfigured, and her lips are burned. She will never play the flute again." She stopped to sob, and then added, "I smashed your flute with a hammer and threw it away."

"I have to go see her."

"No, I forbid it! Go to your room at once, and stay there."

Instead, Maryam put on her burqa for the street and went out by herself, which was both forbidden and very dangerous, but she didn't care. With only a little care to step aside when she saw men coming, she managed to reach Tamara's apartment.

The door was standing open. Someone had scrawled words across the wall outside, big ugly red letters. Maryam didn't know what it said, because no one had ever taught her to read.

She went inside. The interior of the apartment was a wreck. Everything had been torn apart, but the men had attacked the books with special fury, shredding them and then urinating on the piles of scraps. The music books too. Maryam had never dared ask how to read the ordinary books, but she could read music. She knew "dolce" and "cantabile," Italian words from Europe that meant "sweet" and "singing."

Somehow, in their fury, the men had neglected to look under the couch. Tamara's old, well-played flute was still there, in its case.

Maryam sat on the couch and put the flute together. She lifted her veil and began to play. She played a song called "Sheep May Safely Graze," and another called "Somewhere over the Rainbow." She was crying, but she never stopped playing.

She heard voices muttering, getting louder. She didn't stop playing.

Half a dozen men burst into the apartment. They

knocked the flute out of her hands, knocked her to the floor, and started kicking her savagely.

Through the haze of blood that dimmed her eyes, she saw that one of the men was her brother Mahmoud. She wondered if he had recognized her, and guessed that it wouldn't have made any difference.

In her heart, as she died, the flute was still playing. Her last wish was that everyone would hear the music of the flute.

The men left the apartment, left the whore lying broken in her shame, and went down the stairs to the street. "God is great," one of them said. Mahmoud was among the chorus who replied, "God is great!"

"Listen," one of the men said. "Do you hear that?"

They paused. They all heard it. Not far away, someone was playing a flute.

They rushed back into the apartment building and rushed up and down. The music seemed to come from everywhere and nowhere. They burst into several apartments, alarming the inhabitants. They smashed a couple of radios and a television, and threw women to the floor. But still the flute played, louder than before. The men gazed at one another wildly. Their hands and faces were twitching. They covered their ears and tore at their hair. They ran screaming into the street. The flute music never paused.

One of the men ran into traffic. A taxicab hit him and rolled over him. Another fell to his knees, foam and blood gushing from his mouth. A third began clawing at his face with his fingernails, and in moments had torn his own eyes from their sockets. A fourth ran into a wall, backed up, lowered his head, and rammed the wall as hard as he could.

Several blocks away, Maryam's father frowned at

Maryam's mother. "That radio you gave our daughter — go tell her to turn it off."

Maryam's mother looked frightened. "I don't hear the radio."

"Don't argue with me, woman."

She brought the little pink radio out of the bedroom. Its power cord dangled limply. "Here it is, husband."

"Turn it off."

"It's not on. It's unplugged."

"Take the batteries out, then."

"There are no batteries."

He hit her backhanded, and she fell. "Do not argue with me, woman. Stop the radio playing. Here, give it to me." He grabbed it and smashed it against the wall. He smashed it again and again, until the pieces flew apart. "You must stop the music," he said, gasping. "Stop the music!" He pressed his hands hard against his ears. "Make it stop! Make it stop!" He staggered into the kitchen and grabbed a sharp knife. What he meant to do with it even he may not have known. Emerging from the kitchen he tripped. In falling to the floor, he drove the knife into his own belly. His blood pooled around him.

His wife watched as the blood gushed and ripples spread outward with every beat of his heart. She knew that without a husband her life would be very difficult. She knew she ought to kneel beside him and try to stop the bleeding, but she found that she had no wish to do so. After a while the ripples slowed and weakened. Then they stopped.

"Maryam?" she called. "Maryam? Where are you?"

Somewhere nearby, in a place where music flows on and on like an endless river, a flute was playing. Many people heard it. Some who heard it went mad, and died. Others heard it and their hearts were filled with joy. They went to bed in peace, and rose the next morning to begin a new day.

Flute Lessons: An Afterword

"Flute Lessons" is dedicated to the women of Afghanistan, and especially to the female musicians and those courageous enough to teach them. It was inspired by a news item. I no longer remember the details, but while the actual events may have been less horrific than those in my story, there *are* men in Afghanistan who feel perfectly justified in attacking women who dare to play music.

"Flute Lessons" is not specifically intended as an indictment of Islam. It's an indictment of conservative tribal customs that subjugate women, which surely date back a lot further than the days of the Prophet Mohammed. Today, however, Islam provides a convenient refuge for such savage and unforgivable customs. Whether we should blame Islam for the appalling cultural practices that are common across the Middle East, or whether Islam is basically a benign religion (or as benign as any other religion, which isn't saying much) that has appropriated older cultural practices rather than casting them aside, is a question I'll leave others to debate. Those who oppress women, homosexuals, and secular thinkers in such barbaric ways quite often claim that they do so in the name of religion. If they say they're following the teachings of their religion, I believe them.

I know there must be millions of good, kind Muslims in the world. On the whole, I find Islam no more disturbing or objectionable than Christianity or Judaism – and no less disturbing or objectionable. It's all cut from the same cloth. Religion is used so often to justify cruelty that its continued existence cannot really be defended by wise and compassionate people. We can do better. We *must* do better.

A Place to Stay
for a Little While

"**I** CAN'T COPE," CYNTHIA Lutz said to the radio. "I simply cannot cope."

"Oh, come on," the radio said. It was a wooden table model that dated from about 1933. "Things aren't that bad. Things have been this bad before."

"When?" Cynthia snapped.

"Well, they must have been, some time or other," the radio said evasively. "How would I know? My memory isn't worth a damn. What do you expect from vacuum tubes?"

"I've never been turned down for welfare before, that's for sure." Cynthia pushed long loose gray-streaked hair away from her bony face and paced up and down in the kitchen, sandals slapping on the worn linoleum. Her toes were callused and her jeans were frayed. "They told me I make too much money. Too damn much money selling candles, can you believe that? And I can't explain to them that I've got five dependents, or this place will be crawling with social workers, and you know what'll happen then. They'll lock Mrs. Simpston up and send Debby to a foster home and deport Mr. Alvarado,

218

and probably put Toby in a hospital and arrest me for sanitary violations or something. So how am I supposed to feed this menagerie?"

"Fortunately, I require no sustenance," the radio said smugly.

Cynthia narrowed her eyes at the faded grille cloth. "Oh, yeah? What if I can't pay the electric bill?"

"I'm sure it won't come to that," the radio said uneasily. "You'll think of something."

"Your faith is touching." Above a teetering pile of dishes in the sink, an open window let in afternoon breeze through a green tangle of vines. The radio was sitting squarely on the big table against the opposite wall. Cynthia eyed the dishes with distaste — plenty of time for that later — and transferred her attention to the refrigerator. There were still a couple of apples in there....

"There is one other thing," the radio reported.

"What?" She squinted at the naked white interior of the refrigerator. Wilted lettuce and peanut butter. Not quite half a jar.

"Somebody new. He'll be here soon."

"How soon? And what's his problem?"

"That's all the information I'm getting. Sorry."

"You're a big help. As usual."

"I do the best I can. I'm only a radio."

※ II ※

The street was quiet and shady. Here and there tree roots had buckled the sidewalk. He was walking aimlessly, content to let his feet lead the way, whistling soundlessly between his teeth and wondering what it would be like to live in one of these big old houses year after year instead of knocking around on the road. His name was Steven Raleigh, and it had been four months since he had last used his terrible power.

At the attic window of one house he saw a pale shape that moved and was gone, leaving a curtain swaying. He stopped and looked up at the window, shifting the duffel bag on his shoulder, but the shape failed to reappear. The house was a little more decrepit than its neighbors; the paint was badly peeled, nobody had swept the dead leaves off the porch roof, and long spears of grass had grown up around the bone-dry birdbath in the yard. It looked like the kind of place where they could use some odd jobs done. On impulse, he stepped long-legged over the low picket fence and climbed the creaking steps to the porch.

He started slightly when he saw the old man sitting in deep shade on the porch swing. The old man stared straight ahead, not noticing Steven at all. He was a small, frail-looking old man wearing a threadbare but immaculate three-piece suit and a cream-colored hat that had been very fashionable forty years before.

"Excuse me," Steven said.

The leather face turned slowly toward him. "You wish to speak to Cynthia," the old man said in the meticulous accent of a Mexican whose English is very good. "She is inside." His hand twitched on his thigh, a gesture much too small to be called a jerk of the thumb, and his face rotated slowly away again.

Steven rapped on the glass pane in the door, and when nobody came he turned the knob and stepped inside. The hallway smelled of dust and cooking and scented candle wax. "Anybody home?" he called.

Cynthia Lutz set down her peanut butter sandwich and headed for the hall. She saw a slim, well-knit young man with a badly trimmed crop of fine blond hair, an expressionless mouth, and wary, haunted eyes. He was wearing boots, jeans, and a work shirt. He thumped the duffel bag on the floor and looked at her uncertainly.

"Let me guess," she said, setting her hands on her hips. "You turn into a penguin."

"You shouldn't make jokes with me," he told her.

"Oh, I'm sorry. Why not?"

"Never mind. It's not important. I thought maybe you had some odd jobs you needed done."

She put back her head and laughed. "Is that what you thought? There's plenty of work to be done, you got that right, but haven't got a cent to pay you. Would you like something to eat? Anything you like, as long as it's peanut butter. I could make you a peanut butter sandwich."

When he had washed down some sandwich with a swig of the strawberry Kool-Aid she had found gathering dust on a top shelf, he said, "Why feed me? You don't know me."

"I take in strays." She was sitting across from him, admiring his healthy appetite. "What did you mean when you said I shouldn't make jokes?"

"Did I say that? I didn't mean anything." He ran his finger through a ring of the Kool-Aid, making a long wet red smear across the table.

"I think you meant something."

"Just that it might not be safe. When I get mad, I do things, sometimes. But don't worry," he added, holding up a palm, "I won't do anything. I promise."

She chewed on her lower lip. "What kind of things do you do that aren't safe?"

"It's hard to explain. It doesn't matter."

"It does matter. You think I won't believe you, if you

tell me. You think nobody could possibly believe you."

He gave her a smoldering dark look from under his eyebrows. "You'd believe me all right, if I showed you. But I don't dare." He took a big bite of sandwich. The muscles in his jaw clenched as he chewed.

"Why do you think you came here?" she asked conversationally.

"I told you. Looking for an odd job."

"Stopping at all the houses? Or did you just come straight here and walk in the front door?" Outside the window a hummingbird was nuzzling among the vines. She watched until it darted away.

"I didn't stop at every house, no."

"Something about this house in particular attracted you. Shall I tell you what it was?"

He shrugged. "You're doing the talking."

"It was me."

"You?" His forehead wrinkled in disbelief.

"I attract people. But not just anybody. People who have strange gifts. People to whom things happen, things that can't be explained, things that aren't even possible. If you weren't one of those people, you wouldn't be here."

"I don't know what you're talking about."

She took a sip, without asking, of his Kool-Aid. "You saw that old man on your way in?"

"Sitting on the porch? Yeah, what about him?"

"That's Mr. Alvarado. He's resting. Would you like to know why he's resting?"

"I guess."

"Mr. Alvarado patches up the holes in the world. It's hard work. Or I guess it is. When he comes back afterward you can see he's worn out. In between times, when there aren't any holes that need patching, he stays here. When a new hole opens up somewhere, he senses it somehow, and he has to go off and patch it. He's never been able to explain to me *how* he patches the holes in the world, but he did tell me once that he's one of only two or three hole-patchers that are left. Maybe the only one left, by now. When all the hole-patchers are gone, the world is going to come apart, or unravel or something. He couldn't explain that very well either, but I have a feeling it may be serious. Anyhow, he takes it seriously. That's why he's resting. It's hard work patching holes, and he's eighty-three years old."

Steven made motions with his mouth, as though he were rolling the idea around on his tongue, or possibly cleaning peanut butter off his teeth. "You're kidding," he stated.

"I'm not kidding. I hope he's wrong about the end of the world, but I believe he does what he says he does. He's not the strangest person here."

"You're putting me on. That's crazy."

"Any crazier than whatever is going on with you?"

"I don't want to talk about that."

"Suit yourself." Cynthia shrugged. "You belong here. That much is obvious. We've got an empty room upstairs. All it's got is a mattress. Nobody will steal your stuff. The house rules are simple." She ticked them off on her fingers. "Don't pay any attention to anything Mrs. Simpston says; she fell through a hole in the world a long time ago, though I don't guess it was one of Mr. Alvarado's holes. Under no circumstances go into the attic — the person living in the attic does not like visitors."

He remembered the vague shape at the window.

"If you hear noises or see flashing lights, ignore them. Likewise people walking through walls or floating around a foot off the floor. Don't annoy Mr. Alvarado when he's resting. And as of this afternoon, if you want to eat, go out and hustle yourself some grub. The hostess is flat broke."

After looking at her for a minute with his hands half-curled in front of him on the table like an exhausted boxer, he stood up. "I've gotta think about this. Can you show me the room?"

⚓ III ⚓

The mattress was thick and soft, and the blanket that went with it smelled of wood smoke. Steven had walked a long way. Within minutes he was asleep.

Somewhat later, he woke to a presence in the room — gentle breathing, the rustle of a garment. He lifted his head. The intruder's eyes met his for a startled moment, then dropped to the floor. The longish untidy hair and pale hollow-cheeked face could have been that of either a man or a woman. The contours of the body were concealed in a shapeless robe that fell almost to the floor.

"Oh, I'm sorry. I didn't mean to wake you." The voice was a husky contralto. Cynthia said we had somebody new, and I wanted a look. I should go."

"No, don't." Steven raised himself on an elbow. "Stay a minute."

"I can't. Cynthia won't like it." The figure glided toward the door, but hesitated.

"Do you live here?"

"In the attic. But you won't see me. I don't come down much."

"What's your name?"

"I don't know. I kind of like 'Toby.' Mostly that's

what they call me."

Toby's head cocked sideways, asking a silent question, and Steven remembered that posture. Her name had been Laurel. She had looked at him just that way, standing in the darkened living room of her parents' house, that first night when she invited him into her bedroom. Laurel's voice came back to him: "Listen — do you want to do it, or what?" He hadn't thought of her for a long time, and the memory flooded in with an unexpected ache. There had been plenty of other women since; it was easy, and it didn't matter whether they wanted to or not. But with Laurel it had meant something, because that was before the power came to him.

"Are you all right?" Toby asked.

"Fine. I was thinking. You remind me of somebody I knew a long time ago."

Fear flashed in Toby's eyes. "Oh, no, it's starting already. I really do have to go. I can't stay around you any longer."

"Why not? I won't hurt you." He meant it.

"It's not you, it's me. Whenever I'm around somebody, I change. I can't help it. I'm sorry. I have to go." The figure slipped out the door, and light footsteps pattered away down the hall.

Steven sat up and rubbed his neck. "I change," Toby had said. What the hell did that mean? Still, Cynthia was right — the inhabitants of this house were odd.

He pulled on his boots and clomped down the stairs. There wasn't much furniture, and what there was had seen better days. The stained glass above the window seat had a forlorn look of lost elegance. On the sagging couch a large brown dog was asleep. As he went by, it lifted its head and blinked amiably at him.

Entering the dining room, he thought at first it was empty, but a voice halted him. An old woman said, "Twenty of them. My, my. How nice for you." She was sitting on a straight chair in the corner, a round little woman with wispy white hair and twinkling, if somewhat cloudy, eyes. She was smiling and nodding at a point up near where the chandelier would have been, if there had been a chandelier.

"Hello," Steven said.

"Oh. Oh, goodness, you startled me. Orlanoi was just showing me the flaming chariots of the Eastern Kingdom. What a spectacular sight! I do declare!"

"You must be Mrs. Simpson," he deduced.

"Simpston. With a 't.' And who might you be?"

"My name's Steven Raleigh. I just got here." He leaned forward and spoke loudly and distinctly to her, a courtesy to which she did not seem averse.

"Oh, that explains it." She smiled and nodded.

"Explains what?"

"The purple and silver robes, of course. You've been traveling."

He looked at his shoulders. Nobody had come up and draped purple and silver robes around him. "Have you seen Cynthia?" he asked.

"I believe she's at the palace."

Steven considered this. "The palace."

"She's often there."

He went on into the kitchen. Cynthia was at the sink, her sleeves rolled up, steam roiling thinly around her. "I met Mrs. Simpston-with-a-tee," he said. "And Toby."

"Toby."

"Toby came to my room."

"Toby's not supposed to do that," she said, pressing

her lips together. "But Toby gets lonely up there."

He sat down at the table. "What was that you said before, about us having to scrounge our own food?"

Scrubbing a saucer savagely, Cynthia said, "And when she got there, the cupboard was bare. You heard right. We're going to have a meeting in a little while, as soon as I get things cleaned up. We need to brainstorm. If you're going to stay, you should be here for the meeting."

"No problem. I wasn't going anywhere. Anyway, I'd like to meet everybody."

"If they're here, you'll meet them. Sometimes I can't find Frank. He has a tendency to fade."

"You said there was somebody who walks through walls," Steven said, making the connection.

"Right. It's an effort for him to become visible. About three times a week I go up to his room and bang on a garbage can lid and yell at him until he condenses, or whatever it is he does. I'm afraid if I don't do it, he'll evaporate completely."

"Must be tough." Steven stared at a tattered poster on the wall. Under a green spray of marijuana was the legend, *Let a Thousand Parks Bloom*. "You don't expect me to believe any of this," he said.

"Believe what you like. Or better still, talk to the radio. That might do the trick."

"The radio." He noticed it for the first time.

"I can't offer him any proof," the radio said. "Why should he listen to me?"

"Don't worry about that," Cynthia said. "Just talk to the nice man."

"What should I say?"

"Hey," Steven said. "That thing is *talking*."

"Mm-hmm," Cynthia said agreeably, turning back

to the dishes. "Are you starting to feel less alone?"

Seven stared at the radio, breathing through his mouth. "You've got wires hooked up somewhere," he declared. He craned his neck to look under the table, stretched out an arm to pull the plug and examine it, and after replacing the plug straightened up and lifted the radio in both hands to look at the tabletop under it.

"Hey, don't do that!" the radio protested. "Put me down! Some of my components are *very* fragile."

He glared at the radio, then set it down gently. "That doesn't prove anything. You could have a microphone hidden anywhere. Or it could be, like, a cell phone built into a special box."

"Just to fool you?" Cynthia asked sarcastically. "Come on."

"Okay, okay. You've got a radio that talks. You've got a guy that fixes holes and a guy that walks through walls. What else?"

Wiping her hands on her apron, she said, "No. You first."

"Well, at least tell me what it is about *you*. You read minds, or you're a thousand years old or something, right? What is it?"

"Nothing so exciting. As far as I can tell, I'm depressingly normal — except that I attract people who aren't. Nobody has walked into this house uninvited in a long time who wasn't some kind of a case. That's how I knew there had to be something odd about you. So tell. What is it?"

He swallowed with an effort. "I — I control people."

A cold lump congealed in her stomach, and her scalp prickled. She looked at him silently, measuring him. This one could be dangerous.

"I don't do it very often. I try not to."

"Why try not to?"

"Because I start to like it. It feels good. Like a drug. So I try not to. It's been four months."

"When you say you control people, what do you mean?"

"I control them, that's all. I give them orders, in my head, in a certain way, and they do whatever I say. They don't have any choice."

"Show me," Cynthia said impulsively. "Make me do something."

He shook his head stiffly, savagely. "I don't dare. Weren't you listening? I might — I'd start to like it. I'd do it more and more. I wouldn't be able to stop. I think — sometimes I think I'm God. I can do anything. So far I've only used it on people, but what if people weren't enough anymore? What if I could make the Moon fly away, or spell out words by moving the stars around? I don't want to find out."

✞ IV ✞

There were seven of them around the table (eight counting the radio): Mrs. Simpston in her shiny black dress smiling and nodding, Toby chewing slender fingertips and darting dark looks this way and that, Mr. Alvarado sitting very still and straight with his hat in his lap, Cynthia, Steven, and two people Steven hadn't encountered yet. Debby Weibel was a solemn, fidgety girl of nine or ten who looked like she wanted to kick somebody, Frank Reeves an unremarkable middle-aged man who sauntered in through the door without bothering to open it. "Okay," Cynthia said without preamble. "Here's the situation. We've got no money, and no food. Any hot ideas?"

They looked at one another uneasily. "We could help you make some more candles," Frank Reeves suggested. Reeves appeared to be sitting in a chair, and Steven found himself wondering whether this was an act, put on to put the others at ease, or whether Reeves could solidify himself when necessary. Probably the latter. It would be too hard to maintain a sitting posture if you weren't sitting on anything. Unless your body didn't weigh anything, in which case you could sit that way for hours.

"I'm counting on you to help with the candles," Cynthia said. "We'll need the money to pay next month's rent. But business has been slow. Anyway, the street fair isn't until Saturday, and we're out of food *now*. Next idea?"

Debby Weibel started to cry. At the same moment, the room was filled with fat green sparks that swooped and darted like a flock of birds and a huge buzzing groaning noise that rose and fell like a siren while pulsing painfully. "Debby, honey," Cynthia yelled, going over to the girl and squeezing her shoulders, "please try to control yourself. It's okay. Everything will be all right. We'll work it out somehow. Go ahead and cry if you want to, but please try not to make any of the big noises, okay?" Snuffling, Debby nodded. The green sparks faded and winked out, and the horrendous sound dwindled, moment by moment, until it merged with the hum of the refrigerator. Steven realized he had been sitting on the edge of his chair. The sound affected him the way a dentist's drill did.

The kitchen door swung open and the dog floated in, all four paws dangling limply a foot above the floor. The dog, Steven noticed now, was not only large but rather fat. "Come on in, General," Cynthia said. "Join the party. How would you like to hunt some rabbits?"

"Woof," said General. His tongue lolled out.

"I suppose I could apply to the county," Mrs. Simpston ventured. "Not that I like to beg, you understand, but I should like to do my part."

Cynthia shoook her head. "We've been through that, Ursula, remember? If Orlanoi happened to drop by while you were at the welfare office, they'd take you down to the county hospital and give you Thorazine or electroshock. You wouldn't like the county hospital at all."

"I know, dear. It must be so hard on all of you, not being able to see the world as it really is. I can't blame you for getting confused."

"Why can't Mr. Alvarado apply for welfare?" Steven demanded. "He looks like he could cope."

"He's an illegal immigrant," Cynthia explained. "Why don't you apply?"

"No identification. Also, I'm wanted for questioning."

There was some more silence.

"Pardon me for interrupting," the radio said, "but couldn't Mrs. Simpston or Mr. Reeves distract a grocery clerk while the rest of you take things from the shelves and put them in your pockets? I mean, I've never seen the inside of a grocery store, so I wouldn't know, but might that work?"

"I hope we're not reduced to shoplifting," Cynthia said. "For one thing, it's not a long-term solution. Sooner or later we'd get caught."

"You could plant a vegetable garden," the radio suggested.

"Gardens take months to grow, wirehead."

"Oh. I guess I didn't know that."

The little girl started to snuffle. Cynthia patted her shoulder absently.

"Isn't there some sort of charity soup kitchen downtown?" Frank Reeves asked.

"I'd thought of that already. It's five miles each way, and we don't have bus fare. It would take so long to walk back and forth, we'd end up down there living on the street. Anybody ready for that?"

"I have some money," Mr. Alvarado announced quietly. "A little money. Not a lot."

"No, Mr. Alvarado," Cynthia said gently. "What if you need it to get to the hole next time? What if you have to take a plane?"

"I do not like to see my friends in need. I will find a way to get to the hole. I will walk."

"No, Mr. Alvarado. What you're doing is too important."

"Nothing," he said with quiet vehemence, "is more important than helping my friends."

Steven sat forward. "Wait a minute. If he's willing to make a sacrifice like that, what am I doing sitting here on my butt?" An aside to Mrs. Simpston: "Excuse the language, ma'am." To the table at large: "I just got here, but I'd like to stay for a while, if it's all right with you folks. If we've got to have some food, I'll get us some food. You," addressing Frank Reeves, "can you carry stuff without it slipping out of your hands?"

"It takes a little concentration, but I can manage."

"Okay, so you come — and you," nodding at Cynthia. "We're gonna get us some groceries."

※ V ※

I don't think we ought to be doing this, Cynthia told

herself. It felt real bad. Not the stealing — she could live with that. She was worried about what it would do to Steven. He had said he tried not to do it, and she didn't like the spring in his knees or the way he breathed through his teeth. But with all those mouths to feed, what choice did she have?

Steven was buzzing with reckless energy. Pushing the cart down the aisle while Cynthia selected boxes and cans, he felt his stomach twitching. Large, soft things that had been securely moored inside him had come loose and were drifting in the dark, bumping into one another. But could he even do it after all this time? What a mess if they got up to the checkout counter and it didn't work! A fat woman was inspecting an apple, and he focused on her. She put the apple down, picked up an orange, tossed it high in the air, caught it, and set it down among the bananas. Oh, yes. Oh, yes. His whole body tingled. The woman looked around in embarrassment and confusion. Steven winked at her.

"I think that's everything," Cynthia said a couple of minutes later. "Are you sure this is going to work?"

"I'm sure."

They had two heavily laden carts; Frank Reeves was pushing the other one, frowning in concentration at his hands. "How do you shave?" Steven asked.

"It's tricky."

They stood waiting while a disinterested woman ran the groceries across the scanner. Cynthia was squeezing her knuckles. She noticed, pulled her hands apart, and wiped them nervously on her pants. "That comes to two hundred forty-two seventy-seven," the woman said at last.

We've already paid you. Give me the change. Those are the ones, in that slot.

233

Cynthia gasped. The woman was counting out twenty-dollar bills into Steven's hand. He tucked them into a pants pocket.

"Do you folks want help out to your car with this stuff?"

"We can manage," Steven said.

There were too many sacks to carry, so they loaded a cart and Cynthia pushed it while the men carried two sacks each. When they had walked half a block Cynthia said, "That's frightening. You can do that any time you want to?"

"Sure. It's easy. Pretty nifty, huh?" He grinned, pleased with himself.

"But what about the clerk? She'll come up three hundred short at the end of the day. If she doesn't lose her job, she'll have to pay it back."

Steven tried to meet Cynthia's gaze and failed. "You're right," he admitted sourly. "See, I know that. That's the trouble with it. I always end up hurting people."

"Couldn't we have just loaded up the carts and wheeled them out the door without going through the checkout line? I don't want to seem ungrateful, but...."

"That's too complicated. I'd have to control ten or fifteen people at once, to keep them from noticing. I'm not that good. The best I could manage would be to make them all fall down so they couldn't follow us. They'd still call the cops, and the cops would see us on the video surveillance. So it wouldn't work. This way is a lot safer."

"Except that you may have cost that woman her job."

He looked at her coldly. "*We* may have cost that woman her job. You're gonna eat this stuff too, so don't get on your high horse. Anyway, would you rather have used Mr. Alvarado's plane fare?"

She sighed. "I guess not."

They walked along in silence for a while. The tingle had worn off, and Steven was beginning to feel depressed. After what had happened last time, he had promised himself he would never use the power again. It only led to trouble. But hell, he wasn't responsible for the while damn world, was he? If that woman didn't get fired today for losing three hundred bucks, she'd get fired tomorrow for showing up drunk or something. What difference did it make?

The difference, his conscience pointed out, is that you wouldn't be the one making her get drunk. But it's not my fault! I didn't ask to have this power!

To escape this oppressive line of thought, he said to Cynthia, "Tell me about the radio."

"Well, it's a nice old radio. I'm fond of it, even if it doesn't have much to say."

"So it just wandered in, the way I did?"

"Not exactly. We've had maybe two dozen different people staying with us at one time or another. For a while there was this nice old guy — a farm hand from Missouri, he could barely read or write — who did things to machines. He never touched them. All he did was stare at them."

"You mean he could fix things that were broken?"

"It wasn't quite that simple. What things did after he got done with them was never exactly what they'd done before. The trouble was, he couldn't plan it. He never knew ahead of time what would happen. Anyway, somebody had given us an old radio that didn't work, and I asked him if he couldn't see about fixing it up somehow. He was tickled pink when it started to talk — said he'd never gotten anything to do something like that before."

"What happened to him?"

"We had an old car sitting in the driveway, and whenever he got tired of playing checkers with the radio he'd go out and stare at the car. One day he announced that he'd got it running and was going to take it out for a spin. We haven't seen him since. I figure the first time he tried to make a left turn, he took off into the fourth dimension."

❧ VI ❧

"You know, I'm starting to like it here," Steven said. He was sitting at the kitchen table snapping green beans the way she had shown him and throwing them in a pot.

"We like having you," Cynthia said. "You've been a big help."

"I could do a lot more. I could get you a car, and some good furniture, and some nice clothes. Maybe if Debby had a piano and some piano lessons, she'd stop making those damn noises."

"It's sweet of you to think of that, Steven. But we already have everything we really need. I thought you didn't want to use your power unless it was an emergency. You said it did something to you."

"I can handle it," he said. His voice had a surly edge. "I *want* to help. Why won't you let me help? You didn't mind when I got that money last week for Mr. Alvarado."

"Helping Mr. Alvarado is important. But I don't know. Maybe you shouldn't have done that either."

Mr. Alvarado had announced one morning that he must be off within the hour. Cynthia had packed some sandwiches for him, and Steven had slipped out and hit a couple of stores at a nearby shopping center. When he pressed the bills into the old man's hand, Mr. Alvarado said, "Gracias, amigo," and even though the glorious buzz from using the power had already worn off, leaving Steven bleak and gloomy as usual, Mr. Alvarado's "gracias" made him feel good again. But now Cynthia was saying he'd done something wrong? He pushed back the chair and got to his feet.

"Where are you going?"

"Out."

"You aren't going to — do anything to anybody, are you?"

"What if I am? Maybe I need to keep in practice. You don't expect me to stay cooped up in here all day."

"You just said you liked it here. I don't want you to get in any trouble, that's all."

"I can' take care of myself."

But he didn't go out. He knew she was right. Every time he used the power he felt dirty afterward — dirty and defeated. Instead he went upstairs to his room and lay down on the mattress with his fingers laced behind his head and stared at the ceiling. Why did it have to be so complicated? All he wanted was to have that feeling flowing through him like sweet fire, the thrill of being absolutely in command.

Things had been simpler once. There had been other ways to feel good. Playing touch football. Staying up late to watch a meteor shower with his dad, sitting out in the back yard in the dark and the fireflies looping around like crazy little meteors. And the good times with Laurel. Laurel had liked him a lot, and he had been crazy about her. No telling where she was now. Married, probably, with kids. He remembered the silky contours of her body sliding over him, the delicate fragrance of her sheets, the sound of a moan catching in her throat.

Tears stung his eyes. He was alone. Even in a house full of people who ought to understand, he was alone. Cynthia didn't understand, she just wanted to keep him penned up so he wouldn't get into trouble. Besides, she was fifteen years too old for him, and she didn't do anything to make herself sexy. Didn't even shave her legs. The closest he'd get to Laurel in this house was Toby. He hadn't seen Toby since that first day, but he remembered how Toby had reminded him of Laurel. The more he thought about it, the clearer the resemblance became. Drowning in the thought, he rolled to his feet. It couldn't do any harm to get another look, could it?

He climbed the narrow attic stairs and tapped on the door.

"Who's there?" came the husky contralto.

"Steven."

"Go away."

"I wanted to talk to you."

"Talk to somebody else. Talk to the radio."

"You're not being very friendly," he said.

"I can't afford to be friendly."

"It must get lonely, living up here."

A thick silence descended on the other side of the door.

"I got to thinking about that girl," Steven said, leaning his cheek on the wood of the door. "The one you remind me of. You do look like her, just a little. She was real pretty."

"I don't look like her," said the voice. "I don't look anything like her. Now go away. Please."

"Do we have to talk like this? Can't you let me in for a minute? I won't hurt you."

Again, silence. Bitterly, Steven slammed his fist into his palm. Shut out again. They were afraid of him. And he hadn't done anything to deserve it this time, not a thing! Why should he have to put up with this crap? *Come open the door.*

Soft footsteps, and the door swung open. The first glance shocked him — Toby looked nothing at all like Laurel. He brushed past the motionless figure. "I wanted to see where you live," he said. The attic was warm and musty-smelling under the sloping roof. An unmade bed with a brass frame stood against one wall. There were two small curtained windows, one at the front of the house and one at the back.

"Did you make me open the door?" Toby asked.

"What if I did? Is that such a crime? I wanted to see you."

"You've seen me."

"I remembered you looking different."

"I always look different."

"Stand over here where the light's better," Steven said. "Tilt your head a little. That's it. You *do* look like her." Even though he wasn't using the power, Toby seemed to have no will, and obeyed like a mobile mannequin.

"I don't look like her. At least, I didn't. I'll start to before long. The longer you stay, the more I'll look like her. I change."

"Like a chameleon," he said. "So that's why you have to stay up here."

Toby sank into a tattered overstuffed chair by the front window. "When I'm around somebody I start to turn into whoever they love. I can't help it. If I stay around them long enough, I become their ideal lover."

"You mean it's some kind of illusion? They look at

you and think they're seeing somebody else?"

"No, it's a real change. My body molds itself according to whatever is in the other person's mind. Even my sex changes. Around you I'd become a woman. I can feel it happening already. Once it gets started, it happens very fast."

Steven squinted in the washed-out light that sifted in at the window. Already Toby's face hinted at Laurel's. The cheeks and mouth were filling out, and the hair, black a moment before, now glinted with an auburn highlight. "But you're still you. You don't lose your identity or anything."

Toby laughed humorlessly. "What identity? I thought I had an identity once, but it was only a cruel trick. Before I came here I lived with a man named Tom Kittredge. He kept me locked up. He must have known what I was, but he never told me. I thought I was his wife. But then one day he didn't come home, and I started to get scared. After a while I ran out of food, and he still hadn't come, so I climbed out a window.

"When I got out on the street, I started changing. I was sure I was going crazy, because as far as I knew, I was Kitty Kittredge. But when I saw my face reflected in a store window it was *melting*." Toby pressed a hand against cheek and jaw, stretching the skin. "That was a bad time. I don't remember everything that happened. I think I was in a hospital for a while, but then I wasn't. I was just wandering down the street in a daze, and Cynthia found me.

"Once I'd had a chance to sit here by myself for a while, I figured out how it is for me, how I have to live. Maybe understanding that counts as an identity, or anyway a piece of an identity. Do you think so? But I still don't know who I might have been before I was

Kitty Kittredge. I'm not even sure I'm human."

The voice had grown higher and more animated as Toby talked. The nose had shortened and acquired a faint dusting of freckles. Steven's pulse quickened with desire. "Don't do that," Toby said. "I can feel it. It goes through me like a wave. You have to go." But the protest had no force.

"How is it any better living like this—" Steven sat down on the bed and waved a hand at the attic "—than living with a man and thinking you're his wife? You're still a prisoner."

"At least this way I have my own thoughts. That's a precious thing. Maybe it doesn't make any sense to you. You always have your own thoughts, or I guess people do. If I become your friend, the one you're remembering, I'll lose whatever identity I have. The library books Cynthia gets for me, that's a life, it's mine, and it will all go away. I'll start to think I'm her. I'll want to be with you all the time, and make you happy. Making you happy will be the only thing that matters to me. And that's not right."

His groin was throbbing, his erection pressed against his jeans. As he stared, fascinated and aroused, the figure in the overstuffed chair flowed like a lump of wax under a sculptor's caressing fingers, becoming less Toby every moment and more Laurel. Toby's arms were plumper now, and tanned. Her hair was longer and lighter, her eyes set wider in a rounder face.

"Don't. Please don't. Please go away." But it was Laurel pleading with him, not Toby. The shapeless bathrobe fell open, revealing a smooth thigh.

Come over here. Sit beside me. Toby/Laurel obeyed. Tears were streaming from Laurel's gray eyes. He touched Laurel's cheek gently. "Don't be afraid," he said. Erotic excitement and the thrill of control surged in his blood, and it was the finest feeling in the world. "I won't hurt you. It'll feel good, I promise. I know how to make it good for you."

"Oh, please...."

"Laurel. Laurel, baby." He kissed her neck. The perfume was Laurel's. He spread the robe open so it fell around her waist, and they were almost Laurel's breasts. He kissed her mouth, and her lips parted and her tongue darted out, seeking his. He lay back on the bed and drew her over him so the long auburn hair stroked his face, and her face was in shadow. *Unbutton my shirt,* he commanded. But he hardly needed to have bothered. Her fingers were doing it already, and her hips pushed against his. *Now my pants.*

⚇ VII ⚇

"How *could* you?" Cynthia stormed. "After I specifically told you not to go into the attic."

"She did, you know," said the radio.

"I don't have to justify myself." He grabbed a glass from the cabinet and filled it from the tap in the sink, not to have to meet her eyes.

"Do you have any idea how much harm you've done? We've been working for months at strengthening its personality, so it can be around other people and not start changing. And now this! Anybody else, it knows to keep the door locked. There's only one way you could have gotten in."

"You don't know what you're talking about," he said. "She loved it. You should have seen how happy she was. So I'm happy, and she's happy, and what's *your* problem?"

Cynthia sighed in exasperation. "Of course Toby is

happy. The trouble is, it won't say happy. First it will want to move into your room, to be close to you. Then it will start following you around. But every time you're with somebody else, it will get confused and start to change again. We've been through this before, Steven. Last time it was Mrs. Simpston. Toby turned into her Archangel Orlanoi — you know, the one that visits her? She was in heaven having her archangel around all the time, though she did get terribly confused whenever the real Orlanoi showed up. And I'll admit it was interesting for us to see what it is Mrs. Simpston has been having tea with, all these years. Toby became a Radiant Being.

"Until one afternoon when Mrs. Simpston wandered out into the garden and Toby spent an hour in the living room with the dog. When Mrs. Simpston discovered that her Radiant Being now had the muzzle and hindquarters of a Labrador retriever, she had hysterics. She tried to kill General with a fireplace poker. Poor General was so traumatized he hasn't walked a step since.

"So tell me — how are you going to feel when your 'Laurel' takes it into its head to help me out in the kitchen and winds up with a big black beard like my friend David used to have? Not to mention the rest of David's anatomy. What are you going to do then?"

Steven scowled at her. "So what if Mrs. Simpston tried to kill the dog? That's not my fault. I'm just trying to live my life, and I've got as much right as anybody. I don't know why everybody's always blaming me for things."

"Because you create problems, dear heart. That's why. It's what you do, isn't it?"

"I don't see any problem. She can stay in the attic, just like always. If we have to, we can padlock the door from the outside."

"That would be cozy," the radio said. Steven glared at it.

Cynthia spread her fingertips as wide as they would go. "I'm not going to ask you if you think it's fair that we have a being in the house who could give any one of us the complete fulfillment of our erotic fantasies, but *you're* the one who gets to have that being all to yourself. I'm not going to ask that. And I'm not going to ask you why, when you could have your way with anybody in the world, you pick somebody as helpless and vulnerable as Toby instead of somebody who might even be strong enough to deal with it, or at least run away from you afterward. I just want you to think this one over." She leaned forward and spoke with quiet intensity. "You said before that you felt bad about controlling people. But this is worse than controlling. You're completely wiping out another person's life." Her voice rose. "That's not Laurel up there, it's just a projection that came from your mind. You're destroying everything that makes Toby a real person, as little as that might be, and replacing it with some kind of phantom out of your fantasies. Whatever Toby really is, you're killing it. How do you feel about that? How does it feel to be a murderer?"

Go away. Leave me alone.

Cynthia turned on her heel and left the kitchen. Steven slammed his fist into the wall.

"You're certainly causing an uproar around here," the radio said.

He willed it to burst into flames, but nothing happened. "That won't work on me," the radio said. "I'm an inanimate object."

He picked it up, hefted it, and set it down again.

He was still sitting at the kitchen table an hour later, slumped forward with his chin on the heel of his hand, when Mrs. Simpston toddled in. "Oh, there you are, dear. Cynthia asked me if I wouldn't find you. Would it be too much trouble to come out on the front porch and undo whatever it was you did to her? She says she can't come back into the house — and it's nearly dinnertime."

Reaching out with his mind, he found Cynthia Lutz nearby and released her. A minute later, having poured herself a cup of lukewarm coffee with shaky hands, she sat down across from him and looked at him sorrowfully. "We've got a new house rule," she said. "As of right now. You don't do that to anybody who lives here. Not in any way, shape, or form, and not for any reason. Not ever. If you ever do that again, you'll have to leave."

"You can't make me leave if I don't want to," he mumbled.

She touched his wrist. "You've been in situations like this before, haven't you, Steven? Wherever you go, sooner or later this kind of trouble starts."

His throat filled with tears. He nodded, mute.

She said, "I'm sorry. I'm so sorry."

"I only wanted to help with the groceries," he said, choking. "And then I got lonely. You can't blame me for that."

"But once you start, it's hard to stop. Isn't that what you said?"

He nodded, teeth clamped down on his upper lip.

"Steven, listen to me. We want you to live here with us, for as long as you want to. We want to help you learn to control this power, so you can have real friends. We want to be your friends. Do you understand?"

"Yeah, I guess so."

"But you mustn't used your power on your friends.

That's what's hurting you."

"Using it at all is what's hurting me. What difference does it make if it's a friend or a total stranger?"

"Okay, maybe you're right about that. But there's a difference between using it for good and using it to hurt people." Her eyes glowed with a new light. "What if you were a lifeguard at the beach? Nobody could ever drown! You could just sit up there in your tower and if anybody got in trouble you could take over and swim for them and guide them back to shore. Wouldn't that be wonderful?"

"I don't know. What if I decided to drown them instead?"

"You wouldn't do that, would you?"

"I might. Why shouldn't I?" Half to himself, he added, "What's scary is knowing that I *could* drown them if I wanted to. Nobody in the world could stop me."

"That would be awful. But I think you're missing something. The reason you need to learn to use your power wisely isn't to keep from hurting other people, though you *can* hurt us very badly. The reason is to keep from hurting yourself. You're the one I'm worried about. I'd like to see you have a healthy, happy life. And you can do it, I believe that! But unless you learn to control your power, it will destroy you."

"I can take care of myself," he said sullenly. But after glaring at the tabletop for a minute his eyes softened and grew troubled. "I don't know, maybe you're right. I gotta think." He struggled to his feet and left the kitchen, his shoulders slumped.

✄ VIII ✄

For the next two days, wanting to prove how cooperative he was, Steven threw himself into yard work. He swept the roof and gutters, shored up a sagging railing, and hacked at weeds with a rusty hoe. Three dozen times he glanced up at the attic window, but always it was curtained and empty. He knew Cynthia was right, but at the same time he resented her for confronting him. "What does she know?" he muttered. "Hell."

At night he lay on his back, stared at the ceiling, and envisioned scenarios in which he and Laurel ran away from this place to start a new life together. But in every scenario, he had to use the power again and again — to get them money and a place to stay, to keep other minds with other erotic imaginings away from Laurel. And he knew that wouldn't work, because he knew what using the power did to him. The only way to keep Laurel isolated without using the power was to stay here — and as long as he stayed here, he couldn't see her at all. There she was, a few feet overhead, unreachable and untouchable. He shuddered and wept in frustration.

The third morning, as he was dragging the sprinkler around to the front to water the brown patches of grass, Mr. Alvarado came back. The old man shuffled slowly up the sidewalk, like a paper cutout inching forward frame by frame, and turned in at the gate without even looking up at the house. Steven paused, holding the hose. "How did it go?"

Mr. Alvarado ceased his forward progress and considered the question remotely. "The hole — I got it closed. It was bigger than usual. Hard to bring the edges together."

"Cynthia was putting some bread in the oven."

"Ah." An imaginary whiff of baking bread stirred the old man's impassive features. He slid one foot forward, then the other, and resumed his motion in the direction of the house. At the front steps he paused with one hand on the railing, gathering his strength.

Steven dropped the hose and went to him. "Here, let me help you."

"No. Gracias. If I cannot do this myself, it is finished. We are all finished." After deliberating for another moment he hoisted a foot onto the first step.

"Cynthia said what you're doing is important."

"Yes. I close the holes in the world."

"Closing holes — how do you do it?"

The old man's eyes went soft as he looked into inner distances. "It is like wires. Like lightning. The world unravels, and I must knit it up. I seize the strands in my hands, so—" He clutched both hands into fists, suddenly and with surprising strength "—and weave them back together." His torso moved sinuously from side to side, like a snake. "Sometimes they whip this way and that, very fast. I have to grab them and hold them. It tires me."

They had reached the porch. "This power," Steven said. "It just came to you? One day you found you could do it?"

"No. Many years ago, I had a teacher. My teacher found me by the lightning he saw in my hands. I had not yet learned to see it. He taught me. When I was his apprentice there were two others like him in Mexico alone, and others around the world. And it seems to me that the holes were smaller then, but perhaps that is only my memory." He paused in the hallway to hang his hat on the rack. "Now the others are gone. Soon there wil be nobody left to patch the holes."

"Couldn't you teach somebody else?"

"Always, as I travel, I search for one who has the lightning in his fingers." He spread his fingers, palms facing one another from opposite sides of his chest as if he was holding a cat's cradle. "But I find no one."

"Does it have to be somebody like that? Couldn't you teach somebody else?"

"No. Impossible."

"Mr. Alvarado, I don't know what you're saying, about lightning in your fingers, but I've got a kind of power, and maybe it's a little like yours. Maybe we could team up. You could teach me about this lightning stuff, and maybe I could learn it. I might surprise you. But even if it took me a while to learn, I could go along with you when you go somewhere and make sure nobody gives you any trouble."

"I am sorry. I must go to my room now and lie down."

"But Mr. Alvarado, you don't understand. I want to help! I've never done anything in my life but cause trouble, and I want to make a fresh start. I want to do something good for once. If you'll just let me...."

Cynthia appeared in the door to the kitchen, wearing an apron and holding a big blue ceramic bowl under her breast as if it were a baby. "Steven," she said, waving a long wooden spoon at him, "don't annoy Mr. Alvarado."

He glared at her, but then he put his head down. "Sorry, Mr. Alvarado. I only thought maybe I could — never mind."

But the thought ate at him. The old guy needed somebody, that was for sure. Cynthia wouldn't let him near Laurel, and now this. What was he supposed to do around here, with Cynthia giving the orders? Just go for groceries whenever she snapped her fingers, and slave away in the yard, and talk to Mrs. Simpston, who never made any sense, or to the radio, which made sense but had nothing to say. He stomped back out the front door and scowled at the sprinkler, which hadn't been turned on yet, and instead of turning it on went back inside and upstairs to his room.

He had been lying there only a few seconds when the concert started. At first the low rumble pulsed soothingly, like a passing train, but suddenly he was assailed by the screech of metal parts grinding against one another and a prolonged shriek with an uncomfortably human voice. He sat up, grimaced at the wall beyond which was Debby Weibel's room, and shouted, "Shut up!"

Far from abating, the noise erupted. After an avalanche of thumps and crashes, his own voice was thrown back at him distorted and echoing shut-up-shut-up-shut-up. The wall began to waver and shimmer in a moist organic rhythm that made him nauseous. He staggered out into the hall. Here a waterfall of pink globules was oozing sinuously down, accompanied by a dizzying antiphony of invisible mourning doves. He leaned against the wall outside the girl's door to gather his strength. *Stop that.*

The waterfall evaporated and the doves fell silent.

He listened at the top of the stairs, expecting to hear Cynthia coming to point an accusing finger, but the stairwell remained empty. I wasn't supposed to do that, he told himself. Well, what if I did? A guy's entitled to a little peace and quiet, isn't he? Am I gonna let that bitch run my life? Why should I let her?

He went up the attic steps two at a time and pounded

on the door. "Laurel! Laurel, open up!"

There was no response. He knocked again, more gently. "Laurel, it's me. I just want to see you for a minute. That won't hurt anything, will it?"

"Go away," said the muffled voice.

"Laurel—"

"I'm not Laurel. Can't you understand that?"

"But you could be," he said. "Remember how good it was? It could be that good again. Better. Wouldn't you like that?"

Below him the noise surged up again. This time it was a grinding of huge gears that rolled and swelled until the walls rattled. Holding his years, Steven staggered down the narrow stairs, meaning to make the girl eat her fingers, when suddenly Cynthia was below him, eyes flashing, wiping flour on her apron. "What's going on here?" she demanded. "What are you doing?"

"Nothing. I was going to ask her to stop the racket, that's all."

Over the din, Cynthia yelled, "What were you doing in the attic?"

"I wasn't in the attic! Can't you get her to stop?"

"Don't lie to me. You were in the attic."

"I can't stand this any longer." He strode to the girl's door and yanked at the knob, but it was locked. He stood back and kicked. The latch splintered. Debby Weibel was standing in the middle of the room, head back, eyes closed, swaying, hugging herself with thin bare arms.

Stop that. Stop that noise. Silence fell like a thick curtain. Debby faltered, and then crumpled in a heap and lay on the floor, twitching.

Behind him when he turned Cynthia stood, arms folded, eyes leveled at him. "You go," she said. "Right now. Leave this house."

Go back to the kitchen. Bake your bread.

She turned and marched down the stairs.

Oh, yes. Yes. Exulting, he mounted again to the attic. "Laurel, honey. Come on, open up. Don't you know how I've missed you?"

Silence.

"Lau-rel."

Silence.

"I can make you open the door. I'd rather not do that, sugar. I'd rather you do it because you want to. Don't you want to?"

"No! Go away!"

He worked his jaw stiffly. *Open the door.*

The door opened. She was more disheveled than before, and some of the gauntness had returned, a hunted look. He stepped in and closed the door. "Hey, baby. Aren't you glad to see me? Not going to give me a kiss?" He tilted her chin with a forefinger.

"I hate you. You're a monster."

"Oooh, strong language. Well, if I'm a monster, what does that make you?"

"I don't know what I am," Toby/Laurel said.

"Tell me you don't like being with me. Go on."

"I *do* like being with you, Steven. I can't help liking it. That's the trouble. Don't you see? Your strength and my weakness fit together perfectly. That's why you've got to stop. It feeds on itself. I get more and more dependent, and you get more and more cruel."

Shut up.

Laurel/Toby stared at him in mute appeal, the terrified eyes of a fawn caught in a bear trap. He stroked her hair away from her cheeks and held her head immobile, bringing her mouth slowly closer to his own.

Laurel's lips were trembling and wet. "Now, see," he said. "This isn't so bad, is it? You might even start to like it. Mmm?"

✻ IX ✻

"We've got to do something," Cynthia said to the radio.

"Agreed. What do you have in mind?"

"I was hoping maybe you'd have a suggestion. For once." She was leaving nervously through the recipe book. The problem was, she had been ordered to bake bread, and she was running out of ingredients. The flour and eggs and yeast were lined up in neat loaves to the right of the oven, waiting their turn, with a misshapen oblong of Bisquick with onion and dill bringing up the rear. Somewhere in here, she remembered vaguely, there was something about corn starch, sunflower seeds, and zucchini....

"You've already tried asking him to leave," the radio said.

"Right."

"Why not ask him to stay. Flatter him."

"Make him king of the mountain." She considered the idea. Didn't like it much.

"Only until you have a chance to dispose of him," the radio added.

"What if I don't want to be disposed of?" Steven leaned in at the kitchen door with a grin. "You know, that's quite a little piece of action you've got up there. I might be starting to like it here."

He took in a noseful of air. "Smells good. Did we get any strawberry jam, or are you gonna have to go get some?" He fished in the refrigerator. "He-e-ere we go." He set the jar on the table, grabbed an uncut loaf from the already-baked-and-still-warm row on the other counter, pawed through the drawer under the drainboard, and brought out a big sharp knife. Brandishing it with a slightly ironic flourish, he said, "An implement of destruction." He threw himself into a chair and stabbed the loaf of bread. When he had carved out a thick slice, he dug jam from the jar with the blade and smeared it on the bread. Staring into her eyes with a wicked grin, he took a big bite and chewed.

Inside she was squirming with fear, but she met his eyes. "Steven," she said slowly, "we have to talk."

He munched bread.

"Steven, sweetie—"

"Don't you sweetie me. You only want me to back off so you can take charge of this place again. You're scared of me."

"That's right, Steven. We're scared of you."

"You want to run everything. You want to tell me what to do. Isn't that what you want? To tell me to go to my room? You try to tell me I'm *nasty* because I take over a lousy grocery clerk in a lousy supermarket. I'm nasty, huh? I'm not fit to associate with nice people like you. That's what you're thinking, isn't it? Well, I'll show you nasty. *I'll* show you nasty." He hefted the jellied butcher knife. "Here. Catch."

He tossed it to her. She caught it by the hilt.

"That's good. Now dance."

The knife rotated inward toward her belly, and her shoulder and arm vibrated with the double effort of bringing the point closer and pushing it away. She bit her lip and tasted blood. Very slowly she backed away from her own hand, and the hand followed, bringing the smeared and gleaming blade in to press an indentation into the apron. She heard a spastic moan and realized it was coming from her own throat.

"Let her alone!" cried the radio. "Stop it, do you hear? Stop it!"

Steven picked up the radio in both hands and hurled it across the kitchen. It crashed into the wall. But in the moment when he was distracted, Cynthia flung the knife away and plunged toward the door.

He dashed after her. She lurched across the hall and out the front door and across the porch and hit the first step crooked and twisted her ankle and went down hard, banging an elbow and a hip and her head.

He leaned over the porch railing and grinned down at her. *Die, bitch, die. Don't breathe. Forget how to breathe.*

She goggled up at him. Gradually her face turned rosy. Her torso heaved.

Oh, yes. Oh, yes. It was hot wine coursing in his veins.

But in a flash he saw how it would be. This was what he loved, not Laurel. In another moment the image of Laurel would be burned forever out of his brain, and this purpling monstrosity would take its place. He would go back up to the attic and the attic-dweller would have the same staring hideous face, the tongue dripping bloody foam, the eyes popping, and wherever he went in the world the creature with this face would pursue him and call out endearments and reach out to hold him in its cold sticky embrace.

He let go. He let go of her throat and ribs and diaphragm and turned and stumbled back into the house. Behind him came the rasp of air in tortured lungs. From the kitchen he grabbed an unsliced loaf of bread and scrambled upstairs for the duffel bag. Got to get out of here, get out, get out. He looked around the bare room. He had left nothing.

Back down the stairs, he staggered out into the blazing afternoon. Cynthia was lying on the lawn, up on one elbow, coughing. He took the steps two at a time, sprinted past the dry birdbath, and leaped the short fence.

She saw legs flash past, but she was busy sucking in air. When her brain swam into focus, he was already out of sight. Away down the sidewalk the thud of running boots thinned and was gone.

⚜ X ⚜

The next day they held a funeral for the radio. Cynthia had to call about twenty places before she found the right tubes, but when they plugged them in the radio only hummed and got Fresno through a lot of static no matter how much they begged and pleaded with it. So Cynthia dug a hole in the back yard and they buried it. She couldn't think of anything to say at the funeral of a radio, and that made her so damn mad she cried. Mrs. Simpston had picked a bouquet of wild mushrooms, for no reason that anybody could fathom, to put on the grave. Mr. Alvarado clutched his hat before him in both hands, and Frank Reeves put in a wavering appearance. Debby Weibel held Mrs. Simpston's other hand and snuffled. And from the attic window a face looked out.

When Cynthia had tamped down the dirt and put the shovel back in the garage, she looked in the kitchen cabinets to figure out how much food they had left. They were going to eat a lot of bread for the next few days, that was for sure. She made a list and planned some meals. It came to about a week, depending on how many meals Frank Reeves did or didn't show up for. After that, they would be back where they started.

She looked over at the empty spot on the table where there wasn't any radio. "Got any hot ideas?" she asked. The empty spot didn't say anything. After a while she said softly, "Thanks for saving my life."

The empty spot didn't say anything to that either.

From Many, One

[Advisory: Disturbing content.]

AT THREE THAT AFTERNOON I woke from a hazy dream of creeping vines that squirmed like blood-red snakes. Atavan the one-eyed dwarf was shaking me urgently. "Downstairs, Sally-bitch. Special delivery."

I groaned. I knew what that meant. It would be messy. No sense showering until afterward.

At 3:15 I was strapped in the chair and Lugo was tearing my tongue out with a clamp. Lugo doesn't care if he's rough, he just gets the job done. Lugo and Rensie always strapped me in. They told me it was because I squirmed too much, but I think they just enjoyed it, watching a woman strain against the straps.

Blood all down my front, making sticky on my boobs. That's what happens when they tear out your tongue. Rensie held my chin while Lugo extracted the new tongue from the jar and lowered it into my mouth. He got it seated in position and flooded my mouth with tissue sealant. The sealant tastes truly awful, and you don't want to swallow any if you can help it. It can cauterize your small intestine, and then they have to tear it out and put in a new one. I've had that done a couple of times. Also new boobs and cunt when a customer got too crude with his teeth or a skewer from the buffet table, a new face whenever Rensie got tired of looking at the old one, plus fingers, a leg, whatever. Having your face ripped off is no fun, but the intestines are the worst.

They rewired my brain a long time ago. Instead of traumatizing me, the pain makes me yearn to integrate the new tissue and get comfortable in it. I don't know who I am, anymore. Maybe there's none of the original me left. All I have is memories, and who knows? Maybe they've replaced a few of those too.

Rensie held up a porcelain bowl beside the chair. "Lean sideways and spit." He smacked the back of my head with his open palm, as if that was going to help. I spit blood, and drooled, and spit more blood. Rensie is a pudgy man with a smooth face and wispy snow-white eyebrows. He looks like your favorite uncle who gives you candy. I guess in a sense that's what he is. Or was. What's present and what's past in people's personal history has gotten a little confusing lately.

I lay back in the chair for a few minutes while the sealant did its work. The new tongue felt thick and puffy, and my jaw ached from having it pried so wide. "Who's the lucky guy?" I said. At least, that's what I tried to say. It came out, "Oo-uhh uhh-eh ai?"

"Captain Smith," Rensie said. He was mopping up the spatters. "The ship is docking right now. He should be itching for a little bitch by suppertime. You know the drill."

He didn't have to spell it out. Smith was one of my regulars. Smith ran a big freighter up and down the coast from Seattle. With the border between Oregon and California sealed up tight, men like Smith, who pass legally from one zone to the other, have a lot of leverage. And whoever was loading my tongue wanted leverage over Smith. By midnight the smart viruses I was going to squirt into his mucus membranes would be invading his brain, making him do things he might not otherwise have done. Maybe he would forget to list a passenger on the manifest, and a spy would slip quietly over the side when the freighter docked in Seattle. Maybe this trip he was going to dump something nasty at sea and not remember afterward that he'd done it. I neither knew nor cared. My job was simple: Make him happy with my nice new tongue, then wash out my mouth with neutralizer and mind my own business. Or rather, Rensie's business. Rensie owned me. I had no business of my own.

Who owned Rensie, you ask? Technically — that is, legally — nobody did. But when he jumped, you could bet it was the Mariposa family that had jabbed the electrodes into his scrotum and pressed the button. Rensie was a sort of second cousin twice removed of the Mariposas, and Lugo was a lieutenant in their security apparatus. The new faces and boobs and tongues came straight from a Mariposa organ farm. Always the best for us girls.

Captain Smith rolled in around nine that night. He'd already had a few pops, and the tiny red veins in his cheeks were throbbing. He was a big, raw-knuckled man, and usually smelled of mackerel and machine oil. I always called him "Hayward." I wasn't supposed to know his last name, or what he did. Not that it would have mattered to an ordinary bitch. "Hey, Hay," I said, wrapping my arm through his. "Are we gonna have a little fun tonight, or what?"

He winked at me. "I've got somethin' special for you, Sally-bitch."

"Oooh!" I wriggled. "Can I have a peek?"

"Wait 'til we get upstairs."

By the time we got upstairs I had pretty much forgotten about him saying he had something special. I mean, was he gonna give me a pearl necklace? Not likely. I let him paw me while I got his pants down, and then he laid back on the bed and I did him. Then he wanted to do me, which — I don't know. I guess I was just in the mood, but there may have been more to it than that. He may have prepped me with a spritz of something. I'm hardly ever horny, even when I haven't had my tongue yanked out that same afternoon, but by the time he finished, I was as wrung out as an old dishrag.

So I was lying there, kind of on my side, my heart slowing, when he chuckled and said, "Now it's your turn, Sally-bitch. No, don't look. It's a surprise." I heard a tiny zip noise, like a plastic bag opening. I must have turned my head when I heard it, and like I said, he'd had a few, so he was clumsy. This cold wet piece of glop hit my cheek and oozed down my face onto the sheet.

The glop was green and glistening, and it didn't just lie there, it was rippling and writhing as if it was alive, which it was, more or less. Some of its ancestors had been slugs.

He grunted and leaned down on the side of my neck with his forearm. His leg was up over my torso, and I had one arm trapped underneath me. I started bucking to try to get out from under him, and he leaned down harder. "Don't make me kill you," he said. "This won't hurt a bit." He scooped up the green slug thing with his free hand, and this time he didn't miss. It landed on my ear, cold and wet and still moving.

I could feel it start to burrow in. It was tunneling into my head.

It worked fast. In ten or fifteen seconds I had gone from screaming (normal in Rensie's establishment — no cause for alarm) to gurgling and cooing and strangely numb. I didn't feel too different, but I did feel a little disconnected from myself, as if the various body parts that had been grafted onto and into me over the years had started to come awake and have ideas of their own.

Captain Smith waited another minute or two before he let me up. "See, I told you it wouldn't hurt."

"What was that?" I didn't mean, what was it? I knew it was an earworm. I meant, what kind of earworm was it? What was it going to do to me?

"Somethin' special."

Those two words exploded in my mind like a bell, a bell that rang and rang and never got any quieter. The words were the trigger. The earworm had poured all through my brain, and when it heard those words it activated. Rensie didn't own me anymore. Somebody else — or something else — did.

Captain Smith sat back on the bed and smiled in a satisfied way. Then a puzzled look crept over his face. He started to raise one hand, as if he wanted to look at his fingers, but before he could get the hand up to his face he turned to dust. It only took a few seconds. His features froze, and thousands of hairline cracks spread across him, and he collapsed in a heap on the bed with a kind of sad sifting sound. Pinkish brown dust slid off the sheets onto the floor. The same trigger that activated me had destructed him. Whoever had sent him was done with him.

I put on a chemise and went downstairs. Rensie was

in his office. He has a home, but I don't think he ever went there. At night he liked to watch the girls on the monitor while he played with himself. When I went in he was ogling a session up on the third floor. I guess he hadn't checked in on my session with the captain, because he looked at me blankly and said, "There's practically a line outside. You on your lunch break?" Lunch break, that was Rensie's idea of a witticism.

I went around to his side of the desk and put my hand on the side of his neck, like I was feeling affectionate or, more likely, was pretending to feel affectionate because I wanted him to do me a favor. When I pulled my hand away, the outer layer of skin and tissue stayed behind, on his neck. He shoved me back and stood up, and I could still feel the skin of his neck where my hand was pressed against it, even though I had fallen back against the wall six feet away. I was in two places at once.

That was where the folks who had jacked the captain to deliver their earworm miscalculated. They must have known Rensie had the passcodes to the outer areas of the Mariposa palace. They couldn't figure out a way to get an earworm onto him directly, so they came up with a brand new two-stage delivery system — give me the earworm and then have me shed flesh on him, flesh containing the instructions that would turn him into an assassin. But they had no idea how often I had been ripped apart and put back together, or how my brain had been tied in knots so I could integrate strange bits of flesh and bone without losing the thread of myself. They must have thought I was an ordinary bitch.

When the disconnected flesh of my hand started to melt into Rensie, he screamed and fell to the floor. His limbs spasmed and foam bubbled from his lips. Poor Rensie. He was only one ordinary man. He had no useful experience in staying integrated through bodily change.

I stood up and wiped the foam from my mouth and chin. Sally-bitch smiled at me. I smiled at me, and I smiled back and winked. I don't think this kind of pure telepathy is supposed to be possible, but I guess maybe it's an emergent property of a complex system. I never knew words like "emergent property" before, but Rensie is educated. There's lots of stuff like that in his brain.

"You'd better get dressed," I said to myself. "We've got work to do."

While I was upstairs wrapping my hand in bandages and throwing on my street outfit, downstairs I had a look through a few of Rensie's private files. No need, as it turned out: My access to his memories was complete.

I came back downstairs zipping up a tight black plastic pantsuit that showed off my figure and left my arms bare to the shoulder. I had put on fresh makeup, and I whistled when I saw me. "I always thought I was one sexy bitch," I said. "But seeing it from over here...."

"Thanks," I said. I laced my fingers through my fingers, kissed me on the cheek, and off we went to the palace.

Using Rensie's memories, I had no trouble passing through the perimeter checkpoint. I drew one of the guards aside and touched him, and in a few seconds there were three of me, one heavily armed and with a DNA print that would get us through the next checkpoint. The other guard got suspicious, so I had to kill him.

By the time we reached the Mariposa family's private suite, there were five of me. Both of my Sally hands were stripped to the bone, and I was so dizzy from loss of blood I had to help me stagger up the stairs.

When we burst into the suite, Dawn Mariposa leaped up from the couch and tried to run. She was a beautiful, refined-looking woman (I still am) with fine blond hair and sculpted Nordic features — not original issue, but the Mariposa clan enjoys the best. I went around both ends of the couch and grabbed her, and while I held her, scratching and flailing, I came forward and rubbed my upper arm along the side of her face. She tried to scream, but the flesh of my arm flowed into her mouth.

Her two darling children became me next. Then we hunted down Eric Mariposa and his brother Paul. Convenient that they were all home, but once I was Dawn I could have phoned Eric and brought him running. Now I'm Eric and Paul too. Sorting it all out in my heads took some work, but like I said, I have a deep yearning to integrate new body parts.

By the time I was finished, I was lying on the floor unconscious, close to dead. So I phoned Lugo. "The Mariposa Suite. You'll be buzzed in. Bring two new arms for Sally-bitch. Plump ones." I listened to him and interrupted. "Dumb question, Lugo. One left and one right."

When Lugo got there, I could tell he was surprised to see me lying on the bloodstained white carpet in such exalted company, but I didn't bother to explain. He got me laid back on an ottoman, yanked off my arms, and installed the new ones while I watched from nine pairs of eyes to make sure he didn't try anything sneaky. I think I may want to make Lugo me too, in case I need emergency repairs. But that will wait until my new arms finish integrating. In the meantime he's locked in a closet, snoring.

I had no personal grudge against the Mariposa dynasty. The earworm was supposed to use Sally-bitch to jack Rensie so he would kill them, and in some sense I was still operating under that imperative. But the imperative had gotten twisted by who I am, by what they made me.

I run California now. I *am* the Mariposas. And thanks to Eric Mariposa's memories and flair for political intrigue, I can guess who sent the earworm down from Oregon. He'll be in for a rude shock in a day or two. In Paul's memories is a report about a new species of fire ant that will colonize your intestines and eat you from the inside, while excreting healing agents that keep you from dying for a long, long time. If I can't think of anything juicier, the fire ants will do the job.

Not that I have anything against the man. He did me a huge favor. But I spent enough time on the bottom to know: Once you make it to the top, you do whatever it takes to make sure you stay there.

Cleaving

THEY PUT HIS WIFE ON the table and strapped her down and slipped the gleaming machine over the very naked surface of her skull. A sourceless hum blossomed, and the thing on the other table, the thing that was not his wife, began to jerk and twitch. He stood it for as long as he could, knowing he had to, but then inside him the spring coiling tighter and tighter snapped. He dashed across the room shouting, and they clawed at him but they were moving slow motion underwater....

ii

It began, as so many things in the world begin (and end), with numbers. Somebody in an office somewhere scanned a psychomath abstract and spotted the stirrings of a trend toward public resentment of Forever Incorporated. Little things — increased drug consumption in key sectors, the frequency of certain types of jokes on the comedy shows — but psychomath correlated them. Nothing so crude as knocking on doors to ask people how they felt. The modern methods were much more reliable.

Equations showing preferred methods of trend

reversal danced across a screen and were sifted for applicability. Budget analysis showed that Forever Incorporated's fabulously successful but high-overhead operation would comfortably accommodate a campaign of thus and such size. An n-dimensional matrix was plotted showing the points at which a change of psychovector would introduce the desired opinion shift. Citizen ident profiles were combed to find individuals who fit the matrix points. Other numbers — the phone and bank account numbers of certain key influencers — served to generate the necessary buzz. That's right, guys and gals, ain't it great, ain't it grand? They're *givin'* it away! You could be a winner the very next time the phone pings. What do you have to do? Not a thing! And what do you get out of it? You get to live forever....

iii

Howard Kusco shifted the grocery basket to his other hand and pressed his thumb to the doorpad. The door slid aside. Quiet steps took him across the threadbare rug to the kitchenette. The apartment was dim, the air stale with its burden of dinners past, human odors, and the off-sweet tang of medicine. Heavy curtains soaked up the encroaching hiss of passing trains and the whine of hovercycles.

When he had put tomorrow night's Quik N Reddy Kelpburgers in the stasis and dropped a Keesh-4-2 in the oven slot, Howard tiptoed to the bedroom door. By the cool cream glow of the phone cube, he saw Helen was sleeping. Her head sagged sideways on the pillow, and her labored breath rattled. The upper bedclothes were tangled from tossing, while those below her waist lay smooth.

Howard lowered himself gently to sit on the other bed and kicked off his shoes, his eyes never leaving the woman's face. It was drawn in lines of pain and blotched from old fevers. A thin strand of hair, blond going gray, straggled across the forehead. Once she had been pretty. She was not pretty now.

She stirred, though her eyes didn't open. "Howard?" she called weakly. "Howard, are you home?"

"Yes, dearest. I'm right here."

"Oh. Goodness, you startled me. Come over here so I can touch you." He sank onto the edge of her bed. Her hands, as nervous as small birds, came plucking at him, then gripped with surprising strength. "I missed you," she said.

"I missed you too." He leaned over and brushed his lips across the dry forehead.

"How was your day at work?"

"As usual," he said, as usual.

"What did you buy for dinner?"

"A quiche."

They sat silently, fingers intertwined, for several minutes. When the oven chimed, Howard padded out to the kitchen in his stocking feet and cut the quiche onto two plates. He poured Helen a glass of white wine, which the doctor said was all right for her, and himself a root beer. He brought her the supper on a bed tray. She had sat up straighter and was attempting, without much success, to make herself and the tangled sheets more presentable. She had pipped on the light so that Howard could see better. He always left it for her to pip on; she needed to feel she was doing something for him, too.

He set the tray over her lap. "Mmm, that smells good." She fumbled for the fork.

"Do you want the tridee on?"

"No, not yet."

When they had eaten he ran the dishes through the vibrasonic. Then he came back into the bedroom, lifted Helen up very carefully, and carried her into the bathroom. He was always amazed at how light she seemed. While she was in the bathroom he went around the apartment picking up odds and ends (there weren't many) so as not to confuse their persnickety old robo-sweeper. Carrying her back to bed, he was struck powerfully by how much he loved this woman. His eyes filled with tears, and he nearly stumbled.

"Are you all right, Howard?"

"Yes, dear. I'm just fine." He lowered her slight body into the bed.

He pipped the tridee and they watched *Exoticon* and part of the new deGracchi hypnoswirl. Helen said she liked the music, but she couldn't really enjoy a hypnoswirl because it was mostly visual. Then Howard put on his pajamas and they went to bed.

iv

The smooth green sides of the tube slid downward as Howard rose toward Level 17. A force field held him in the air, his feet dangling above the chasm.

As he passed Level 5 a familiar figure, broad of shoulder with a big square face and thinning mat of brown-red hair, stepped into space beside him.

"Morning, Clay."

"Mornin', Howard. Hey, you comin' to the game Saturday?" This was a standing joke. Clayton knew Howard always stayed home on weekends. He had even come to dinner a couple of times and regaled Helen

Kusco with stories (probably mendacious) about his exploits in the Andes. These visits had cheered her for days afterward.

"Thanks, Clay. Maybe next time."

"Helen gets along without you all day. C'mon, I'm not taking no for an answer."

They glided up through the hub of radiating corridors of Level 10. "Sure, she could get along for a Saturday. And I'd have a great time. And then there'd be another Saturday, and then a Tuesday night card game. Pretty soon she'd be nothing but a burden I was stuck with, and whenever I was home I'd resent it. She'd sense that. Sooner or later it would kill her."

"Yeah, I guess so. You got guts, Howard."

"Does it take guts to love your wife? Maybe it does."

When they got to the cubicle they shared, the phone was chiming. Howard pipped it. Helen's face formed in the air above the cube.

"Howard, is that you?"

"It's me, dear. Is everything all right?"

"I don't know. I think it's better than all right. I just got a phone call, Howard."

"From Mary Beth?"

"No, no, it was from — oh, what did he say his name was? Gron, that was it, Amberton Gron. He was calling to let me know I've been selected as a recipient — that was how he put it, *selected as a recipient* — in a new program they have. It's — oh, Howard, you won't believe it. I didn't believe it, I made him repeat it twice. They're going to give me a new body. *Give* it to me, Howard, can you believe that? For free!"

"Oh, darling, that's wonderful! It's amazing! There's not some kind of catch? It's not for experiments or something?"

"Howard, you're such a pessimist. It's Forever Incorporated, just like the astronauts and the billionaires, and they want to give me a body! I'll be able to see. I'll be able to walk. We'll be able to take that vacation after all." She choked with happy tears. They had been planning the vacation eleven years before, but canceled it when she fell ill.

Howard found himself crying too, and Clayton was pounding him on the back and whooping, and Ms. Bunshah and Mr. Nakamura heard the commotion and came running, so Helen had to explain it all over again for them.

Howard made it through the day in a daze. He slipped out twelve minutes early (with Mr. Nakamura's okay) to catch the early train.

"I'm home, darling."

"Come sit with me." She held her arms out, and they embraced. "Isn't it wonderful?"

"I hardly know what to think," he said. "It doesn't seem real somehow. It's like a dream."

"A dream come true! Oh, Howard, I'm so happy! They want us to come down on Saturday and make the arrangements. They have to do tests to make sure I'm compatible, and you'll have to pick out a new body for me. It's all so exciting!"

"Have you thought what you want to look like? You could be a long-legged brunette, or a flaming redhead."

"I think I want to look mostly like I did before, only maybe with a turned-up nose and dimples."

"One set of dimples comin' up, ma'am."

The phone chimed. He pipped it. A face he'd never seen before floated up from the cube. "Mr. Kusco? I'm Deed Brenner, from Channel Twelve. How does it feel that your wife is about to turn into a beautiful young woman?"

"Well — great, just great."

"Only great?"

"Terrific, I guess."

"You *guess*?"

"Terrific, then, sure. Terrific!"

"Mrs. Kusco — can I call you Helen? They tell me Forever Incorporated is doing you a little favor."

"A huge big favor!"

"What's the first thing you're gonna do when you can see and walk again?"

"Maybe we'll rent a cottage by the beach for a few days. If Howard can get time off from work, that is."

"Sounds like a wrinkle. Pip the web at nineteen and glom yourself." He winked out.

Helen made Howard get out the red kimono, which she wore for company. After he helped her on with it, he went and dropped the kelpburgers in the oven slot. There were three more brash and breezy calls from reporters before they finished eating.

After supper he pipped up a Forever Incorporated briefing on the tridee and they listened to it together, holding hands. It explained how the Forever machine read the complete electrochemical pattern of the brain, including subconscious memories, emotional patterns, and latent potentials, and then impressed the pattern onto a fresh, empty brain. The new bodies were grown in tanks, with enzymes to speed up their growth and exercise machines to produce real muscles. Doctors monitored the bodies at every step. Growing them was *expensive*.

Forever Incorporated had two types of customers: multiple transfers and individuals. The multiple transfers, informally known as "dupes," were people whose special talents made them worth duping a hundred times or more. The government had strict controls on who could be duped. The individual clients ("That's me," said Helen) were mainly rich people who were getting old, but there were also accident and disease victims who were eligible for the process. The original person the dupes were copied from was left to continue his or her own life, in case more dupes were needed later. The individuals had their old body put painlessly to sleep after the Forever machine verified that the transfer was complete.

The briefing ended with a sampling of the new body styles, faces and torsos in dozens of shapes and shades with fanciful names like "The Samurai" and "The Milk Maid." Helen asked him to describe them to her. There was one, "The Aphrodite," that was blond with a turned-up nose and dimples. Her flawless beauty brought a lump to Howard's throat. It was Helen — not Helen as she had ever been but as, in a brighter and more perfect world, she might have been.

After he had pipped out the light, Howard lay awake for a long time in the dark, staring up at the ceiling, thinking.

v

"I can't do it, Clay." Howard shook his head. "I can't let them do that to her."

"You *what*?"

They were sitting in the Tonk, a booze and smoke pit halfway between the office and the train station. Howard was having a scotch on the rocks, Clayton something tall and blue called a Phobos Phizz. Green and violet mermaids swam through the room, eerily silent, translucent, smiling, undulating seductively in the air. It was a typical neighborhood bar.

"You know what they do to them? They kill them. They put a needle in them and their heart stops. I can't let them do that to her."

"Howard, jeez, it's not killing her. How can it be, if she's still there afterward talking to you?"

"It wouldn't be her. She'd be ashes in an urn. Or in landfill. Something they grew in a tank would be walking around thinking it was her."

"So you're just gonna turn 'em down?"

"I'd like to. But if you saw how *happy* Helen looks...."

"Crelt flakes and toasted smurt. I'm gonna talk straight with you. I don't want to see you throw away the only chance you and your lady got for happiness. You'd do it, too. I saw a science show one time. They said every atom in your body changes every seven years. Who you were seven years ago, that's all mud someplace. Maybe you keep your same teeth, I don't know.

"But you're still the same person you were before, see? So what's the same? Not the atoms, and not the teeth. You can lose all your teeth and still be you. What's the same is the pattern, see? It's the pattern of the way you think and how you feel and who you think you are. That's all you are. That's all any of us is, and it's all Helen is. That's all she'll be after they do what they do, is that same pattern. It's the pattern you love, too. You'll forgive me speaking frankly, but it's not that shriveled-up shell you love. That ain't Helen anyway, and you'd both be better off rid of it and have some fun outta life while you're still young enough. You ask me, that's what I think. You ask her, she'll tell you the same."

"I can't ask her."

"Why not? It's her they're giving the new body to. If

it ain't her business, I don't know whose it is."

"If I ask her, she'll agree with you. She's been cooped up all these years...."

"Know what I think? I think you got cold feet. How many years has it been since you been with a woman?"

"That's not it, Clay."

"And now somebody wants to put you in the sack with some eighteen-year-old hottie, who happens to be your wife, and you think you're not gonna be man enough for her. Yeah, that's it. You better hang onto that old cripple woman. She's not goin' anywhere."

Howard's hands were shaking. "You take that back."

"Aw, I'm sorry. I didn't mean it. I take it back. But you gotta think about these things. Lotta times people do damn fool things for what sounds to them like the best reasons. Then they put 'em under the psych scanner and the holo says, 'I wanna kill Daddy and marry Mommy.' Know what I mean?"

Howard stared at a green and violet mermaid as she glided by. "I guess you're right. It's only, I don't know what to do. I love her, and I want her to be happy more than anything. But how can you be happy when you're dead?"

"I don't know. It still sounds to me like you're talking yourself out of an awfully sweet deal."

"Thanks for the drink, Clay. I've got a train to catch."

"Any time, Howard. Sorry I couldn't be more help."

The bartender gazed after Howard's retreating back. "What's eatin' him?" The bartender was wearing a skindiving suit covered with iridescent green and violet scales. His gloved fingers were webbed.

"He just won the sweepstakes," Clay said.

"Oh. Yeah, right. I shoulda known."

vi

The salesman was dapper and round-faced. A bland, personable, meaningless little smile was permanently affixed between his nose and his chin. He had received instructions from Very High Up that Mr. and Mrs. Kusco were to receive every courtesy. In their drab, worn clothes they looked alien among the prisms of polished glass. A hovercaster floated discreetly nearby to capture their every gasp of delight.

The cases, on pedestals, were cunningly lighted. Each case held a single nude human form, motionless and perfect. The little party strolled slowly, Howard nudging Helen's chair occasionally to guide it. Murmurs of other voices came to them, echoing, drained of meaning, but the other visitors in this mausoleum of the unborn were not nearby. They wandered alone, Howard and Helen and the salesman, in a glass forest of exquisite naked people, a timeless funhouse of the ideal.

"The Aphrodite is right over this way," the salesman murmured. "She's not chosen nearly as often as some of our models." In fact the Aphrodite was very popular indeed, but the sales manual wisely pointed out that clients for individual transfers didn't like to feel they were going to look like dupes. "But the more I look at you the more firmly I'm convinced she's perfect. The similarity is quite striking. I'm sure you'll feel very natural when you've become her. Ah, here we are."

The blond goddess in the case stood with one leg slightly raised, as though she had been caught in a stop-motion tridee while taking a graceful step. Her eyes were closed, her coral lips slightly parted. Her hands were poised, palms forward, just out from her thighs, as though in invitation. Her pubic hair was a curling cloud of ringlets, a tawny nest that diffused so subtly its tendrils seemed to dissolve into smoke.

Howard looked, and not just at the pubic hair, though it was hard to look away. He paced slowly around the case, examining the dimpled back, the shoulder blades, the graceful curve of the neck.

"Well?" Helen demanded. "Well? Tell me."

"She's very lovely." Howard felt a sigh rising in him, and caught it before it surfaced.

"Tell me what you see."

"She's blond. I don't know how." Howard appealed silently to the salesman.

"The Aphrodite was crafted by a team of our most gifted young genetic engineers, and I have to say that in my personal opinion they outdid themselves. She stands 168 centimeters tall and weighs 48 kilograms. She has perfectly formed features, small dimples in her cheeks and chin, blond hair with a natural wave, and blue eyes flecked with lavender. Her skin is pale, but you'll find that hours in the sun will bring out a deep golden tan. She never suffers from sunburn. And like all of our models, she is certified completely free of genetic and structural defects of any kind, however slight."

"She sounds just right. What do you think, Howard? I'll trust you to decide."

"I think you'd like being her. I'm sure you would."

They went back to the salesman's private office, which was paneled in warm wood and had a wide balcony overlooking the forest of glass prisms. When they had gotten Helen comfortable, Howard drew the salesman out onto the balcony. "I have to know," he whispered. "After they do the transfer, is it her? Or is it just a copy?"

The salesman smiled. "That's a very astute question, Mr. Kusco, one that the great religionists of the age have pondered. Is there a soul? Does the soul leap the gap like a spark to dwell in the new body? Many of them feel sure it does.

"You're not the first person who has wondered about this, though usually it's the client himself or herself who asks, rather than a spouse. We at Forever Incorporated are not equipped to answer religious questions. What we offer is not a religious service but a scientific service. Naturally, if you're religious you'll want to consult your preferred spiritual adviser. Are you religious, Mr. Kusco?"

"No."

"That's all right, then. Rather than talking about the soul, we prefer to talk about the essence of the personality. The soul may or may not exist — nobody is even sure how to define the term. But the personality essence is a biochemical and micro-anatomical reality that we can measure. And I assure you, Mr. Kusco, that to the limits of our most advanced testing equipment, the personality essence in the new body after transfer is fine-nines identical to the essence in the donor body prior to transfer. Point nine-nine-nine-nine-nine, Mr. Kusco — five nines. Need I say more?" The salesman smiled.

"No, I guess not."

The salesman laid out a stack of forms for Howard to fill out, including three to take to Helen's doctors. Some of the usual forms were waived because the Kuscos weren't paying for the transfer, but others were substituted whereby Forever Incorporated was authorized to use and/or dramatize Helen Kusco's story in their public education programs. Howard wanted to take the forms home and read them through, but the salesman hinted politely that Howard should be a little more trusting of a company that was being so lavishly charitable, so in the end he signed them. Helen made shaky X's in the right places, and Howard and the salesman signed as witnesses.

"I do have a couple more questions," Howard said.

"Certainly, Mr, Kusco. Ask away."

"Will it be all right for me to come watch the transfer? In the same room, I mean?"

"Oh, Howard." Helen laid her hand on his arm.

The salesman remembered what the person Very High Up had told him about extending every courtesy. "It isn't usual," he said, "and of course there are sterilization protocols. But I'm sure we can arrange it. Was there something else?"

"The Aphrodite. Is she going to get the one out there, the one we saw, or will it be another one like it?"

"I don't—"

"Because I don't think it would be right to give her one everybody has been staring at."

"No, of course not. I understand perfectly. Mrs. Kusco's Aphrodite will be identical to the one you saw in every respect, but I'll make a note in the file that on no account is she to be given the floor model."

"I'm getting tired," Helen said. "Can we go home now?"

The salesman escorted them to the drop tube, smiling all the while.

vii

Helen was tired from all the excitement and went

to bed right after supper. Howard pipped up the library index on the tridee, found the technical article that he wanted, and sat far into the night reading the words that spilled out of the cube.

viii

The morning of the transfer, Howard watched the gray light creep up outside the window. A steady drizzle softened the hard outlines of the next building over. His fingers twisted and untwisted in the corner of the tablecloth. "Can I do it?" he asked himself. "Can I just sit there and let them murder her?"

The silken contours of the Aphrodite beckoned to him. He wrenched his thoughts away, but the vision coiled in his mind like perfume. It would be so easy to do nothing, to let them replace her with — with what? Hikes on the beach, carefree laughter, deeper intimacies.

But just as he couldn't let it happen, he couldn't allow himself to try to stop it. How could he deny her a chance at a new life, after eleven years of blindness, pain, the endless indignities of the sickbed?

Though he had never been religious, he had told the salesman the truth about that, he found himself saying, "'Father, if thou be willing, remove this cup from me; nevertheless, not my will, but thine be done.'" His fingers twisted and untwisted in the tablecloth.

At half past seven he woke her and carried her to the bathroom. By eight (no breakfast; it would disturb the metabolism) she was at the door in her chair, a long unused handbag in her lap, humming a happy tune and bobbing her head from side to side. Howard fought back tears. How could they do this to a woman? To anyone, really, but especially to one so good, so patient, and so helpless?

During the taxi ride his hands were slick with sweat. Helen prattled gaily. It was all he could do not to scream at her, "For God's sake, woman, don't you know what they're planning to do to you?" He pressed his lips together and bit them 'til they bled, then dabbed the blood away with a handkerchief.

A distinguished but faintly perfunctory dignitary greeted them in the enormous opalescent lobby. "You can leave the chair here," he said. "We have a chair of our own."

"That's all right," Howard said tightly. "I'll take her up myself."

"Stepping into a tube with a chair can be tricky. The force fields can oscillate when they merge."

"I'll manage."

They rose slowly past the green tube walls. In the upper lobby, he kissed her tenderly as she was put on a gurney and whisked away. "See you in a little while," she called.

He parked the chair in an alcove near the tubes. "I'll show you to the lounge," the dignitary said.

"They told me I could watch the transfer."

"Oh, but that's quite impossible. I'm sure you understand."

Howard's gut clenched into ice. "They promised me. Isn't there someone you can check with?"

"There's really very little to see. And the technicians mustn't be disturbed. I'm sure you'd be more comfortable in the lounge."

Fighting to keep his voice calm, he said, "Well, maybe I could at least see the machine beforehand."

"You must have seen it in the tridee briefing." The

dignitary's voice was tinged with annoyance.

"I'll only be here this once. I'd like to see it for real."

"Oh, all right. You'll need to stand well back. And don't touch anything."

The transfer room was a riot of cheerful yellows, with the entwined triangular emblem of Forever Incorporated prominently displayed on two of the wall panels. Three technicians bustled around the misshapen bulk of the machine. Tiny lights winked and glittered. The Aphrodite was already in place, a close-fitting metal mesh covering her head. A mask covered her nose and mouth. With a start, he saw that she was already breathing.

"If you've seen all you care to see, I'll show you to the lounge."

Howard's shoulder muscles bunched with suppressed jitters. "How long 'til they do it?"

"Ten or fifteen minutes, I suppose. Right this way." The dignitary held the door open.

As they traversed the hall, Howard looked around for something to hit the dignitary in the back of the head with, but saw nothing he could use. Just as well; he had no idea how hard you'd have to hit a man to knock him out.

There were two other people in the lounge. "Is there a washroom?" Howard said dseperately.

"Just around the corner there."

Around the corner was also a door that led to a side hall that led back to the tubes. Nobody stopped him. Breathing fast and shallow, he opened the hooded robe he had stored under the chair and spread it on the seat. From its folds he removed the opticutter he had bought the day before.

The door to the transfer room was locked!

Fighting down panic, he circled through unfamiliar halls, light on his feet, and found the room's other side. He slipped in the rear door unnoticed and stood back against the yellow wall, making himself as still and small as he could. The room was cold and full of small unfamiliar noises. Time dilated, seconds stretching out forever. His feet were frozen in stone somewhere far away.

At his shoulder the door slid back and an orderly brought Helen past him on a gurney, unconscious, so close he could have touched the fresh nakedness of her scalp. He had never learned why they shaved the donor but not the recipient. Vanity, probably — and to dehumanize the donor. She was lifted onto the table and a broad strap pressed across her. His stomach was moving in a hot buzz now. He swallowed, swallowed again. The metal mesh cap was fitted onto her head.

Technicians consulted their monitors and called out checks and cross-checks. At a word, at a click, a sourceless hum blossomed, and the thing on the other table, the thing that was not his wife, began to jerk and twitch under the inrushing formation of mind.

Howard shrank tighter against the wall and counted. He had practiced the count a hundred times on the clock at home, but now nineteen seconds stretched out in an endless vista. If the machine had been improved since the library reference material was written, nineteen seconds was too long. If the machine ran into a hitch, nineteen seconds was too short. Either way, he wouldn't know. He could only wait.

Eleven. Twelve. Thirteen.

Fourteen.

Fifteen.

ix

Sixteen.

x

Seventeen a green light flashing above the Aphrodite a chime sounding, the other door opening the dignitary pushing through, his eyes blazing, and Howard was in motion shouting NO YOU CAN'T I WON'T LET YOU startled faces turning toward him slowly underwater eyes wide and he was past them, the opticutter slicing at the strap pulling it free someone scrabbling at him from behind he sent one elbow back connecting solidly with something and then he scooped her up a little ragdoll woman and staggerdashing from the room bolting down the hall to the tubes shouts behind him setting her tenderly in the chair and pulling the robe shut the hood over her ugly scalp and sledding into the down tube sinking slowly slowly feet dashing at his face sinking and sledding *out* he steered the chair across the lobby like a bongo racer and more shouting but the taxi was waiting and they got her in and left the chair and tore out of there in one damned big hurry.

xi

She was stuffed with thick drug sleep. He called her regular doctor and then pipped the phone to auto-answer. Outside the window it was still drizzling. He thought about what he was going to tell her, how to say it. He went and peeked in at her. The doctor arrived and looked at him with eyes steeped in doubt, but said she was none the worse and would wake soon. When the doctor was gone he nulled the door. After a while he went and sat on the edge of the bed so he'd be there when she woke.

She stirred.

"Helen?"

"Howard?"

"Just lie still and rest, darling."

"Howard, I can't — I can't — what happened?"

"The transfer didn't work." He took a deep breath. "The doctors told me this happens once in a while. It just didn't take. There's nothing they can do. They asked me to bring you home."

"It didn't—" She sobbed. He put his arm around her and rocked her.

In a high, pain-wracked voice, "Can't they try again?"

"No. I'm sorry."

xii

In a white room with blue curtains, a woman lay on a bed. She was blond and had a turned-up nose and dimples. She stirred on the pillow. A man with a black beard leaned forward. The woman opened her eyes.

"Don't try to talk yet if you don't feel up to it," the bearded man said. "I'm Doctor Barnacker. You're going to be just fine."

"Howard?" the woman said. "Where's Howard?"

"Howard will be here as soon as he can. How do you feel?"

"I don't know. Oh. I can see. I'm seeing. Oh."

xiii

The man on the phone was thin-lipped, his voice brusque. "Our legal department has informed us, Mr. Kusco, that what you did, however shocking, was not illegal. However, you are definitely *persona non grata* on the premises of Forever Incorporated. As per our original agreement, we will take care of Mrs. Kusco — that is, the post-transfer Mrs. Kusco — for a few days, until she achieves sufficient bodily atunement to be released. If you attempt to see her or communicate with her in any way, you will be stopped. You have made your choice, Mr. Kusco, repellent as it may seem to outsiders, and under the circumstances we can hardly do otherwise than insist that you stick by it. I'm sure you understand."

"Yes," Howard said meekly. "I understand."

xiv

"You blew it, Howard," Clay said, shaking his head in disbelief.

"Yeah, I guess I blew it."

"You coulda had that hot little number, the goddess of love, but you had to go and screw it up."

Howard didn't say anything. No point arguing. Clay would never understand.

xv

"Howard, I had the strangest dream last night. I dreamed I was in a room with blue curtains, and a man with a black beard was telling me you couldn't come to see me." Her face, more pale and drawn than ever, turned fretfully on the pillow.

"Hush, darling. It was only a dream."

xvi

She came to see him when they let her out. He had hoped she wouldn't, but he knew she would. The apartment was dim behind the curtains, and smelled of cooking and medicine. Helen was asleep when the door chimed. He closed the bedroom door before he opened the outside door.

She was so beautiful she tore at his soul. Her eyes were uncertain.

"Howard? You look—"

"Older. Yes. She's sleeping. You can't come in." He stepped out onto the landing.

"I had to come. I want to try to understand."

"I couldn't let them kill her, that's all. She didn't deserve that."

"But I'm not dead. It isn't death."

"Not for you, no. That was the other part of it. I had to give you a chance. You deserved a chance."

"Come with me. Howard. I need you." The blond aura radiated, its heat washed through him.

"You don't need me. You can make your own way now. *She* needs me. Please don't ask. I don't want to be tempted."

"Then nothing has changed for you."

"No. Or — no, that's not right. Something has changed. I don't know how to explain it. I had to do something hard, and I had to do it exactly right, and I did it. So I have that. I'll always have that. And maybe what I'm doing now is even harder, but I'm going to keep on doing it. Please don't make it any harder. Please go away."

She turned toward the stairs, but paused. "Howard — thank you. For everything. Thank you." They were both crying, silently, their eyes locked together.

"Good luck," he said. She turned and was gone.

He went back inside. He heard Helen stirring in the other room. "Howard?"

He went to her. "Yes, dear?"

"Who was that out there? I heard voices."

"It was nobody. A lady who got lost on the wrong floor, that's all." He sat on the edge of her bed and took her hand. "How are you feeling?"

"Oh, I'm all right. Are we going to watch tridee tonight?"

They sat together in silence for a long time.

Silver Dancer

DRIFTING SAND HAD buried much of the city. From the sloping faces of dunes broken segments of wall jutted, windows open on both sides to the glaring desert sky. Pillars that no longer held roofs marched along a ruined avenue toward a cracked fountain basin awash in grit. Before the crushed and sagging remains of what might once have been a palace, a massive statue of a noble beast lay fallen on its side, headless.

Lazan stood at the top of a low hill and gazed across acres of desolation. He held his uruma's harness, the creature whuffling softly, and shaded his eyes with his free hand.

"There? You see it?" Bouric pointed.

Far across the city, near the horizon, a spark of light brighter than the sun twinkled and shifted and leaped. Ripples of heat rising from the ruins hid the spark, tossed it playfully, yet always it returned, moving slowly along a distant crest.

"We'll need to get closer," Lazan said.

"You're plannin' to trap it without we get closer? Tell me somethin' I don't know."

"I mean closer to study it. We're not ready to trap it yet." The silver speck drifted along a looping course down the face of a dune and disappeared from view. "Does it always follow the same route?"

"How would I know?" Bouric turned to the head imp, whose name was Ergul, and said, "We make camp down there." A half-buried building had blocked the march of a dune across what might once have been a plaza, leaving a wide flat space.

Ergul jabbered something to his two helpers, who were perched in high-backed saddles on the lead urumas. Lazan and Bouric remounted, and the string of beasts glided into motion. The urumas' undulating six-legged gait made them ideal pack animals in the shifting desert terrain. Lazan had never ridden an uruma until Bouric hired him for this expedition, had barely heard of urumas. Imps he knew about; the study of other races was part of his training. The imps were elves, but smaller, bolder, and more quarrelsome than the woods-elves Lazan had known growing up. Imps were reputed to be fierce fighters, and to have little love for humans. There had been nothing on this trek for them to fight, but Lazan now knew for certain that an imp would spit on you when your back was turned — or even if your back wasn't turned. And turn away contemptuously when you protested.

Fractionally taller than the other imps, Ergul stood nearly shoulder-high to the two men. Four inches of this height was a handsome pair of corkscrew-curled black horns. The imps' skin was deep red, with black spots. They wore knee-length canvas trousers, possibly in a concession to human ideas of modesty, but were otherwise naked in the broiling sun.

The imps pitched tents for the two men in the ruined plaza and stowed the boxes containing Lazan's books and apparatus in his tent. The urumas hunkered down in the narrow strip of shade cast by a building and went to sleep. Tilted paving blocks made the footing treacherous, but Bouric strode about looking satisfied and eager. When Lazan started up the side of the nearest dune empty-handed, Bouric said, "We brought all that crap all this way, and you're not gonna set it up?"

"Where would you suggest I set it up? I've got these." Lazan opened the leather pouch at his waist and held up the far-seeing spectacles. "Until we learn what paths the dancer favors, we'll be able to get close to it only by accident. If it follows no path, we may never get close enough."

"Makin' excuses already." Bouric made a disgusted face. "Wizards."

"I'm going to find a high spot and watch," Lazan said, stifling his impatience. "Possibly for several days. You may as well get comfortable, if you can figure out how."

Lazan had begun to dislike his employer even before they set sail from Cathua. Bouric was loud, profane, impatient, irritable, arrogant, belligerent, disrespectful, manipulative, contentious, deceitful, and, when all else failed, simply disagreeable. His repertoire of invective seemed inexhaustible. But he had money, and he had wanted to hire a wizard. Lazan was a wizard, and he needed money. Thus the deal was struck.

They spent four days at sea (Lazan sick, Bouric surly) and three days in the port of Neyseur, where Bouric managed to alienate the first three imp guides he tried to hire and swore foully and at length about currency exchange rates, foreign food, and the perfidy of imps. Once he had secured the services of Ergul as a guide and purchased a string of urumas, they set out southward across parched, uninviting terrain that gradually merged with utter desert. After a miserable six days on uruma-back, here they were.

Lazan climbed a dune and turned slowly, scanning the horizon. A jagged undulation of bleakness greeted him. The city — or rather, what had once been a city — covered several square miles. A sketchy pattern of gullies and hollows among the dunes hinted where broad avenues must have run.

His prey was not in view.

Bouric had insisted the dancer never left the city, but Bouric might be wrong. Even if he was right, the dancer might wander at whim, never traveling the same path twice. And if it did have a habitual path, it might still be too wary to let them get close. Lazan had searched the literature before they departed, trying to learn what sort of creature he had been hired to trap, but the references were few, scattered, and ambiguous. The city had been called Amabis (or Amanbis, or Amanpes, spellings differed). No two maps put it in quite the same place, but all of the legends agreed: Once a cultural beacon and a cradle of beauty, Amabis had been swallowed up by the desert a very long time ago.

A flicker of light caught his attention. It might be only a shard of glazed pottery baking in the sun, but it seemed to be moving. He donned the far-seeing spectacles.

There it was! His heart beat faster. The silver dancer was gliding, skipping, pirouetting among the parched hummocks, a humanlike figure, slim and graceful, its limbs as smooth and featureless as a mirror. Heat-haze shimmered across it. Its legs moved, but its feet seemed to float above the cracked ground, kicking up no dust.

It passed behind a dune. Lazan realized he had been holding his breath.

An eternal spirit invoked and then abandoned by the wizards of Amabis, one tattered scroll had called it, which will abide unchanged until the end of time. A species of guardian demiurge, another source said; reputed to be beneficent, but impervious to human entreaty, and still active though the city it once guarded is no more. "Though human eyes see only desolation," a third author claimed, "to the silver dancer Amabis is now as it has always been, a perfect city — so perfect that it has withdrawn into a finer place, safe forever from the rude trampling of history." This worthy gave no indication how he had ascertained what, in its perambulation of the ruins, the dancer saw, but he claimed to have visited this place. "The silver dancer," said a fourth authority, more circumspect or more cynical, "was originally an amusement for the citizens of Amabis. It has outlasted both its creators and its audience." Said a fifth, more a prophet than a scholar, "When the dancer ceases to dance, all the world will be as Amabis is today. We owe our prosperity, our very lives to its ceaseless celebration of all that it has witnessed."

Lazan sipped from his water bottle, slipped the spectacles down his nose, and patiently watched the place where, unless the silver dancer changed course, it would reappear.

The next morning he brought a piece of paper up the dune and started sketching a map. The city was large, the task nearly overwhelming. In the afternoon he climbed a different dune and drew another map. The dancer made three circuits of the city that day, not always following the same route but always covering roughly the same ground.

There was one place, Lazan soon found, where the dancer descended what remained of a broad staircase and wove a crooked trail among a low tumble of blackened, broken boulders. It might approach the staircase by a different route and leave the stony maze by a different exit, but it traversed the staircase on every circuit.

At sundown he trudged back to camp, ate as much as he could stomach of the imps' foul cooking, and fell into an exhausted sleep. At dawn the air was cooler. He made sure his water bottle was full and set out to hike to the staircase.

It was a long walk, and the staircase when he reached it proved grander in scale than he had expected. The far-seeing spectacles had made it seem both closer and smaller than it was. The steps were a hundred feet wide, and each was three feet lower than the last. He descended the first dozen steps easily by sitting and swinging his legs down. Looking back up, he was startled at how far he had come, and discouraged by how steep the climb back up would be.

Flanking the steps were weathered stone panels into which figures and designs had been cut. He recognized a few of the symbols from his days as an apprentice, but most were strange to him. A few of the symbols glimmered a deep trickle of bright, pure yellow, as if they had once been filled with gold. He wished he had time to stop and examine them; his fingers itched to pull out a piece of paper and make copies. But he wasn't here to study. He was here to commit an act of almost unimaginable barbarity.

As he moved down the staircase, the monstrous size of the black and broken stones at the bottom became clear. Lazan felt like a morsel dropping into a vast mouth of grinding teeth. The fact that the stones were motionless was not, somehow, reassuring. It was as if they were waiting for him.

He wondered how the silver dancer would react if it saw him on the staircase. Had it noticed their camp? Noticed him as he perched on the dunes mapping its paths through the city? If it had, what sign would it give?

The dancer had left no footprints on the stairs. He had expected none. At the bottom, after dropping off of the last step, he stood among the black stones. They were twelve feet high on average, rough-edged and rough-faced, and set in the sand haphazardly, as if they had been poured down, in some bygone age, out of a giant dice-cup in the sky. The lanes among them were narrow and crooked.

With difficulty Lazan scaled a flat-topped stone. Its surface was so hot he feared it would raise blisters. He sat cross-legged, tilted his broad-brimmed hat to shade the back of his neck, had a sip from his water-bottle, and waited. After a while he dozed.

The dancer was halfway down the staircase before he saw it and jolted awake. It moved not in a straight line, not purposefully, but edging and skipping and looping back and forth as it came. Nearer, its torso swirled with the flat blue of sky and teasing reflections of the symbols carved beside the staircase. Its limbs were longer and leaner than a human's. It swayed, shoulders rolling from side to side, and then gracefully leaped. Its pace as it neared the bottom of the staircase was anything but steady: It skittered to one side with small steps, stopped to spin entirely around, strode back the other way with its arms raised, then extended the arms like the wings of a bird about to take flight as it bent forward to race toward Lazan on tiptoe. It turned a cartwheel and regained its feet without breaking stride.

Reflected sand and sky leaped across its impossibly smooth skin.

As it angled toward the stone lane nearest Lazan, it slowed. Or perhaps he only thought it had slowed because the moment seemed to stretch out. The dancer had no eyes and no mouth, though a raised ridge hinted at a nose. Hollows between brow and cheekbone showed where eyes would be, but the dancer lacked eyes. He thought it must be looking at him, but then, with a shake of its head and a complicated flourish of its arms, it passed beneath the stone where he sat, not quite close enough for him to lean down and touch, and flowed on.

He thought it was the most beautiful thing he had ever seen. Long after it had vanished into the maze of jagged boulders, he sat watching the place where it had gone. The swirling rhythms of its movement filled him.

He had the impression that the dancer had noticed his presence. Noticed, and been glad. Something in the rhythm of its movements hinted at it, as if each leap or gesture was a word in a language he had known in early childhood, and had forgotten.

Getting down the staircase had been easy. Climbing back up, he found, was harder. He cursed Bouric, cursed the desert, cursed the imps, cursed every bad choice he had made in life and every bit of ill luck that had brought him to this pass. The golden designs carved in the flanks of the staircase mocked him. An early, ornate form of the runic syllabary? Possibly. Were the zigzag lines on that panel related to the angular jottings of the Pei'i nomads? Were those broken circles a remnant of astrologers' signs for the nine planets and fifteen constellations of the zodiac? The knowledge that had flowed in the veins of this place had died centuries ago. He gritted his teeth and tried not to care.

Sunset had stained the western sky with copper and bruised plum before he staggered back into camp.

"Wondered if you'd run off," Bouric said laconically. Bouric was wolfing down the imps' foul stew from a metal plate, and talked with his mouth full. "Or was you just sight-seein'? There's nothin' here, you know. No gold, no treasure. First time I was here, we dug for a month, never found nothin'. Place was picked clean a thousand years ago."

"There are other kinds of treasure."

"Well, yeah. That's what we're here for, ain't it?"

Lazan had been thinking about the inscriptions on the staircase, not about the silver dancer. "I may have found our spot," he said.

The next morning he directed the imps to load his apparatus onto one of the urumas.

"What about the cage?" Bouric said.

"Tomorrow the cage," Lazan told him. "First I have to sample the creature's essence."

"I wanna see how you do it."

"It would be better if I weren't disturbed. The procedure requires concentration."

"Who's payin' for this, eh?"

In the end he was glad Bouric had insisted. When the imps got to the head of the staircase and saw that they were supposed to lead the uruma down to the bottom and unpack the apparatus there, they balked. "Here," Ergul said, pointing at the ground. "We put here. You want down there, you carry!" Bouric threatened them with seven kinds of mayhem, and in the end they acceded, though with many a sidelong glance of pure malice. The uruma glided easily down the staircase on its long legs, but the imps had to walk beside it to steady its load, and the steps were nearly as high as the imps were tall. Getting back up would be a worse ordeal for them than it had been for Lazan the day before.

When they jerked the pack straps, the apparatus slid sideways, and Lazan had to dive to catch it before it smashed into the ground. He was sure they had done it on purpose, but he had neither the time nor the patience for another argument. He snapped back the clasps and unfolded the panels with care. Set into the top of a table with folding legs was an array of mirrors, crystals, lenses, brass plates with incised diagrams, weights suspended on pendulums, and fine thread stretched taut between screw-threaded mounting posts. He made delicate adjustments, pulled a small book from his pouch and consulted the columns of numbers, made more adjustments. The long trip had jostled things badly out of alignment.

Bouric fidgeted. "You finished yet? Or are you just doin' all that to impress me?"

"If you're bored, go back to camp. Anyway, I'd suggest you take the imps and the animal and wait somewhere back among the stones, out of sight. Your life essences will disturb the measurements."

Bouric scowled at the wizardly gibberish. "Besides," Lazan added reasonably, "seeing a crowd might alarm it."

"Yeah, all right." Bouric tramped off.

Lazan sipped from the water-bottle. Sweat trickled down his neck. He waited.

The dancer, when it appeared at the top of the staircase, was at first no more than a spinning glitter of misplaced sun. It glided downward, moving to the left and right, coming gradually closer but in no hurry. Hands trembling, he touched, one at a time, the three small brass plates into which were cast the symbols that activated the apparatus.

This time he was sure, again without knowing how he knew, that the dancer welcomed his presence. As it swept past, it almost bowed before pirouetting away.

He switched off the apparatus. A little sphere of gold and ivory at the center smelled faintly of mint. That was reassuring. If it had smelled sour or rotten, the entire expedition would have been for naught. Lazan had been well trained in the magical arts, but no one knew better than a master wizard just how much could go wrong, even with the simplest spell. Capturing the essence of a creature that wasn't human, that might not be a creature at all — not more than a hundred wizards in the world had the art with which to attempt it.

And how many of them would sell their services to a man like Bouric, with such a monstrous goal in view? Lazan thrust the thought away angrily. He had taken the job. Paying off his cartload of debt was only the start. Bouric meant to tour the world, showing off the silver dancer in every city, exhibiting it to kings and princes and selling tickets to gawking crowds. And Lazan would be there at his side, renewing the spells that kept the dancer caged and quiescent. They would both be rich. And if Lazan refused, what good would that do? Bouric would just hire another wizard. Ethical misgivings, ideals — he had had his share when he was an apprentice. But he had shucked them off one by one, like the dried husks of a many-layered fruit left lying too long in the sun. Noble ideals were a fond dream of youth, but only a distant luxury when you had been trampled by a few years of hard living.

With great care, not touching the sphere of gold and ivory with his fingers but elevating it using certain magical gestures, Lazan extracted it from the apparatus and tucked it into the velvet lining of a small carved box.

The imps balked, inevitably, at loading the apparatus onto the uruma and porting it back up the stairs. "Why not just leave it here?" Bouric asked.

"Because it's incredibly expensive," Lazan said.

"Once we got the thing in the cage, what do we care? I'll buy you ten more just like it." They left the apparatus in the minimal shade offered by one of the larger stones, and the imps rode the uruma up the staircase while Bouric and Lazan laboriously climbed. Lazan was pretty sure he heard the imps snickering.

The next morning Lazan assembled the cage. It had survived the trip across the desert broken down into two flat packs, which had been strapped across the back of an uruma. Each pack, seven feet square, held three sides of a cube. The bars were set close together, and augmented by curlicues into which were worked magical symbols of great power. The imps held the sides upright while he fastened them together.

The construction completed, he crept into the cage and installed the sphere of gold and ivory on a little tripod. This was the essence of the spell. Every creature in the world — even including the gods, or so the theory went — had a natural affinity for its own essence. That affinity was what insured every creature's continued identity, kept it from flying apart in an undifferentiated cloud. In Lazan's first apparatus he had captured a bit of the essence of the silver dancer. Only a tiny wisp, less substantial than a hair. The second apparatus, the one in the cage, would magnify that essence a thousandfold. When it was activated, the silver dancer would be drawn to it, would be entirely unable to resist its pull.

The cage itself was the third necessity, and in some ways the most difficult. Constructing it had required days of painstaking magical work. The bars were impervious to any assault Lazan had ever heard of, either physical or magical. If this cage couldn't hold the silver dancer, nothing could.

"We about ready?" Bouric leaned in the door of the cage. His breath smelled rank and bitter.

"Almost." Lazan was on his knees in the cage. The imps were outside, watching. He wondered how he would feel if Bouric slammed the door and left him in here, if the imps used their spears to poke and prod him through the bars while they laughed. He shuddered, and kept working.

"Is it gonna work? It had better work."

"As I told you when you first hired me," Lazan said, "if you want guaranteed results, you need to work with another wizard. And if a wizard guarantees results, you can be sure he's lying."

"Yeah, yeah." Bouric scratched his beard and spat. "Wizards."

Lazan finished settling the sphere in the apparatus and emerged from the cage. The imps led an uruma forward, evidently assuming they were to strap the cage to the uruma's back to transport it across the dunes to the staircase. Lazan told them they had to carry it by hand. The magnifying apparatus was mounted in the cage, and he didn't want it jiggled or bounced.

Ergul shouted, "We not carry! Uruma carry!"

Bouric raised his fist. "If the wizard wants you to carry it, you'll carry it." The discussion grew heated. Ergul renewed an old complaint about low pay, and claimed one of the urumas was sick because the supply of fodder was running low. Bouric waved his arms and shouted, but didn't actually strike the imp, though Lazan could see he wanted to. Eventually the argument burned itself out. Still grumbling to one another in their incomprehensible tongue, the imps picked up the cage and carried it across the dunes.

When the cage was in position near the foot of the staircase, the imps retreated among the black boulders. Even after they had disappeared from view, Lazan could still hear them gurgling to one another. To Bouric he said, "You ought to go with them."

"I wanna watch."

"It has seen me, but it may not have seen you. We don't want to alarm it."

"You said it couldn't resist the spell."

That hadn't been precisely the way Lazan had phrased it. He was a wizard, and always phrased things precisely. But he was weary of the endless bickering. "Stay if you like, then. In fact — would you like to be the one to trap it?"

Bouric scowled at him, as if suspecting a trick.

"I'm sure your sense of timing is good," Lazan went on. "Stand on that side, next to the lever, and stand very still. When it moves into the cage, pull the lever down sharply. That drops the physical gate, and also activates the barrier spell."

They waited. The sun crept across the sky like a lump of molten metal. Lazan couldn't hear the imps anymore. Maybe they had found another route out of the maze of boulders — there must be one, because the dancer never looped back up the staircase after descending — and gone back to camp.

At the top of the staircase, the silver dancer spun into view. It seemed to take forever to drift down the stairs; time had slipped its moorings. The dancer's elaborate, oblique movements and the grace and purity of its body were so beautiful Lazan felt he had been stabbed in the heart.

As the dancer came down the last stair to the level stretch of sand before the boulders, Lazan pressed the touchplate that activated the essence magnifier. It hummed.

The dancer jerked, a sudden, unexpected, jarring movement. It tumbled sideways, righted itself, and scampered toward the cage.

Bouric's arm was on the lever, and Lazan saw the muscles of the man's shoulder bunch. He was going to pull it too soon. Suddenly Lazan hoped he would. To trap such a beautiful thing.... But being outside the cage might be worse for the dancer than being inside. It might batter itself to death on the bars trying to get in, trying to reunite with the filament of its essence caught in the sphere of gold and ivory.

Then the dancer was in the cage. Bouric pulled the lever. The door slid down with a crash.

The dancer's fingers wrapped around the gold sphere. It pulled the sphere free from the apparatus. The apparatus stopped humming.

For a moment the dancer was utterly motionless. Then it started throwing itself at the bars. Faster and faster, a frenzy of motion, a blur of gyrating limbs. The cage lurched from side to side. Both Lazan and Bouric stepped back hurriedly as the cage tumbled on its side and skidded in the sand.

"Stop it!" Bouric cried. "Make it stop! You gotta do something! It's gonna kill itself!"

Lazan knew several calming spells, but his heart was pounding so sharply in his ears he had trouble remembering any of them. The dancer was emitting a sound now, painfully loud, a sound as raw as screaming but far too complex and high-pitched to have come from a human throat. The cage lurched again; it was upside down. Bouric was on his knees, hands pressed against his ears. His mouth was open and moved as if he was shouting, but Lazan could hear only the dancer's impossible keening. Yellow dust boiled up in a cloud around the cage, the sound so loud it stirred the sand to life. The cage jumped and fell back, the dancer within it a silver whirlpool of agitation.

The whole scheme had been a mad mistake, Lazan saw that now. The dancer could never be caged. And how might the world be rocked on its foundations, when a force so potent was wrenched out of its course? As well grab a planet in your fist and toss it at the sun.

He plunged toward the cage, knocking Bouric aside, and threw the lever that held the door. The door sprang open and the dancer spilled out.

Still screaming, if that razor shriek was truly its voice, the dancer ricocheted away, slamming against the nearest of the black boulders, darting up the staircase, down, somersaulting, skidding clumsily, arms flailing, knees flying five directions at once. In a few seconds it had charged up to the top of the staircase and was gone.

The sudden quiet of the desert crackled around them, like pottery breaking in a kiln.

Bouric started swearing. "You stupid miserable worthless hunk of whore filth. You afterbirth-slimed idiot pustule of a—" He went on and on. Lazan didn't listen. He picked up the sphere of gold and ivory where it had fallen in the sand.

Something slammed into him and he was borne to the ground. The something was Bouric. Bouric's hands were at his throat. Bouric's thumbs pressed against his windpipe. Bouric's eyes, glazed with hatred, were inches from Lazan's, and the stink of Bouric's breath was in his nostrils.

He grabbed Bouric's wrists and tried to pry the man's hands apart, but to no effect. He tried to knee Bouric in the groin, but the blow was weak. Bouric only grunted and didn't relax his grip. Dark spots floated before Lazan's eyes.

The raw keening sound swelled again. Lazan thought it was only the sound his ears were making because he was dying, but something smacked into Bouric, tossing him aside like a sack of bones. Bouric rolled over twice and came to rest face-down in the dust. Coughing and choking, Lazan got to his knees. The silver dancer had returned, had struck Bouric as it passed. Now it was spinning away again, still gyrating as madly as before.

Bouric groaned. Lazan looked down at him. A bubble of blood had formed at the corner of Bouric's mouth. Lazan could still feel Bouric's thumbs on his throat, and he was having trouble breathing. Bouric said, "Hurts," and coughed up more blood.

Lazan had left his bag of healing charms back at the tent. "Ergul! Ergul!" He meant to tell Ergul to run get the bag, but his cry was unanswered. He wasn't sure he wanted to heal Bouric, but he knew it would be wrong not to. Somehow, doing what was right seemed more important now than it had a few minutes before.

He left Bouric lying among the boulders, groaning. The man was too heavy; Lazan knew he couldn't carry him back to the camp.

It was a long, weary climb to the top of the staircase, and it took him another half-hour to cross the dunes. When he topped the last ridge and looked down on the camp, he could see something was wrong, but in his befuddled state it took several heartbeats to figure out what it was. His tent and Bouric's were still there, but the urumas were gone. The imps had taken the animals and vanished into the desert.

Lazan stumbled down the hill. The contents of the tents lay scattered across the ground, but evidently the imps had been in a hurry, because not much had been taken. He found the bag of healing charms and a half-full water bottle, which he tied to his belt. It took even longer to make his way back to Bouric. The sun had angled down into the pit of the afternoon; its heat beat down on him like a giant hammer.

Bouric had coughed up a lot of blood, which had already dried to a dark crust on the sand around his head. At a guess, broken ribs had punctured his lung. Lazan fell to his knees beside Bouric and sorted through the bag hurriedly, looking for something that would heal a punctured lung. The amulet of Culapsepnoris, that might work. The white disc of the amulet was almost too bright to look at. Lazan muttered an incantation as he pressed the amulet against Bouric's side.

Only then did he realize Bouric was dead. No heartbeat, no rise and fall of breath. The man's eyes didn't blink. Grains of sand were adhering to the eyeballs.

Lazan sat back on the ground, as out of breath as if he'd run ten miles. No imps, no urumas, and half a bottle of water. There might be an oasis within a day's walk, but without the imps he would never find it. He was as dead as Bouric.

He wondered if the dancer had saved his life intentionally, or by accident. Not that it mattered, now. It would have been a mercy to have been strangled quickly, rather than die of thirst.

He didn't have enough strength left to go back to the tent. He crawled into the skimpy shade of the nearest boulder and leaned back against it. Bouric's corpse lay sprawled in the sun, the open cage tipped on its side not far away.

The sphere of gold and ivory, Lazan saw, had fallen, forgotten, a little way from the cage. He levered himself to his feet, staggered over to the sphere, picked it up, and staggered back into the shade. The sphere seemed to thrum faintly. The filament of the dancer's essence must still be within it.

Cradling the sphere against his gut, he closed his eyes. He might have slept a little. He awoke not refreshed but more muddled than before. A sip of water didn't seem to help. His throat was scratchy and his eyes burned.

He noted idly the texture of the black stone against which his head rested. The surface had looked, up to now, merely pebbled, as if flecks of various dark colors had been ground into it. But now he was close enough to see that the surface was covered with writing. Row upon row of tiny symbols stretched away from him, and up and down the stone's face as far as he could see.

He knew no more what the symbols meant than he had known how to interpret the large ones on the panels beside the staircase. In the way that, in a dream, quite different things can seem to be the same, it came to Lazan that the symbols, small and large, were an elaborate and precise transcription of the movements of the silver dancer. Or perhaps the dancer's movements were a translation of the symbols, from one unknown language to another.

"Once there was a city here," he said aloud. "It was

called Amabis." There didn't seem to be much else to say, so he closed his eyes again.

Dozing, he dreamed that he walked among the broad avenues of the city of Amabis. The air was cool and fragrant. Trees swayed, and golden fruit bobbed heavy among the boughs in an orchard. Spires stood slim and tall and proud, pennants fluttering from their rooftops, and no dunes encroached. The statue of the noble beast in the plaza crouched proudly on its pedestal before the palace, flowers strewn between its paws, and the golden domes of the palace were as bright as a dozen suns.

He dreamed that men and women in festive robes passed him on the street, intent on their own business. Exotic animals in colorful harness paced among them. Somewhere nearby a flute played a limpid melody.

He dreamed that a man greeted him by name, and clapped him on the shoulder. He knew the man was a scholar because of the red tassel on his cap. The man said, "Will you be studying at the university?"

"I can't afford the tuition," Lazan told the man.

The man smiled. "Oh, that has already been paid."

Almost without transition, as dream scenes dissolve into one another, Lazan was in an amphitheater watching a grand spectacle. Or was it a ritual? Hundreds of men and women danced, bright ribbons swirling around them, to the throb of an unseen orchestra. Among them, on a raised dais, a slim silver shape formed and slowly rose. Were the human dancers calling to it? Or were they creating it?

When he woke, he was still sprawled among the black boulders. By the flat angle of the sun, he had slept all night. It was early morning, and his throat was caked with dust. Bouric's body was a dark smudge against the sand, hazy behind a halo of swarming flies.

Beside Lazan, in the lee of the boulder, lay a broad, shallow bowl. He was quite sure it hadn't been there the day before. In the bowl was a single golden fruit. It looked exactly like the fruit he had seen in his dream, the fruit in the orchard in the living city of Amabis.

He picked up the fruit and bit into it. It was delicious. Indescribable. A dozen flavors cascaded across his tongue. The juice quenched his thirst completely.

He wondered whether he was imagining the fruit, whether death's delirium had swept him up. But he felt stronger now — restored, not weaker, and not confused. He stood up and stretched. While he ate the rest of the fruit, he traced the writing on the boulder, first with his eyes and then with a fingertip. What a pity there was no way to translate it! The wisdom of the ages might lie spread out before him, and he could not read it.

But maybe, somewhere in the ruins, there was a key — a plaque inscribed in one of the languages he knew. If he searched, maybe he could find it. Bouric had said there was no treasure here, but Bouric had been looking for the wrong sort of treasure.

Lazan finished the fruit and licked his fingers. His whole body was suffused with well-being. He was sure that he would not need to eat or drink all day.

Tomorrow? Either there would be another fruit tomorrow, or he would die. That made things very simple.

The silver dancer appeared at the top of the staircase and descended, with many a languid slide and joyous sidestep, toward him. When it reached the bottom he bowed and said, "Thank you."

The dancer paused and bowed in return.

"May I learn what is here to be learned?"

The dancer extended a graceful hand, palm up.

"Without this food, this fruit, I'll die. Will you sustain me daily with the gift of it?"

The dancer's head tipped in a slow nod. And then it was dancing again, moving on, always on.

When it had disappeared among the stones, Lazan went back to the camp to get a shovel. First he would bury Bouric. Then he would set out to explore the ruins. One day, perhaps, inscribed on one of the stones, he would find the wisdom that would open a doorway back into the city of his dream.

Or devote his life to searching. That would be all right too.

Into the Gulf

EVEN IN COLOMBIA everybody had cell phones, and at the dock where the sloop tied up there were videocams mounted up on the corners of the old shed buildings, and who knew whether the cameras were working but they probably were, and it made Jake very sad and a little nervous. There was nowhere left that wasn't overrun with ten kinds of civilization. Sometime when he wasn't looking, and probably it was before he was born, the whole world had gotten way too complicated.

Dex told Jake not to worry about the videocams, because the fat dumb policemen sitting in front of the monitors all day long were paid off by the men moving the product, but all the same Jake felt better when they had the product stowed belowdecks and had eased the sloop back out into the Gulf headed for Florida, because there was nothing out here but endless miles of blue sea, maybe an occasional tanker plowing along in the distance but mainly sun and water and a long rolling gentle swell. Some junk floating here and there, bits of styrofoam or an oil slick, but there were fish too, the water so clear you could see them gliding along down there. Jake liked leaning out over the side while he smoked a cigarette and seeing if he could spot any fish. Up in the sky were probably satellites that could read the label on his cigarette pack, but you could pretend they weren't there, it hardly mattered out here so far from anything, so he was feeling all right as the sloop angled north, the warm salty breeze riffling his hair, and when they reached Florida and unloaded the product he would feel even better, he would have enough cash in his jeans not to have to worry about anything for a while. Maybe hook up with a girl.

It was Dex's boat. Or, technically, Dex had borrowed it from a guy without telling the guy, but the guy was rich and never used the boat, he only paid Dex to take care of it. Dex knew boats and he knew sailing, and so did Jake, because after Jake dropped out of high school he tried working in the fishing fleet out of Seattle for a couple of years, until he got bored.

Knowing boats was why Dex recruited him to make this trip. Dex had brought along his girlfriend too, Libby, and she knew how to fold a sheet or keep the lines from getting tangled but she was a hard case. Jake didn't like her at all. Libby was skinny except for the big tits, and her long tanned face had lines etched in it from frowning, and whenever she had the con she liked to give orders and got pissed off when you ignored her. The other guy making the trip was Scooter, a big quiet blond guy, no more than 21 or 22, a bodybuilder. Scooter had dragon tattoos all across his shoulders, and when he flexed his arms you could practically hear his shoulders creak. Scooter didn't know shit about sailing. Dex had brought him along strictly to show the Colombians some muscle, but the truth was, Scooter was a nice gentle guy, and not very bright. Jake liked Scooter okay. Dex he could take or leave.

The other reason Dex brought Libby along, other than her tits and an extra hand with the rigging, she was supposed to be some kind of witch. Before they made port at Baranquilla she spent hours locked up in the cabin, burning incense and candles and chanting and ringing little bells and various kinds of shit, and when she finally came out she said, "It's cool. The local shamans are down for the deal."

Jake snorted. He couldn't help it. Libby looked murder at him and said, "Stay stupid. See if I care."

Dex pulled Jake aside, digging his thumb pretty hard into Jake's elbow. Dex might look like a bullshit Florida nightclub bandito with that little black mustache and chin whiskers, but Jake had seen Dex cold-cock a guy in a bar fight once, so he knew Dex didn't fool around. "First of all," Dex said, "you don't want to get on her bad side. She'll make your dick shrivel and your nuts fall off."

"Yeah, right."

"Are you listening to me?" Dex leaned into Jake's face. "Second of all, she's on our side. These Colombians, man, the motherfuckers got evil juju you wouldn't believe. How do you think they move all this product all these years, and nobody takes them down? You're from Seattle, there's nothin' up there but white people drivin' Volvos, you think you can cover the action. But I'm telling you, from Guatemala all the way over to Barbados, there is stuff going on down here that goes back way before Columbus. The witch doctors up in the jungle, they run this operation. You and me are no better than gnats on their butt. So be cool, you hear me?"

Jake shrugged. "Yeah, whatever."

"No, man, not *whatever*. You stay cool, we all go

home rich. You blow it mouthing off, it's all over. We're dead meat. You got it?"

Jake said he got it. What he got was that Dex wanted him to take Libby's bullshit witch act seriously because Dex had the hots for Libby and didn't want her to stop putting out. But that was okay with Jake. Dex was doing him a favor cutting him in, and putting up with Libby wasn't that hard, especially with her flashing her melons now and then. So they made the buy, enough cocaine to keep every stoner in Miami wasted for a month, and there was a guy sitting there wearing a necklace made out of teeth and carrying a painted stick with some feathers on top, and the guy didn't say a word but the other Colombians waited until he nodded. Jake figured the necklace could be just a local fashion trend. The painted stick he wasn't so sure about. But he kept his mouth shut, and now they were on their way home, sailing free and clear.

They had rounded the western end of Cuba, bearing west almost close enough to Cancun to see the beachfront hotels rise up out of the haze, and were headed up across the gulf toward Cape Coral, but they were still a hundred miles out. The weather was smiling on them, and there wasn't a speck of land in sight. Dex had the con and Libby was up in the bow sulking about something. Jake was lazing back in a deck chair with his eyes closed, basically snoozing, when Dex said, "We've got company."

Jake stretched and stood up. Dex pointed off at the starboard quarter, and Jake shaded his eyes and looked. At first he couldn't see anything, but then the sloop slid up out of a trough onto the crest of a swell and he saw a white blip off near the horizon. No sail, it was a power boat. Hard to say how big, but when he squinted he could see the spray when its bow cut across the swell. He decided it was big, and moving fast.

"I been watching them the last five minutes," Dex said. "They're closing on us."

"Lot of boats out here," Jake said. He sat back down on the deck chair and stretched out. But he didn't go back to sleep. He was thinking it might be a Coast Guard cutter, and he might end up in prison, doing hard time. He had done ninety days in county lockup once on a reckless driving beef, and was in no hurry to go back. After that his old man tried to get him to join the Army. "Get your head straightened out," was how the old man put it. But the Army was exactly the opposite of what Jake wanted. Taking orders from some goon? No, thanks.

Libby came back down the deck, and Dex pointed at the other boat. "Fire up the radio, would you, hon, in case they hail us." Libby turned on the radio and pressed one side of the headphones against her head. The other boat was closer now. It was definitely big, and it was angling straight at the sloop. All you could see was its bow.

Libby punched buttons and twisted dials on the scanner. "Nothing," she said. "Just chatter. Let me — hold on." She threw down the headphones and headed down into the cabin. They heard her hollering, "Out, out!"

Scooter lumbered up on deck, and the cabin hatch slammed. Scooter said, "What's up?" Dex told him. A worry line creased Scooter's forehead. "You don't think it's somebody wants to hijack us, do you?"

"Hijack what? We're just weekend recreational boaters. We been to Cancun, now we're on our way home. Keep that straight in your head, and try not to act nervous."

Down in the cabin there was a rattling noise, like bones in a cup, and Libby started chanting in some language Jake didn't recognize. The rattling and chanting went on for a minute, and then they heard Libby say, "Shit. Shit!"

The other boat was a lot closer now. They could see three or four people leaning out over the bow rail. The boat looked like a Coast Guard cutter, and its engine had that deep throb, but the paint job was white, not gray. Jake wondered if you could buy an old cutter from the government the way you could buy an old police car. The guys leaning out over the rail weren't wearing uniforms, either.

Libby boiled up out of the hatch. She had a .45 automatic in one hand, which Jake had seen stowed below and knew they had on board, and a semi-auto, some kind of Uzi, which Jake hadn't known about at all. She heaved the Uzi across to Dex, and Dex let go of the wheel to catch the gun but he looked kind of surprised, like, what am I supposed to do with this? Libby went down on one knee, braced the .45 in both hands like a pro, and as the cutter glided up she popped off a couple of rounds at the guys leaning over the rail.

The guys on the cutter weren't ducking for cover. They hooted and grinned and waved like they were at a rock concert. A couple of them ran at the rail with a grappling hook and tossed it, and the line behind the hook snaked out and the hook caught in the sloop's rigging, and someone was hauling the line in so the sloop heeled over, the top of the mast clear over the cutter's rail, and its hull thumped against the cutter's hull. The sloop's deck was six feet lower than the cutter's, so Libby had to raise her arms to keep firing, and by now Dex had got the idea and had flipped the safety off the Uzi and let go with a rattling burst, but mostly all he did was stitch a row of holes in the side of the cutter, which almost hypnotized Jake, watching the little dark holes *sping* into the bulkhead so chips of paint puffed out like white dust.

The guys on the cutter were leaping down onto the sloop's deck now, two of them and then two more, so Dex couldn't fire the Uzi without hitting Libby. They were the scummiest looking guys Jake had ever seen, the whole world had come apart suddenly into little glimpses like separate reflections in pieces of broken glass but he was very aware of how ragged the guys' clothes were, practically falling off of them in flaps, and how one had oozing sores on his arms and another had bleeding gums when he grinned and their skin had kind of a greenish tinge, not the tan you get if you're out in the Caribbean any length of time at all. Libby shot one of them in the gut and he fell back against the rail and tipped over the side between the sloop and the cutter in a flail of arms and legs, and there was a crunching noise when the hulls swung together. Another one had a Taser gun, and he Tased Libby and her back arched and she jumped about a foot in the air and the .45 flew out of her hands in a clean arc, a little piece of black metal tumbling end over end against the sunny blue sky. Dex clubbed a guy with the butt of the Uzi, and the blow hardly seemed to faze the guy, the guy had some kind of big machete and he jabbed and the machete went right into Dex below his rib cage, and the guy was twisting it and Dex's guts were spilling out and Scooter was on the guy trying to rip his arm off, and they could hardly Tase Scooter without Tasing the guy he was hanging onto so about three of them started hitting Scooter in the head with clubs. Jake saw all of this very clearly in slow motion because another guy with a Taser had come up on his blind side and Tased him and the whole world turned this funny purple color and quite distinctly as the purple color got deeper he felt his heart lurch a couple of times in his chest and then stop, no more heartbeat, no more heartbeat, and he sank all the way down into the purple and he was gone.

※ ※

The next thing he knew, he was lying down with a cool wet cloth plastered over his face, and his whole body hurt, a hurt that was like aching and burning and itching all at once, itching clear down in his bones. The inside of his mouth tasted of metal, and his fingers were a wadded mass of tingles.

A voice said, "He's comin' around." It wasn't a voice Jake recognized. It was gravelly, and too loud. There was a deep rumble too, behind the voice and around it. Jake decided that was the cutter's engine. He must be on the cutter. He didn't exactly remember what had happened, but he remembered the cutter closing on them and the scummy-looking guys jumping down on the deck, and then he remembered his heart stopping, and that scared him so much his arms and legs spasmed, and he tried to sit up.

A heavy hand on his shoulder pushed him back down. "Don't rush it, cowboy," said a different, softer voice.

"You ever known that stuff to fail?" said gravel-voice.

"Oh, yes," said soft-voice. "It depends on their condition, of course. The ritual is always efficacious when it's performed properly, but if the corpse is too far gone the reanimation can be — quite ghastly to behold."

Gravel-voice emitted a harsh caw that was probably laughter. "Compared to what we got now."

"Well, yes."

A hand removed the cloth from Jake's face, and he blinked his eyes open. He was lying on his back in a narrow, low-ceilinged bunk. Seated beside the bunk and bending forward toward him was a bald man wearing round-lensed, rimless glasses. Another man, standing, hovered behind him.

The bald man said, "Can you understand what I'm saying?" His was the soft, well-modulated voice.

Jake tried to swallow. That didn't work too well — he could feel the burning all the way down his gullet. The second time it went better. He thought about a couple of cutting replies, but settled on, "Yeah."

"Good." The bald man sat back, closed up a black bag that had been lying at his feet, and rose. "He's all yours." He stepped past the other man and went out.

Jake levered himself up on one elbow. "I feel like shit. I never felt this bad in my whole life."

The man said, "Get used to it." He was tall, with greasy black hair that hadn't been cut for a while. He was standing with his arms folded on his chest, looking down at Jake with a sour expression. Jake wasn't sure if he was one of the guys who had boarded the sloop.

"It's almost dinnertime," the man said, "so I'm gonna make this short. Ask questions later, if you got any. I'm Crocker. You can call me 'sir.' Or not, it's all the same to me. But if I tell you to do somethin', you hustle. No back-talk. Got that?"

Jake decided he would kill Crocker the first chance he got. Right now he didn't feel up to it.

"The guy you just saw, that was Dr. Bishop. I'm the guy you gotta be afraid of, and Dr. Bishop is the guy you want to be nice to. Every couple of days, Dr. Bishop'll call you in and give you an injection. You want those injections. You don't want to do anything that would piss off Dr. Bishop. If you do, the rest of us will make sure you regret it."

"Injections."

"Yeah, injections. He's got this magic juice. As long as you get your shots on schedule, you'll be fine for a year or so. If you don't get your shots, you'll start to rot a lot sooner than that." Crocker held out his hands, palms up, as if hefting a pair of canteloupe to judge their weight. "Shots, rot, take your pick. Personally, I'll take the shots. I seen guys rot. You wouldn't care for it."

"I thought — I thought my heart stopped. I thought I died."

"Yeah. You did."

"So this doctor did, like, CPR or something?"

Crocker threw back his head and cawed a laugh. "No. No CPR. You're still dead."

Jake was having trouble putting it together. "You're shitting me, right?"

"You wish I was."

Well, he could remember dying, and this guy Crocker was telling him that's what happened. It sure didn't feel like heaven, though. "Is this hell?"

"I dunno. When you been here a couple of weeks, you tell me. What's your name?" Jake told him. "Well, okay, Jake, I hear the dinner bell, so if you still got questions later, you can ask me, or ask any of the guys. C'mon. Stand up." Jake hadn't heard any bell, but he hadn't been listening. Crocker grabbed his arm and jerked him to his feet. Jake stumbled and fell to his knees, narrowly avoiding slamming his head against the corner of a table. Crocker jerked his arm up again and propelled him out the door.

The deck of the cutter was drenched in sun so bright Jake thought it would burn right in through his eyeballs and scorch his brain. Crocker had let go of his arm and was striding aft, where a tight knot of nine or ten men was pressed around something that was lying on deck. The something that was lying in the forest of legs was moving. Crocker elbowed his way brutally into the group.

Whatever was lying in the forest of legs screamed. It was a raw, full-throated man's scream.

Jake's mouth started watering. Since he woke up he hadn't been able to smell anything except an awful chemical reek. The reek was so powerful it made him want to gag. But now a different smell, a wonderful smell, blossomed. It was coming from the middle of the knot of men. Still unsteady on his feet, he staggered toward them.

The screaming hadn't stopped. The men were moaning and grunting. Their arms reached and groped and stretched inward toward the center. Jake couldn't quite make out what was going on, his eyes ought to have been watering from the bright light but they weren't, they were still as dry as sandpaper, though his mouth was drooling. He tried to press his way into the knot of men but he didn't have the strength, and someone hit him in the face and he went down backwards and sat there for a minute, too stunned to get up but not too stunned to watch.

The thing in the middle of the knot of men, the thing that was writhing on the deck and crying and trying to get away and couldn't, was Scooter. Jake recognized the tats on Scooter's shoulders, just for a second, lost in the forest of legs. The men had knives, little short sharp pocket knives, and they were slicing bloody bits out of Scooter and stuffing the bloody bits into their mouths. There were more of the men now, at least twenty, all of them pressing in, howling and moaning and grunting, and Jake crawled toward them on his hands and knees because he was so hungry, he had never been this hungry in his life, he needed just one bite, just one mouthful of that fresh juicy meat, but he couldn't force his way into the circle, and for sure nobody was going to help him.

By the time the mob frenzy tapered off, all that was left of Scooter was a big messy pile of wet glop and the bones sticking out of it. Most of the meat had been hacked out already. Jake didn't have a knife, and he didn't much feel like asking anyone else if he could borrow theirs. He crawled toward the pile of glop doggedly, knowing he would kill anybody that got in his way. Nobody did. He managed to pull a long bone free by twisting and tugging on it, and gnawed at the meat that was still clinging to it. If there hadn't been any bones he would have licked the blood off of the deck, he was that hungry. The meat was tough, but he was able to tear off some bits with his front teeth. He shut his eyes and chewed. He chewed for a long time, until the meat was still stringy but softer. After he had swallowed a little he started to feel better. Not a lot better, but enough that he noticed. The burning/aching and the sandpaper-all-over and the chemical reek that went all the way up his nostrils into his brain subsided a little. He found a few more bits of meat on another bone, and gnawed them off.

When he sat back and wiped his sticky hands on his pants, not that it did much good, he saw Libby. She was standing close to Dr. Bishop, who had an arm around her waist. There was a long wet smear of blood from one side of her mouth down along her chin and jaw. Scooter's blood, Jake had no doubt. Her eyes were glazed over with a dreamy expression. She didn't have a knife either, and Jake hadn't seen her in the mob, so he figured Dr. Bishop had made sure she got fed. Dr. Bishop got her turned around and led her away without ever taking his arm from around her waist or taking his eyes off her tits.

Crocker squatted down beside Jake. He looked almost friendly, except that when he grinned you could see about half his teeth were gone, the gums black and cracked. "You get a little?" Jake mumbled a reply, and Crocker slapped his shoulder. "That's good. Sometimes it's a while before anything comes along. Got to keep the crew happy." He gestured around at the deck, where the men were sitting or lying, satiated. They looked stoned. All of them were dressed in rags and tatters and had the same sickly green pallor. Three of them had gone back to sit beside Scooter's bones and were quarreling over the remains in slow motion, groping and thrashing like drunken squid.

The sun was going down, sinking into the haze like a blob of peach jelly. It cast a golden pall across the deck, and long shadows crept up the aft bulkhead. Jake thought about Scooter. Sweet, dumb Scooter. All that meat on the bodybuilder. Like a steer. Jake felt bad about wolfing down a few scraps of Scooter, but he didn't feel too bad. The hunger was too primal. Trying to fight the hunger wouldn't have done Scooter any good. He thought about Libby, Dr. Bishop taking her off somewhere to fuck her brains out, if he wasn't into anything more inventive with clamps and shit, which he probably was. On the whole, Jake decided, he was better off than either Scooter or Libby. That wasn't saying much, but it cheered him up a little.

He said, "It's voodoo, right?" His throat felt like ground glass, and he had to pause to cough. "It's voodoo. We're all zombies."

"You got it," Crocker said, and cackled. "Except for Dr. Bishop and the captain and the engineer. Couldn't trust a zombie to run the boat. We're not real dependable."

"Dex told me there was black magic down here. I thought he was bullshitting. So one bunch of Colombian witch doctors is shipping product, and another bunch has a boatload of zombies hijack the product." Jake was thinking, this was about as bad as it could possibly get, but at least he was an outlaw. There was some faint consolation in that.

"Well, almost," Crocker said. "There's just one thing, though. Dr. Bishop, he's not with the Colombians."

"Haitians, then. Panamanians."

"Keep guessin'. No, he's DEA. Drug Enforcement Agency. The feds wants to stop those bad boys smugglin' blow, they have to use the same exact tactics."

Jake felt like somebody had kicked him in the stomach. "This is a DEA boat?"

"Very unofficial. But yeah." Crocker grinned, showing off his hideous teeth and gums. "You're now a full-time employee of the United States Government. There's no pay, no retirement plan, no vacation, no sick leave — but on the bright side, the weather's mostly good, and if you're nice to Dr. Bishop he'll see to it you don't start to rot. Not for a while, anyhow. You want me to show you how to suck the marrow out of bones?"

Dancing Among Ghosts

THE ALMOND SAUCE wasn't thickening properly under the chicken, only scorching on the sides of the pan, and of course she had discovered halfway through mixing the salad dressing that she was completely out of tarragon, and Tony was being no help whatever, which was a disappointment, though not one she had time to dwell on just now, but he came from an old-fashioned Italian family, so Carla guessed she had to make allowances. When she asked him to run down to the store for the tarragon and a couple of other things, he had wandered out of the room without actually saying no, and now he was sitting in the living room banging out the same seven and a half bars of some Fifties rock song over and over on the piano, which belatedly she realized she ought to have had tuned, in case Guy or Dory played, or asked her to play. Tony was making the same thick-fingered mistakes every time, losing the beat, and starting over, meanwhile moaning tunelessly but emphatically, like a walrus flopping around on the floor of a shower stall. Carla wiped her hands on the brand-new apron, reached for the lid of the electric skillet to sniff the zucchini — and jerked her hand back, burned. The lid fell, slid, and bounced clattering to the floor. "Damn!" She sucked vigorously on her finger, then turned on the faucet and ran cold water over it.

The piano and the walrus noises stopped. Tony appeared in the doorway, appraised the situation swiftly, and put on a grin that was more amused than solicitous. He leaned against the door jamb and folded his arms. "Everything under control?"

She grabbed a dish towel and retrieved the lid, which went into the sink for a quick rinse. "I didn't know you played the piano."

"We had one for a couple of years when I was a kid." If he noticed her sharp tone, he ignored it. That was one of the things she liked about him — not only handsome with his dark curly hair and square jaw, but willing to put up with her when she wasn't at her best. "My brother was the one who got the lessons," he went on. "Lot of good it ever did him. You burn yourself?"

"A little."

He took her hand gently, examined and then kissed the red place, and murmured, "*Cara mia.*" Which was really very nice. It almost made up for not going to get the tarragon.

"What time did they say they'd be here?"

Carla glanced at the clock. "Seven. It's only twenty past. Why don't you set the table?"

As he was looking around in vague discomfort at the shuttered mystery of the kitchen cabinets, the downstairs buzzer buzzed. Not bothering to call down to find out who it was, she thumbed the black button, held it down for a couple of seconds, and went back to the kitchen. The cabinets and drawers were still firmly closed, but in the other room the stereo came unobtrusively to life with the first notes of the new

Pat Metheny album. She throttled her annoyance. He *is* trying to be a good host, she chided herself. He's a bachelor, that's all. He's not domesticated yet.

Or maybe all men were like that. What did she know about home life, growing up the way she had? She turned everything on the stove down low, so it would keep for a few minutes, and hung her apron over the back of a bar stool.

When the doorbell rang, she sprang down the hall like a colt, but forced herself to pause in the entry to take a deep breath and survey herself swiftly in the mirror. Makeup in good order, the rest of her much as usual — the straw-colored eyes set wide apart, nose a bit too large, generous mouth, hair cut fashionably short and streaked blond. A sudden stab of insecurity: she should definitely have worn something more conservative than the tight gray leather jeans and bright turquoise sweater. Guy and Dory Rossiter were nearly old enough to be her parents, but she had persuaded herself that a dress would look too obsequious, that they would feel more at home if they thought she felt at home. Now it was obviously the wrong outfit. Too late. She squared her shoulders, smiled, and opened the door.

The solitary figure outside, huddled inside a large dark coat and clutching a wide rectangle of cardboard under one arm, was not Guy and Dory Rossiter. Carla blinked stupidly. A single luminescent green eye peered back at her, set deep in a putty-colored face; the other eye was hidden behind a drooping shock of unwashed black hair.

"Joelle. Hello. I was expecting somebody else." She realized how awful that must sound. "I mean, gee, it's good to see you. It's been — how long has it been? Weeks. Come in, come in."

"I can't stay. I came to drop this off." Joelle Cogburn lifted the cardboard rectangle a few inches, let it fall back to her side.

"You've got to come in, at least for a minute. I never see you anymore. You're always hiding in your studio." Awkward seconds passed; Joelle made no move to enter. Carla realized she was still blocking the doorway. She stepped aside. "You're looking good." A transparent lie. Joelle looked dreadful. Maybe it was that horrible coat. The fabric was clumped and threadbare, and it was several sizes too large for Joelle's emaciated frame. If she had bought it in one of the secondhand shops where she got most of her clothes, it probably smelled, too, sour and musty. "Let me take your coat."

"I can't stay, really." Joelle's gaze slid uneasily. "You're expecting company. You're cooking. Anyhow, I'm in the middle of something. I have to get back." But she allowed Carla to herd her into the living room.

"You know Tony, don't you? You mean you two haven't met yet? Oh, I don't believe it. Well, I must have told you about him. He's—"

"I don't—" Joelle began.

"Tony, this is my friend Joelle. Joelle the painter. We went to college together. I told you about when we went to Paris, didn't I? Joelle is the one I went with. Now Joelle, be nice to Tony. He's special." Carla wrapped an affectionate hand through Tony's arm.

If Tony was nonplussed by Joelle's awful coat, he gave no sign. He extended his hand with perfect aplomb. "It's a pleasure." Joelle tried to raise her right arm, noticed that it was occupied holding the large cardboard rectangle, started to maneuver the rectangle, which was covered with stiff, crinkling brown paper, around to her other side, changed her mind, grunted, turned her back to

Tony in order to set the rectangle with great care on the coffee table, and then, instead of turning back at once, proceeded to shrug, in a series of bony contortions, out of the coat, which Carla snagged before it could touch the floor, and picked the rectangle up again and tucked it after a moment of uncertainty under her left arm, before extending her right hand to be shaken. During this entire ballet, poor Tony stood with his hand out, smiling the indulgent smile of a man who is used to dealing with wayward children and has nothing more important to do. Having permitted him a quick, nervous handshake, Joelle trapped the rectangle against her body again with her left arm and right hand both, as though afraid a gust of wind might tear it from her.

Now where to put the coat, Carla gazed around in muted alarm. Not on the couch. There might be fleas. Roaches, even. At the very least, spots of wet paint. Not in the hall closet. The Rossiters would be here at any moment, and it would be awkward trying to warn Tony not to hang theirs next to it. And certainly not in the kitchen, not with dinner on. She bore it away into the bedroom, where it collapsed reluctantly in a corner on the floor, like a mangy bearskin whose bear has gone on to better things.

How could she explain Joelle to Tony? She certainly didn't want him to get the impression that, well, not street people — Joelle wasn't a bag lady or anything — but people who didn't take proper care of themselves, were in the habit of dropping in on her. That wasn't Tony's style at all. Carla rooted in the top drawer of the bureau and found, beneath the hairpins and eyeliner, the snapshot taken the week before she and Joelle left for Paris. They had gone off after graduation to study art and music and drink red wine with earnest young

Marxists in the cafés on the Left Bank. Carla's Marxist, she remembered, ate quantities of garlic, and Joelle's stole her passport. The whole fiasco lasted less than two months. They had been in the hostel only three days when Carla picked up a newspaper and learned that Nadia Boulanger had died, which made confetti of the elaborate schemes Carla had concocted for getting introduced to her so she could show her the score of the *Nocturne for Orchestra*. Then Joelle's psoriasis flared up, and Carla got a bladder infection, and when an Atlantic storm started tossing the liner around in its teeth like a puppy with a favorite rag, they were both miserably seasick all the way home. But the girls in the photo didn't know that yet. One blonde and one dark, they were as alike as sisters, arms draped across each other's shoulders, grinning at the camera. Neither of them, when Carla looked closer, looked like anybody she knew. Or like anybody Tony would especially want to know. Feeling obscurely sad, she pitched the picture back into the drawer.

Back in the living room, Tony was saying, "Actually, if anything, sales is *more* creative than the so-called creative side of the business. What the artist produces is just a lump of coal. My job is turning coal into diamonds." He fingered a cuff link.

Joelle, in a paint-spattered sweatshirt and baggy trousers, was standing with one fist parked on her bony hip, head cocked sideways. Carla knew the pose. Expecting to see the disgusted sneer that would mean Joelle had decided Tony was a jerk, Carla stepped to Tony's side to protect him from Joelle's scorn, but then she saw that Joelle was barely listening. The iridescent green eyes were staring vacantly at some inner vista.

Carla leaned against Tony and walked her fingers

affectionately up his back. "Actually," she told Joelle, "it's a real coincidence, your dropping by tonight. The people that are coming, Guy Rossiter and his wife, Guy is in charge of the d'Arle account. He's the one who will give the approval for your work. If he likes it, he might commission a whole series."

"I don't know if this is such a good idea," Joelle said. "I mean, I need the money. I don't want to sound ungrateful. But it didn't come out the way I think you want. It started going off in a new direction."

The downstairs buzzer buzzed. "That'll be them," Carla said. "Could you get it, hon?" Tony headed for the door. To Joelle Carla said, "You did it the way I explained, didn't you? The woman rushing down the long hall? And her gown and everything?"

"That part's all right. But I wasn't sure where she was going, or why. I needed to find out. I kept asking her, 'Who are you?' And then finally she told me, and I couldn't just ignore what she said, could I? It's hard, getting it all the way it's supposed to be." She trailed off into silence.

"Joelle, you're beating yourself up again. We've had this conversation before."

"Yes, Mommy." Joelle wouldn't meet Carla's eyes.

"I'm not your mommy, but somebody's got to talk some sense into you. You're incredibly talented, Joelle, you know that. But you always assume the worst. You assume people are going to despise your work. It's like you're walking around with a big sign on that says, 'Spit on me, I'm no good.' Is it any wonder people reject you? You don't give them a chance to do anything else. Honestly, how are you ever going to be successful the way you deserve to be, if you always let your feelings get in the way?"

Joelle looked up at her. For a moment something golden danced in Joelle's eyes, so like flame that Carla thought, *Oh, Tony lit a fire in the fireplace, how nice* — and actually turned to admire the burning logs before she remembered the apartment didn't have a fireplace. But all Joelle said was, "You're going to be mad at me."

"Don't be an idiot. I *will* get mad if you don't start showing some self-confidence."

But Joelle wouldn't budge. "I *am* confident. I'm absolutely sure you're going to be mad at me."

The doorbell rang. Carla touched Joelle's arm and said in a lower voice, "Are you doing okay? You don't look well."

"I'm okay," Joelle blurted. "I'm a little behind on the rent, is all."

"I thought Richard was helping with the rent."

Joelle's mouth went wooden. "I don't want to talk about Richard."

"I don't want to pry, but — are you eating? Have you got enough money for food? When was the last time you ate?"

Joelle sank down on the edge of the couch and rubbed her knuckles stiffly. "I'm doing okay."

Into the living room sailed Guy and Dory Rossiter, plump and glittering, moving like sleek ships in a calm sea. Carla performed introductions. "Joelle didn't even know you were going to be here tonight," she finished. "She just came by to drop off her proposal for the d'Arle account, and I insisted that she stay at least long enough to meet you."

"Perhaps she should stay for dinner," Guy murmured agreeably, "so we can get better acquainted."

Which put Carla in an impossible bind. Joelle certainly needed a good meal, to say nothing of the value of getting her name and face firmly planted in Guy Rossiter's notoriously slippery mind. As simple a thing as an evening of sociable conversation might do her a world of good. And sending her off into the cold would be unthinkably cruel. On the other hand, she certainly wasn't dressed for dinner, and her abrasively turbulent moods could easily turn the party into a disaster. The occasion was important to Carla — not only her first evening of domestic entertaining with Tony as a couple, but her first chance to socialize with one of the agency vice-presidents on something like an equal footing. Joelle would have been an intrusion, a disruption, even if she hadn't looked so disreputable.

All this flashed by in an instant. Carla smiled. "I don't see why not." If Guy was going to issue the invitation, though, at least let him make an informed decision. Carla gestured at the coffee table. "She was just going to show us her art for the layout. We haven't even seen it yet." They all looked down at the brown rectangle. "Well, go ahead," Carla said to Joelle. "Unwrap it."

"I don't think this is such a good idea." Joelle twisted her fingers around one another miserably. "I think I should just go. Where did you put my coat?"

Carla was getting irritated. Here she was, trying to do Joelle a favor, and Joelle was too obtuse even to cooperate. Not only that, but what would Guy think the next time Carla recommended a freelancer, if this one never even got out of the starting gate? "Joelle's always shy about having people see a new painting," Carla explained. Which was true, as far as it went. "She has a big bedsheet rigged up in her studio, like a stage curtain on a curtain rod over the easel, so when you visit you can't see what she's working on unless it's finished."

"I can feel it afterward," Joelle said in a sepulchral

monotone. "Their eyes leave smears, and I can't ever get them out." If the sheet was raised when you came into the studio, Carla knew, it meant the painting was finished. You could look at it all you wanted, say whatever you liked. Joelle accepted praise and criticism alike with a bored expression, nodding abstractedly, often changing the subject without acknowledging the comment. Once a painting was done, it was a child abandoned by its mother; Joelle seemed to want nothing further to do with it. Yet here she was, fingering a corner of the brown paper and nibbling at her lip. Carla had never seen her display this kind of diffidence.

"My dear," Dory Rossiter gushed, "artists are so sensitive. I adore art. You must show us what you've done. We insist."

"Okay, I guess. If you say so." Joelle held the carboard out crookedly in front of her. "But don't say I didn't warn you." The paper crackled as she lifted it.

They pressed forward. Standing on tiptoe so she could peer around Tony's shoulder, Carla was at the wrong angle to take in details. At first glance, the gouache looked to be exactly what she had told Joelle the d'Arle perfume campaign called for — a young woman from the pages of a Gothic romance novel, fleeing (from some unnamed terror? toward the muscular arms of a young cavalry lieutenant?) down an endless hallway of brooding arches, her full skirt trailing behind her on the flagstone floor. The rich browns and floral highlights were perfect. Carla felt a moment of relief. Joelle had captured just the right mood to sell a perfume that, while not expensive, was meant to seem both romantic and elegant.

Dory Rossiter drew in her breath sharply, and Tony made a strangled sound. Carla wedged herself between Tony and Guy for a better look, and her warm glow drained into cold shock. The central figure in the painting, while wearing the right costume, fell somewhat short of a Gothic heroine's physical perfection. Her arms were slim, yes, and gracefully extended in poetic agitation. Her snow-white breast all but visibly heaved. But her face was not lovely, not delicate, not alluring. The face was a bestial distortion, the jaw jutting forward to reveal vulpine lower teeth, the thick-boned hairy brow plainly modeled on a gorilla's. And from the walls around the woman, an elaborate frieze of imps and gargoyles leered menacingly down, demonic eyes glowing coal-red, their naked limbs pornographically intertwined.

Guy cleared his throat delicately. "It's really remarkable," he said. "I don't know that I've ever seen anything quite like it." He leaned forward to examine the brushwork. "Technically superb, of course...."

Tony came to the rescue. "Guy, can I get you a drink? Dory, anything for you?"

Carla clamped her hand on Joelle's elbow. "If you'll excuse us for a minute?" She propelled Joelle in the direction of the bedroom. Over her shoulder she called, "Fix me a highball, Tony, would you?" When the bedroom door was safely closed, she glared at Joelle. "How could you?"

Joelle's green eyes glistened with tears. "I tried to warn you. But you wouldn't listen."

"Cover it up, for God's sake. I don't want to look at it. Was this supposed to be some kind of sick joke, or did you seriously expect...?" Carla made a throat noise through clenched teeth. "*Agghh.*"

Joelle's hands trembled as she fumbled the wrapping paper back over the painting. "I did the best I could. I didn't want to, but I thought maybe somehow.... I knew you'd be mad. I knew I shouldn't have wasted the time on it. I should never...." Her body twisted crooked, like a puppet whose strings are tangled.

"Well, for once you were absolutely right." But when Carla saw the hurt-puppy look in Joelle's eyes, her rage drained away suddenly, exposing the rocky bed of shame beneath it. "Oh, shit, Jo. I'm sorry. I'm so sorry. It's all my fault. Can you forgive me? I never should have—"

"No, it's my fault. You were only trying to help. I'm no good, no good to anybody. I shouldn't be allowed to live."

"Come on, Joelle, don't talk like that. It scares me when you talk like that." Carla rubbed Joelle's shoulder lightly, tentatively, wanting to embrace her and afraid she'd spring away like a startled fawn. Joelle rocked woodenly on her heels, staring at the rug. "How are you and Richard getting along?" Carla knew it was the wrong thing to ask, but she couldn't think of anything better.

"I told him to take his mud pies and clear out."

"Oh, no. I'm so sorry." Richard, Carla recalled vaguely, sculpted in clay, great brooding lumps stuck with broken dowels and scraps of burlap.

"Don't be. He called me an *illustrator*." Joelle's voice vibrated with contempt.

"Because you were working on this?"

"Before that. Another painting, a big one. Why do I have to get stuck with these creeps? Why?"

"Peter wasn't so bad."

"Peter was gay."

"Well, I suppose that did have some drawbacks. Joelle, I wish you'd at least think about getting some kind of job. I hear they're hiring at Bloomingdale's for Christmas."

"You know what they do to you at Bloomingdale's?" Joelle's voice rose, an edge of hysteria creeping in. "They make this nice, neat cut around the top of your head, and they lift a section of the skull off—" Joelle mimed the action. "—and they make you sit under a big conveyor belt in the basement while they stuff you full of bits and pieces of *dead toys*." The last two words shook with an acid mixture of laughter, loathing, and dread.

"Joelle, are you feeling all right? You don't look well."

"They're all walking on glass."

"Well, all right. I guess maybe Bloomie's is not such a good idea." Carla reached for her purse and brought out the checkbook and a pen. "How much do you need?"

"It's seven hundred a month for that place. Do you believe that? Seven hundred a month, and no heat. The super wouldn't even come to the door, no matter how much I pounded on it. So I called the owner. I had to go down to the pay phone at the laundromat."

"What's his name?"

"Weintraub. Morris Weintraub."

Carla hesitated, licked her upper lip, and inked a check to Morris Weintraub for seven hundred dollars. It would put a big dent in her budget, but maybe she owed Joelle something for making such a mess trying to get her a commission from the agency. She ought to have been more sensitive to what Joelle was trying to tell her. Besides, she couldn't stand the thought of Joelle ending up on the street, especially in this weather. "Give him this. And tell him to turn the heat back on."

Joelle stared at the check stupidly. "You don't have to do this," she asserted. "I don't need charity. I'll get by."

"It's a loan, until you get on your feet. And here." Carla dug in her purse again and found some cash. "Here's fifty dollars for groceries. I want you to be strong enough to take your work around to some more galleries. I just know somebody's going to love it. I can feel it. All you have to sell is one painting, and you can pay me back."

Joelle crushed the check shoving it into her pants pocket. "You should come by," she said. "As soon as I'm done with the new one, you have to come see it. I think maybe it's the best thing I've ever done."

"One of your ice palaces?" For the past year Joelle had been painting the interiors of oddly angled buildings, in the blue depths of whose translucent walls weirdly refracted faces could sometimes be glimpsed, elongated like rubber masks and smiling gleefully or crying out in pain.

"No. No more ice. At least, not — You'll like this one. It's got music in it."

"Music in a painting?"

"At first I thought everybody could hear it. Dum-da-dum dum dum dum." Joelle's hand twitched in a spastic parody of an orchestra conductor. "It got so loud I couldn't sleep, and underneath it there were voices, a bunch of conversations all going at once. I thought they were having a party downstairs, and I went down and banged on the door to tell them to knock it off, but then I saw there wasn't any party. That's when I knew I had to paint it."

Auditory hallucinations. Great. "Joelle, I really think maybe you ought to see a doctor. I can find out—"

"There's nothing wrong with me," Joelle snapped. "I'm fine. You're just jealous. You're trying to confuse me into thinking I'm one of your ghosts."

"Ghosts?" Carla was drifting into the hazy headache she usually got sooner or later trying to follow the twists and turns of Joelle's private labyrinth.

"I have to be getting back." Joelle picked up the horrid coat. "They need me."

"What's this about ghosts?"

"The painting. Only, see, they're *my* ghosts." She smiled thinly. "That makes all the difference."

"I still don't understand."

"You used to." After a queer, crooked, piercing look at Carla from under the lank lock of greasy hair, Joelle said again, "You used to." She squirmed into the coat, and seemed to shrink a little within its dark folds. "But you forgot."

II

A week after their first dinner party, they had their first argument. Tony wanted her to fly down to Fort Lauderdale with him for Christmas. For some reason that she couldn't quite put her finger on, Carla was desperate not to go.

"You don't like flying," Tony suggested.

"It's not that. I like flying. It's just — I don't know. It's hard to explain." She didn't want to refuse point-blank, for fear he'd think she was rejecting him. If he thought that, he might start to lose interest in her. So she stalled, hoping he'd take the hint, hoping he'd let her off the hook.

But he kept after her. "You'll have a great time, I promise. The weather is fantastic. Not like this crap." He gestured through the windshield at the lowering sky. Swirling down between the tall buildings, snowflakes were beginning to settle like a crust of powdered sugar on the rutted slush.

"I like New York at Christmas. All the Santas, and the lights. It wouldn't be the same in Florida. Wouldn't you like to stay here and have our own little tree and everything?"

"Mama is pestering me to meet you. And hey, I want to show you off. Anything wrong with that?" Tony flipped the Porsche into the left lane, accelerated around a truck, and plunged through a yellow light. "My brothers will be there with their wives, and they will *die* of jealousy. You're gorgeous, in case you hadn't noticed. You'll be the star of the show."

"Well, it would be nice to get away from the cold for a few days."

"They'll warm you right up. Real Italian hospitality. Make you feel like a member of the family."

A lump of cold grease congealed in Carla's throat. That's what it was — family. After five foster homes in nine years, and the convent school in between, she was terrified she wouldn't know how to act around a real family. "I don't know. It sounds lovely. I just — maybe it's too soon. Anyway, I've got so much to do at the office."

"Not a problem. I'll talk to Guy. Mama's got the guest room all fixed up for you, and—"

"Whoa. Slow down a minute. The guest room?" Carla covered her eyes with her hand, laughing but not really laughing. "Let me see if I've got this straight. They're going to treat me like a member of the family, but you sleep in your old bedroom and I sleep in the guest room?"

"Mama's old-fashioned. You have to understand."

"I spent too many years in guest rooms when I was a kid. If you can't admit to your mother that we're sleeping together, or if she's not okay with that, then there's no way I'm going."

Tony's face darkened. "She's my mother."

"And how old are you, thirteen?"

"What's that supposed to mean? I live my own life. But she's entitled to respect."

"So am I, buster." Her voice was shaking. Thirteen. That was the year she lived with the Martins in Cincinnati, Mr. Martin with his big red face always drinking beer at the kitchen table, Mrs. Martin forever sniffling and wiping her nose and whining about what a burden Carla was, and how ungrateful if she asked for anything, anything at all. Carla had prayed for the Martins to send her away, but when they did she was surprised to find that it hurt just as much as all the other times.

"It's only for a couple of days. What are you making such a big deal about?"

"If you don't know...."

"Honestly, I don't. And I'm not sure I *care*." They rode for several blocks in a thick silence punctuated by Tony's savage jerks on the gearshift. By the time he pulled into the parking lot, Carla was feeling thoroughly wretched. Wasn't this what she had always wanted — to be part of a real family? What right did she have to march in and impose her own standards on them? You're not being sensible, she told herself sternly. What's so bad about a few days in sunny Florida? You'll have to meet them sooner or later. Either that, or break it off with Tony, and that would be idiotic. Where are you going to find another guy this good-looking, with such hot career prospects? And if you do find another guy, and he falls for you, guess what? He'll want to take you home to meet his family.

Still scowling, Tony marched around the front of

the car and opened the door for her, and she stepped out into the biting wind. Well, all right. She'd go. She'd force herself. And probably end up having a wonderful time. But it wouldn't do to give in too quickly. Let him stew for a few minutes.

The elevator, not plush but reasonably modern, whisked them up five flights. Tony took off his gloves, folded them, and put them in his coat pocket, still staring straight ahead.

The door he knocked on was opened after a minute by a spiky-haired young man in a rumpled shirt, who nodded and said, "Mr. Da Costa, come in. We're just finishing up the backing tracks."

The loft was larger than Carla's flat, but had less free floor space. The main room was crammed with gear — a tall rack studded with knobs, winking lights, and twitching needles, a tape deck with fat spools, and several keyboards on a tiered stand. Mounted on the far wall were two pairs of speaker cabinets, one large and one small. She stopped just inside the door, awestruck as always by the mysterious alchemical apparatus of modern music. At college she had once shepherded a piece of hers through the recording process, but that was with a two-track Sony reel-to-reel on a table at the back of the recital hall, and a pair of microphones on tall stands stuck up in front of a student string quartet. This setup was in another galaxy.

Two electric guitar players, one with a six-string and one with a bass, eyed the newcomers coolly. The spiky-haired young man didn't introduce them. "Let me play you what we've got. See what you think." He tapped a button. The tape whizzed, braked, reversed itself, and rolled forward. The big speakers had no grill cloths, and the black cones pulsed and trembled with every beat.

The tune was only sixty seconds long. When it had wrapped itself in a fast fadeout, Tony said, "What the hell was that crap? I thought you were doing the Cato jeans spot today."

The young man blushed. "Uh, that was the Cato jingle, Mr. Da Costa."

Carla had recognized the tune, but she wasn't surprised that Tony hadn't. The guitarist had built a haunting series of jazz chords that somehow meshed with the hackneyed melody, and poured them out over a submerged girderwork of weirdly accented percussion, the drums bouncing and echoing like distant cannon fire. "It's slow motion, is all," the young man said, "like you wanted it."

"I know how the Cato jingle goes," Tony stated. That was *not* the Cato jingle."

"Uh, Tony...."

"Not now, Carla. Look, Stu—"

"Steve," the young man corrected. If you'll just let me explain, Mr. Da Costa. We were trying to do something a little creative here. It's a concept. Just listen to it once more before you make up your mind; that's all I ask."

"You're not getting paid to be creative," Tony snapped. "You're not getting paid to have fucking concepts. Let the people be creative who know what the public wants."

Steve squared his shoulders and suppressed a grimace. "Sure, Mr. Da Costa. Anything you say."

"Because you won't last long in this business pulling stunts like that. Now let's get this thing turned around. I've got a deadline." Tony turned to the guitar players. "You boys know the Cato jeans jingle, right?"

The guitar players, both of whom were black, exchanged a glance. "We know it," one of them admitted.

"Well, play it. Play it slow. Dah, dah da-dah, dah." Tony's arm pumped up and down as he snapped his fingers. The musicians fell raggedly into line with him. "That's it. Keep it simple." Tony turned to Steve. "Well, what are you waiting for? Roll the tape."

"It'll be a lot easier if we program the drum machine first, Mr. Da Costa. We'll get a tighter groove."

"Drum machine? What the hell are you talking about?" Tony looked around, apparently noticing for the first time that there was no drummer in the little room, only an empty trap set huddled in one corner. "Where's the drummer?"

Steve patted a black box studded with big square buttons. "In here, Mr. Da Costa."

"Did the drummer just not show up?"

"It's cheaper this way," Steve said patiently. "Plus, it sounds cleaner. Just give me a minute to program a beat, okay?"

Embarrassed that Tony was behaving so badly, Carla did her best to wander away, which in the confines of the little room was difficult to manage. She leaned forward to examine one of the keyboard instruments. The knobs and buttons and sliders on the panel were intimidating, but she twiddled a bit at random, just to see what it felt like. At least the black-and-white keys were familiar. She poked a key — and instead of a musical note, the big speakers erupted in a cacophony of breaking glass. She jerked her hand back. But rather than shutting off, the crashing echoed on and on in a tangled, lurching roar. Both Tony and Steve turned to glare at her. Cheeks burning, she smiled meekly and sidled out the door. She wanted very much to stay and learn more about how the studio worked. One of the reasons she had been so excited about getting the job at the agency, two years ago now, was that she wanted someday to get into music production. Well, today wasn't going to be the day.

The runner in the hall was badly frayed, and the kitchen showed no signs of domesticity, though the stove had evidently been cooked on a great deal. The table was littered with electronic components, tools, and bits of wire and solder, in the midst of which, like a plastic temple erected in the jungle, a small computer sat, its screen glowing. She sank onto a chair. She wondered whether she might be disturbing some delicate process of assembly or repair by setting her purse and gloves in the midst of the clutter, but the computer seemed to be intact. The table looked more as if bits and pieces of the insides of things had simply collected here, items that might once have had a function but now languished, forlorn.

The computer, on the other hand, looked coolly functional. On the screen a video game was going through its demonstration loop. The game was called "The Amazing Snake." In the demo the snake crawled out of its hole at the bottom of the screen and tried to wriggle up through the maze to the top. Blue daggers fell, and the snake twisted sinuously as it dodged them. A pair of red lips with white teeth came chomping toward the snake, and it had to dodge those, too. It ate a golden apple, and the daggers and teeth froze for a moment. But always the snake got hit by one of the daggers before it got to the top. With a sad little noise, it would curl up into a ball and shrivel — only to appear a moment later at the bottom of the screen, as idiotically cheerful and determined as before.

Usually Carla had no use for computer games, but for some reason this one captivated her. If nothing else, it provided a distraction from the music and the rumble of Tony's voice coming from the other room. She drew the keyboard to her and started punching keys at random. In a minute she got the game to start, but she had no idea how to control the snake. It lay writhing cutely at the bottom of the screen until one of the daggers impaled it. She got three snakes, and the same thing happened to all of them. After the third snake, the screen flashed "GAME OVER" and went back into the demo loop.

In another minute she had figured out how to manipulate the snake with the cursor keys, but it was still getting killed every time. She hunched over the keyboard and started a new game. There had to be a pattern in the way the daggers came down the screen, if only she could figure out what it was. Scraps of music floated in from the other room, woven around a wordless rise and fall of voices.

After a while the two guitar players ambled in. Carla didn't even look up at them. One drew himself a glass of water from the tap, shook his head, and said, "Man, what a way to earn a living." The other said, "You got that right." After watching the game over her shoulder briefly, they wandered out again. The keyboard chords from the other room broke off, leaving only naked drum hits, which went on and on in an irregular pattern. "I'm getting it," she heard Tony exclaim. "I'm getting it!"

Carla was getting it too. Throwing her body from side to side in useless sympathetic exertion, she nearly succeeded in steering the snake to the top, but the spastic drum sounds broke her concentration, and the snake died again. And again. And yet again.

"That's a blind alley. You've got to start off to the right, wait 'til the first barrage falls past, and then buttonhook back to the left."

She looked up. Steve was standing beside her, looking more harried and disheveled than he had half an hour before. She hadn't heard him come in. "I'm no good at these things," she said.

"It's nothing, once you get the hang of it. My best score is over a hundred thousand." Carla's best score so far was 160. "The better you get, the faster things come at you. Play it for an hour or so, and when you stop you'll keep seeing daggers raining down and the snake twisting away from the teeth. It does something to your brain." In the other room the bass guitar rumbled into life again, marching through a sludgy version of the Cato jingle. Steve shook his head sadly. "Can you beat the stones on that guy?"

"Mr. Da Costa and I," she said coldly, "are engaged to be married."

"Sorry. I don't seem to be doing anything right today."

She wanted to say, *The way you were doing the jingle, before Tony butted in, that was right. That was wonderful.* She wanted to say, *Can you show me those chords?* But this was Tony's account, and she didn't want to cause any more friction. "He has strong ideas," she said.

Steve shrugged. "It doesn't matter. The customer is always right. If you want to be a success in this business, you just have to keep plugging away at it."

She nodded. "I wish you could tell that to a friend of mine. She's a painter, and — oh, my God."

"Something wrong?"

"Excuse me." Carla jumped up, rattling all the junk on the table, grabbed her purse, and plunged down the hall. "Tony! Tony!"

Tony, his tie loosened, was frowning in perplexity at the drum machine. "It's not working right," he declared. "Why won't it—"

"Tony, we have to go."

"It's the auto-correct, Mr. Da Costa," the bass player said. "It you hit it too early, it will—"

"Tony, listen to me. You're not listening to me."

"Babe, we're right in the middle of a very important—"

"I know. I'm terribly, terribly sorry, but I just remembered. I was supposed to meet Joelle for lunch, and I forgot all about it."

"So what? Phone her. What's the big—"

"She doesn't have a phone. We'll have to drive down there."

"Carla, darling." He put a hand on her shoulder. "Believe it or not, this is not the first broken lunch date in the history of New York City. If you'd like, we can swing by after I'm finished here."

"Tony, the lunch date was *yesterday*. Why don't I take the car and come back for you? Or you can take a cab and meet me."

"I don't want you going down into that neighborhood by yourself. It'll be dark in half an hour."

"Tony, I will go to Lauderdale with you. I will sleep in the guest room. I will even kiss your mother on the cheek. Only *please,* we have to go down there right now. I'm worried about Joelle. She's not well."

"And this is something new you're telling me?" Tony scowled. "All right. You and the boys can finish this up, Stan. You know what I want. Have a cassette on my desk in the morning."

Steve rumpled his hair. "It'll be there. I'll call the messenger service now and set it up."

As they waited for the elevator, Tony jerked his gloves on, one stiff finger at a time. "Do you believe that kid? Thinking he could get away with a stunt like that. Slipping his own music in instead of the jingle. I think I'll turn the cassette down, no matter how good it is."

"He seems pretty talented," Carla ventured.

"Talented kids are a dime a dozen. Trouble is, they get so full of themselves they're impossible to work with. They get crazy ideas. Look at your friend Joelle. She's talented. She's also a mess. That painting — I still don't believe that painting. Guy and Dory were so polite about it, but I may never live it down. I don't know why you bother with her. You should just cut her off."

Carla didn't know whether to be angry or sad. "You never knew the old Joelle. She had emotional problems, but she was fun. We had some great times together, in college and after. Now she's — I don't know. I feel like I hardly know her. When she phoned me Monday she was barely coherent. I'm sure that's why I blocked it out. She kept rambling on about her new painting. She said she had just finished it. There was something about it that was bothering her, but I couldn't make out what it was. She'd start to give me a straight answer, and then she'd go off on another tangent. No, 'bothered' is the wrong word. She was excited but confused. And scared, and thrilled, and, I don't know, defiant?"

Night had fallen on the city while they were in the loft. A bus rolled by, the passengers immobile profiles framed in trapezoids of light. "She kept saying, 'They're calling to me. They want me to dance.'"

"I thought you said she didn't have a phone."

"She said, 'They need me so the steps will come out right.' That's what it was — 'so the steps will come out right.'"

"The steps." Tony sounded bored.

"It was about dancing. Dancing and ghosts. It didn't make any sense. But it gave me chills."

"She's a wacko. You'd be a lot better off if you got her out of your life for good."

"She needs me. She doesn't have any family." Either. "I'm all she has."

"That's not your problem," Tony said. "Speaking of family, though, I just wanted you to know I didn't appreciate being manipulated back there. I don't want you coming to Florida to do me a favor, in exchange for another favor. I want you to come because you want to come, because it means something to you." He unlocked the car door on the passenger side, but held it open only a few inches, so that she couldn't slide in without facing him.

"Okay," she said. "I had already decided I was coming. I just hadn't told you yet. You're right. I should never have tried to use it against you. Sometimes I just don't think." Say anything. Buttonhook back to the left.

Joelle's studio was on the top floor of a dilapidated walk-up on the edge of the Village. The door of the building was ajar. Tony maneuvered the car expertly into a tiny parking spot half a block down, and dragged a garbage can away from the curb so Carla could get out. She had left her gloves lying beside "The Amazing Snake," and the metal edge of the car door was a knife of ice cutting across her fingers.

Even the cold couldn't rinse the smells of cabbage, cheap wine, and unwashed humanity from the vestibule. Up three creaking flights, Tony stood scowling at the unsavory darkness while Carla stunned her knuckles pounding on the door. The door was scarred and stained; the pale outline of a 6 was still visible at the center of the upper panel, punctuated by three rust-streaked wounds where nails had held the numeral in place. A TV set, blaring faintly from the floor below, was the only response to her knock. After a minute she pounded again, and called Joelle's name.

"She's gone out," Tony said.

Carla rattled the doorknob. "Maybe. I've got a bad feeling about this. Maybe we ought to get the super to let us in. Once, when we were in college, she—" Carla pressed her lips together, unwilling to say the words.

"She what? Went out for a walk?"

Go find the super, please, Tony? I'll wait here."

Their sophomore year, Joelle had swung precipitously between outbursts of hysterical good humor and spells of sullen withdrawal. For days at a time she sat on her bed, hair uncombed, responding to overtures with vague grunts, or by averting her face, or not at all. Coaxing did no good, but periodically some internal balance would tilt the other way. She would rouse herself, dress, and plunge into life with feverish glee, running everywhere rather than walking, fidgeting when she tried to sit still, chattering interminably about whatever lanced across her mind. Her laugh was like breaking glass.

It was Carla who rode beside her in the ambulance, who sat in the waiting room while they pumped the pills out of her stomach. That one had been hushed up, but the next year it was a razor blade, and they kept Joelle a week for observation.

Cooped up in a tiny room in a youth hostel while the Paris skies dumped rain, Carla was finally irritated enough, by her own urinary distress and by Joelle's obtuse defiance and self-pity, to bring the incident up. "You know what you are?" she said. "You're just selfish.

You don't give a damn about anybody or anything. You remember that time you made such a mess out of killing yourself? It was me that cleaned up the bathroom — me on my hands and knees, mopping up your damn blood! Did I get any thanks? Did you even bother to ask who took care of your mess?"

The rain drummed on the Paris roof. "What did you use?" Joelle asked after a while.

"What do you mean, what did I use? A towel."

"What did you do with it? Did you keep it?"

"Please. I threw it away."

"You ought to have kept it," Joelle said. "I wish you'd kept it."

Tony's head appeared in the stairwell. "No luck," he announced.

By standing halfway down the stairs and looking up at her, he was trying to will her to give up and come down. She turned back to the door and surveyed it dubiously. "Maybe we ought to pick the lock," she said. "She might be hurt."

With a little sigh, he trudged the rest of the way up the stairs and put a heavy arm around her shoulders. "You're letting your imagination run wild," he said. "She's probably downstairs watching TV with the neighbors."

"Do you know how to pick locks?"

"No, and I'm not—"

"Neither do I. Let's break it down."

"Sweetheart, that's against the law. It's breaking and entering. Would you please try to be a little bit rational here? This is not *Cagney & Lacey*."

"Break it down, Tony. If you don't, I will." Tony raised a condescending eyebrow. She set her jaw. "I will. Watch me."

He shrugged. "Okay. First rule of television detective work: Never break down a door until you've checked to make sure it's locked. Saves a lot of trouble." He jiggled the doorknob, but it failed to turn. He shoved experimentally, and the latch and hinges rattled. Placing both palms flat against the door panel, he tried lifting sideways to pull the latch clear of the strike plate, but this did no good. He rubbed his jaw for a second, and then stood back a pace and drove his foot squarely into the door just beside the knob. At his second kick the flimsy wood splintered and tore. By pushing the ragged tear open with both gloved hands, he was able to force it wide enough to reach through and twist the dead bolt. "Nice security," he commented. Downstairs the TV was still blaring; if the other tenants had heard the noise, they had chosen not to investigate.

The apartment was as cold as the landing. To the left a bare bulb glowed in the kitchen ceiling. The refrigerator was standing open, nothing inside but a blue-and-white milk carton. Pans and plates were piled in the sink, and the spigot dripped a measured *plonk, plonk, plonk*. To the right the studio was deep in shadow, a streetlight throwing the shapes of windows faintly on the ceiling.

"Joelle? Joelle?"

III

They found her sprawled on the bathroom floor. Her face was mottled blue and gray. The eyes and mouth were open, and a crust of foam had dried on her lips. She was naked below the waist, and the bones of her knees stood out like chalk, as if they were already trying to force their way through the skin. The door of the medicine cabinet yawned wide, and empty pill containers lay scattered across the floor. A water glass had fallen among them and shattered, and sharp bright shards glinted. Carla swayed against the wall, turned her head away, and gripped the edge of the sink to keep from fainting. Glass chips whirled behind her eyes. "Call—" She bit back the high-pitched wail that was forming in her throat. "Call an ambulance."

Tony knelt and pressed a thumb into the notch below Joelle's ear. Carla couldn't look at the face. There was dried paint in the crevices around Joelle's gnawed fingernails. Tony shook his head heavily. "She's been dead for hours. Maybe days."

"Shit. *Shit.*" Carla slammed her open hand against the wall. It stung.

"I'll call the cops." Tony stood up and moved past her toward the stairs. She stood leaning against the bathroom door for a while longer, not looking at the cold, stiff, naked thing lying contorted on the floor. "I'm sorry, honey," she said softly. "I tried. I tried to tell you, but you never did listen." After a while she pushed herself upright and walked unsteadily away. The kitchen was uninviting. She turned and went into the studio.

She had to grope for the light switch. At the heavy snap, a white glare flooded the room. Joelle's last painting stood braced between the twin pillars of the easel, which stretched from floor to ceiling. Ten feet long and six feet high, the canvas leaped with color, swirled with grand sweeps of glittering detail. Tears, wrenched free by the painting, flooded Carla's eyes, smearing the image into thick cobwebs of light. Gasping and sniffling, she pulled a handkerchief from her purse.

When she could see again, she found that the painting was of the interior of a ballroom, a magnificent high-ceilinged chamber in some palace of a century gone by, bejeweled with mirrors and chandeliers. Joelle had never been seduced into impressionism or abstraction; her subject matter had always been as anachronistic as her craft was meticulous. In the ballroom a masked ball was in progress: across the broad parquetry floor nearly a hundred figures were poised in the patterns of a complex courtly dance. On a balcony between marble pillars, musicians were playing.

Carla stepped closer, fascinated. There were several sorts of people in the painting. What caught her eye first were the silhouettes. Six or seven figures, scattered here and there, were nothing but black cutouts, oddly jarring against the riot of three-dimensional color that flowed around them. The silhouette of a lady whose hair was piled in high curls curtsied to her partner, her mouth open in gay laughter behind a fan. In the midst of a group standing to one side against a wall, a silhouette of a gentleman was taking a pinch of snuff.

More of the dancers were unreal in a different way. They were ghostly, tenuous, only half visible. Though their features were discernible in the pastel light with which they glowed, the room behind them could be glimpsed through them. Some of the ghosts were wearing elaborate masks — boars' heads, tragicomic painted faces of stiff plaster, confections of feathers and lace. A few of them, though their bearing was aristocratic, were naked.

Among the silhouettes and ghosts were ten or twelve fully rendered, solid people. A young girl in adult finery stood framed by a doorway, her mouth half open in surprise or delight. Her mother's translucent hand rested on her shoulder. One of the musicians, his eyes closed, cheeks ruddy, his head thrown back, sawed contentedly on a viol. A young woman in a cat mask lifted her skirt as she executed a turn, so that her petticoats and ankle flashed. A jolly gentleman with a long wig of tight ringlets stood gazing at the punch bowl, his portly stomach threatening to burst his trousers. These figures were as real as the walls around them, but though they danced among and conversed with and laid their hands upon the hands of ghosts, they gave no sign that they knew; or, if they knew, that they cared.

The painting quite literally took Carla's breath away; for long seconds she breathed shallowly through her mouth, afraid the slightest stirring of the air would sweep the magical vitality of the canvas into a meaningless jumble, like a living animal made of fallen leaves. She was unsure at first why the painting had such a palpable effect. Not simply because its vibrancy contrasted so forcibly with the cold, still body on the bathroom floor. Nor that it was the last work that would erupt from Joelle's fevered brush. Nor the extraordinary ballroom scene itself. At last Carla thought she understood: Of Joelle's perpetual torment, the angst that had throbbed within her for as long as Carla had known her, the painting bore not a trace. Even with the sense of barely contained chaos, even with the shadowy silhouette figures, it was a testament of joy.

Or was there more to it than that? Something maddeningly elusive and yet urgent. But what? Carla's eyes darted into the painting, drinking up clues: the folds of a satin skirt, the polished buckles on a gentleman's shoes, the shifting scintillation of the chandeliers. A ghostly oboist's cheeks huffed as he tootled. The opaque viol player's arm was raised to push the bow across the strings, and the knuckles of his other hand stood out, tense but graceful, at the instrument's neck. Carla felt she could almost hear the seductive throbbing of that viol. She stepped closer. Now the painting was all she could see. It wrapped itself around her, the grand sweep of the dance cascading toward her and away. The ballroom was a sea of faces, hands, ribbons fluttering, sparkling tiaras — and her head whirled, she was falling into the sky, the translucent dancers swathed in pulsing light, smiling at one another, at her, an unfolding web of turning, stepping, a nod, a hesitation, the oboe's carefree tune skipping across a low river of conversation, the mingled scents of perspiration and perfume.

A hand tugged at her hand, and she curtsied to the gentleman in a powdered wig who stood bowing before her. He offered his arm, she took it, and they promenaded down the room. Her petticoats rustled. Three paces and a dip to the left, three more and a dip to the right. Her feet knew the steps. (Petticoats?) Now sweep forward, now back. She smiled at her partner, whose eyes twinkled. Something very odd was going on, but she was too busy dancing to think what it might be. Weren't these people supposed to be translucent? But what an odd thought! Why should she think that? Their flesh was as solid as hers.

A face flashed past, another of the dancers, hauntingly familiar, iridescent green eyes and gaunt cheeks under severe center-parted black hair. Carla stumbled. Suddenly her legs were heavy and stupid. She frowned at her feet, invisible in their soft slippers beneath the layers of flaring skirt. Concentrate. If you spoil the dance, the other ladies will whisper about you behind their fans. You won't be invited back.

Twice more she glimpsed the black-haired woman, now across the room, now swept down the line as the harpsichord trilled out a march rhythm. There was some reason, Carla felt, why she ought to know that woman, something urgent she must say to her. But it was difficult to think about anything while keeping step.

The intricacies of the dance seemed interminable. Twirl to the left, a kick, and place her hand atop the next gentleman's. But at last the musicians wove a final ornate phrase into a flowery cadence. She curtsied again to her partner. He murmured some pleasantry, but she wasn't listening. She felt thoroughly confused and rather frightened. Where was she? How had she come here? Did she know these people? It seemed so natural, and yet —

"Does milady feel faint?" her partner inquired solicitously. "Perhaps a breath of fresh air...."

"I thank you, sir, for your kind concern. I assure you, I feel quite well." But she didn't feel well. She gazed distractedly around the room, desperate for some clue. There! The black-haired woman was just now turning away, as if she might have been looking in this direction. Carla forged a path among the couples milling on the parquet floor, but the black-haired woman, after a swift backward glance, slipped out a door.

Carla pressed forward. What am I doing? she asked herself. Am I insane? Why am I following this person? Who is she? Who am I, for that matter? No, I know who I am, concentrate on that. I just don't know where I am or how I got here, that's all.

She faltered, uncertain, at the door. Was this the right door? A long hallway stretched out before her, rows of pillars flanking dim arches. Was that the black-haired woman rushing away from her down the hall? Or was it only a shadow, a gust of wind that set the candles flickering?

A footman in livery materialized before her, bearing a silver tray laden with a crystal decanter and a goblet. "Wine, milady?" The wine lay as motionless in the heart of the decanter as an enormous ruby.

"Did you just see a woman come this way?"

"The wine is of an excellent vintage." The footman proffered the tray. Around its rim undulated a design of embossed snakes, the tail of each snake in the mouth of the one behind it. As she stared at the snakes, she saw they were actually rippling.

She tore her eyes away from the snakes. "Why won't you answer me? Did a black-haired woman just now come this way? Did you see where she went?"

"Milady seems troubled, if she will forgive my saying so. The wine, she will find, is an excellent physick. Those who drink of it cast aside all care. The burden of memory is forever lifted."

Impatiently she brushed the footman aside and plunged down the hall. It was longer than she had thought at first — quite long, in fact — and she felt sure she was being watched. But when she turned to look back, the men and women laughing and drinking in the grand ballroom were paying no attention to her. The festive scene beckoned, and in her breast a flame leaped in answer to the candle flames in the chandeliers. Determined not to be deflected, she set her jaw and hurried on.

Ahead, on the left, a door set with beveled panes of glass stood just slightly ajar. Beyond the door was darkness. After taking a deep breath, which failed to quell the tripping of her heart, she opened the door and stepped through.

Night. Jasmine. A dove calling. Soft moonlight, and

overhead ten thousand stars. The black-haired woman had stopped by a low stone balustrade. Beyond her stretched dark lawn smudged with pale statues, the curving hedges of a formal garden.

"Joelle!"

The black-haired woman turned slowly to face her, head held proudly high, porcelain neck as slender as a swan's above bare shoulders. For a moment Carla thought she must be mistaken. She remembered Joelle now, the memories were returning. But Joelle had never radiated this calm grace. "Begging madame's pardon," the woman said, "but it seems she has confused me with somebody else." The green eyes flashed.

"Joelle, don't be like that! It's me! At least I think I'm still me. This is all crazy. Where are we? What is this place?"

Terror flickered across Joelle's face, and was gone so quickly Carla wasn't sure she had seen it. "Are you enjoying the festivities?" Joelle said. "You haven't drunk the wine yet, have you? You must have some wine at once. It brings surcease of all sorrow."

"I don't want any wine. I want you to tell me what's going on. I was in your studio. We had just found—" No, she couldn't say that. "It was cold and dark, and there was broken glass all around on the floor. And then I heard the music and saw your painting — and the next thing I knew, I was here, dancing."

"A place that was dark," Joelle said. "And cold. Perhaps I could remember being in such a place, if I had not drunk the wine. It is of no importance. Now I am here, and now you are here, and you must drink the wine. Soon the dance will begin again."

Carla looked out across the dark formal garden. The statues weren't at all where she remembered seeing them only moments before. Or were they? They seemed to have shifted somehow, like smoke.

"I find it peaceful here," Joelle said.

Carla shivered. "I don't like it at all." Or was that true? Her body felt buoyant, tingling, electric. But everything she saw or heard or touched was so strange! "I don't want to be here," she insisted. "I want to be back in — in that other place. You brought me here. You may not know it, but you did. You've got to tell me how to get back there!"

"Well, there is one thing you might try." Joelle's cool facade melted into an impish smile. "Click your heels together three times," she said with a twinkle, "and say, 'There's no place like New York.'"

"Aha! You admit it!"

Joelle smiled seraphically, and spread her hands and cocked her head in a graceful shrug.

Carla looked at her friend appraisingly. "So you haven't drunk the wine either."

"How much fun would it be if I didn't know the difference? But I don't have to think about the other place if I don't want to. Your being here reminds me. You have to go away. Either that, or drink the wine. The way you are, you don't belong here."

"Neither do you. This place isn't *real*. You created it somehow."

Joelle laughed, a humorless bark. "You don't know how wrong you are. That other place — that was the place that wasn't real. All the nasty things clawing at me, getting their slime all over me. You kept dragging me back, but this time I was too smart for you. I fixed it so you can't ever make me go back."

"And you think you can just stay here? Forever?"

Joelle nodded vigorously. "Why not? That's the

kind of place this is. All the shapes and patterns fit. The colors work together. The movement never gets tangled. Do you have any idea how nice this feels? After all those years, I finally got it right!"

"It sounds lovely," Carla admitted. "It looks lovely too. I guess I ought to congratulate you."

"There's just one thing. You don't belong. I could feel it when you got here. The steps of the dance started not being right. You have to go back now."

"I don't want to leave you here. We'll never see each other again."

Joelle shrugged, but looking away, not meeting Carla's eyes. "Maybe I'll think about you once in a while."

"I'm supposed to say that about you. You make it sound like I'm the one that's dead."

Joelle said nothing.

"It *is* nice here." The scent of the night flowers was as thick as syrup. Carla's body was made of bubbles, made of cloud. "Could I — do you think I could stay for just a little while?"

"I told you. This isn't your place. You make the steps come out wrong."

"Just one more dance, Joelle! Please!"

"That's not my name now. My name is Lucy." Within the palace a fanfare flourished. "If you want a place like this, you have to make your own."

"What do you mean? How?"

"That's what you have to find out. It's hard."

"I wouldn't even know where to start."

"Either you know or you don't know. I think you used to know, but you forgot. I think your coming here was an accident. I sucked you in after me, like a tornado." Joelle pointed at Carla's feet. "See? You're walking on glass."

Carla looked down. On all sides the broad paving stones were solid blocks — but the one directly beneath her was transparent. Through it she could see, below her, a nether sky thick with stars. Not a reflection, either. When she lifted her skirts to look, no upside-down Carla peered back at her. Suddenly dizzy, she staggered backward and sank down on a bench.

The fanfare sounded again. "The next dance is starting," Joelle said. "They need me. Goodbye." Framed by the light that spilled through the prismatic panes of the door, she raised her fan and spread it before her face, then turned and swept back into the palace.

Carla shivered, and hugged herself. I won't let her turn me away like that, she vowed. I have as much right to be here as she does. I'll stay for another dance, at least. And I won't drink the wine, either. But she felt too weak to stand. Something tugged at her deep within, something that slid like heavy oil. She closed her eyes.

Loud masculine footsteps came clumping toward her. "They asked us to wait. Said they'd be here in a few minutes."

She opened her eyes, and started in alarm. She was back in the studio, sitting on a bare wooden chair, wearing not a ball gown but her heavy alpaca coat. Tony was standing over her, between her and the painting, blocking her view. "Are you okay?"

"I — I'm not sure. I felt — peculiar for a minute. Faint. I felt faint. That must have been what it was."

"You want a glass of water?"

"I'll be all right."

Tony wandered off. The painting was jarringly active in the bleak room, like a greenhouse seen in a fever. She stood up and moved toward it. Her legs were wobbly. "Tony, talk to me. Say something."

His voice behind her. "What do you want me to say?"

"Anything." Throw me a rope. Pull me back. With his presence like a rock behind her, she could look at the dancers, could feel the ache in the bones of her fingers yearning to reach out to them, and still jam her hands deep into her coat pockets and hear the traffic noises echoing up from the street.

Tony said, "I think it's a miracle she could paint at all, living in a dump like this. I would have killed myself years ago."

"You don't get the impression that it's almost — almost *moving* or anything, do you?" Distantly, threaded through the traffic noise, she could still hear the throbbing of the viol. She scanned the crowd for the black-haired woman with the slim neck and bare shoulders, but didn't see her.

"Moving? You mean like an optical illusion? Like one of those things where you put red against green, and every time you move your eyes, it jumps?"

"Something like that." Suddenly she was frightened that Tony *would* see the painting move, that he would be drawn into it as she had been. No, Tony was too down-to-earth for that ever to happen. But what if someone more susceptible came along, and looked, and plunged in to upset Joelle's perfect world?

"I want it," Carla said decisively.

"What?"

"The painting. We have to take it with us."

"Why, for God's sake? It's way too big for your apartment."

"It's not. I know exactly how to work it. I'll rearrange the living room. I'll put the bookcase in the bedroom and move the piano across—"

He put his hands on her shoulders. "Slow down.

You're babbling. They'll have to seal the place up. It's a crime scene."

"A crime? What crime?"

"We don't even know her death was an accident. The cops have ways to deal with these things."

She's not dead, Carla wanted to say. I spoke with her. Sensibly, she said nothing aloud.

"I guess you could arrange to get your hands on it in a couple of weeks," Tony conceded, "if you haven't come to your senses by then. Who's her next of kin? Do you know if she left a will?"

Carla had forgotten that real life could be so complicated. "I think she has a cousin out in Ohio someplace. But if she ever made out a will, I think she would have told me."

"In that case, forget it. If the probate court doesn't lose her stuff, which they do once in a while with indigents, you'll be lucky to get it by next summer. And they'll bill you for storage. Not just on the one painting, on all of them." He gestured at the rack in the corner, where large rectangles jostled. "And somebody will have poked a hole in the canvas by then, or else there'll be water damage. Better forget the whole thing."

"No, I can't. She wanted me to have this one, Tony. I can feel it." Maybe I can even go back, if I can figure out how to make the steps come out right. Whatever that means. No, don't be crazy. In the first place, you don't *want* to go back there. Who knows what it's really like? It could turn into a nightmare. In the second place, Joelle doesn't want you there. And in the third place, there's no there there. Even if you did want to go back, you couldn't, because there's no place to go back to. It wasn't real. Whatever just happened, it wasn't real.

This is real. This, right here, right now. I'm trying

to protect Joelle, that's all. Wherever she is now. No, even that is crazy. All I want is, I want something to remember her by. "Look — the police aren't here yet. Could we just take it outside now, before they get here, and kind of put it someplace?"

"Like on the sidewalk?"

"Or in somebody's apartment. *Please,* Tony. Please say you'll help."

The corner of his mouth quirked up in amusement. "You really have a thing about this painting all of a sudden, don't you?"

"So I'm being silly. Humor me."

"You're not being silly. I like you when you're being silly. Right now you're being completely unreasonable."

"All right," she snapped. "Be that way." Stepping up beside the easel, she lifted one side of the painting. It was heavier than she expected. Tony watched, his arms folded. After glaring at him, she moved in behind the canvas and tried to find a way to grip it. Joelle must have been able to manage somehow. Grab the top stretcher bar like this, and then the crossbar.... She thought she had it, but then the other corner dropped free of the easel, and she swayed dangerously. "Tony, help me!"

"I'm having more fun watching."

"If you don't help me, you can forget about Fort Lauderdale."

"I told you before, no wheeling and dealing." From behind the painting she couldn't see him, but she could imagine his scowl.

"Okay, okay. I'm sorry. I'll go to Fort Lauderdale whether you help me or not. Now will you please help me?"

She heard knuckles on a door, and new footsteps. A man's voice said, "You the guy that called?"

"That's right, officer. The body is—"

"Hey, that's a new one. A painting that walks." The cop peered around the end of the canvas. Carla felt herself blushing. "You, lady. You plannin' to go somewhere?"

"No," she said, feeling like a complete idiot. "It was crooked. I was trying to straighten it."

"Sure. Look, I gotta go look at a stiff, and then radio in for Homicide. You be here when I get back, don't go runnin' off, okay?"

"A stiff? Don't talk about her that way. She was my friend."

"Whatever. You just stay put." The big square face and the mustache went away. Carla stood helpless, the painting gripped in both hands. Her arms and shoulders were starting to hurt, and she was crying again. She needed to wipe her eyes and blow her nose, but she couldn't get into her purse for her handkerchief. "Tony!" she wailed.

He didn't come. She lowered the painting carefully so its lower edge rested on the floor, sidled out from behind it, and leaned it back against the easel. The vivid rectangle of blues and greens and yellows radiated into the streaked and shadowed browns and grays of the room, perfection bleeding into misery. The cop's walkie-talkie coughed a few times. Carla shivered. She didn't want to see what they were doing to Joelle, even if it was just standing over her staring at her, but it seemed disloyal to Joelle to wait here, so after a while she crept softly down the hall.

Tony and the cop were standing pressed close together in the narrow bathroom, their backs to the door. Tony was saying something. The cop nodded. Tony turned, came down the hall toward her, and took her arm. "Come on. Let's go."

"Don't we have to give a statement or something."

"Yeah. Officially, we never left the apartment. We're just going to take the damn painting down to the second-floor landing and stash it behind the stairs. And if you're real nice and say, 'Yes, officer,' and, 'No, officer,' maybe he'll let me keep the painting company while you're talking to the coroner or whoever shows up, so the neighbors won't get any ideas about taking it down to the pawnshop."

Relieved and excited, but confused, she helped him lift the painting. They moved awkwardly toward the stairs. "What happened? I thought you said—"

"Yeah. I gave him a hundred bucks." Tony paused to get a better grip on the stretcher bar. "You owe me."

✌ IV ✌

But what with the rush of Christmas shopping, and packing to fly down to Lauderdale, and unpacking when she got back, and then in January her promotion, which meant she suddenly had hours of work to bring home every night, and then getting ready for the wedding, which Tony wanted to have in April because his parents had already scheduled their Mediterranean vacation for June — what with all that, she never did quite get around to hanging the painting. At first she had it leaning against the couch, but then there was nowhere to sit except on the piano bench. After a couple of weeks she wrestled it onto one end and leaned it against the bookcase. Now at least she could sit on the couch, but the painting, being too long to stand vertically in a room with a normal ceiling, protruded into the center of the living room like a garage door that would neither open nor close, forcing her to detour around it twenty times a day. No matter where it was, it unbalanced the room drastically. Sometimes the couch and the piano seemed to be in danger of sliding down into it, as if they were leftover vegetables and it was the drain in the kitchen sink. Other times it was obviously much higher than the rest of the room, so that the furniture looked as if it had tumbled out like dice from a dice cup.

"Why don't you put the damn thing in storage?" Tony wanted to know.

"I'm going to hang it," she said. "Next week for sure." She wasn't about to admit that she had been foolish to insist that they bring it home, three miles with the two of them leaning out the windows of the taxi in the cold wind! And when they went back to pick up the Porsche, of course three of the hubcaps had been stolen.

But it wasn't just not wanting to give Tony something to complain about. She felt she owed something to Joelle. Keeping her last painting on display in the living room, where any visitor could see what genius the world had scorned, was certainly a small enough gesture. All the same, she found day by day that she was less fascinated by the ballroom and the dancers, and more apprehensive every time she looked at them. They seemed a little less threatening now that she had to turn her head sideways to look at them, but not by much.

At night, lying awake in the dark, alone or with Tony snoring beside her, she was sure she could hear the low throb of the ghostly viol in the other room. Some nights it was so soft she could mistake it for her own heartbeat, but if she listened closely it seemed to get louder, to the point where she could make out the ground bass of a whole movement, complete with sequences, repeats, and the modulation to the dominant. It was only her imagination, of course. The painting was an ordinary painting, no more than that, a thing of canvas and pigment. However evocative they might be, paintings did not make actual audible music. Thinking they could was just — well, it was because she still couldn't get Joelle out of her mind, that was all. One night, feeling enormously embarrassed even though Tony wasn't there to see, she set a cassette recorder on the nightstand and started it recording when the music started. And of course, when she played it back the next morning there was nothing on it but tape hiss.

Somehow, this was less than reassuring. Now she was sure she was hearing things. Could Joelle's mental instability have been contagious? No, that was ridiculous. Obviously the whole episode was a hallucination brought on by shock. Incredibly detailed, yes, but her own unconscious had supplied whatever details the painting itself hadn't provided. Dwelling on such a bizarre and meaningless incident was morbid, morbid, morbid. Thinking she heard the viol at night had to be some kind of weird displaced grief. She ought to see a shrink, deal with the feelings, get it over and done with. To think she had seriously considered, even for a moment, something as lunatic as trying to make the steps come out right! Whatever that might mean. The idea that anything out of the ordinary might actually have happened wasn't even worth considering. This was New York, after all. This was the 1980s. Dead women simply did not go around sucking their friends into paintings.

Now that she was a junior account executive rather than a mere administrative assistant, Guy Rossiter put her in charge of an actual account. It was a very small account, but she knew she had to handle it exactly right. This was the opportunity she had been working toward ever since college — real responsibility, and the stability and respect that went with it. The client, Mr. Edward Abernathy, was short and fat and quite bald, and when he got angry, which he did at every opportunity, his voice squeaked and his upper lip beaded with sweat. He was in Persian rugs. The rugs were ridiculously expensive ("A Hakim says you've arrived"), and Abernathy expected Carla to help him sell an improbable number of them. He made disparaging remarks about the art department's roughs, he whined about the color reproduction when he saw the proofs, and he flatly refused to believe how much a two-thirds vertical cost in *The New Yorker.* He ordered her to get him a discount. "Yes, Mr. Abernathy," she found herself saying. "Certainly, Mr. Abernathy. I agree completely, Mr. Abernathy. We'll look into it, Mr. Abernathy." When she hung up the phone, she felt as if an army had marched over her.

The viol's tune snaked across her mind, clearer than ever. G major, of course. A dotted rhythm. What would the melody be, above a bass line like that? She scrabbled in a desk drawer looking for music paper. She thought she remembered dropping some in there one day when she was making room in her briefcase for a stack of media abstracts, but it was gone now. A notepad, then. She drew quick, wobbly staves. 3/4 time. A pickup. Continuo?

She listened for the tune, but it was gone. Something like this, though. She sketched four bars, frowned at them, erased one note and then another, scribbled furiously. The second and third versions of the line looked no more correct than the first. She wadded the sheet of paper up and pitched it at the wastebasket. It bounced onto the carpet. She drew more staves, carefully this time, and tried again. Maybe it wasn't 3/4. Maybe it wasn't a sarabande. Maybe an allemande. Must be. Sarabandes never had pickups. Or did they? She couldn't remember. Or maybe there was more than one movement. That would explain the confusion. Allemande, courante, sarabande, minuet, gigue. Some kind of motivic cell to tie them together. Up a third and back down, then up a fifth. That would invert nicely starting on either the root or the fifth, or even on the seventh over the dominant....

She skidded to a halt, realizing what she was doing. This was ridiculous. Sitting in an office in midtown Manhattan, roughing out a Baroque dance suite. A twelve-tone row, that you could take seriously, at least, but this would still be the wrong time and place for it. She tore the second piece of paper out of the pad, retrieved the first and smoothed it, placed one atop the other, and tore them both into tiny squares. As she was dumping the scraps into the wastebasket, Tony came in. He nodded approvingly. "Getting rid of the evidence. Always a good idea. Mind if I look?" Bending over, retrieving a wad of bits.

"It's nothing," she told him. "Nothing at all."

In the big mirror in the upstairs lobby, on her way out for lunch, out of the corner of her eye, she thought for a moment that she saw a gentleman in periwig and knee breeches taking a pinch of snuff.

She whirled and stared. There was nobody, only an old man in coveralls pushing a broom.

She dismissed the idea that she was being haunted, but she admitted that she was obsessed. She didn't like being obsessed. Her unconscious had turned traitor. It was throwing out ballroom imagery at random because the stuff never had a chance to drain away. Every time she walked past the painting, it gave her a fresh dose. That evening she tried to drape a sheet over it, but none of her sheets was big enough. Even when she safety-pinned two of them together, a band of bright color leaked out.

All right, then. Let Tony make fun of her, if it suited him. She had had enough. After a quick trip downstairs to make sure there was room in the basement, because she knew she'd never be able to get the painting back up the stairs by herself if there wasn't, she dragged it out and down three flights — bump, bump, slide, bump, turn, slide, bump, bump.

Halfway through the basement door, breathing hard, she thought she felt a hand touch her hand. She dropped the painting and shrank back with a stifled cry. But the touch — and of course it couldn't actually have been a touch — was not repeated. Under a single forty-watt bulb, the ballroom scene was less imposing than it had been upstairs. It glittered dimly, rippling with hypnotic allure, but failed to enfold her. Gathering her courage, she wrestled the canvas against the handlebar of a rusty one-wheeled bicycle. She got thoroughly dusty clearing a space against one wall, and when she finally got the painting maneuvered into place and discovered how obscenely exotic the ballroom looked surrounded by shipping trunks and old end tables, she was too exhausted to drag it out again and turn it around to face the wall. Instead, she went back upstairs for the sheets and safety pins. Having installed the makeshift shroud, she dusted her hands off, locked the basement, and went upstairs without looking back.

For a week or so, she rose early, plunged into her

work at the agency with deliberate enthusiasm, and came home at night dead tired to fall into a dreamless sleep. The night came, however, when she awakened to hear scraps of music whispering under the bedroom door. Scalp prickling even as she damned herself for her own foolishness, she unplugged the table lamp and tiptoed out brandishing it as a club, expecting, as in a bad *Twilight Zone* episode, to see that the painting had magically returned to haunt the apartment.

It hadn't. But she felt too fidgety to go back to bed. Instead, she sat down and tried to pick out the notes of the gavotte (was it a gavotte?) on the piano. Something like that, yes. She hopped up and dug the score paper out of the piano bench. Now a pencil. In the kitchen drawer. She jotted down a phrase, crossed it out, sketched another, added an alto line, alternately chewing on the pencil and using it to conduct in the air the way she had in college.

Do you suppose this would be easier, she chided herself, if you did a little composing once in a while? But that was ridiculous. Whatever she would be composing, if she were composing, it certainly wouldn't be gavottes.

After an hour or so, she had the sensation that she was actually getting somewhere, that at least the first phrase of a binary-form gavotte was down on paper and that it did closely resemble the piece the viol had been playing. Eyelids grainy, she dragged herself back to bed. But in the morning she could barely tell which notes were on lines and which were on spaces. Some of the bars clearly had too many beats, or too few. Disgusted, she tossed the scribbled sheets in the garbage.

The next afternoon, Guy Rossiter called her into his office. Mr. Abernathy was there, pacing up and down in an eddying cloud of cigar smoke. "Ah, Carla," Guy said smoothly. "I'm afraid we've got something of a problem. Mr. Abernathy has just received his bill."

"It's outrageous," Abernathy said.

Carla said, "I checked the bill myself, Mr. Rossiter. It looked correct to me."

"It's about this item here." Guy pushed the bill toward her across the desk and tapped it with a manicured nail. The *New Yorker* insertion. Mr. Abernathy tells me you promised him there would be a fifteen percent discount."

"I promised him I'd look into it, and I did. There was no basis for a discount, not unless we went to a ten-time rate, and that would have been only five percent. My understanding was that Mr. Abernathy wanted the ad to run only once, so we had to pay full price."

"That's not what you told me," Abernathy squeaked. "You told me there'd be a discount. This is totally unacceptable."

"It's only a verbal agreement by a junior employee," Guy said, looking faintly embarrassed, "but of course we'll be happy to honor it. Carla, please draw up a new bill that reflects the discount."

She opened her mouth to protest — and stopped. Where Guy's hand hovered above the desk she could see the edge of the blotter quite distinctly *through* the hand. And the back of his chair through his chest. Head spinning, she turned to Abernathy and reached for his arm to steady herself, but he was shimmering slightly as well, not really transparent but not fully opaque either. She stifled a gasp. She had a wild impulse to turn and run, but a sensible scrap of her mind hauled her back. This was her first account after a promotion. She *had* to keep herself under control, no matter what. With a supreme effort of will, she stared straight at Guy until he stopped being gauzy and was once more reassuringly solid. "Of course," she said evenly. She turned to Abernathy. "I'm terribly sorry about the mix-up," she said. "I'll take care of it right away."

"That's more like it." Abernathy stuck his cigar into his face and turned to stare out the window.

"Will that be all, Mr. Rossiter?"

"For now, yes. I'll want to talk to you a little later."

As she shut the door very quietly behind her, she was fighting her legs, which wanted to buckle. Nothing had happened, nothing at all. It was just the cigar smoke drifting in odd patterns and irritating her eyes. Once she had gotten a drink from the drinking fountain and started to calm down, she could see that Guy must know she would never have promised a discount. But in the interest of keeping the account, he was perfectly willing to shame her in front of a client. Later he would be fatherly, might even apologize. And she'd tell him, she knew, that it was all right, that it wasn't important, that he'd done the right thing. It *was* the right thing, too. Keeping the account happy was worth a few dollars. Abernathy would be good for ten times as much business if he thought he'd put one over on them. Or maybe he actually had misunderstood. Either way, it was silly of her to get mad. Silly and dangerous. She'd have to keep a tighter rein in the future.

The week before the wedding, Tony had to fly down to New Orleans to supervise a TV spot that was being shot on location, so Carla was left to close up her apartment by herself. He already had furniture, of course, and dinnerware, and sheets and towels. She sorted her possessions into one stack to keep and another stack for Goodwill, but things kept bouncing from stack to stack. If she kept everything that had sentimental value, Tony's flat — their flat — would be jammed. It was a struggle deciding what simply had to go, no matter how she might feel about it, and what she was actually justified in keeping. Tony, being more sensible about such things, would have been a big help, but Tony was in New Orleans. There were the cartons of books she'd kept from college, for instance — ethics, comparative religions, Greek tragedies. Why keep carting all that around? And the bust of Mozart that the Sisters had given her when she got the scholarship. It was too large, and not in very good taste, but the piano would look lonely without it. She wasn't sure how Tony felt about the piano, if it came to that. It was only an old Ivers & Pond spinet, with deep scuff marks on the legs, a spongy action, and a muffled nasal tone. On their combined salaries they'd be able to afford a really nice six-foot grand. Maybe she ought to have the spinet hauled away. On the other hand, getting Tony to agree to buy a good piano might be easier if there was a bad piano in the living room for him to be embarrassed by.

At last, knowing that Tony would be back in a couple of days and that he wouldn't be pleased to see that she was still entangled in the packing process, she talked Honey Maxwell into coming over on Saturday on the pretext of needing help wrapping dishes. Honey was from Tennessee, and had drifted into the secretarial pool at the agency after an unsuccessful modeling career. She had long legs and flawless skin and curly hair the color of her name. During the first weeks when Carla was going out with Tony, she had worried that he was casting an eye too often and too appreciatively in Honey's direction, stopping by Honey's desk on too many transparent pretexts. But Honey drew her aside and drawled, "Don't worry, sugar. I never touch another woman's man. My mama tried it once. The other woman shot her." Since then, Carla and Honey had gotten along fine.

Honey arrived in jeans and a work shirt tied at the midriff and stood, fists on hips, surveying the wreckage of the living room. "How much rent do you pay on this place? Have you given notice yet? Me and a girlfriend could sublet from you. Put up some lace curtains and things."

"Oh, that reminds me. Look at this." Carla dug in a box and carefully unwrapped the tissue from around a pair of dolls in period costume. They were a souvenir from her days in Paris.

"Well, aren't they cute?"

"This one's ear broke off," Carla confessed. "I glued it back on."

"You can hardly see the crack. They are darlin'."

"Do you want them? I can't keep everything, but I just hate to throw them away."

"Why, sure, I guess. What else you got in there?"

So they spent an hour on the floor, drinking coffee and delving into cartons and oohing and ahhing over this and that. Every item reminded Carla of some story from her past. She talked about growing up and college and her job and Tony and Tony's parents and how they were flying up for the wedding even though it was to be a small civil ceremony.

"You gonna have anybody stand up for you?"

"No." Carla stared into the dregs at the bottom of her coffee cup. "I had a friend in college that for years I thought would just naturally be my maid of honor, but we kind of drifted apart. And then last winter she died. She killed herself."

"No! That is so sad."

"I miss her. I didn't always treat her as well as I should

have, but she made it hard. She was crazy, basically."

"I had a cousin once went crazy," Honey said, nodding soberly. "They had to lock him up. Said he was a menace. He was, too. Slashed ever so many tires one time before they caught up with him."

"Joelle wasn't a menace, except to herself. She just never could quite figure out how to live in the real world, you know?"

"Elmer was like that. He *definitely* was not livin' in the real world. Some of the things he said he saw — aliens from outer space and who knows what-all. Mama made us all go down and visit him one time in the nut-house, and the way he carried on! Said the whole place was on fire, I remember that. And I was the Blessed Virgin Mary, he said — not that we was R.C., you understand, just his mind worked that way. And I hadn't been a virgin for a good two years, only I didn't dare set him straight, not with Mama standin' there." Honey laughed merrily. "Good old Elmer. I hadn't thought about him in I don't know how long."

"Thanks. I needed to hear that. I think I was starting to build Joelle up into more than she was, because of the way she died. I got to thinking she was in touch with some weird power, some mystical force. But she wasn't. She was just a poor, scared, confused woman. I mean, her paintings were great, they were wonderful, but there was never anything more to it than that."

"I'm not followin' you, sugar. What more would there have been?"

Carla laughed uneasily. "Well — promise you won't tell anybody at work. I would die if it got back to Tony."

"My lips are sealed."

"I'm glad this came up. I guess I needed to tell somebody. What happened, I had this sort of psychic experience the night Joelle died. She had just finished a painting the day before, and — how can I put this? I thought I saw her in the painting. It was incredibly vivid. I mean, she spoke to me. In the painting. After she died."

Honey's shoulders bunched in a shiver. "You're givin' me the willies, girl."

"It gives me the willies too. I try not to think about it. I don't believe in ghosts. It was a shock, that's all. We'd just found her, on the bathroom floor in her flat, and I kind of blacked out for a minute. Come on." Carla scrambled to her feet. "I'll show you."

"Show me what?"

"The painting. Bring your coffee. It's downstairs."

Honey unfolded her legs and stood up. "Do I want to see this?"

"It won't hurt you, I promise. It's just a big painting. It's a ballroom scene. There are like a hundred people in this big ballroom, and they're dancing a gavotte or something. It's right out of the eighteenth century."

"You mean with the petticoats and all?"

"And the wigs and shoes with brass buckles." Carla snapped back the deadbolt and led the way down the hall. "I haven't figured out yet what I'm going to do with it. Maybe give it to Goodwill."

"I don't know if they take paintings."

"No, I guess not. What we ought to do, we ought to just haul it out to the dumpster right now. Unless you want it. Hanging onto it is like hanging onto Joelle. It'd be healthier if I put the whole thing behind me."

"Well, let me take a look at it. It doesn't sound like my style, but you never know."

Carla unlocked the basement door and groped for the light switch. The bulb flared. A rat, or something that sounded like a rat, skittered away into a corner. She led the way across the cold and musty room. Honey, looking dubious, picked her way gingerly among the cartons and broken things.

The painting was still draped with the pinned sheets, but they had sagged in uneven folds. Standing at one end of the canvas, Carla flipped the sheets up and back. Dust billowed, and Honey sneezed and waved it away from her face. "She really was quite a painter," Carla said. "What do you think?"

Honey's brows pinched. "I don't get it. You said there was a bunch of people dancin'?"

Carla turned to look at the painting — and cried aloud in dismay. A chill struck at her core, as if her blood were being sucked away into some icy underground reservoir.

The ballroom — and clearly it was the same ballroom — was shrouded now in night. Blue moonlight pooled beneath a window. A single candle was guttering in its holder on one of the music stands on the balcony, and at the edge of its fading glow a yellow sheet of parchment, tattered and dog-eared, lay forgotten where it had fluttered to the floor.

Of the dancers, the musicians, the servants, of the ghosts and silhouettes and all the rest, not a trace remained.

"You suppose she used some kind of disappearin' ink? Or is this just a different painting?"

"It's the same painting." The heaviness in Carla's heart was as thick as the day she found Joelle lying dead. But this time it was a part of herself she had lost. Half blinded by a spurt of tears, she stepped toward the painting and reached out to pick up the little sheet of parchment, but her fingers bumped against the canvas. She grasped again, at the air, knowing it was futile, feeling as if it was a solid thing the emptiness where her fingers met the thumb.

"Brr," Honey said. "It's chilly in here."

"Let's go upstairs." Carla stepped back — and her foot hit something that clattered and clanked. A tray and a bottle. The tray was badly dented, and cheap tarnished metal showed through the ragged gaps where the paint had flecked off. The bottle had fallen on its side when she kicked it; it was dark green and had a plain cork. She picked it up. There was no label, only smudged dust. By its heft and gurgle it was nearly full, and by its dark opacity the wine was red. "Where did this come from?"

"It must have been there all the time. I didn't notice. You must have stepped right past it. If it'd been a snake, it woulda bit you."

Snakes. Of course. Carla knelt and examined the tray. In the patches of paint that still clung to the scratched metal, she could just make out a crude design of snakes with other snakes' tails in their mouths.

She tossed the tray aside and stood up. "Let's go upstairs," she said with forced enthusiasm. "You want a glass of wine?"

Honey looked at the bottle doubtfully. "My mama taught me never to drink liquor from a bottle that didn't have a label on it."

"Well, maybe I'll have a glass myself." Carla switched off the light and pulled the basement door shut. "Or maybe I won't."

Which would be better, she wondered as she followed Honey up the stairs. To know, always, what you had missed in life? Or not to know?

www.ingramcontent.com/pod-product-compliance
Lightning Source LLC
Chambersburg PA
CBHW022242020726
47496CB00004B/1025